VINCENT

PUB FARE AND APPS FOR LUNCH? MY DREAM!

SUPER GENIUS

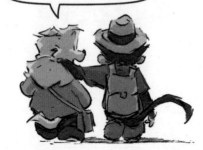

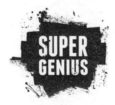

GRAPHIC NOVELS AVAILABLE FROM SUPER GENIUS

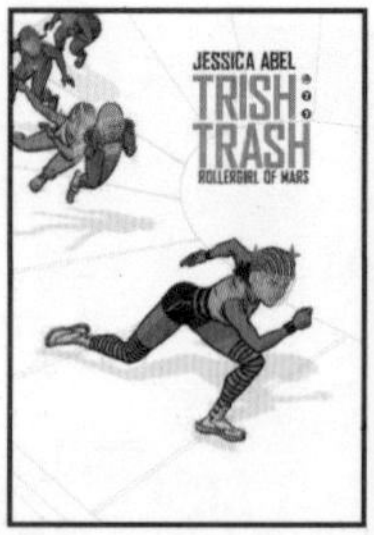
JESSICA ABEL
TRISH TRASH
ROLLERGIRL OF MARS

TRISH TRASH #1
Rollergirl of Mars
By Jessica Abel

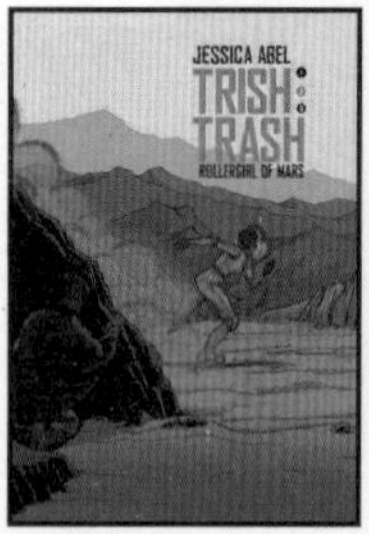
JESSICA ABEL
TRISH TRASH
ROLLERGIRL OF MARS

TRISH TRASH #2
Rollergirl of Mars
By Jessica Abel

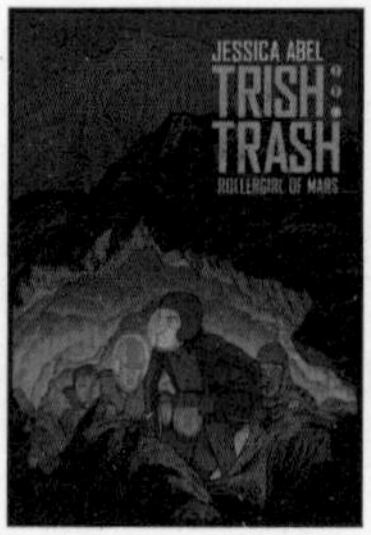
JESSICA ABEL
TRISH TRASH
ROLLERGIRL OF MARS

TRISH TRASH #3
Rollergirl of Mars
By Jessica Abel

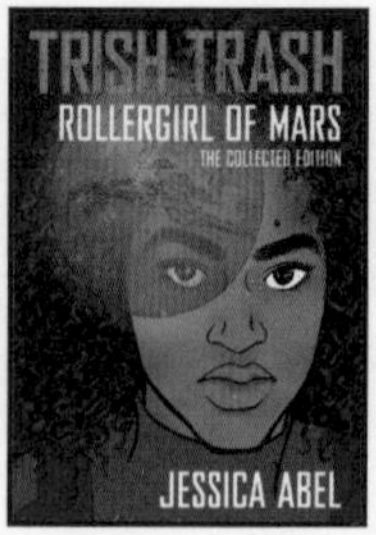
TRISH TRASH
ROLLERGIRL OF MARS
THE COLLECTED EDITION
JESSICA ABEL

TRISH TRASH
The Collected Edition
By Jessica Abel

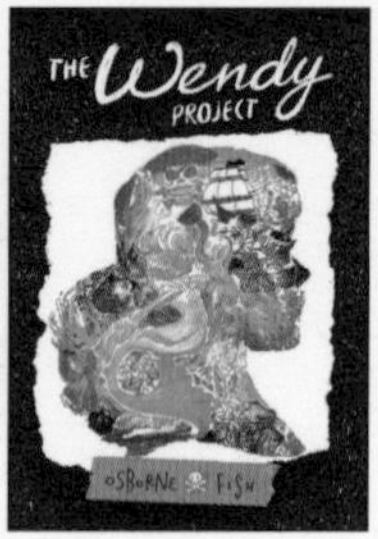
THE Wendy PROJECT

THE WENDY PROJECT
By Melissa Jane Osborne & Veronica Fish

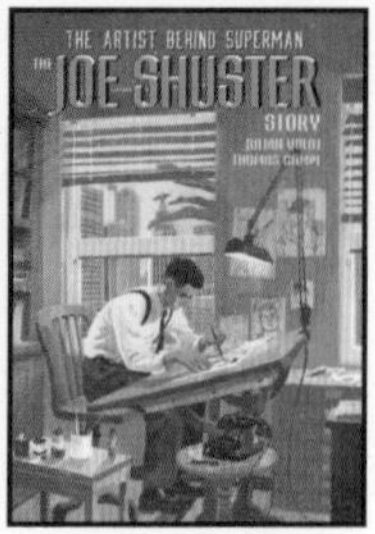
THE ARTIST BEHIND SUPERMAN
THE JOE SHUSTER STORY

THE JOE SHUSTER STORY
By Julian Voloj and Thomas Campi

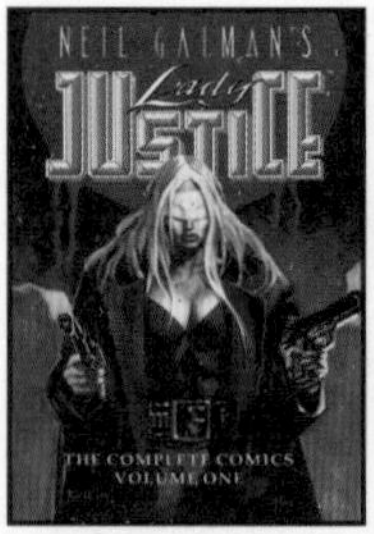
NEIL GAIMAN'S
Lady JUSTICE
THE COMPLETE COMICS
VOLUME ONE

NEIL GAIMAN'S LADY JUSTICE
Volume One

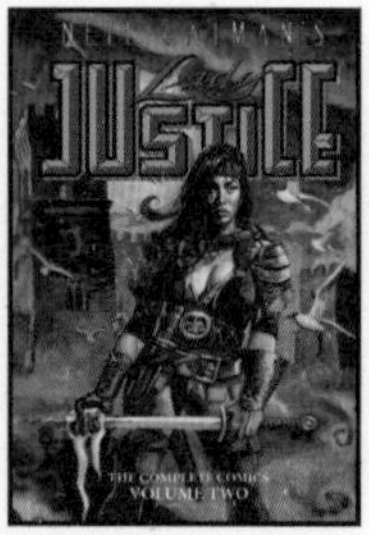
JUSTICE

NEIL GAIMAN'S LADY JUSTICE
Volume Two

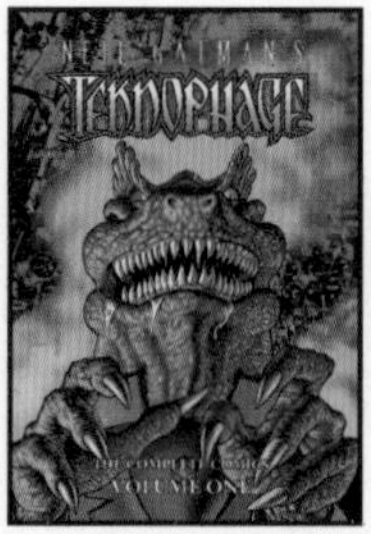
TEKNOPHAGE

NEIL GAIMAN'S TEKNOPHAGE
Volume One

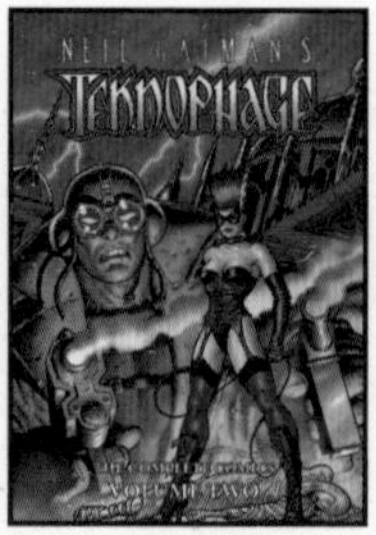
NEIL GAIMAN'S
TEKNOPHAGE

NEIL GAIMAN'S TEKNOPHAGE
Volume Two

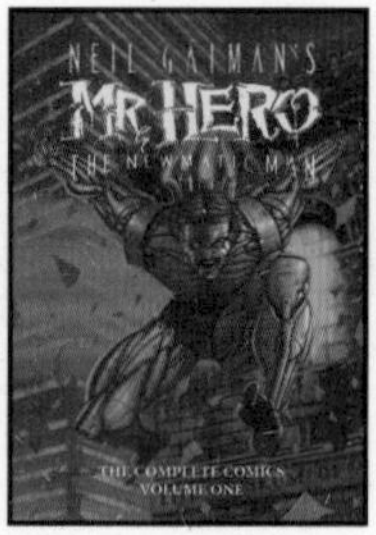
NEIL GAIMAN'S
MR HERO

NEIL GAIMAN'S MR. HERO
Volume One

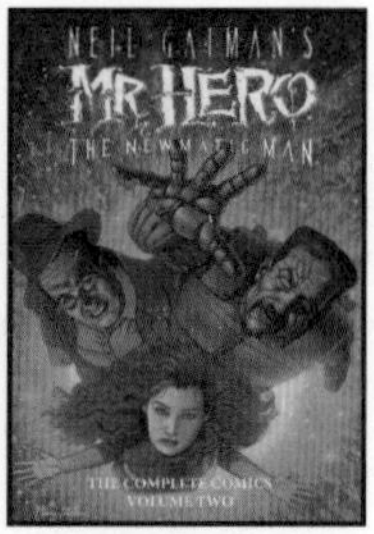
NEIL GAIMAN'S
MR HERO

NEIL GAIMAN'S MR. HERO
Volume Two

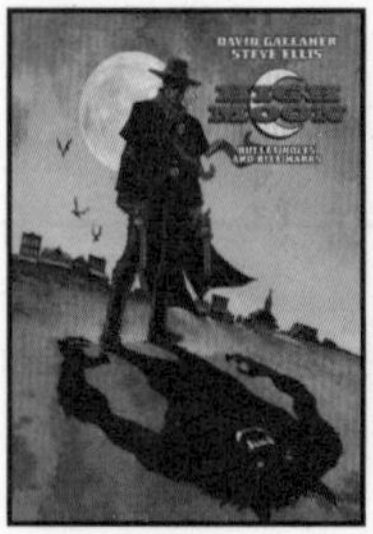

HIGH MOON #1
By David Gallaher & Steve Ellis

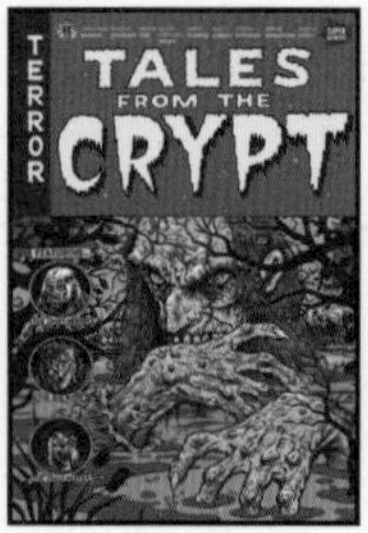
TERROR
TALES FROM THE CRYPT

TALES FROM THE CRYPT
By Miran Kim, Bernie Wrightson, Jolyon Yates & others

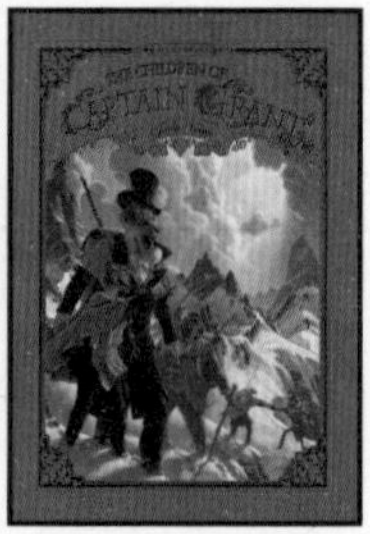

THE CHILDREN OF CAPTAIN GRANT
By Jules Verne
Adapted by Alexis Nesme

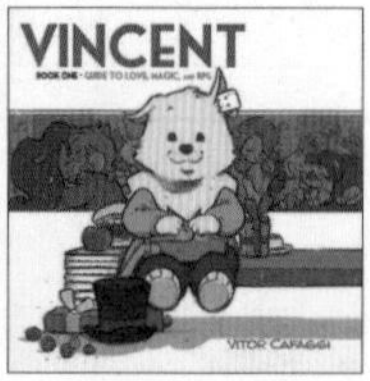
VINCENT

VINCENT
Book One
By Vitor Cafaggi

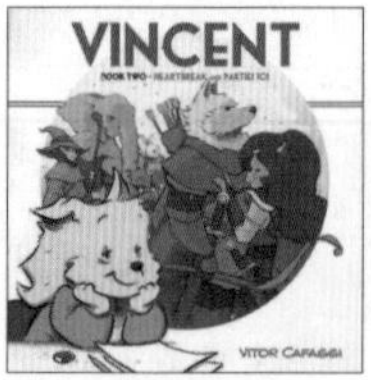
VINCENT

VINCENT
Book Two
By Vitor Cafaggi

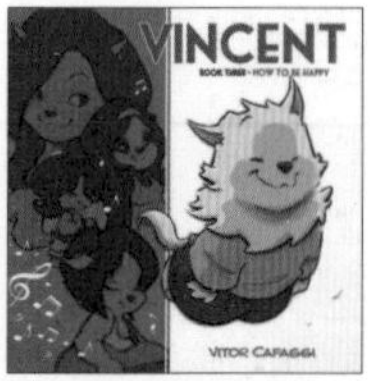
VINCENT

VINCENT
Book Three
By Vitor Cafaggi

See more at www.supergeniuscomics.com

VINCENT

BOOK THREE - HOW TO BE HAPPY

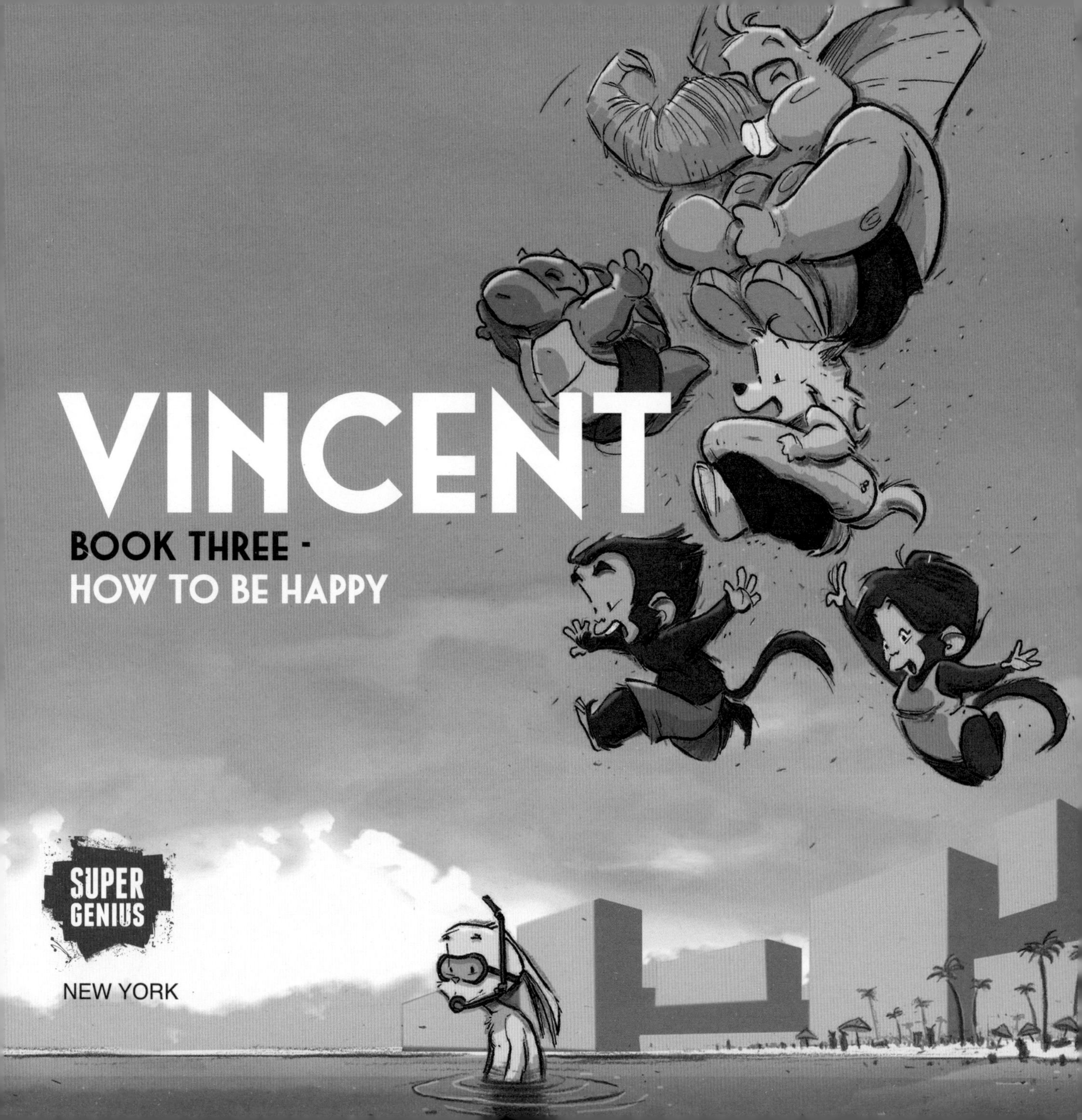

SUPER GENIUS
NEW YORK

VINCENT

BOOK THREE · HOW TO BE HAPPY

Created by VITOR CAFAGGI

JEFF WHITMAN —Translation, Lettering, Editing, and Design
ERIC STORMS — Editorial Intern
JIM SALICRUP
Editor-in-Chief

Copyright ©2017-2020 Vitor Cafaggi. All rights reserved.
English translation and all other editorial material © 2020 Super Genius.
VINCENT Book Three — How to be Happy was originally published in Brazil under the titles "*Valente para onde você foi?*" and "*Valente Por Você*."

Super Genius is an imprint of Papercutz.
www.supergeniuscomics.com

ISBN: 978-1-5458-0411-7

Super Genius books may be purchased for business or promotional use. For information on bulk purchases please contact Macmillan Corporate and Premium Sales Department at (800) 211-7945 x 5442.

Printed in Turkey
August 2020

Distributed by Macmillan
First Super Genius Printing

Previously in **VINCENT:**

Our story began when Vincent met **LADY** on the bus and fell in love instantly. But things didn't work out. To get over his heartbreak, Vincent spent a good chunk of his time playing RPG with his friends and listening to the wise advice of his best friend, Bu. Months later, Vincent met **PRINCESS.** And fell in love instantly. While Princess was deciding if she wanted to be official or not with him, Lady resurfaced. Lady and Vincent agreed to a date. At that very same moment, Princess, finally, accepted Vincent as her boyfriend.

Vincent went out to an empanada dinner with Lady and realized that he still liked her, and worse, she liked him back. Vincent then went out with Princess and realized that he liked her too.

After he thought a lot about it, Vincent decided to start officially dating Princess. But not long after, Princess went to Australia to study abroad for six months. After two weeks there, she ended her relationship with Vincent over the phone.

Vincent graduated high school. A regretful (and single) Vincent chased after Lady, only to discover she had a new boyfriend. Drowning his sorrows in pizza, Vincent missed his first chance to meet **CINDY**, the girl of his dreams. Two weeks into his college career, Vincent falls for a mysterious girl. Vincent then lost his second chance to meet Cindy by sleeping in a park. Vincent then got to know the mysterious girl, **LUNA**, on the bus. Then Princess returned. Vincent grew closer to Luna, but this closeness was interrupted abruptly with spring break.

Thinking that Princess wants to get back together and still confused about his feelings for Luna, Vincent once again ran to Bu for her advice. What Vincent felt for Luna was very strong. This made him get out of his comfort zone and even go to the club where Luna works as a DJ, where he got her number. After many text messages, Vincent and Luna scheduled a date. On the next day, Princess also set up a date with Vincent. On his date with Luna, Vincent realized he is definitely completely in love with her. The same did not happen with Princess.

Vincent had his second date with Luna with hopes of a third... that never happened. His relationship with Luna grew cold when she decided to drop out of school for the semester. Together with his friends, Vincent became a regular at college parties and barbecues. He even went to a costume party dressed like the obscure Disney character Hard Haid Moe. There, Cindy (dressed as an inflatable Stay Puft) bumped into Vincent by accident, unbeknownst to Vincent.

The next day Vincent saw Luna again. Vincent invited Luna to meet up, but she let him know how hurt she was by Vincent. Vincent then surprised everyone by showing up at Luna's front door, ready to show her how he feels about her.

BEING ADULT

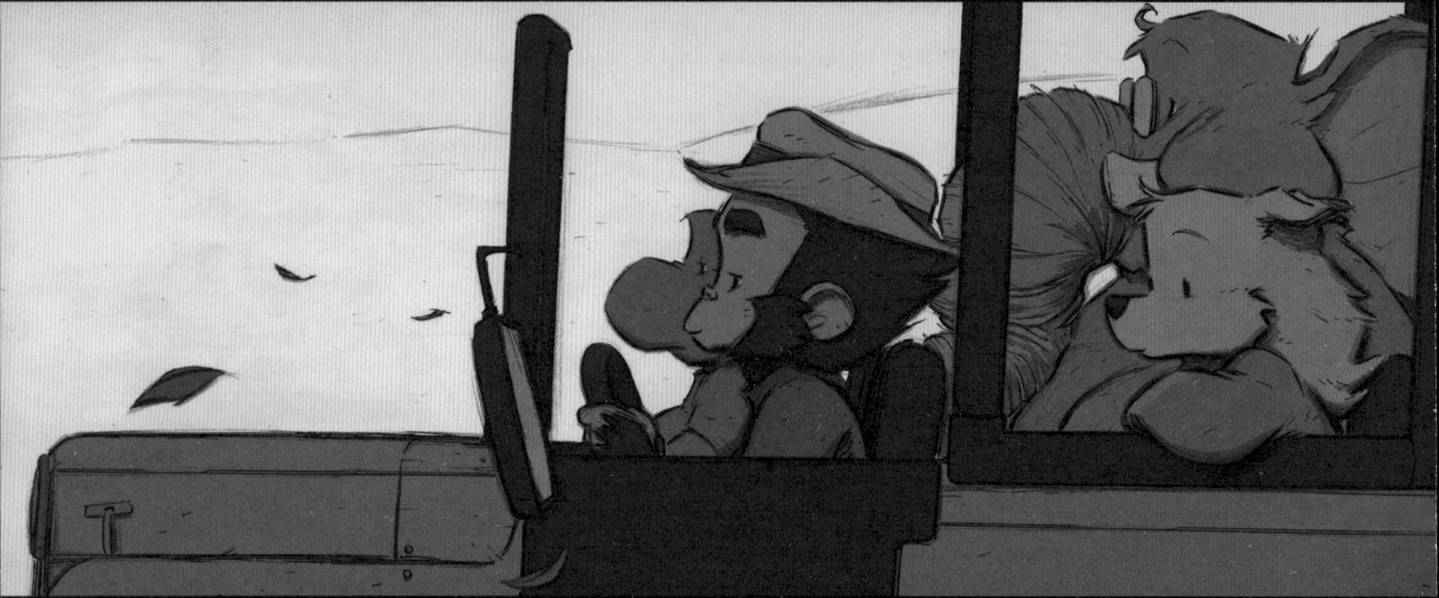

SATURDAY,
APRIL 11TH,
58 MINUTES
AND
19 SECONDS
PAST 11 PM.

WHEN HER BEST FRIEND INVITED HER TO A COSTUME PARTY AT SCHOOL, CINDY THOUGHT: "HOW BORING..."
AFTER PLENTY OF INSISTING FROM HER FRIENDS, SHE WAS CONVINCED TO THROW TOGETHER A COSTUME AND HEAD TO THE PARTY.

DESPITE SOME GUY BLOWING SMOKE IN HER FACE AND ANOTHER GUY VOMITING ALL OVER THE ENTIRETY OF THE GIRLS BATHROOM, WHEN SHE GOT HOME, CINDY THOUGHT: "I'M GLAD THAT I WENT."
SHE LAUGHED A LOT, ONE OF HER FAVORITE SONGS PLAYED AT THE PARTY, AND THE MOJITOS WERE VERY STRONG...AND SHE EVEN SAW SOMEONE DRESSED UP AS HARD HAID MOE.

HEH. HARD HAID MOE...

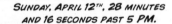

SUNDAY, APRIL 12TH, 28 MINUTES AND 16 SECONDS PAST 5 PM.

AFTER LAST NIGHT'S PARTY, TODAY, CINDY WOKE UP READY TO ADOPT HEALTHIER LIVING HABITS.

KNOWING THAT TOMORROW STARTS A NEW PHASE IN HER LIFE, SHE THOUGHT: "WHY NOT START MY NEW PHASE ALL AT ONCE?"

CINDY NEVER ENJOYED PARTICIPATING IN PHYSICAL ACTIVITIES. SHE NEVER MANAGED TO RUN FOR MORE THAN TWO MINUTES. SHE DOESN'T KNOW HOW TO RIDE A BIKE OR ROLLER SKATE.

ALL HER ATHLETIC APTITUDE WENT TO ONE ACTIVITY: POGO BALL.

CINDY WAS A PHENOMENON AT POGO BALL WHEN SHE WAS SEVEN.

VARIOUS OLD HOME MOVIES PROVE THIS.

CINDY HAS GREAT EXPECTATIONS FOR HER NEW PHASE IN LIFE.

AND DOING LAPS AROUND THE PARK IS SOMETHING THAT DEFINES THIS NEW, AND MORE MATURE, PHASE.

THAT'S JUST WHAT SHE'LL DO. SHE'LL KEEP WALKING.

UNTIL THE DAY COMES WHEN POGO BALL IS BACK IN STYLE AGAIN.

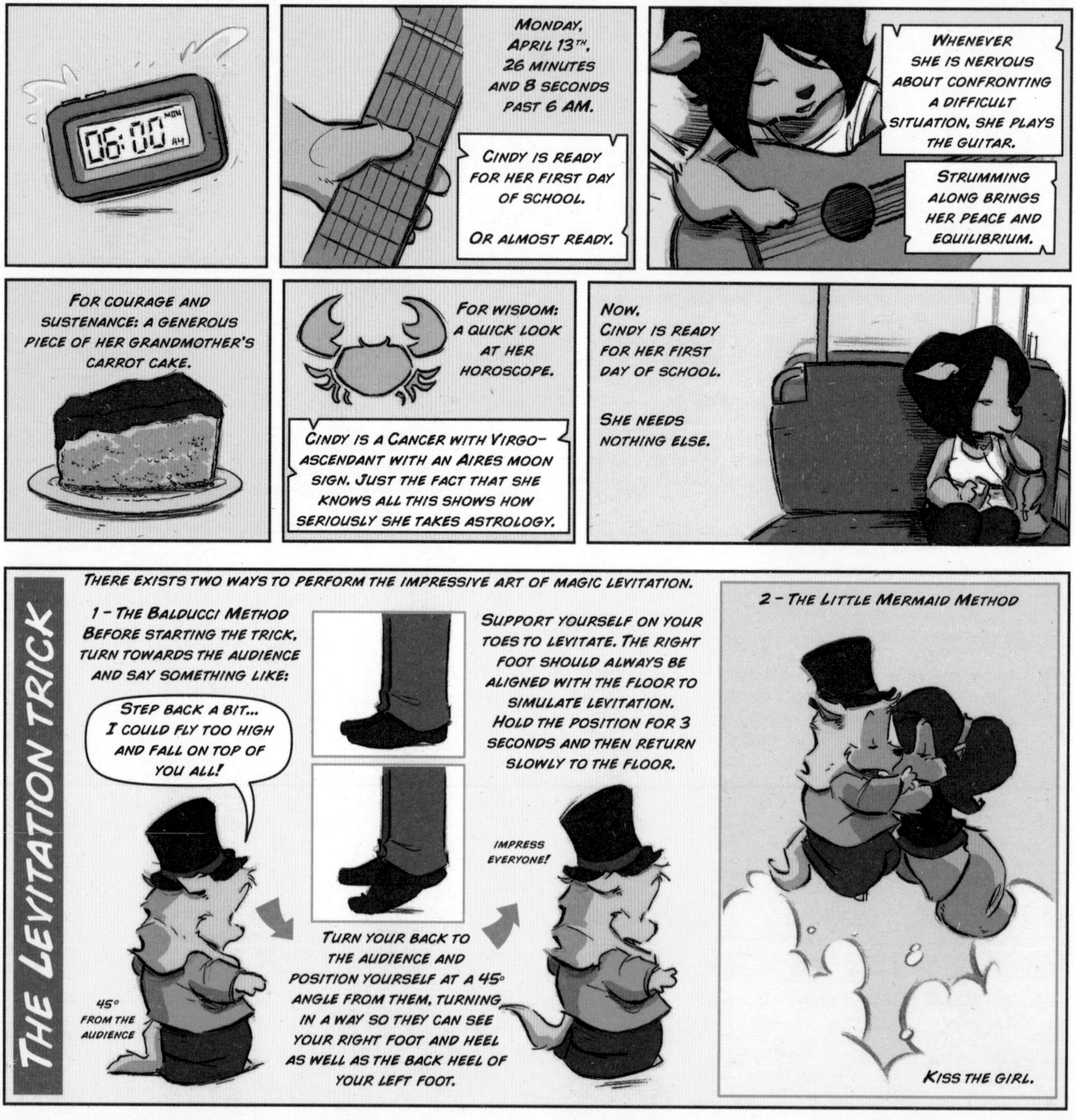
06:00 MON AM
MONDAY, APRIL 13TH, 26 MINUTES AND 8 SECONDS PAST 6 AM.
CINDY IS READY FOR HER FIRST DAY OF SCHOOL.
OR ALMOST READY.
WHENEVER SHE IS NERVOUS ABOUT CONFRONTING A DIFFICULT SITUATION, SHE PLAYS THE GUITAR.
STRUMMING ALONG BRINGS HER PEACE AND EQUILIBRIUM.
FOR COURAGE AND SUSTENANCE: A GENEROUS PIECE OF HER GRANDMOTHER'S CARROT CAKE.
FOR WISDOM: A QUICK LOOK AT HER HOROSCOPE.
CINDY IS A CANCER WITH VIRGO-ASCENDANT WITH AN AIRES MOON SIGN. JUST THE FACT THAT SHE KNOWS ALL THIS SHOWS HOW SERIOUSLY SHE TAKES ASTROLOGY.
NOW, CINDY IS READY FOR HER FIRST DAY OF SCHOOL.
SHE NEEDS NOTHING ELSE.
THE LEVITATION TRICK
THERE EXISTS TWO WAYS TO PERFORM THE IMPRESSIVE ART OF MAGIC LEVITATION.
1 - THE BALDUCCI METHOD
BEFORE STARTING THE TRICK, TURN TOWARDS THE AUDIENCE AND SAY SOMETHING LIKE:
STEP BACK A BIT... I COULD FLY TOO HIGH AND FALL ON TOP OF YOU ALL!
45° FROM THE AUDIENCE
TURN YOUR BACK TO THE AUDIENCE AND POSITION YOURSELF AT A 45° ANGLE FROM THEM, TURNING IN A WAY SO THEY CAN SEE YOUR RIGHT FOOT AND HEEL AS WELL AS THE BACK HEEL OF YOUR LEFT FOOT.
SUPPORT YOURSELF ON YOUR TOES TO LEVITATE. THE RIGHT FOOT SHOULD ALWAYS BE ALIGNED WITH THE FLOOR TO SIMULATE LEVITATION. HOLD THE POSITION FOR 3 SECONDS AND THEN RETURN SLOWLY TO THE FLOOR.
IMPRESS EVERYONE!
2 - THE LITTLE MERMAID METHOD
KISS THE GIRL.

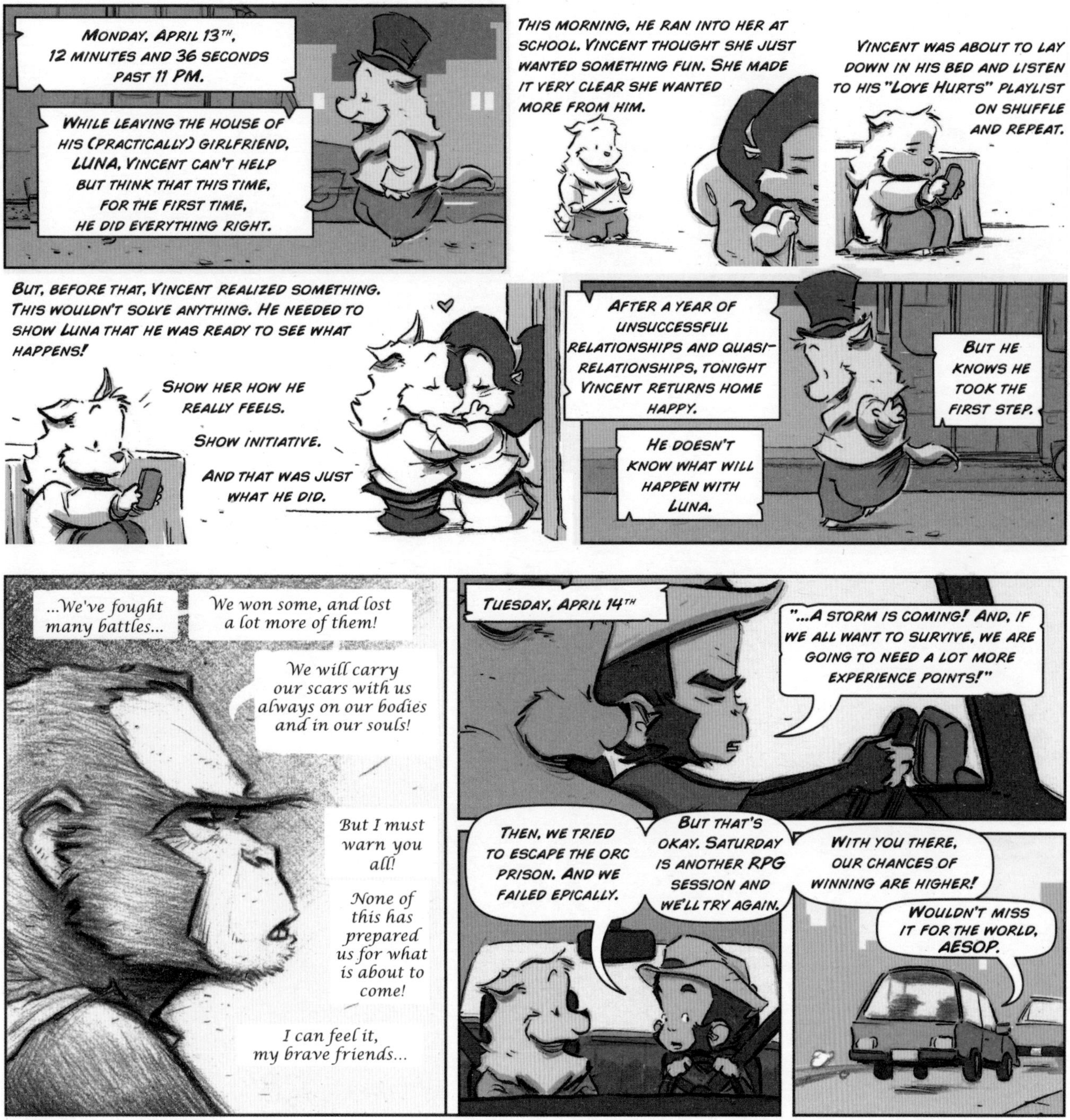
MONDAY, APRIL 13TH, 12 MINUTES AND 36 SECONDS PAST 11 PM.
WHILE LEAVING THE HOUSE OF HIS (PRACTICALLY) GIRLFRIEND, LUNA, VINCENT CAN'T HELP BUT THINK THAT THIS TIME, FOR THE FIRST TIME, HE DID EVERYTHING RIGHT.
THIS MORNING, HE RAN INTO HER AT SCHOOL. VINCENT THOUGHT SHE JUST WANTED SOMETHING FUN. SHE MADE IT VERY CLEAR SHE WANTED MORE FROM HIM.
VINCENT WAS ABOUT TO LAY DOWN IN HIS BED AND LISTEN TO HIS "LOVE HURTS" PLAYLIST ON SHUFFLE AND REPEAT.
BUT, BEFORE THAT, VINCENT REALIZED SOMETHING. THIS WOULDN'T SOLVE ANYTHING. HE NEEDED TO SHOW LUNA THAT HE WAS READY TO SEE WHAT HAPPENS!
SHOW HER HOW HE REALLY FEELS.
SHOW INITIATIVE.
AND THAT WAS JUST WHAT HE DID.
AFTER A YEAR OF UNSUCCESSFUL RELATIONSHIPS AND QUASI-RELATIONSHIPS, TONIGHT VINCENT RETURNS HOME HAPPY.
HE DOESN'T KNOW WHAT WILL HAPPEN WITH LUNA.
BUT HE KNOWS HE TOOK THE FIRST STEP.
...We've fought many battles...
We won some, and lost a lot more of them!
We will carry our scars with us always on our bodies and in our souls!
But I must warn you all!
None of this has prepared us for what is about to come!
I can feel it, my brave friends...
TUESDAY, APRIL 14TH
"...A STORM IS COMING! AND, IF WE ALL WANT TO SURVIVE, WE ARE GOING TO NEED A LOT MORE EXPERIENCE POINTS!"
THEN, WE TRIED TO ESCAPE THE ORC PRISON. AND WE FAILED EPICALLY.
BUT THAT'S OKAY. SATURDAY IS ANOTHER RPG SESSION AND WE'LL TRY AGAIN.
WITH YOU THERE, OUR CHANCES OF WINNING ARE HIGHER!
WOULDN'T MISS IT FOR THE WORLD, AESOP.

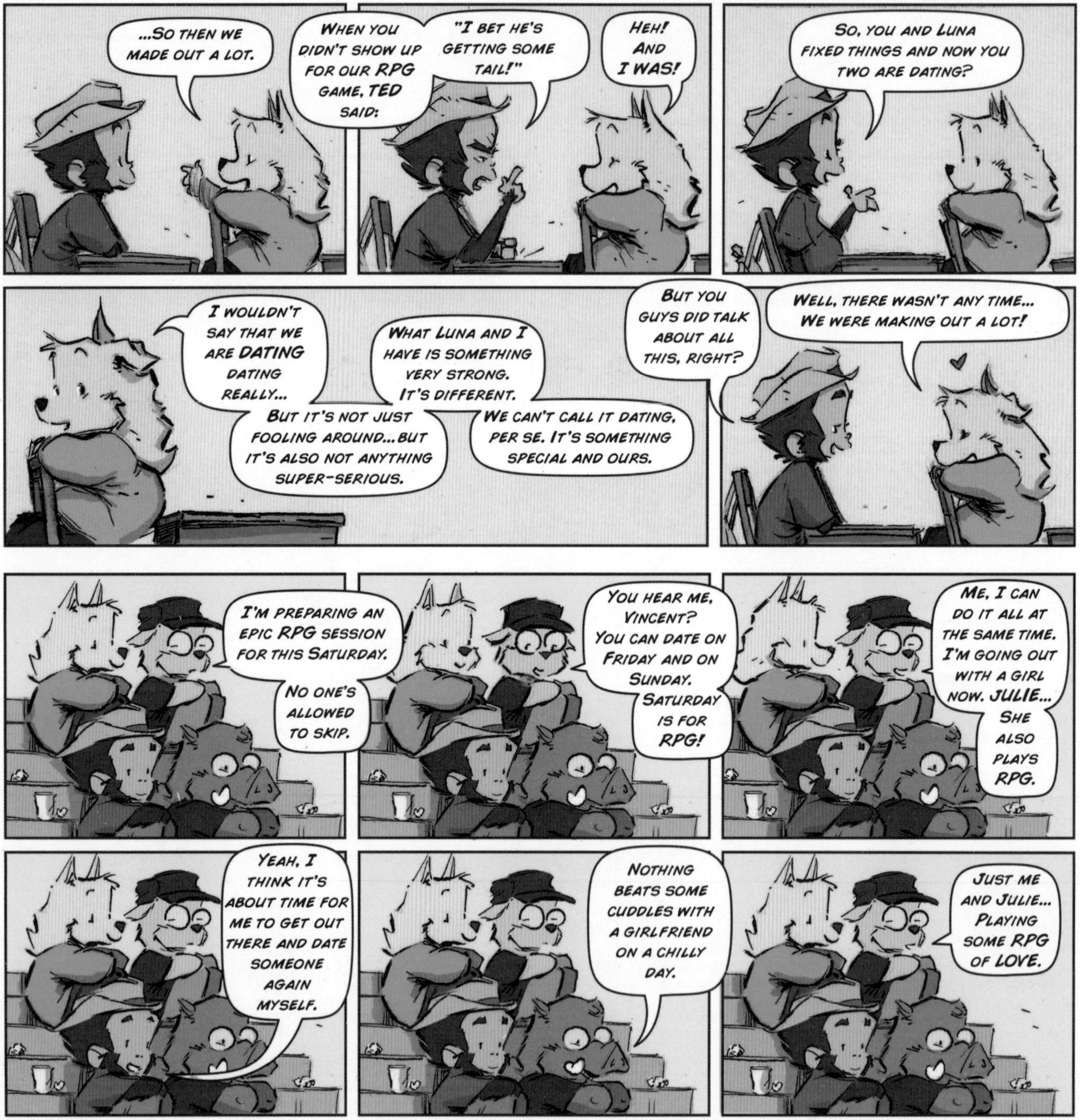
...So then we made out a lot.
When you didn't show up for our RPG game, TED said:
"I bet he's getting some tail!"
Heh! And I WAS!
So, you and Luna fixed things and now you two are dating?
I wouldn't say that we are DATING dating really...
But it's not just fooling around... but it's also not anything super-serious.
What Luna and I have is something very strong. It's different.
We can't call it dating, per se. It's something special and ours.
But you guys did talk about all this, right?
Well, there wasn't any time... We were making out a lot!
I'm preparing an epic RPG session for this Saturday.
No one's allowed to skip.
You hear me, Vincent? You can date on Friday and on Sunday.
Saturday is for RPG!
Me, I can do it all at the same time. I'm going out with a girl now. JULIE...
She also plays RPG.
Yeah, I think it's about time for me to get out there and date someone again myself.
Nothing beats some cuddles with a girlfriend on a chilly day.
Just me and Julie... Playing some RPG of LOVE.

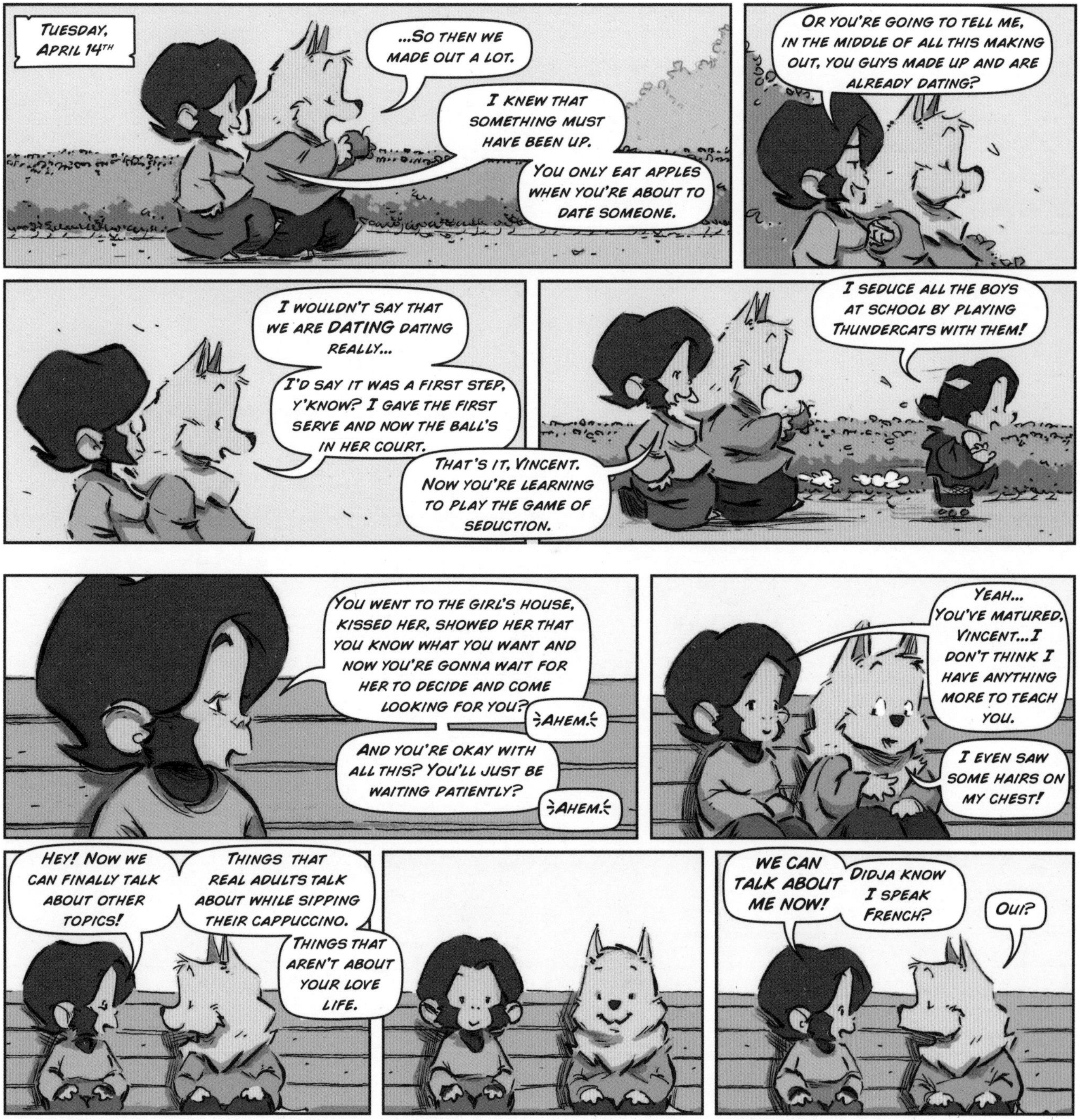
Tuesday, April 14th
...So then we made out a lot.
I knew that something must have been up.
You only eat apples when you're about to date someone.
Or you're going to tell me, in the middle of all this making out, you guys made up and are already dating?
I wouldn't say that we are DATING dating really...
I'd say it was a first step, y'know? I gave the first serve and now the ball's in her court.
That's it, Vincent. Now you're learning to play the game of seduction.
I seduce all the boys at school by playing Thundercats with them!
You went to the girl's house, kissed her, showed her that you know what you want and now you're gonna wait for her to decide and come looking for you?
Ahem.
And you're okay with all this? You'll just be waiting patiently?
Ahem.
Yeah... You've matured, Vincent...I don't think I have anything more to teach you.
I even saw some hairs on my chest!
Hey! Now we can finally talk about other topics!
Things that real adults talk about while sipping their cappuccino.
Things that aren't about your love life.
We can talk about me now!
Didja know I speak French?
Oui?

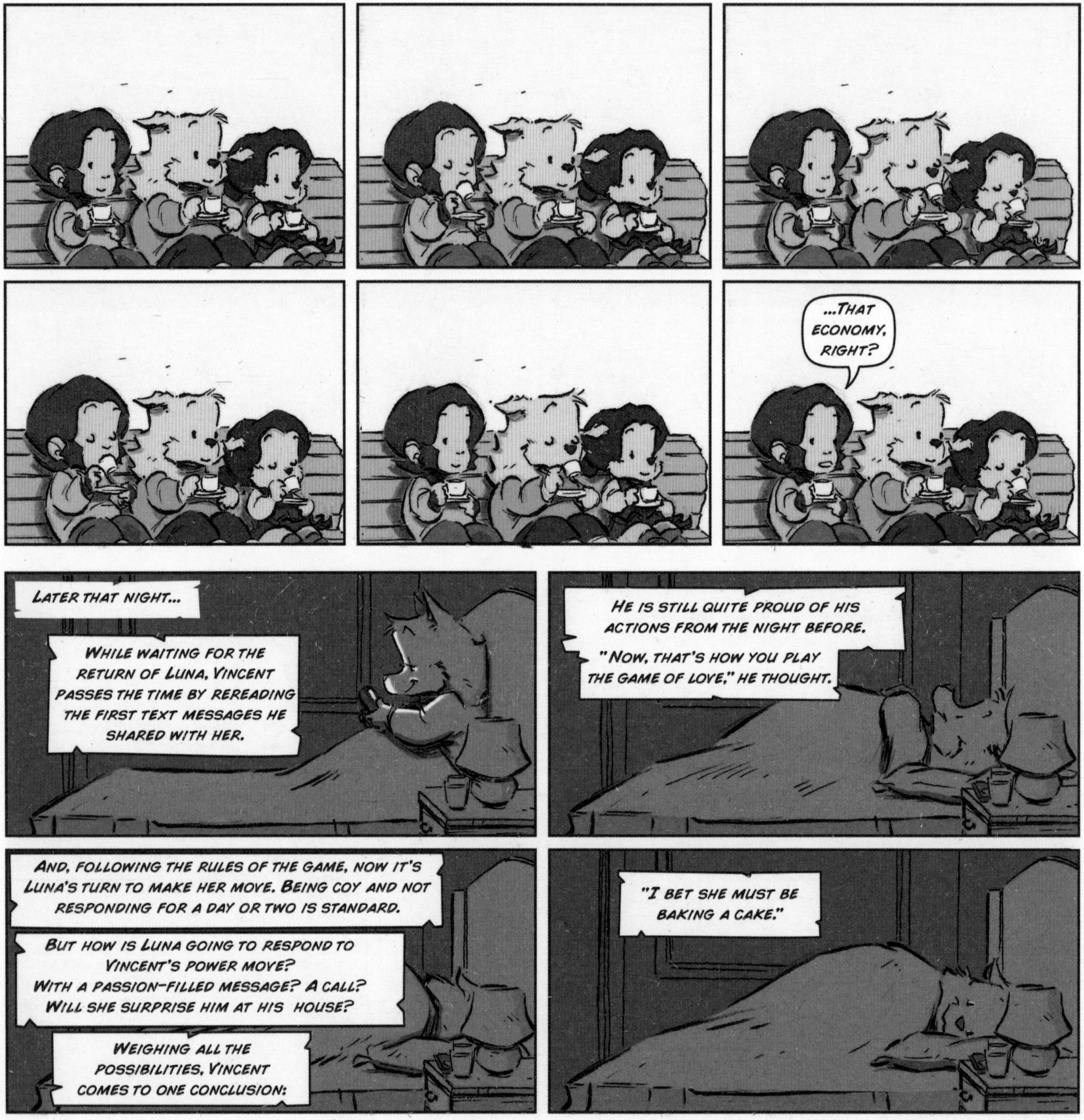
...THAT ECONOMY, RIGHT?
LATER THAT NIGHT...
WHILE WAITING FOR THE RETURN OF LUNA, VINCENT PASSES THE TIME BY REREADING THE FIRST TEXT MESSAGES HE SHARED WITH HER.
HE IS STILL QUITE PROUD OF HIS ACTIONS FROM THE NIGHT BEFORE.
"NOW, THAT'S HOW YOU PLAY THE GAME OF LOVE," HE THOUGHT.
AND, FOLLOWING THE RULES OF THE GAME, NOW IT'S LUNA'S TURN TO MAKE HER MOVE. BEING COY AND NOT RESPONDING FOR A DAY OR TWO IS STANDARD.
BUT HOW IS LUNA GOING TO RESPOND TO VINCENT'S POWER MOVE? WITH A PASSION-FILLED MESSAGE? A CALL? WILL SHE SURPRISE HIM AT HIS HOUSE?
WEIGHING ALL THE POSSIBILITIES, VINCENT COMES TO ONE CONCLUSION:
"I BET SHE MUST BE BAKING A CAKE."

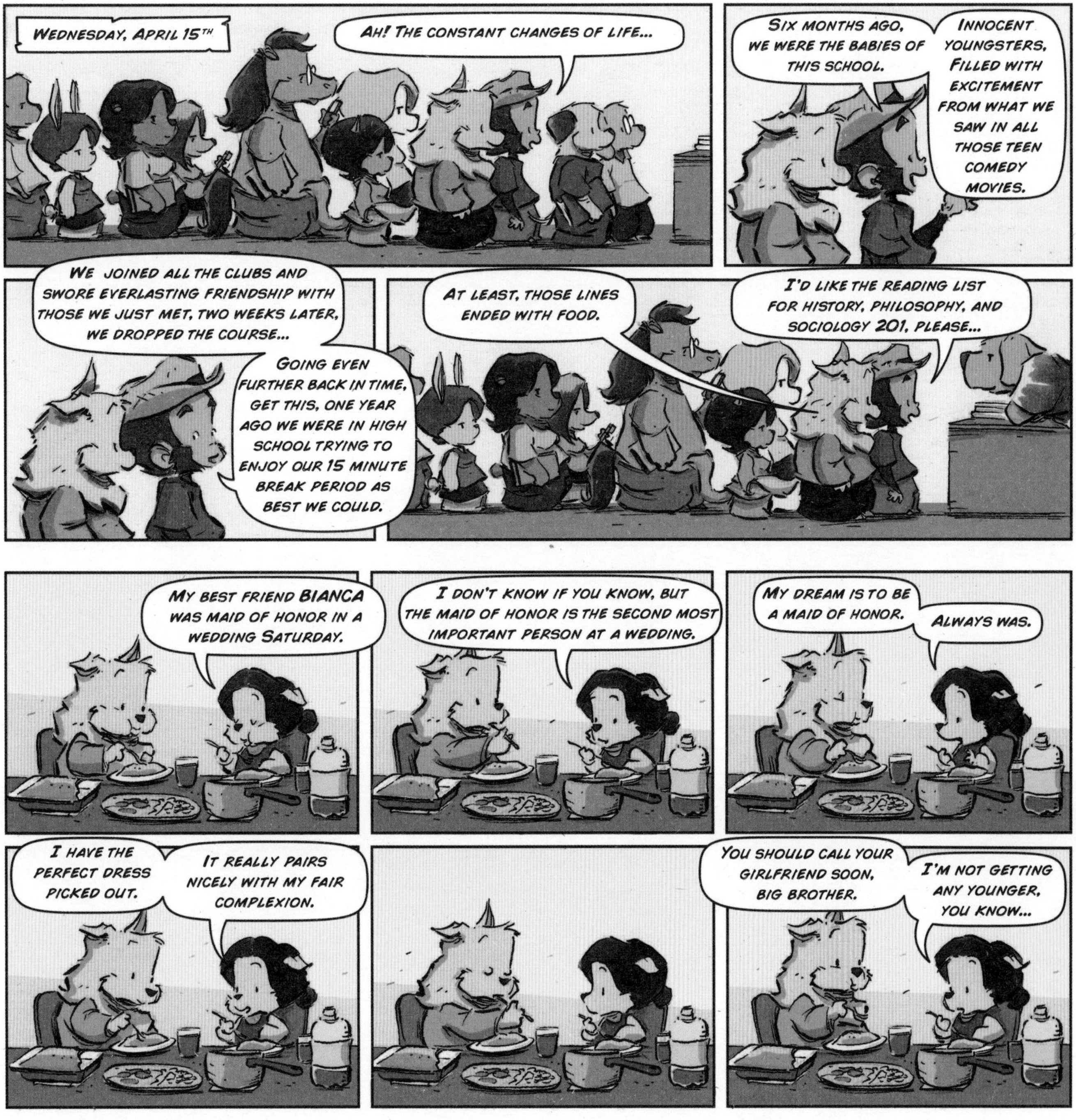
Wednesday, April 15th
Ah! The constant changes of life...
Six months ago, we were the babies of this school.
Innocent youngsters, filled with excitement from what we saw in all those teen comedy movies.
We joined all the clubs and swore everlasting friendship with those we just met, two weeks later, we dropped the course...
Going even further back in time, get this, one year ago we were in high school trying to enjoy our 15 minute break period as best we could.
At least, those lines ended with food.
I'd like the reading list for history, philosophy, and sociology 201, please...
My best friend BIANCA was maid of honor in a wedding Saturday.
I don't know if you know, but the maid of honor is the second most important person at a wedding.
My dream is to be a maid of honor.
Always was.
I have the perfect dress picked out.
It really pairs nicely with my fair complexion.
You should call your girlfriend soon, big brother.
I'm not getting any younger, you know...

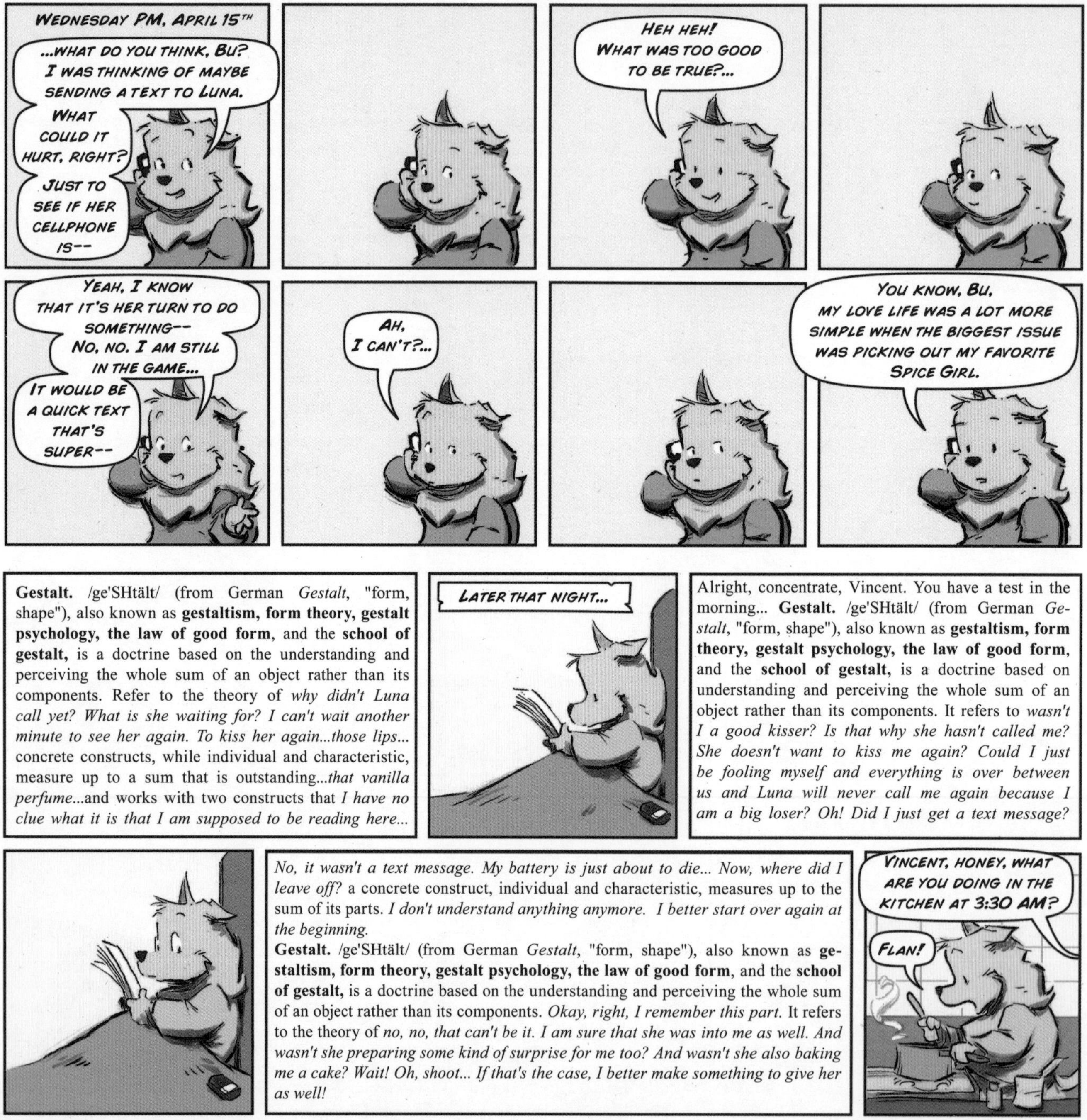
WEDNESDAY P.M. APRIL 15TH
...WHAT DO YOU THINK, BU? I WAS THINKING OF MAYBE SENDING A TEXT TO LUNA.
WHAT COULD IT HURT, RIGHT?
JUST TO SEE IF HER CELLPHONE IS--
HEH HEH! WHAT WAS TOO GOOD TO BE TRUE?...
YEAH, I KNOW THAT IT'S HER TURN TO DO SOMETHING--
NO, NO. I AM STILL IN THE GAME...
IT WOULD BE A QUICK TEXT THAT'S SUPER--
AH, I CAN'T?...
YOU KNOW, BU, MY LOVE LIFE WAS A LOT MORE SIMPLE WHEN THE BIGGEST ISSUE WAS PICKING OUT MY FAVORITE SPICE GIRL.
Gestalt. /ge'SHtält/ (from German *Gestalt*, "form, shape"), also known as **gestaltism, form theory, gestalt psychology, the law of good form**, and the **school of gestalt,** is a doctrine based on the understanding and perceiving the whole sum of an object rather than its components. Refer to the theory of *why didn't Luna call yet? What is she waiting for? I can't wait another minute to see her again. To kiss her again...those lips...* concrete constructs, while individual and characteristic, measure up to a sum that is outstanding...*that vanilla perfume*...and works with two constructs that *I have no clue what it is that I am supposed to be reading here...*
LATER THAT NIGHT...
Alright, concentrate, Vincent. You have a test in the morning... **Gestalt.** /ge'SHtält/ (from German *Gestalt*, "form, shape"), also known as **gestaltism, form theory, gestalt psychology, the law of good form**, and the **school of gestalt,** is a doctrine based on understanding and perceiving the whole sum of an object rather than its components. It refers to *wasn't I a good kisser? Is that why she hasn't called me? She doesn't want to kiss me again? Could I just be fooling myself and everything is over between us and Luna will never call me again because I am a big loser? Oh! Did I just get a text message?*
No, it wasn't a text message. My battery is just about to die... Now, where did I leave off? a concrete construct, individual and characteristic, measures up to the sum of its parts. *I don't understand anything anymore. I better start over again at the beginning.*
Gestalt. /ge'SHtält/ (from German *Gestalt*, "form, shape"), also known as **gestaltism, form theory, gestalt psychology, the law of good form**, and the **school of gestalt,** is a doctrine based on the understanding and perceiving the whole sum of an object rather than its components. *Okay, right, I remember this part.* It refers to the theory of *no, no, that can't be it. I am sure that she was into me as well. And wasn't she preparing some kind of surprise for me too? And wasn't she also baking me a cake? Wait! Oh, shoot... If that's the case, I better make something to give her as well!*
VINCENT, HONEY, WHAT ARE YOU DOING IN THE KITCHEN AT 3:30 AM?
FLAN!

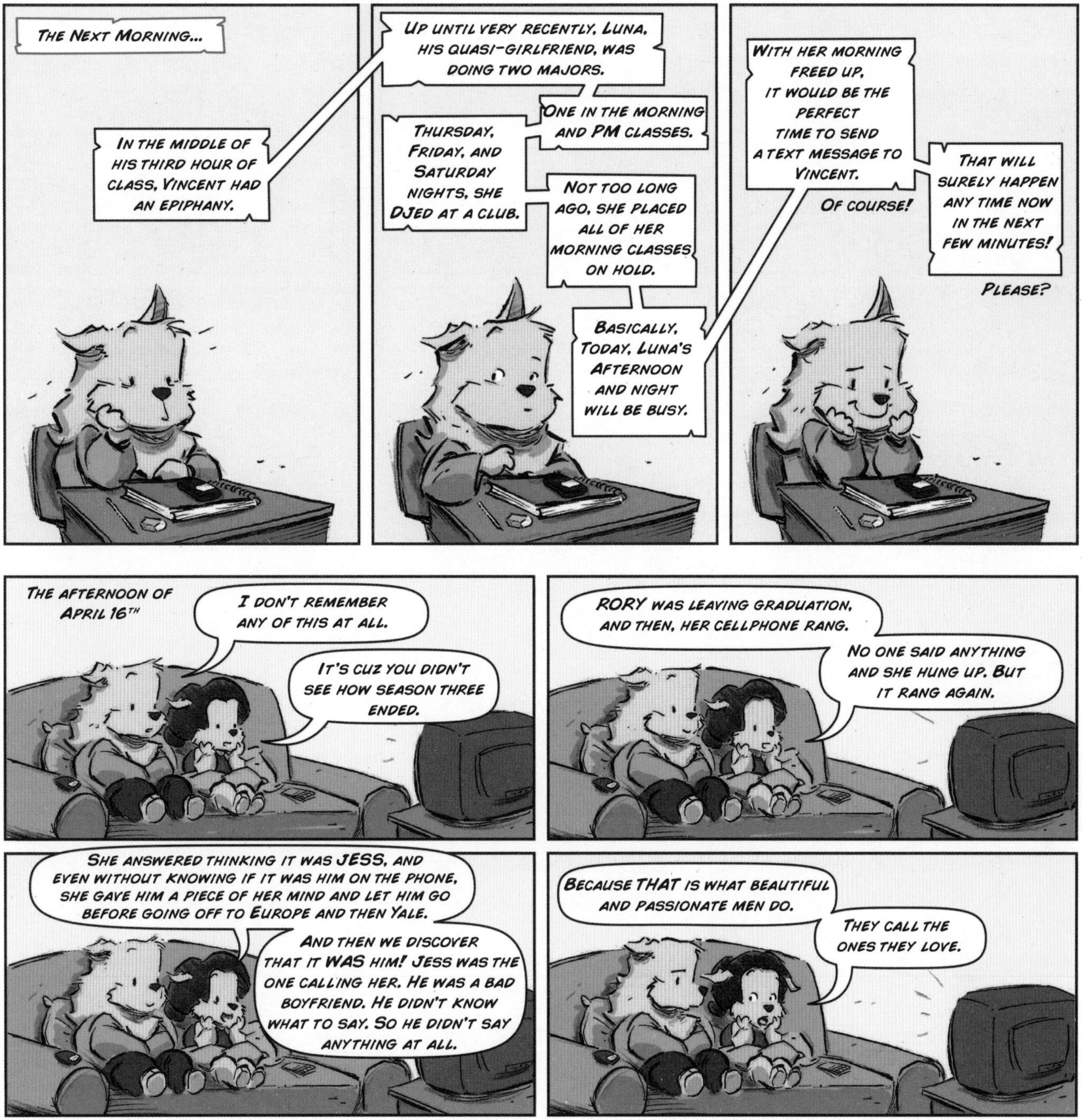
THE NEXT MORNING...
IN THE MIDDLE OF HIS THIRD HOUR OF CLASS, VINCENT HAD AN EPIPHANY.
UP UNTIL VERY RECENTLY, LUNA, HIS QUASI-GIRLFRIEND, WAS DOING TWO MAJORS.
ONE IN THE MORNING AND PM CLASSES.
THURSDAY, FRIDAY, AND SATURDAY NIGHTS, SHE DJED AT A CLUB.
NOT TOO LONG AGO, SHE PLACED ALL OF HER MORNING CLASSES ON HOLD.
BASICALLY, TODAY, LUNA'S AFTERNOON AND NIGHT WILL BE BUSY.
WITH HER MORNING FREED UP, IT WOULD BE THE PERFECT TIME TO SEND A TEXT MESSAGE TO VINCENT.
OF COURSE!
THAT WILL SURELY HAPPEN ANY TIME NOW IN THE NEXT FEW MINUTES!
PLEASE?
THE AFTERNOON OF APRIL 16TH
I DON'T REMEMBER ANY OF THIS AT ALL.
IT'S CUZ YOU DIDN'T SEE HOW SEASON THREE ENDED.
RORY WAS LEAVING GRADUATION, AND THEN, HER CELLPHONE RANG.
NO ONE SAID ANYTHING AND SHE HUNG UP. BUT IT RANG AGAIN.
SHE ANSWERED THINKING IT WAS JESS, AND EVEN WITHOUT KNOWING IF IT WAS HIM ON THE PHONE, SHE GAVE HIM A PIECE OF HER MIND AND LET HIM GO BEFORE GOING OFF TO EUROPE AND THEN YALE.
AND THEN WE DISCOVER THAT IT WAS HIM! JESS WAS THE ONE CALLING HER. HE WAS A BAD BOYFRIEND. HE DIDN'T KNOW WHAT TO SAY. SO HE DIDN'T SAY ANYTHING AT ALL.
BECAUSE THAT IS WHAT BEAUTIFUL AND PASSIONATE MEN DO.
THEY CALL THE ONES THEY LOVE.

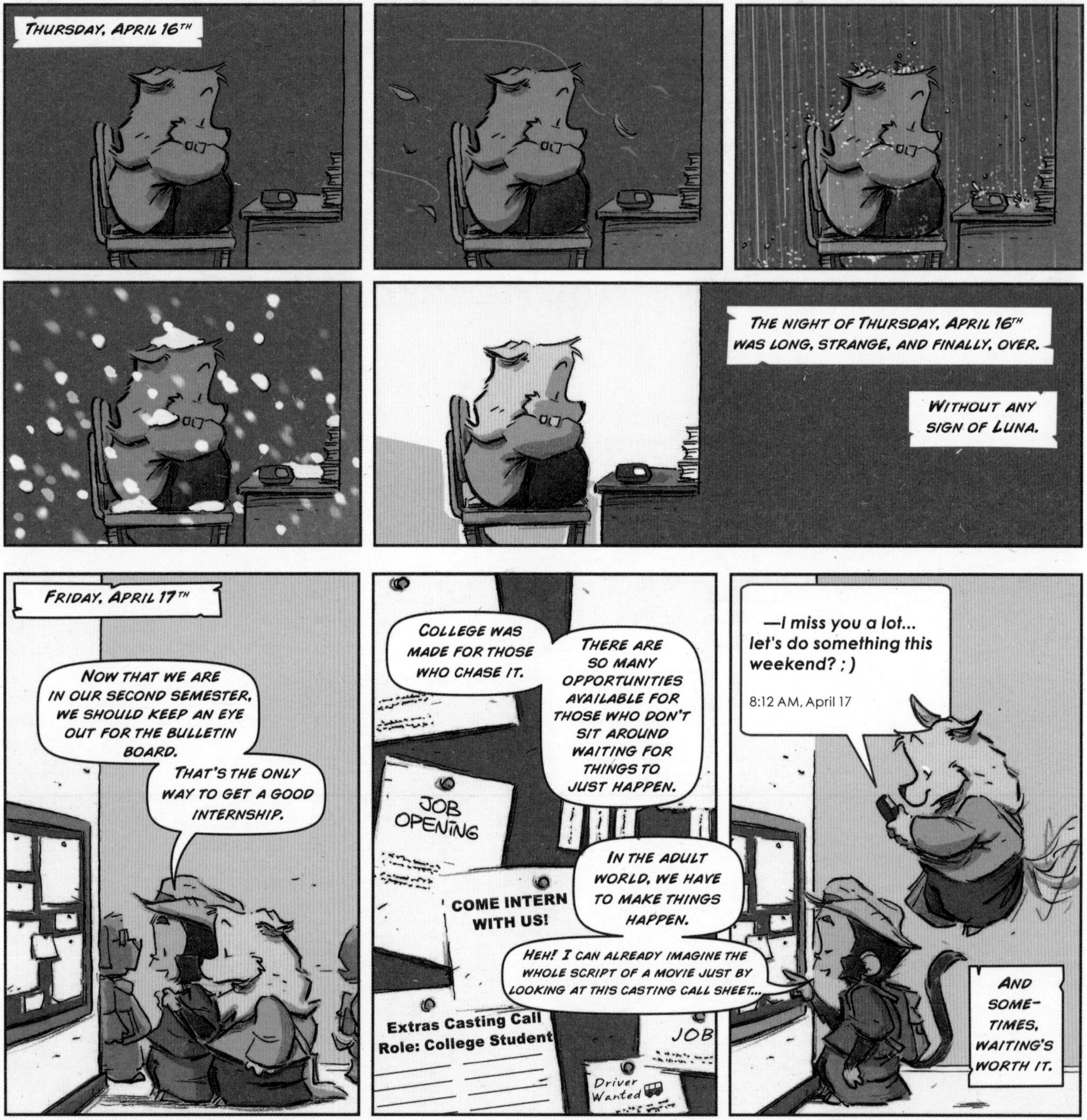
THURSDAY, APRIL 16TH
THE NIGHT OF THURSDAY, APRIL 16TH WAS LONG, STRANGE, AND FINALLY, OVER.
WITHOUT ANY SIGN OF LUNA.
FRIDAY, APRIL 17TH
NOW THAT WE ARE IN OUR SECOND SEMESTER, WE SHOULD KEEP AN EYE OUT FOR THE BULLETIN BOARD.
THAT'S THE ONLY WAY TO GET A GOOD INTERNSHIP.
COLLEGE WAS MADE FOR THOSE WHO CHASE IT.
THERE ARE SO MANY OPPORTUNITIES AVAILABLE FOR THOSE WHO DON'T SIT AROUND WAITING FOR THINGS TO JUST HAPPEN.
JOB OPENING
IN THE ADULT WORLD, WE HAVE TO MAKE THINGS HAPPEN.
COME INTERN WITH US!
HEH! I CAN ALREADY IMAGINE THE WHOLE SCRIPT OF A MOVIE JUST BY LOOKING AT THIS CASTING CALL SHEET...
Extras Casting Call
Role: College Student
JOB
Driver Wanted
—I miss you a lot... let's do something this weekend? ;)
8:12 AM, April 17
AND SOMETIMES, WAITING'S WORTH IT.

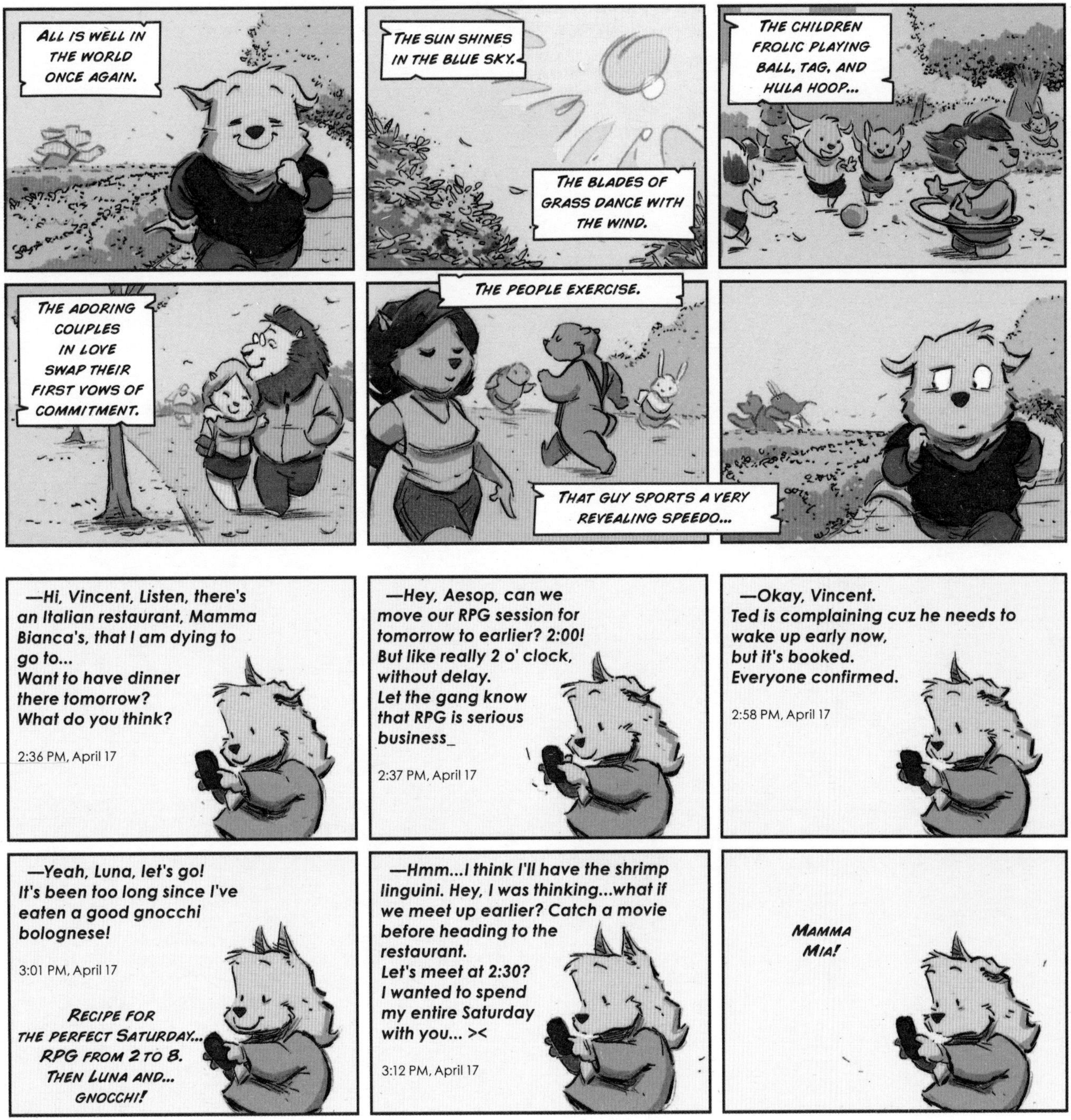
ALL IS WELL IN THE WORLD ONCE AGAIN.
THE SUN SHINES IN THE BLUE SKY.
THE BLADES OF GRASS DANCE WITH THE WIND.
THE CHILDREN FROLIC PLAYING BALL, TAG, AND HULA HOOP...
THE ADORING COUPLES IN LOVE SWAP THEIR FIRST VOWS OF COMMITMENT.
THE PEOPLE EXERCISE.
THAT GUY SPORTS A VERY REVEALING SPEEDO...
—Hi, Vincent, Listen, there's an Italian restaurant, Mamma Bianca's, that I am dying to go to... Want to have dinner there tomorrow? What do you think?
2:36 PM, April 17
—Hey, Aesop, can we move our RPG session for tomorrow to earlier? 2:00! But like really 2 o' clock, without delay. Let the gang know that RPG is serious business_
2:37 PM, April 17
—Okay, Vincent. Ted is complaining cuz he needs to wake up early now, but it's booked. Everyone confirmed.
2:58 PM, April 17
—Yeah, Luna, let's go! It's been too long since I've eaten a good gnocchi bolognese!
3:01 PM, April 17
RECIPE FOR THE PERFECT SATURDAY... RPG FROM 2 TO 8. THEN LUNA AND... GNOCCHI!
—Hmm...I think I'll have the shrimp linguini. Hey, I was thinking...what if we meet up earlier? Catch a movie before heading to the restaurant. Let's meet at 2:30? I wanted to spend my entire Saturday with you... ><
3:12 PM, April 17
MAMMA MIA!

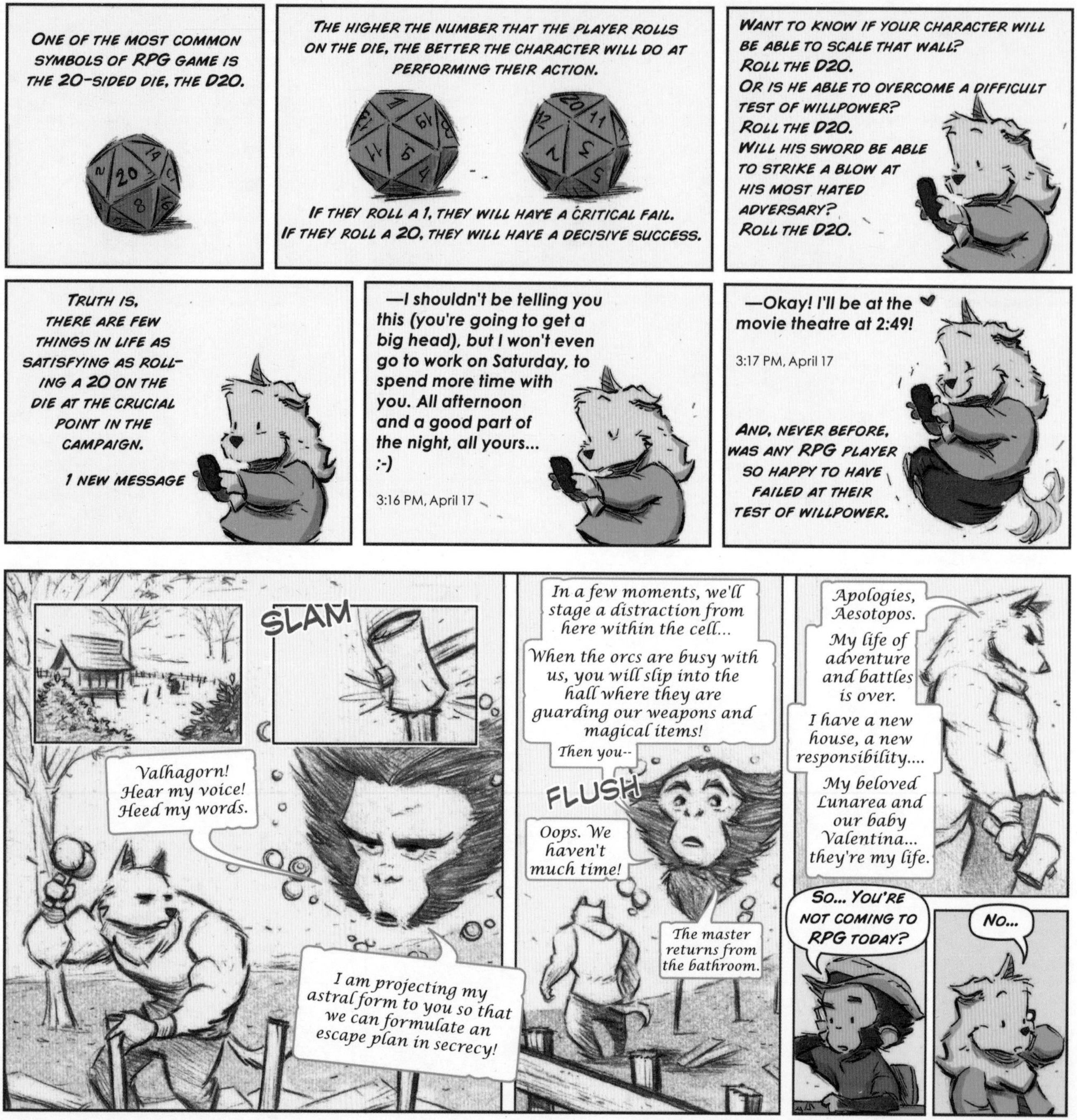

ONE OF THE MOST COMMON SYMBOLS OF RPG GAME IS THE 20-SIDED DIE, THE D20.
THE HIGHER THE NUMBER THAT THE PLAYER ROLLS ON THE DIE, THE BETTER THE CHARACTER WILL DO AT PERFORMING THEIR ACTION.
IF THEY ROLL A 1, THEY WILL HAVE A CRITICAL FAIL.
IF THEY ROLL A 20, THEY WILL HAVE A DECISIVE SUCCESS.
WANT TO KNOW IF YOUR CHARACTER WILL BE ABLE TO SCALE THAT WALL?
ROLL THE D20.
OR IS HE ABLE TO OVERCOME A DIFFICULT TEST OF WILLPOWER?
ROLL THE D20.
WILL HIS SWORD BE ABLE TO STRIKE A BLOW AT HIS MOST HATED ADVERSARY?
ROLL THE D20.
TRUTH IS, THERE ARE FEW THINGS IN LIFE AS SATISFYING AS ROLLING A 20 ON THE DIE AT THE CRUCIAL POINT IN THE CAMPAIGN.
1 NEW MESSAGE
—I shouldn't be telling you this (you're going to get a big head), but I won't even go to work on Saturday, to spend more time with you. All afternoon and a good part of the night, all yours... ;-)
3:16 PM, April 17
—Okay! I'll be at the movie theatre at 2:49!
3:17 PM, April 17
AND, NEVER BEFORE, WAS ANY RPG PLAYER SO HAPPY TO HAVE FAILED AT THEIR TEST OF WILLPOWER.
SLAM
Valhagorn! Hear my voice! Heed my words.
I am projecting my astral form to you so that we can formulate an escape plan in secrecy!
In a few moments, we'll stage a distraction from here within the cell...
When the orcs are busy with us, you will slip into the hall where they are guarding our weapons and magical items!
Then you--
FLUSH
Oops. We haven't much time!
The master returns from the bathroom.
Apologies, Aesotopos.
My life of adventure and battles is over.
I have a new house, a new responsibility....
My beloved Lunarea and our baby Valentina... they're my life.
SO... YOU'RE NOT COMING TO RPG TODAY?
NO...

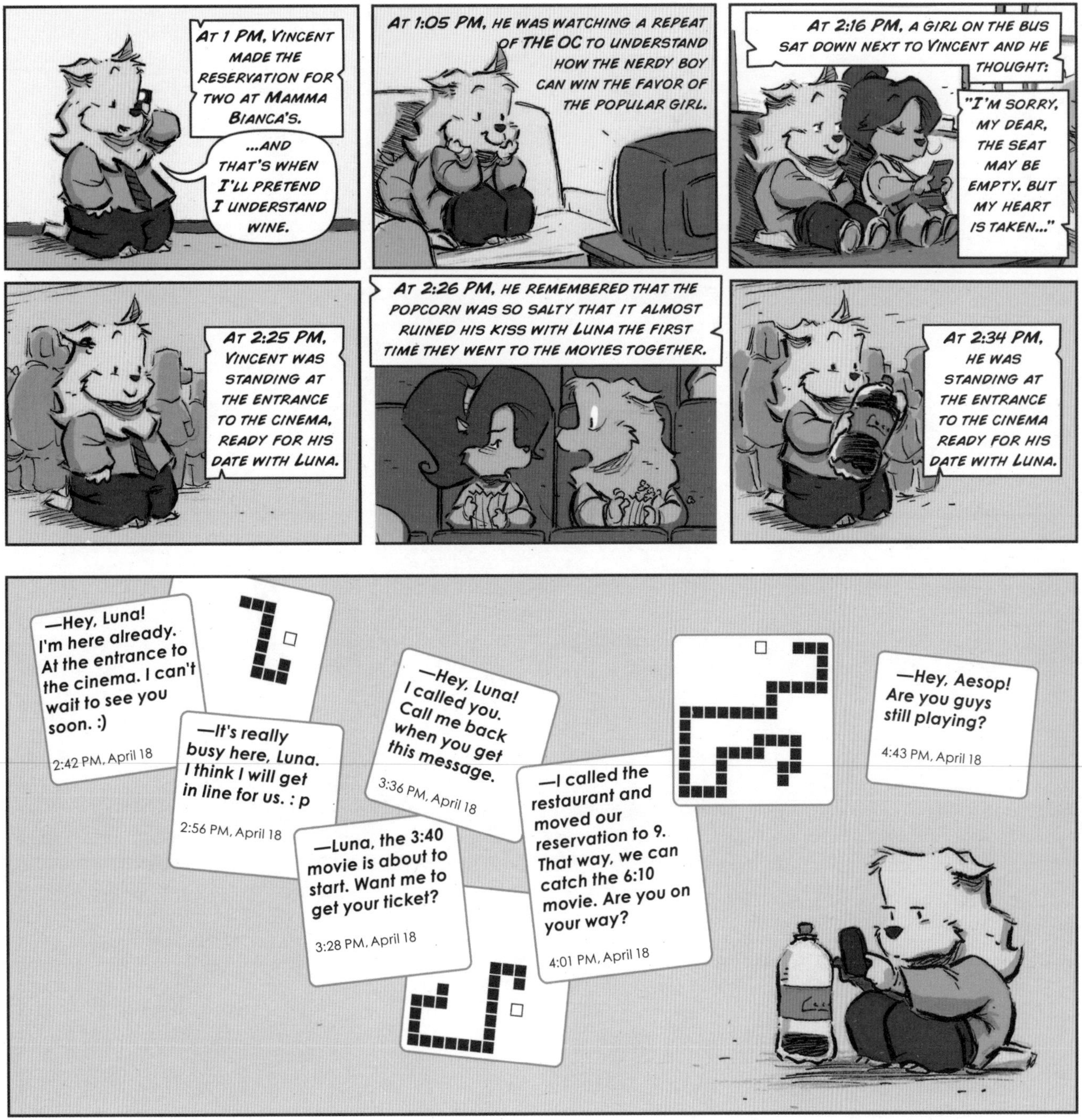

AT 1 PM, VINCENT MADE THE RESERVATION FOR TWO AT MAMMA BIANCA'S.
...AND THAT'S WHEN I'LL PRETEND I UNDERSTAND WINE.
AT 1:05 PM, HE WAS WATCHING A REPEAT OF THE OC TO UNDERSTAND HOW THE NERDY BOY CAN WIN THE FAVOR OF THE POPULAR GIRL.
AT 2:16 PM, A GIRL ON THE BUS SAT DOWN NEXT TO VINCENT AND HE THOUGHT:
"I'M SORRY, MY DEAR, THE SEAT MAY BE EMPTY, BUT MY HEART IS TAKEN..."
AT 2:25 PM, VINCENT WAS STANDING AT THE ENTRANCE TO THE CINEMA, READY FOR HIS DATE WITH LUNA.
AT 2:26 PM, HE REMEMBERED THAT THE POPCORN WAS SO SALTY THAT IT ALMOST RUINED HIS KISS WITH LUNA THE FIRST TIME THEY WENT TO THE MOVIES TOGETHER.
AT 2:34 PM, HE WAS STANDING AT THE ENTRANCE TO THE CINEMA READY FOR HIS DATE WITH LUNA.
—Hey, Luna! I'm here already. At the entrance to the cinema. I can't wait to see you soon. :)
2:42 PM, April 18
—It's really busy here, Luna. I think I will get in line for us. : p
2:56 PM, April 18
—Luna, the 3:40 movie is about to start. Want me to get your ticket?
3:28 PM, April 18
—Hey, Luna! I called you. Call me back when you get this message.
3:36 PM, April 18
—I called the restaurant and moved our reservation to 9. That way, we can catch the 6:10 movie. Are you on your way?
4:01 PM, April 18
—Hey, Aesop! Are you guys still playing?
4:43 PM, April 18

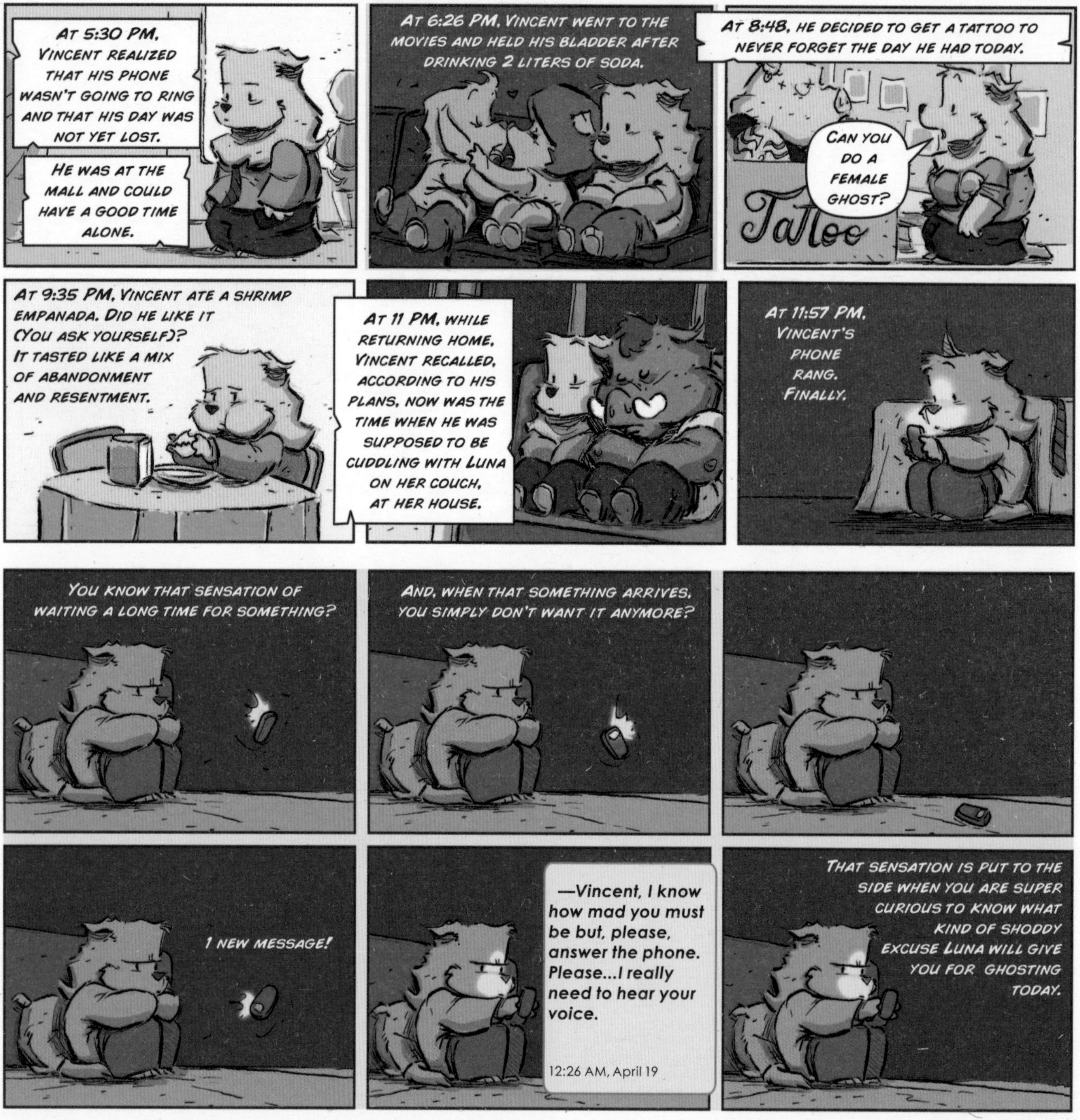
At 5:30 PM, Vincent realized that his phone wasn't going to ring and that his day was not yet lost.
He was at the mall and could have a good time alone.
At 6:26 PM, Vincent went to the movies and held his bladder after drinking 2 liters of soda.
At 8:48, he decided to get a tattoo to never forget the day he had today.
Can you do a female ghost?
Tattoo
At 9:35 PM, Vincent ate a shrimp empanada. Did he like it (you ask yourself)? It tasted like a mix of abandonment and resentment.
At 11 PM, while returning home, Vincent recalled, according to his plans, now was the time when he was supposed to be cuddling with Luna on her couch, at her house.
At 11:57 PM, Vincent's phone rang. Finally.
You know that sensation of waiting a long time for something?
And, when that something arrives, you simply don't want it anymore?
1 new message!
—Vincent, I know how mad you must be but, please, answer the phone. Please...I really need to hear your voice.
12:26 AM, April 19
That sensation is put to the side when you are super curious to know what kind of shoddy excuse Luna will give you for ghosting today.

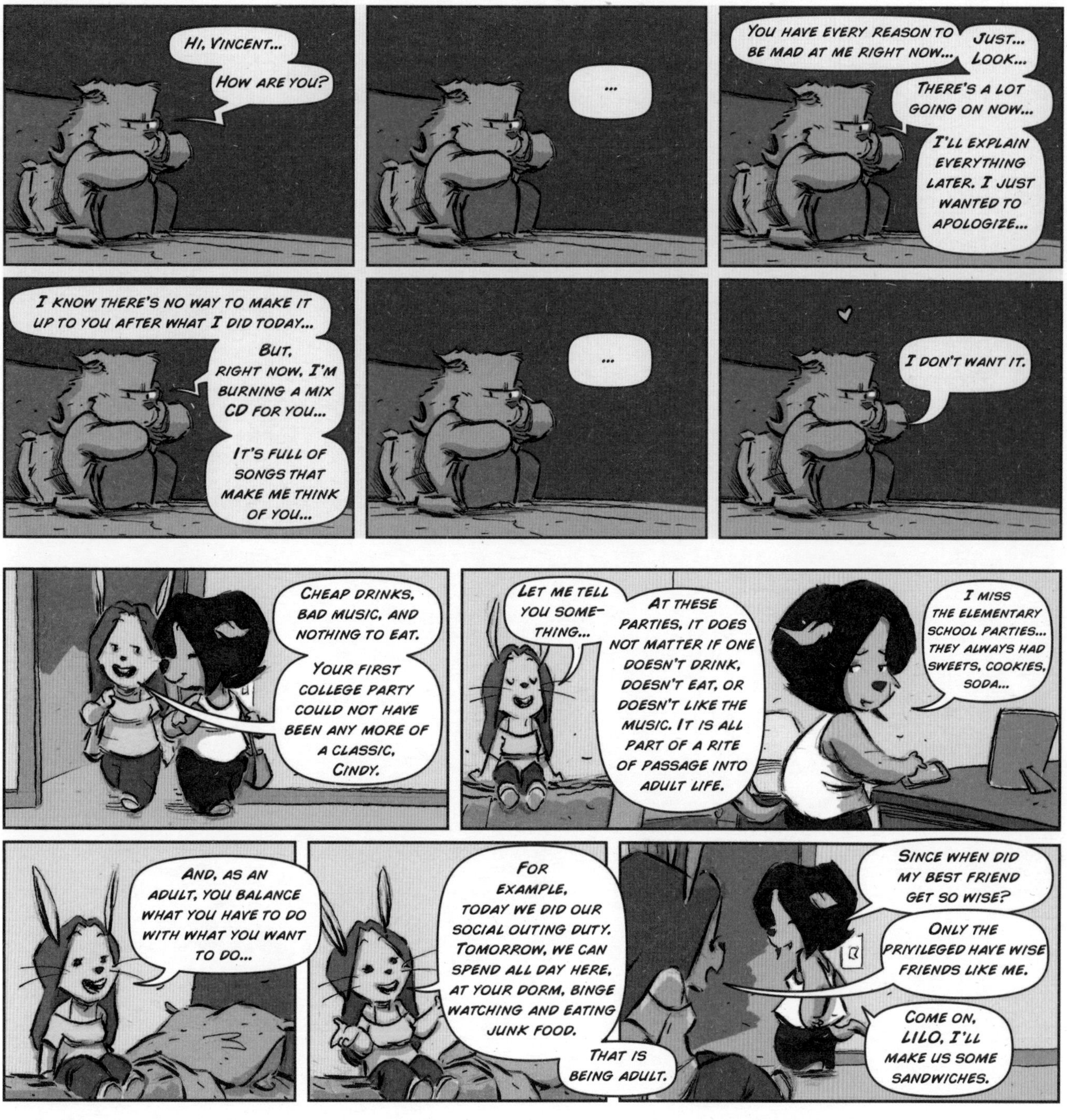
HI, VINCENT...
HOW ARE YOU?
...
YOU HAVE EVERY REASON TO BE MAD AT ME RIGHT NOW...
JUST... LOOK...
THERE'S A LOT GOING ON NOW...
I'LL EXPLAIN EVERYTHING LATER. I JUST WANTED TO APOLOGIZE...
I KNOW THERE'S NO WAY TO MAKE IT UP TO YOU AFTER WHAT I DID TODAY...
BUT, RIGHT NOW, I'M BURNING A MIX CD FOR YOU...
IT'S FULL OF SONGS THAT MAKE ME THINK OF YOU...
...
I DON'T WANT IT.
CHEAP DRINKS, BAD MUSIC, AND NOTHING TO EAT.
YOUR FIRST COLLEGE PARTY COULD NOT HAVE BEEN ANY MORE OF A CLASSIC, CINDY.
LET ME TELL YOU SOME-THING...
AT THESE PARTIES, IT DOES NOT MATTER IF ONE DOESN'T DRINK, DOESN'T EAT, OR DOESN'T LIKE THE MUSIC. IT IS ALL PART OF A RITE OF PASSAGE INTO ADULT LIFE.
I MISS THE ELEMENTARY SCHOOL PARTIES... THEY ALWAYS HAD SWEETS, COOKIES, SODA...
AND, AS AN ADULT, YOU BALANCE WHAT YOU HAVE TO DO WITH WHAT YOU WANT TO DO...
FOR EXAMPLE, TODAY WE DID OUR SOCIAL OUTING DUTY. TOMORROW, WE CAN SPEND ALL DAY HERE, AT YOUR DORM, BINGE WATCHING AND EATING JUNK FOOD.
THAT IS BEING ADULT.
SINCE WHEN DID MY BEST FRIEND GET SO WISE?
ONLY THE PRIVILEGED HAVE WISE FRIENDS LIKE ME.
COME ON, LILO, I'LL MAKE US SOME SANDWICHES.

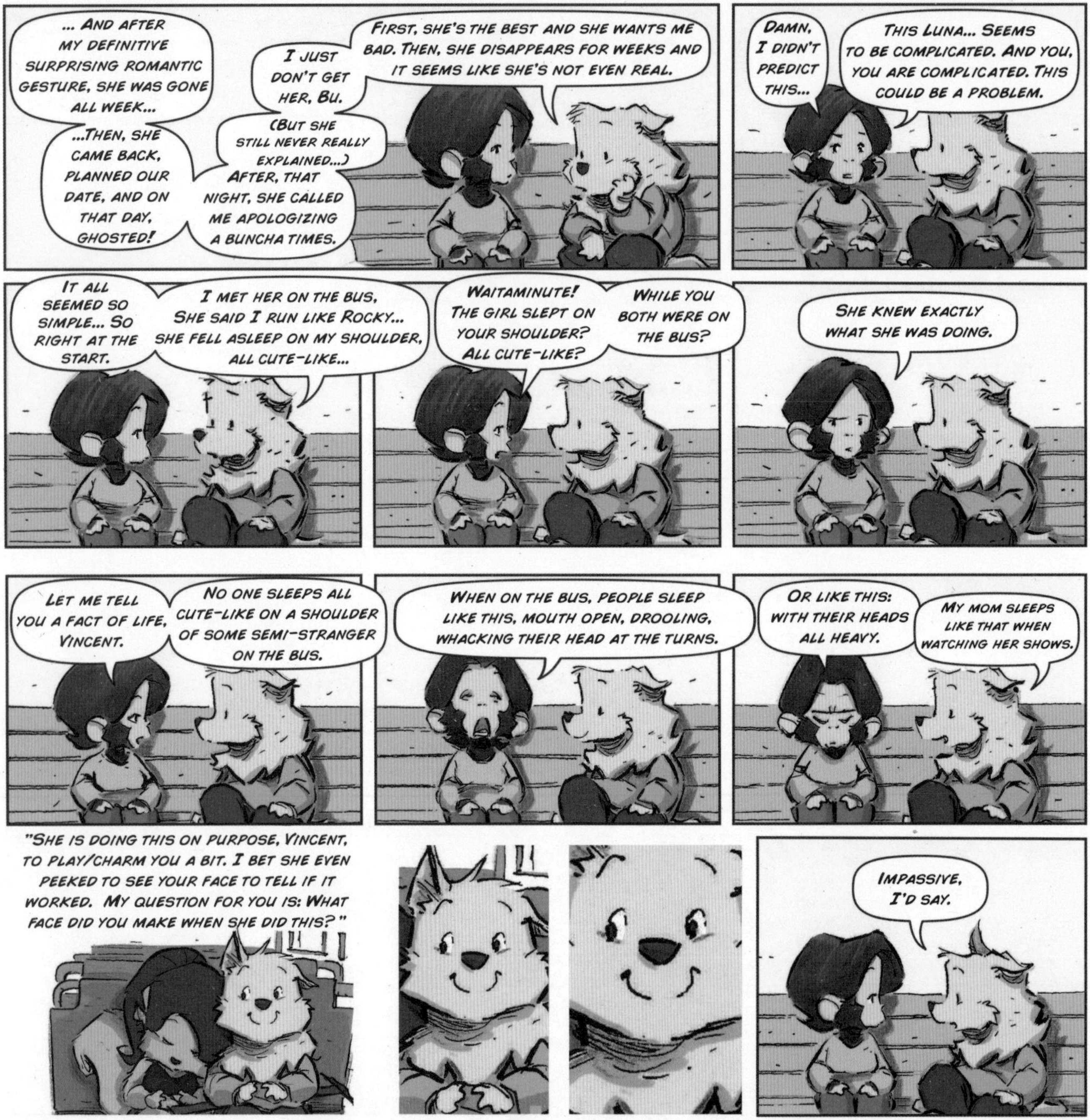
... AND AFTER MY DEFINITIVE SURPRISING ROMANTIC GESTURE, SHE WAS GONE ALL WEEK...
...THEN, SHE CAME BACK, PLANNED OUR DATE, AND ON THAT DAY, GHOSTED!
I JUST DON'T GET HER, BU.
(BUT SHE STILL NEVER REALLY EXPLAINED...)
AFTER, THAT NIGHT, SHE CALLED ME APOLOGIZING A BUNCHA TIMES.
FIRST, SHE'S THE BEST AND SHE WANTS ME BAD. THEN, SHE DISAPPEARS FOR WEEKS AND IT SEEMS LIKE SHE'S NOT EVEN REAL.
DAMN, I DIDN'T PREDICT THIS...
THIS LUNA... SEEMS TO BE COMPLICATED. AND YOU, YOU ARE COMPLICATED. THIS COULD BE A PROBLEM.
IT ALL SEEMED SO SIMPLE... SO RIGHT AT THE START.
I MET HER ON THE BUS, SHE SAID I RUN LIKE ROCKY... SHE FELL ASLEEP ON MY SHOULDER, ALL CUTE-LIKE...
WAITAMINUTE! THE GIRL SLEPT ON YOUR SHOULDER? ALL CUTE-LIKE?
WHILE YOU BOTH WERE ON THE BUS?
SHE KNEW EXACTLY WHAT SHE WAS DOING.
LET ME TELL YOU A FACT OF LIFE, VINCENT.
NO ONE SLEEPS ALL CUTE-LIKE ON A SHOULDER OF SOME SEMI-STRANGER ON THE BUS.
WHEN ON THE BUS, PEOPLE SLEEP LIKE THIS, MOUTH OPEN, DROOLING, WHACKING THEIR HEAD AT THE TURNS.
OR LIKE THIS: WITH THEIR HEADS ALL HEAVY.
MY MOM SLEEPS LIKE THAT WHEN WATCHING HER SHOWS.
"SHE IS DOING THIS ON PURPOSE, VINCENT, TO PLAY/CHARM YOU A BIT. I BET SHE EVEN PEEKED TO SEE YOUR FACE TO TELL IF IT WORKED. MY QUESTION FOR YOU IS: WHAT FACE DID YOU MAKE WHEN SHE DID THIS?"
IMPASSIVE, I'D SAY.

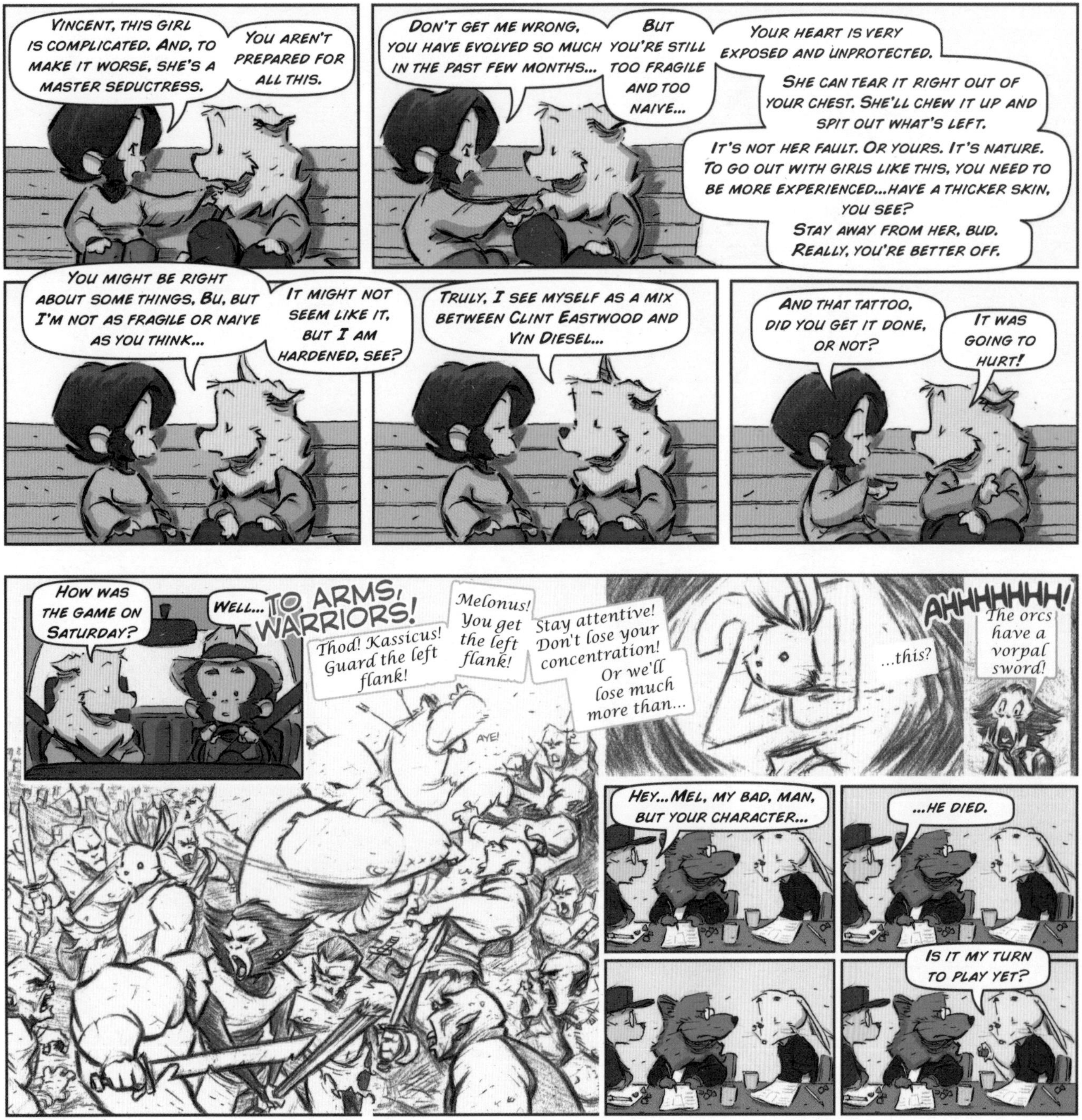
VINCENT, THIS GIRL IS COMPLICATED. AND, TO MAKE IT WORSE, SHE'S A MASTER SEDUCTRESS.
YOU AREN'T PREPARED FOR ALL THIS.
DON'T GET ME WRONG, YOU HAVE EVOLVED SO MUCH IN THE PAST FEW MONTHS...
BUT YOU'RE STILL TOO FRAGILE AND TOO NAIVE...
YOUR HEART IS VERY EXPOSED AND UNPROTECTED.
SHE CAN TEAR IT RIGHT OUT OF YOUR CHEST. SHE'LL CHEW IT UP AND SPIT OUT WHAT'S LEFT.
IT'S NOT HER FAULT. OR YOURS. IT'S NATURE. TO GO OUT WITH GIRLS LIKE THIS, YOU NEED TO BE MORE EXPERIENCED...HAVE A THICKER SKIN, YOU SEE?
STAY AWAY FROM HER, BUD. REALLY, YOU'RE BETTER OFF.
YOU MIGHT BE RIGHT ABOUT SOME THINGS, BU, BUT I'M NOT AS FRAGILE OR NAIVE AS YOU THINK...
IT MIGHT NOT SEEM LIKE IT, BUT I AM HARDENED, SEE?
TRULY, I SEE MYSELF AS A MIX BETWEEN CLINT EASTWOOD AND VIN DIESEL...
AND THAT TATTOO, DID YOU GET IT DONE, OR NOT?
IT WAS GOING TO HURT!
HOW WAS THE GAME ON SATURDAY?
WELL...
TO ARMS, WARRIORS!
Thod! Kassicus! Guard the left flank!
Melonus! You get the left flank!
Stay attentive! Don't lose your concentration!
Or we'll lose much more than...
AYE!
...this?
AHHHHHHH!
The orcs have a vorpal sword!
HEY...MEL, MY BAD, MAN, BUT YOUR CHARACTER...
...HE DIED.
IS IT MY TURN TO PLAY YET?

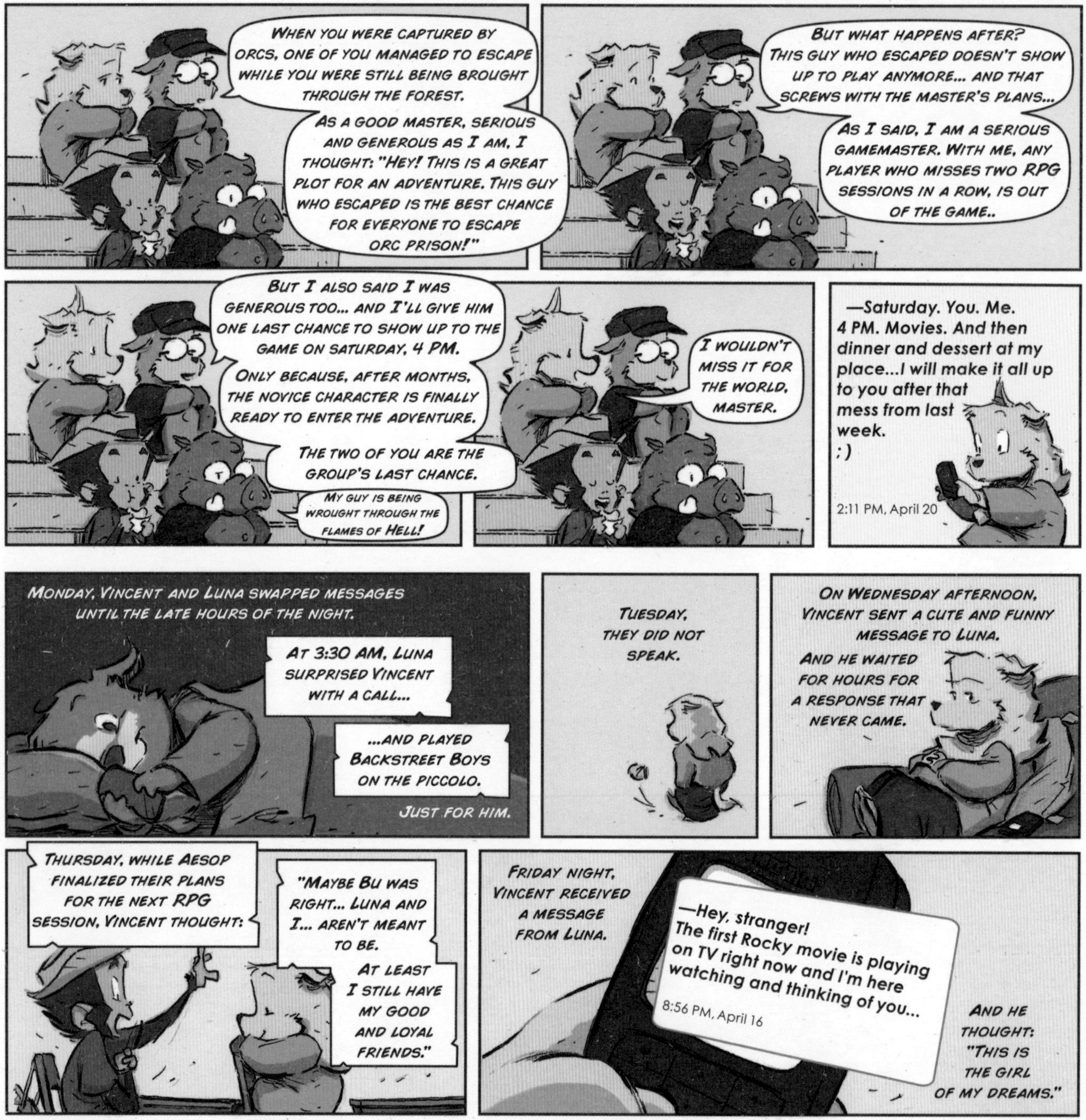
WHEN YOU WERE CAPTURED BY ORCS, ONE OF YOU MANAGED TO ESCAPE WHILE YOU WERE STILL BEING BROUGHT THROUGH THE FOREST.
AS A GOOD MASTER, SERIOUS AND GENEROUS AS I AM, I THOUGHT: "HEY! THIS IS A GREAT PLOT FOR AN ADVENTURE. THIS GUY WHO ESCAPED IS THE BEST CHANCE FOR EVERYONE TO ESCAPE ORC PRISON!"
BUT WHAT HAPPENS AFTER? THIS GUY WHO ESCAPED DOESN'T SHOW UP TO PLAY ANYMORE... AND THAT SCREWS WITH THE MASTER'S PLANS...
AS I SAID, I AM A SERIOUS GAMEMASTER. WITH ME, ANY PLAYER WHO MISSES TWO RPG SESSIONS IN A ROW, IS OUT OF THE GAME..
BUT I ALSO SAID I WAS GENEROUS TOO... AND I'LL GIVE HIM ONE LAST CHANCE TO SHOW UP TO THE GAME ON SATURDAY, 4 PM.
ONLY BECAUSE, AFTER MONTHS, THE NOVICE CHARACTER IS FINALLY READY TO ENTER THE ADVENTURE.
THE TWO OF YOU ARE THE GROUP'S LAST CHANCE.
MY GUY IS BEING WROUGHT THROUGH THE FLAMES OF HELL!
I WOULDN'T MISS IT FOR THE WORLD, MASTER.
—Saturday. You. Me. 4 PM. Movies. And then dinner and dessert at my place...I will make it all up to you after that mess from last week. ;)
2:11 PM, April 20
MONDAY, VINCENT AND LUNA SWAPPED MESSAGES UNTIL THE LATE HOURS OF THE NIGHT.
AT 3:30 AM, LUNA SURPRISED VINCENT WITH A CALL...
...AND PLAYED BACKSTREET BOYS ON THE PICCOLO.
JUST FOR HIM.
TUESDAY, THEY DID NOT SPEAK.
ON WEDNESDAY AFTERNOON, VINCENT SENT A CUTE AND FUNNY MESSAGE TO LUNA.
AND HE WAITED FOR HOURS FOR A RESPONSE THAT NEVER CAME.
THURSDAY, WHILE AESOP FINALIZED THEIR PLANS FOR THE NEXT RPG SESSION, VINCENT THOUGHT:
"MAYBE BU WAS RIGHT... LUNA AND I... AREN'T MEANT TO BE.
AT LEAST I STILL HAVE MY GOOD AND LOYAL FRIENDS."
FRIDAY NIGHT, VINCENT RECEIVED A MESSAGE FROM LUNA.
—Hey, stranger! The first Rocky movie is playing on TV right now and I'm here watching and thinking of you...
8:56 PM, April 16
AND HE THOUGHT: "THIS IS THE GIRL OF MY DREAMS."

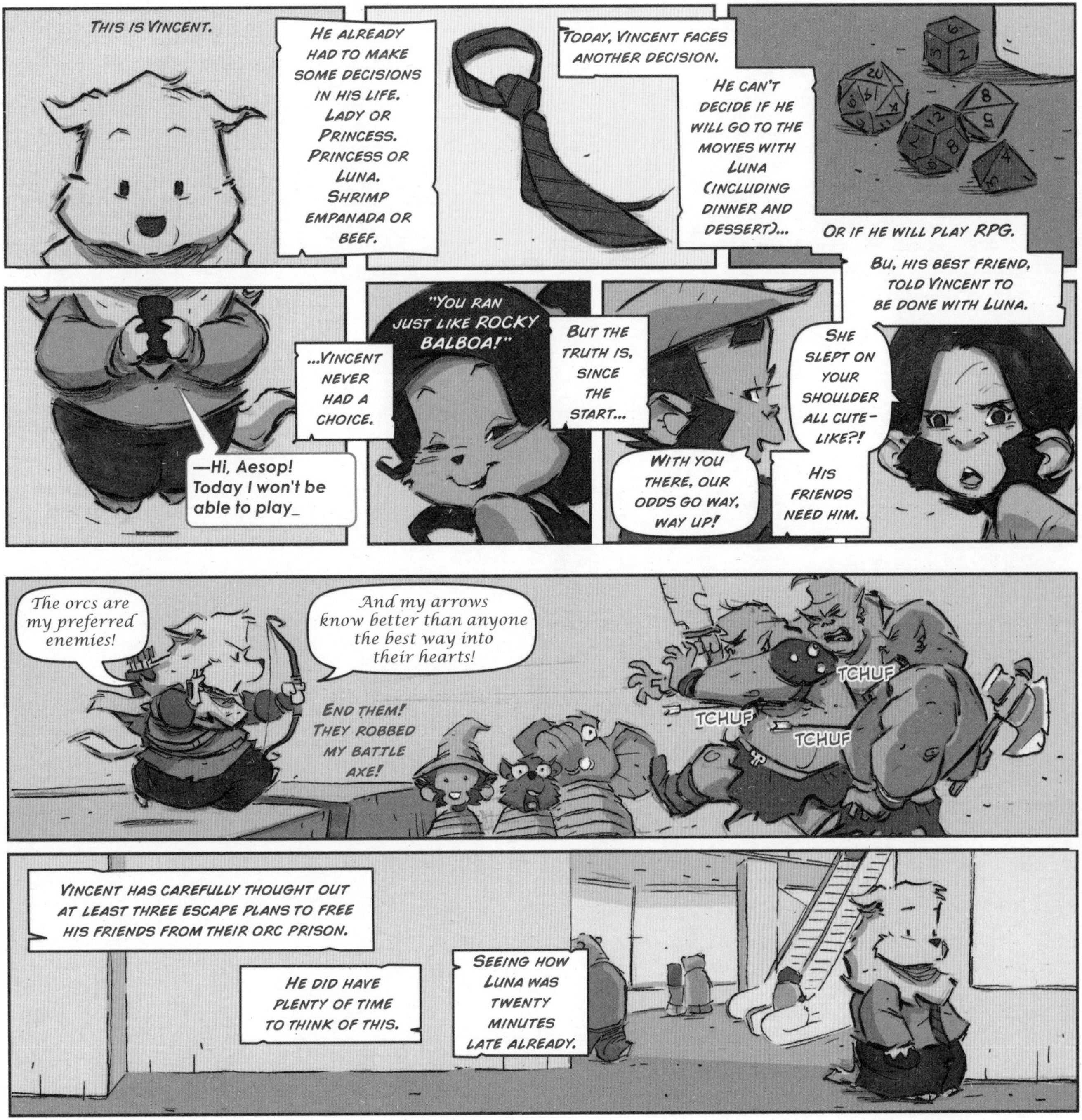

THIS IS VINCENT.
HE ALREADY HAD TO MAKE SOME DECISIONS IN HIS LIFE. LADY OR PRINCESS. PRINCESS OR LUNA. SHRIMP EMPANADA OR BEEF.
TODAY, VINCENT FACES ANOTHER DECISION.
HE CAN'T DECIDE IF HE WILL GO TO THE MOVIES WITH LUNA (INCLUDING DINNER AND DESSERT)...
OR IF HE WILL PLAY RPG.
—Hi, Aesop! Today I won't be able to play_
...VINCENT NEVER HAD A CHOICE.
"YOU RAN JUST LIKE ROCKY BALBOA!"
BUT THE TRUTH IS, SINCE THE START...
WITH YOU THERE, OUR ODDS GO WAY, WAY UP!
BU, HIS BEST FRIEND, TOLD VINCENT TO BE DONE WITH LUNA.
SHE SLEPT ON YOUR SHOULDER ALL CUTE-LIKE?!
HIS FRIENDS NEED HIM.
The orcs are my preferred enemies!
And my arrows know better than anyone the best way into their hearts!
END THEM! THEY ROBBED MY BATTLE AXE!
TCHUF
TCHUF
TCHUF
VINCENT HAS CAREFULLY THOUGHT OUT AT LEAST THREE ESCAPE PLANS TO FREE HIS FRIENDS FROM THEIR ORC PRISON.
HE DID HAVE PLENTY OF TIME TO THINK OF THIS.
SEEING HOW LUNA WAS TWENTY MINUTES LATE ALREADY.

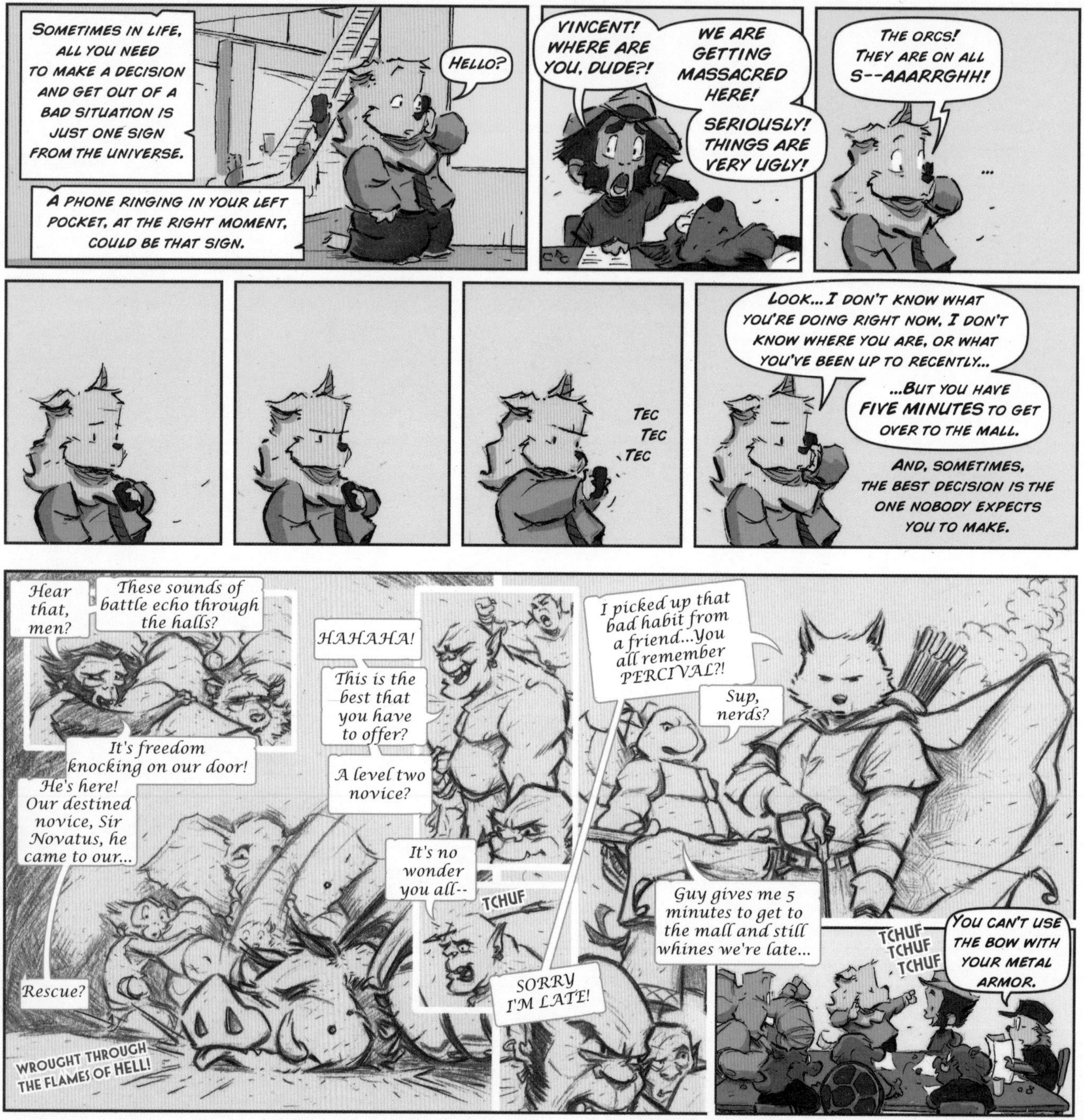

SOMETIMES IN LIFE, ALL YOU NEED TO MAKE A DECISION AND GET OUT OF A BAD SITUATION IS JUST ONE SIGN FROM THE UNIVERSE.
HELLO?
A PHONE RINGING IN YOUR LEFT POCKET, AT THE RIGHT MOMENT, COULD BE THAT SIGN.
VINCENT! WHERE ARE YOU, DUDE?!
WE ARE GETTING MASSACRED HERE!
SERIOUSLY! THINGS ARE VERY UGLY!
THE ORCS! THEY ARE ON ALL S--AAARRGHH!
...
TEC TEC TEC
LOOK... I DON'T KNOW WHAT YOU'RE DOING RIGHT NOW, I DON'T KNOW WHERE YOU ARE, OR WHAT YOU'VE BEEN UP TO RECENTLY...
...BUT YOU HAVE FIVE MINUTES TO GET OVER TO THE MALL.
AND, SOMETIMES, THE BEST DECISION IS THE ONE NOBODY EXPECTS YOU TO MAKE.
Hear that, men?
These sounds of battle echo through the halls?
It's freedom knocking on our door!
He's here! Our destined novice, Sir Novatus, he came to our...
Rescue?
WROUGHT THROUGH THE FLAMES OF HELL!
HAHAHA!
This is the best that you have to offer?
A level two novice?
It's no wonder you all--
TCHUF
SORRY I'M LATE!
I picked up that bad habit from a friend...You all remember PERCIVAL?!
Sup, nerds?
Guy gives me 5 minutes to get to the mall and still whines we're late...
TCHUF TCHUF TCHUF
YOU CAN'T USE THE BOW WITH YOUR METAL ARMOR.

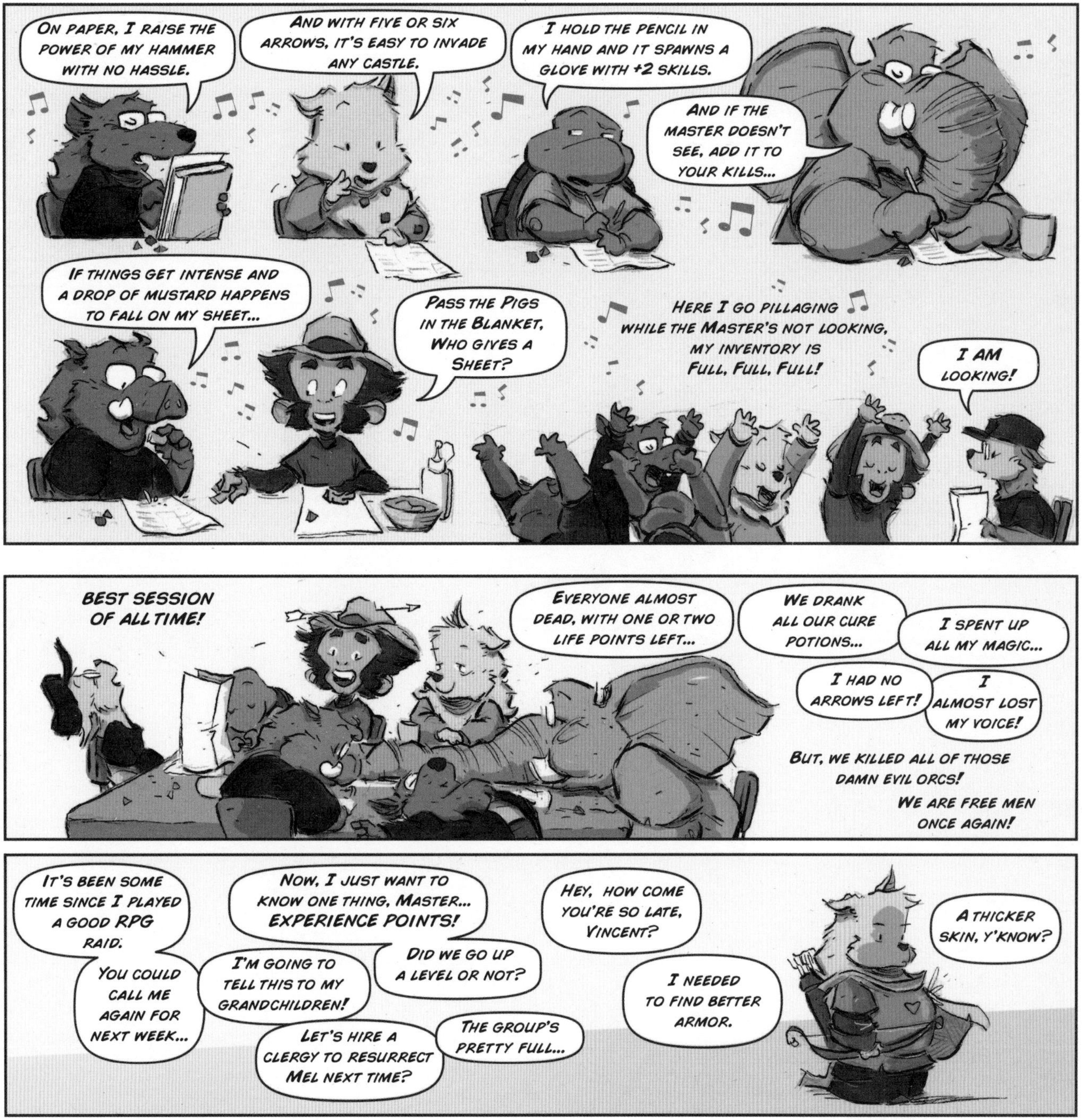
ON PAPER, I RAISE THE POWER OF MY HAMMER WITH NO HASSLE.
AND WITH FIVE OR SIX ARROWS, IT'S EASY TO INVADE ANY CASTLE.
I HOLD THE PENCIL IN MY HAND AND IT SPAWNS A GLOVE WITH +2 SKILLS.
AND IF THE MASTER DOESN'T SEE, ADD IT TO YOUR KILLS...
IF THINGS GET INTENSE AND A DROP OF MUSTARD HAPPENS TO FALL ON MY SHEET...
PASS THE PIGS IN THE BLANKET, WHO GIVES A SHEET?
HERE I GO PILLAGING WHILE THE MASTER'S NOT LOOKING, MY INVENTORY IS FULL, FULL, FULL!
I AM LOOKING!
BEST SESSION OF ALL TIME!
EVERYONE ALMOST DEAD, WITH ONE OR TWO LIFE POINTS LEFT...
WE DRANK ALL OUR CURE POTIONS...
I SPENT UP ALL MY MAGIC...
I HAD NO ARROWS LEFT!
I ALMOST LOST MY VOICE!
BUT, WE KILLED ALL OF THOSE DAMN EVIL ORCS!
WE ARE FREE MEN ONCE AGAIN!
IT'S BEEN SOME TIME SINCE I PLAYED A GOOD RPG RAID.
YOU COULD CALL ME AGAIN FOR NEXT WEEK...
NOW, I JUST WANT TO KNOW ONE THING, MASTER... EXPERIENCE POINTS!
DID WE GO UP A LEVEL OR NOT?
I'M GOING TO TELL THIS TO MY GRANDCHILDREN!
LET'S HIRE A CLERGY TO RESURRECT MEL NEXT TIME?
THE GROUP'S PRETTY FULL...
HEY, HOW COME YOU'RE SO LATE, VINCENT?
I NEEDED TO FIND BETTER ARMOR.
A THICKER SKIN, Y'KNOW?

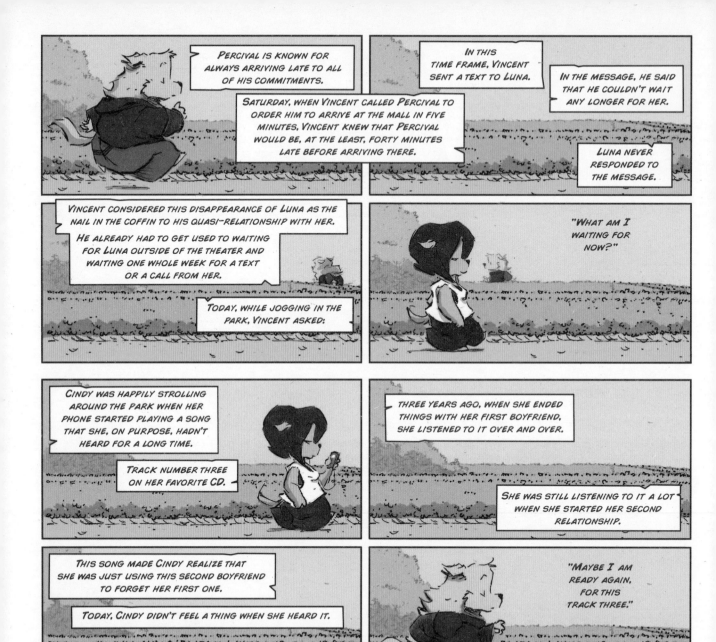

PERCIVAL IS KNOWN FOR ALWAYS ARRIVING LATE TO ALL OF HIS COMMITMENTS.

SATURDAY, WHEN VINCENT CALLED PERCIVAL TO ORDER HIM TO ARRIVE AT THE MALL IN FIVE MINUTES, VINCENT KNEW THAT PERCIVAL WOULD BE, AT THE LEAST, FORTY MINUTES LATE BEFORE ARRIVING THERE.

IN THIS TIME FRAME, VINCENT SENT A TEXT TO LUNA.

IN THE MESSAGE, HE SAID THAT HE COULDN'T WAIT ANY LONGER FOR HER.

LUNA NEVER RESPONDED TO THE MESSAGE.

VINCENT CONSIDERED THIS DISAPPEARANCE OF LUNA AS THE NAIL IN THE COFFIN TO HIS QUASI-RELATIONSHIP WITH HER.

HE ALREADY HAD TO GET USED TO WAITING FOR LUNA OUTSIDE OF THE THEATER AND WAITING ONE WHOLE WEEK FOR A TEXT OR A CALL FROM HER.

TODAY, WHILE JOGGING IN THE PARK, VINCENT ASKED:

"WHAT AM I WAITING FOR NOW?"

CINDY WAS HAPPILY STROLLING AROUND THE PARK WHEN HER PHONE STARTED PLAYING A SONG THAT SHE, ON PURPOSE, HADN'T HEARD FOR A LONG TIME.

TRACK NUMBER THREE ON HER FAVORITE CD.

THREE YEARS AGO, WHEN SHE ENDED THINGS WITH HER FIRST BOYFRIEND, SHE LISTENED TO IT OVER AND OVER.

SHE WAS STILL LISTENING TO IT A LOT WHEN SHE STARTED HER SECOND RELATIONSHIP.

THIS SONG MADE CINDY REALIZE THAT SHE WAS JUST USING THIS SECOND BOYFRIEND TO FORGET HER FIRST ONE.

TODAY, CINDY DIDN'T FEEL A THING WHEN SHE HEARD IT.

WHEN SHE LEFT THE PARK TO GO HOME, CINDY THOUGHT:

"MAYBE I AM READY AGAIN, FOR THIS TRACK THREE."

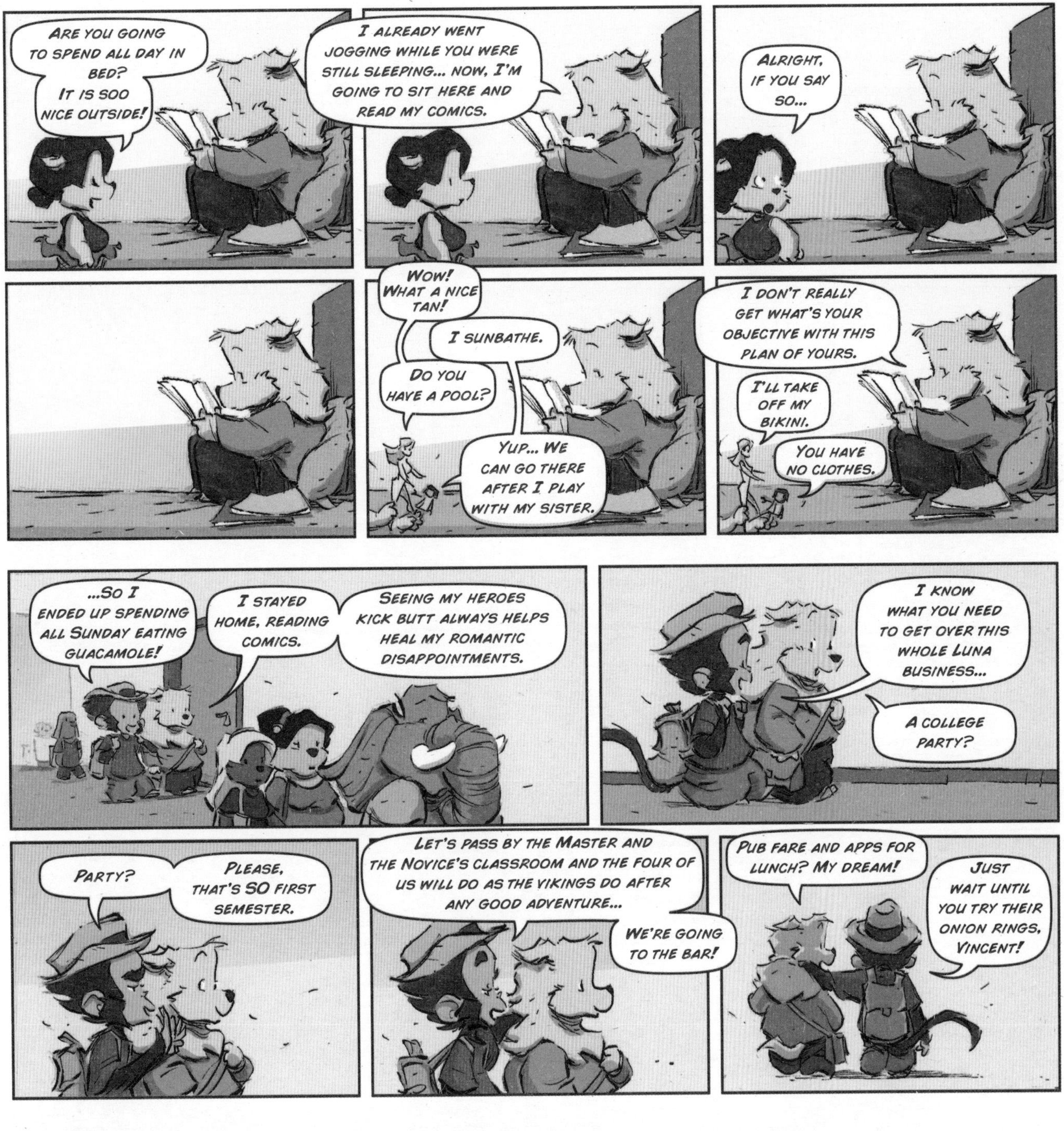
ARE YOU GOING TO SPEND ALL DAY IN BED? IT IS SOO NICE OUTSIDE!
I ALREADY WENT JOGGING WHILE YOU WERE STILL SLEEPING... NOW, I'M GOING TO SIT HERE AND READ MY COMICS.
ALRIGHT, IF YOU SAY SO...
WOW! WHAT A NICE TAN!
I SUNBATHE.
DO YOU HAVE A POOL?
YUP... WE CAN GO THERE AFTER I PLAY WITH MY SISTER.
I DON'T REALLY GET WHAT'S YOUR OBJECTIVE WITH THIS PLAN OF YOURS.
I'LL TAKE OFF MY BIKINI.
YOU HAVE NO CLOTHES.
...SO I ENDED UP SPENDING ALL SUNDAY EATING GUACAMOLE!
I STAYED HOME, READING COMICS.
SEEING MY HEROES KICK BUTT ALWAYS HELPS HEAL MY ROMANTIC DISAPPOINTMENTS.
I KNOW WHAT YOU NEED TO GET OVER THIS WHOLE LUNA BUSINESS...
A COLLEGE PARTY?
PARTY?
PLEASE, THAT'S SO FIRST SEMESTER.
LET'S PASS BY THE MASTER AND THE NOVICE'S CLASSROOM AND THE FOUR OF US WILL DO AS THE VIKINGS DO AFTER ANY GOOD ADVENTURE...
WE'RE GOING TO THE BAR!
PUB FARE AND APPS FOR LUNCH? MY DREAM!
JUST WAIT UNTIL YOU TRY THEIR ONION RINGS, VINCENT!

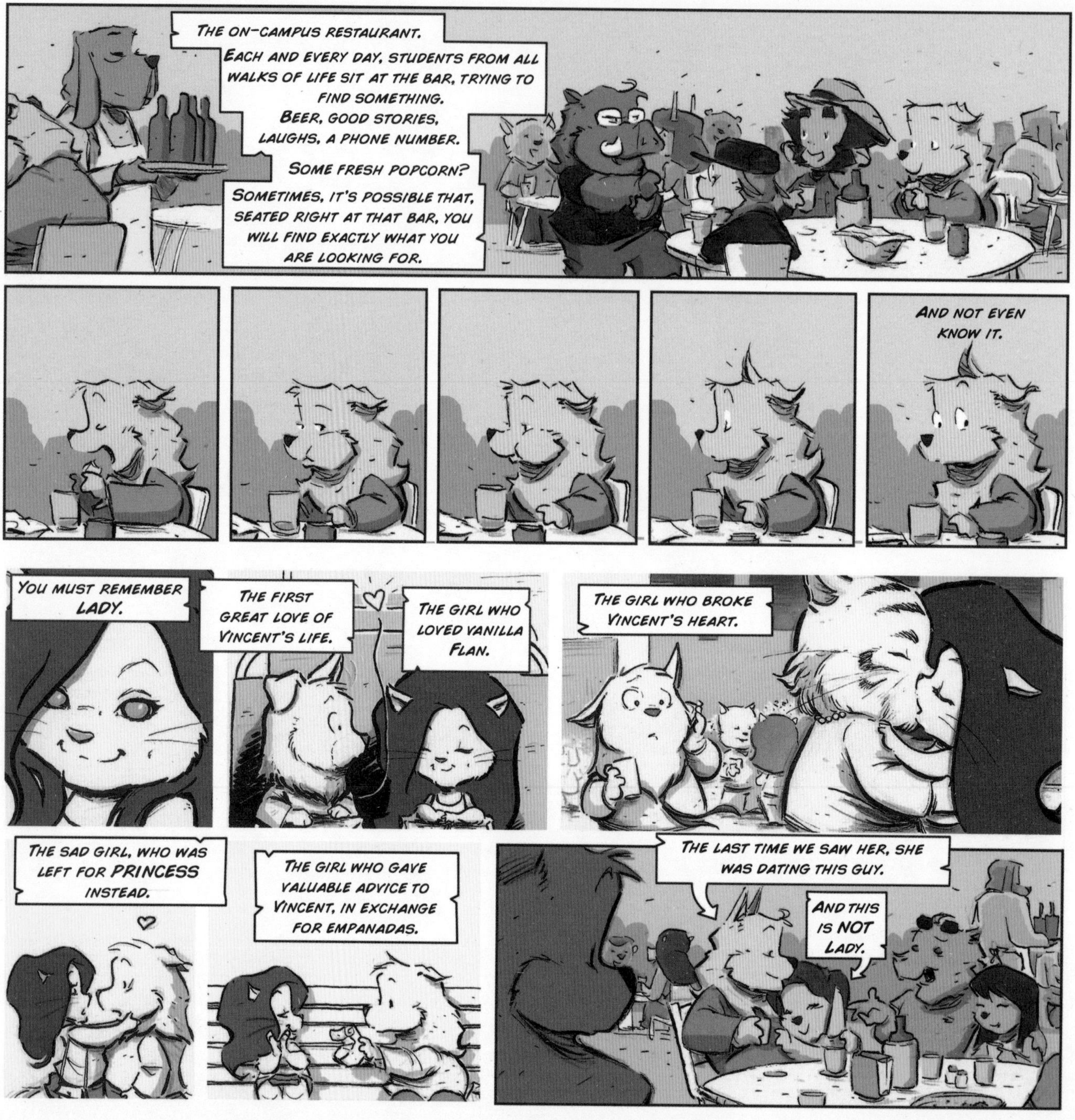
THE ON-CAMPUS RESTAURANT.
EACH AND EVERY DAY, STUDENTS FROM ALL WALKS OF LIFE SIT AT THE BAR, TRYING TO FIND SOMETHING.
BEER, GOOD STORIES, LAUGHS, A PHONE NUMBER.
SOME FRESH POPCORN?
SOMETIMES, IT'S POSSIBLE THAT, SEATED RIGHT AT THAT BAR, YOU WILL FIND EXACTLY WHAT YOU ARE LOOKING FOR.
AND NOT EVEN KNOW IT.
YOU MUST REMEMBER LADY.
THE FIRST GREAT LOVE OF VINCENT'S LIFE.
THE GIRL WHO LOVED VANILLA FLAN.
THE GIRL WHO BROKE VINCENT'S HEART.
THE SAD GIRL, WHO WAS LEFT FOR PRINCESS INSTEAD.
THE GIRL WHO GAVE VALUABLE ADVICE TO VINCENT, IN EXCHANGE FOR EMPANADAS.
THE LAST TIME WE SAW HER, SHE WAS DATING THIS GUY.
AND THIS IS NOT LADY.

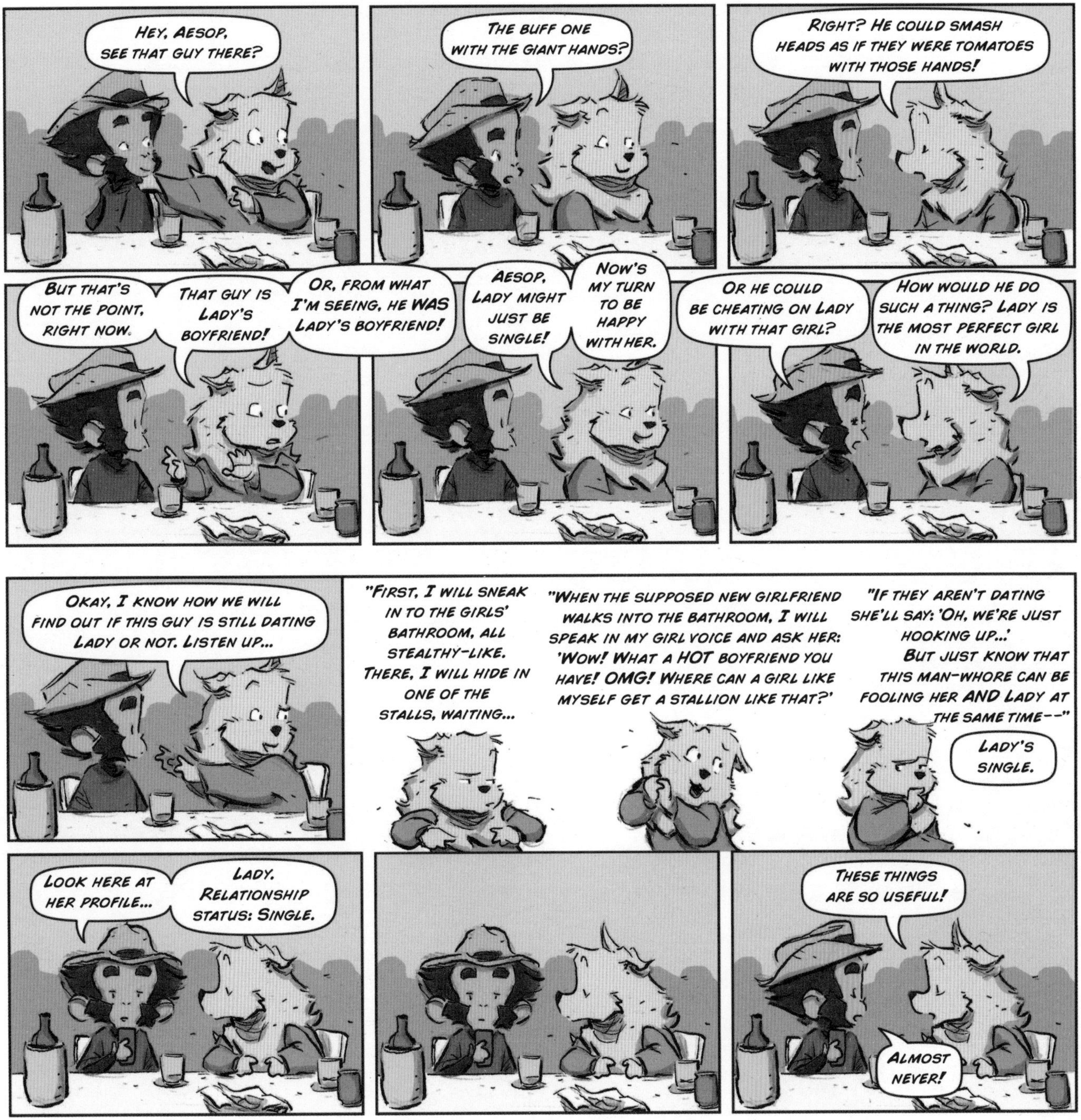
HEY, AESOP, SEE THAT GUY THERE?
THE BUFF ONE WITH THE GIANT HANDS?
RIGHT? HE COULD SMASH HEADS AS IF THEY WERE TOMATOES WITH THOSE HANDS!
BUT THAT'S NOT THE POINT, RIGHT NOW.
THAT GUY IS LADY'S BOYFRIEND!
OR, FROM WHAT I'M SEEING, HE WAS LADY'S BOYFRIEND!
AESOP, LADY MIGHT JUST BE SINGLE!
NOW'S MY TURN TO BE HAPPY WITH HER.
OR HE COULD BE CHEATING ON LADY WITH THAT GIRL?
HOW WOULD HE DO SUCH A THING? LADY IS THE MOST PERFECT GIRL IN THE WORLD.
OKAY, I KNOW HOW WE WILL FIND OUT IF THIS GUY IS STILL DATING LADY OR NOT. LISTEN UP...
"FIRST, I WILL SNEAK IN TO THE GIRLS' BATHROOM, ALL STEALTHY-LIKE. THERE, I WILL HIDE IN ONE OF THE STALLS, WAITING...
"WHEN THE SUPPOSED NEW GIRLFRIEND WALKS INTO THE BATHROOM, I WILL SPEAK IN MY GIRL VOICE AND ASK HER: 'WOW! WHAT A HOT BOYFRIEND YOU HAVE! OMG! WHERE CAN A GIRL LIKE MYSELF GET A STALLION LIKE THAT?'
"IF THEY AREN'T DATING SHE'LL SAY: 'OH, WE'RE JUST HOOKING UP...' BUT JUST KNOW THAT THIS MAN-WHORE CAN BE FOOLING HER AND LADY AT THE SAME TIME--"
LADY'S SINGLE.
LOOK HERE AT HER PROFILE...
LADY. RELATIONSHIP STATUS: SINGLE.
THESE THINGS ARE SO USEFUL!
ALMOST NEVER!

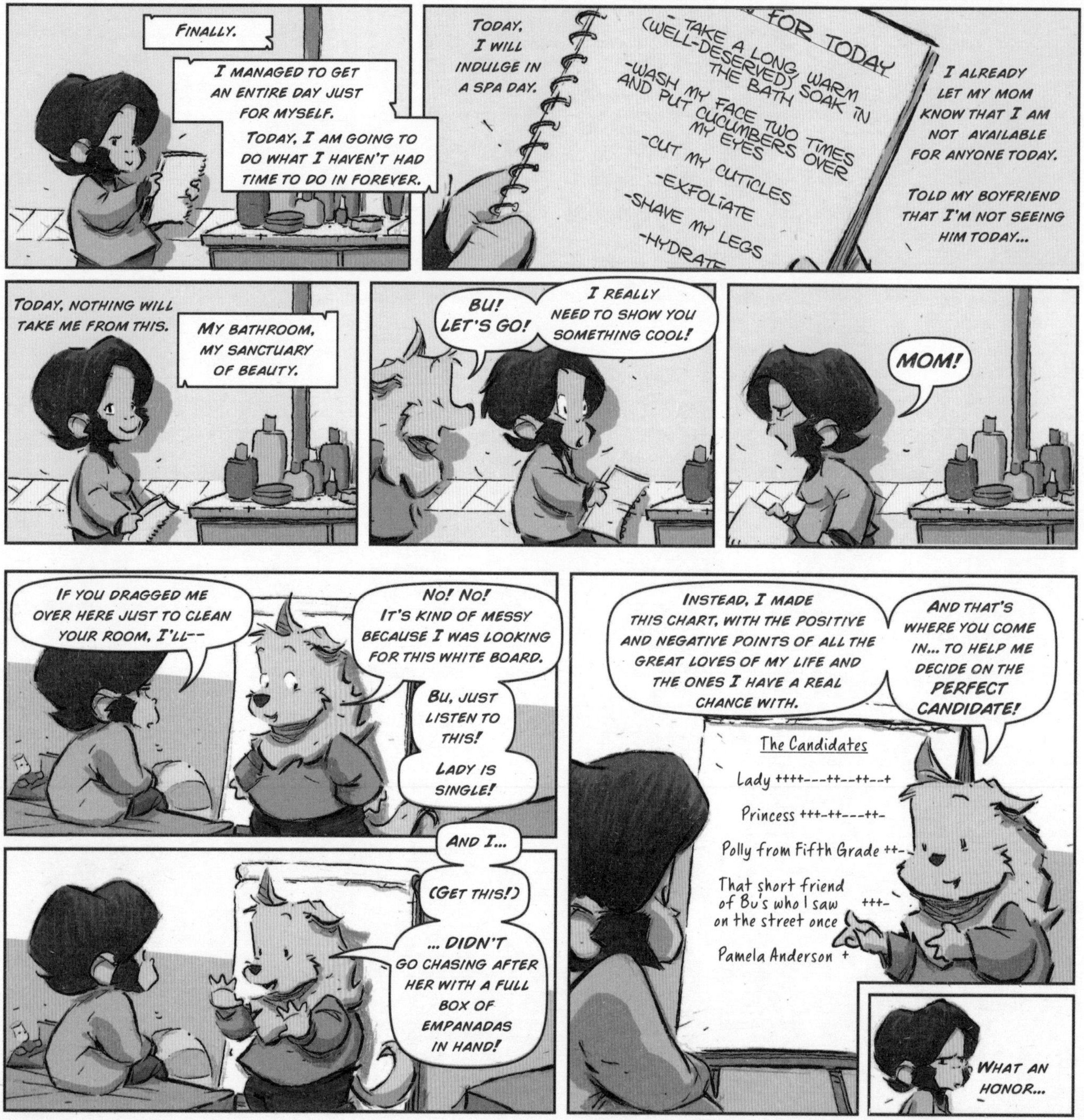
FINALLY.
I MANAGED TO GET AN ENTIRE DAY JUST FOR MYSELF.
TODAY, I AM GOING TO DO WHAT I HAVEN'T HAD TIME TO DO IN FOREVER.
TODAY, I WILL INDULGE IN A SPA DAY.
FOR TODAY
- TAKE A LONG, WARM (WELL-DESERVED) SOAK IN THE BATH
-WASH MY FACE TWO TIMES AND PUT CUCUMBERS OVER MY EYES
-CUT MY CUTICLES
-EXFOLIATE
-SHAVE MY LEGS
-HYDRATE
I ALREADY LET MY MOM KNOW THAT I AM NOT AVAILABLE FOR ANYONE TODAY.
TOLD MY BOYFRIEND THAT I'M NOT SEEING HIM TODAY...
TODAY, NOTHING WILL TAKE ME FROM THIS.
MY BATHROOM, MY SANCTUARY OF BEAUTY.
BU! LET'S GO!
I REALLY NEED TO SHOW YOU SOMETHING COOL!
MOM!
IF YOU DRAGGED ME OVER HERE JUST TO CLEAN YOUR ROOM, I'LL--
NO! NO! IT'S KIND OF MESSY BECAUSE I WAS LOOKING FOR THIS WHITE BOARD.
BU, JUST LISTEN TO THIS!
LADY IS SINGLE!
AND I...
(GET THIS!)
... DIDN'T GO CHASING AFTER HER WITH A FULL BOX OF EMPANADAS IN HAND!
INSTEAD, I MADE THIS CHART, WITH THE POSITIVE AND NEGATIVE POINTS OF ALL THE GREAT LOVES OF MY LIFE AND THE ONES I HAVE A REAL CHANCE WITH.
AND THAT'S WHERE YOU COME IN... TO HELP ME DECIDE ON THE PERFECT CANDIDATE!
The Candidates
Lady ++++---++--++--+
Princess +++-++---++-
Polly from Fifth Grade ++-
That short friend of Bu's who I saw on the street once +++-
Pamela Anderson +
WHAT AN HONOR...

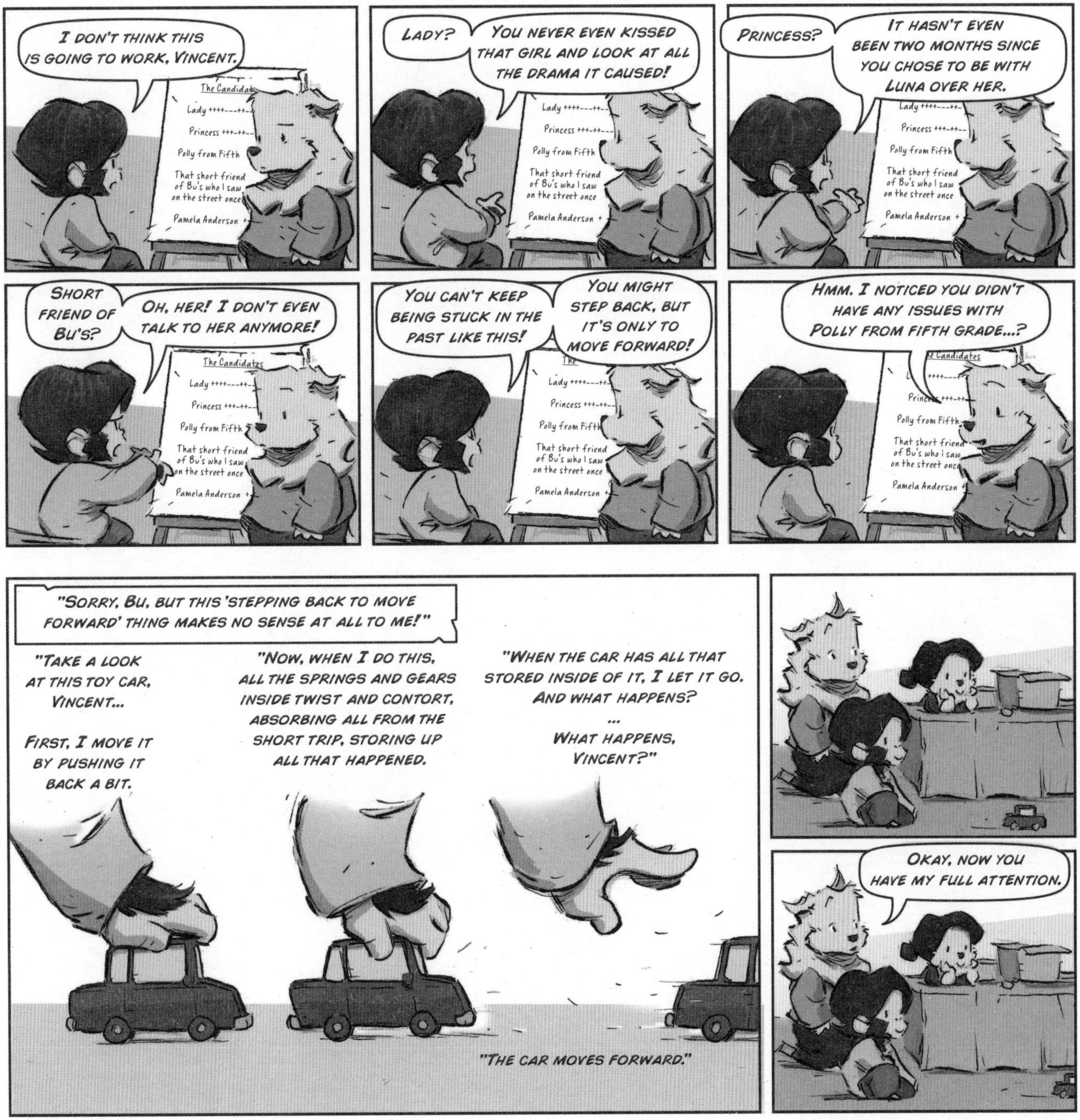
I DON'T THINK THIS IS GOING TO WORK, VINCENT.
The Candidates
Lady ++++---++--
Princess +++-++---
Polly from Fifth
That short friend of Bu's who I saw on the street once
Pamela Anderson +
LADY?
YOU NEVER EVEN KISSED THAT GIRL AND LOOK AT ALL THE DRAMA IT CAUSED!
PRINCESS?
IT HASN'T EVEN BEEN TWO MONTHS SINCE YOU CHOSE TO BE WITH LUNA OVER HER.
SHORT FRIEND OF BU'S?
OH, HER! I DON'T EVEN TALK TO HER ANYMORE!
YOU CAN'T KEEP BEING STUCK IN THE PAST LIKE THIS!
YOU MIGHT STEP BACK, BUT IT'S ONLY TO MOVE FORWARD!
HMM. I NOTICED YOU DIDN'T HAVE ANY ISSUES WITH POLLY FROM FIFTH GRADE...?
"SORRY, BU, BUT THIS 'STEPPING BACK TO MOVE FORWARD' THING MAKES NO SENSE AT ALL TO ME!"
"TAKE A LOOK AT THIS TOY CAR, VINCENT...
FIRST, I MOVE IT BY PUSHING IT BACK A BIT.
"NOW, WHEN I DO THIS, ALL THE SPRINGS AND GEARS INSIDE TWIST AND CONTORT, ABSORBING ALL FROM THE SHORT TRIP, STORING UP ALL THAT HAPPENED.
"WHEN THE CAR HAS ALL THAT STORED INSIDE OF IT, I LET IT GO. AND WHAT HAPPENS?
...
WHAT HAPPENS, VINCENT?"
"THE CAR MOVES FORWARD."
OKAY, NOW YOU HAVE MY FULL ATTENTION.

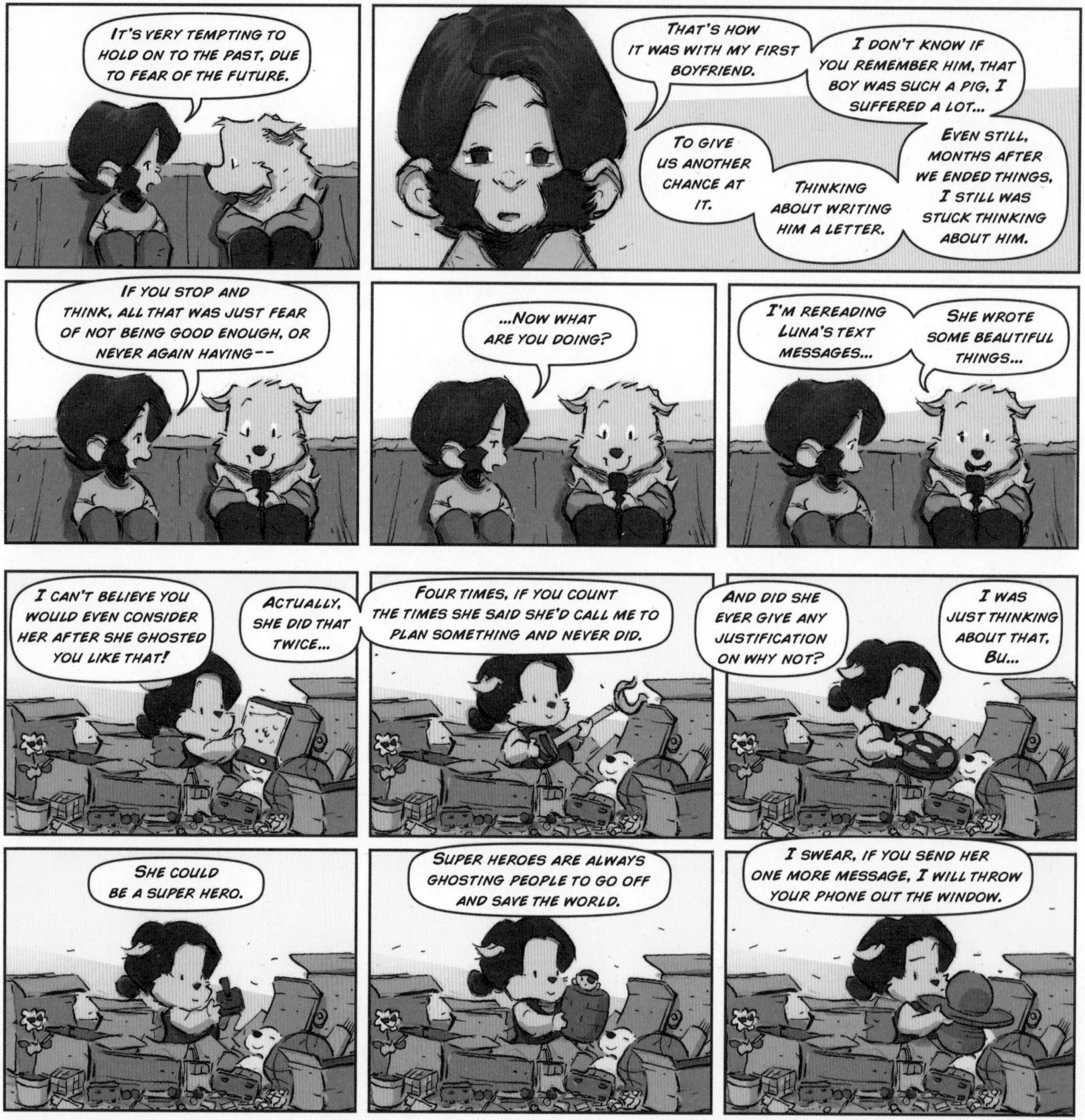
IT'S VERY TEMPTING TO HOLD ON TO THE PAST, DUE TO FEAR OF THE FUTURE.
THAT'S HOW IT WAS WITH MY FIRST BOYFRIEND.
I DON'T KNOW IF YOU REMEMBER HIM, THAT BOY WAS SUCH A PIG, I SUFFERED A LOT...
EVEN STILL, MONTHS AFTER WE ENDED THINGS, I STILL WAS STUCK THINKING ABOUT HIM.
THINKING ABOUT WRITING HIM A LETTER.
TO GIVE US ANOTHER CHANCE AT IT.
IF YOU STOP AND THINK, ALL THAT WAS JUST FEAR OF NOT BEING GOOD ENOUGH, OR NEVER AGAIN HAVING--
...NOW WHAT ARE YOU DOING?
I'M REREADING LUNA'S TEXT MESSAGES...
SHE WROTE SOME BEAUTIFUL THINGS...
I CAN'T BELIEVE YOU WOULD EVEN CONSIDER HER AFTER SHE GHOSTED YOU LIKE THAT!
ACTUALLY, SHE DID THAT TWICE...
FOUR TIMES, IF YOU COUNT THE TIMES SHE SAID SHE'D CALL ME TO PLAN SOMETHING AND NEVER DID.
AND DID SHE EVER GIVE ANY JUSTIFICATION ON WHY NOT?
I WAS JUST THINKING ABOUT THAT, BU...
SHE COULD BE A SUPER HERO.
SUPER HEROES ARE ALWAYS GHOSTING PEOPLE TO GO OFF AND SAVE THE WORLD.
I SWEAR, IF YOU SEND HER ONE MORE MESSAGE, I WILL THROW YOUR PHONE OUT THE WINDOW.

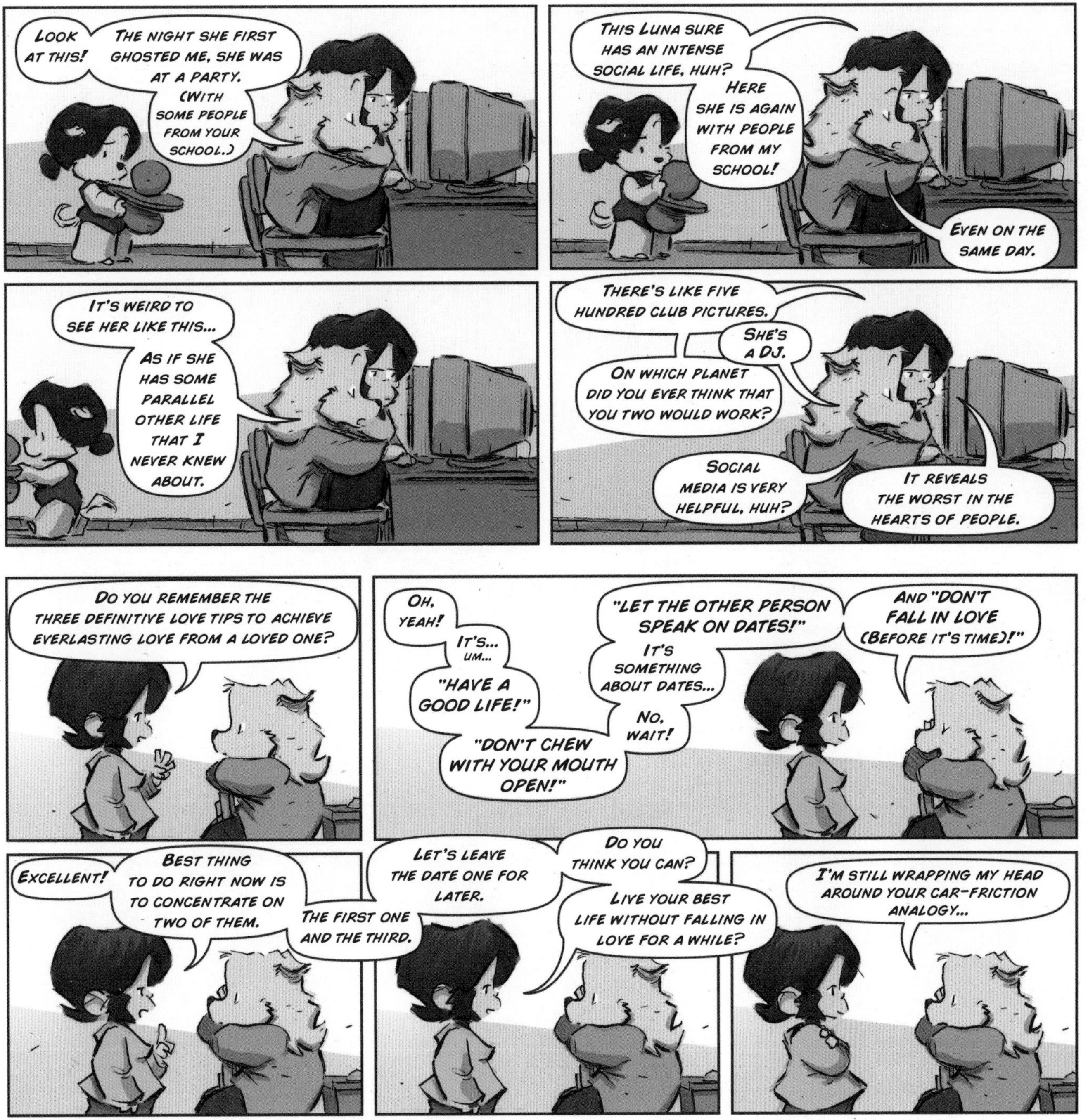
LOOK AT THIS!
THE NIGHT SHE FIRST GHOSTED ME, SHE WAS AT A PARTY.
(WITH SOME PEOPLE FROM YOUR SCHOOL.)
THIS LUNA SURE HAS AN INTENSE SOCIAL LIFE, HUH?
HERE SHE IS AGAIN WITH PEOPLE FROM MY SCHOOL!
EVEN ON THE SAME DAY.
IT'S WEIRD TO SEE HER LIKE THIS...
AS IF SHE HAS SOME PARALLEL OTHER LIFE THAT I NEVER KNEW ABOUT.
THERE'S LIKE FIVE HUNDRED CLUB PICTURES.
SHE'S A DJ.
ON WHICH PLANET DID YOU EVER THINK THAT YOU TWO WOULD WORK?
SOCIAL MEDIA IS VERY HELPFUL, HUH?
IT REVEALS THE WORST IN THE HEARTS OF PEOPLE.
DO YOU REMEMBER THE THREE DEFINITIVE LOVE TIPS TO ACHIEVE EVERLASTING LOVE FROM A LOVED ONE?
OH, YEAH!
IT'S... UM...
"HAVE A GOOD LIFE!"
"DON'T CHEW WITH YOUR MOUTH OPEN!"
"LET THE OTHER PERSON SPEAK ON DATES!"
IT'S SOMETHING ABOUT DATES...
NO, WAIT!
AND "DON'T FALL IN LOVE (BEFORE IT'S TIME)!"
EXCELLENT!
BEST THING TO DO RIGHT NOW IS TO CONCENTRATE ON TWO OF THEM.
THE FIRST ONE AND THE THIRD.
LET'S LEAVE THE DATE ONE FOR LATER.
DO YOU THINK YOU CAN?
LIVE YOUR BEST LIFE WITHOUT FALLING IN LOVE FOR A WHILE?
I'M STILL WRAPPING MY HEAD AROUND YOUR CAR-FRICTION ANALOGY...

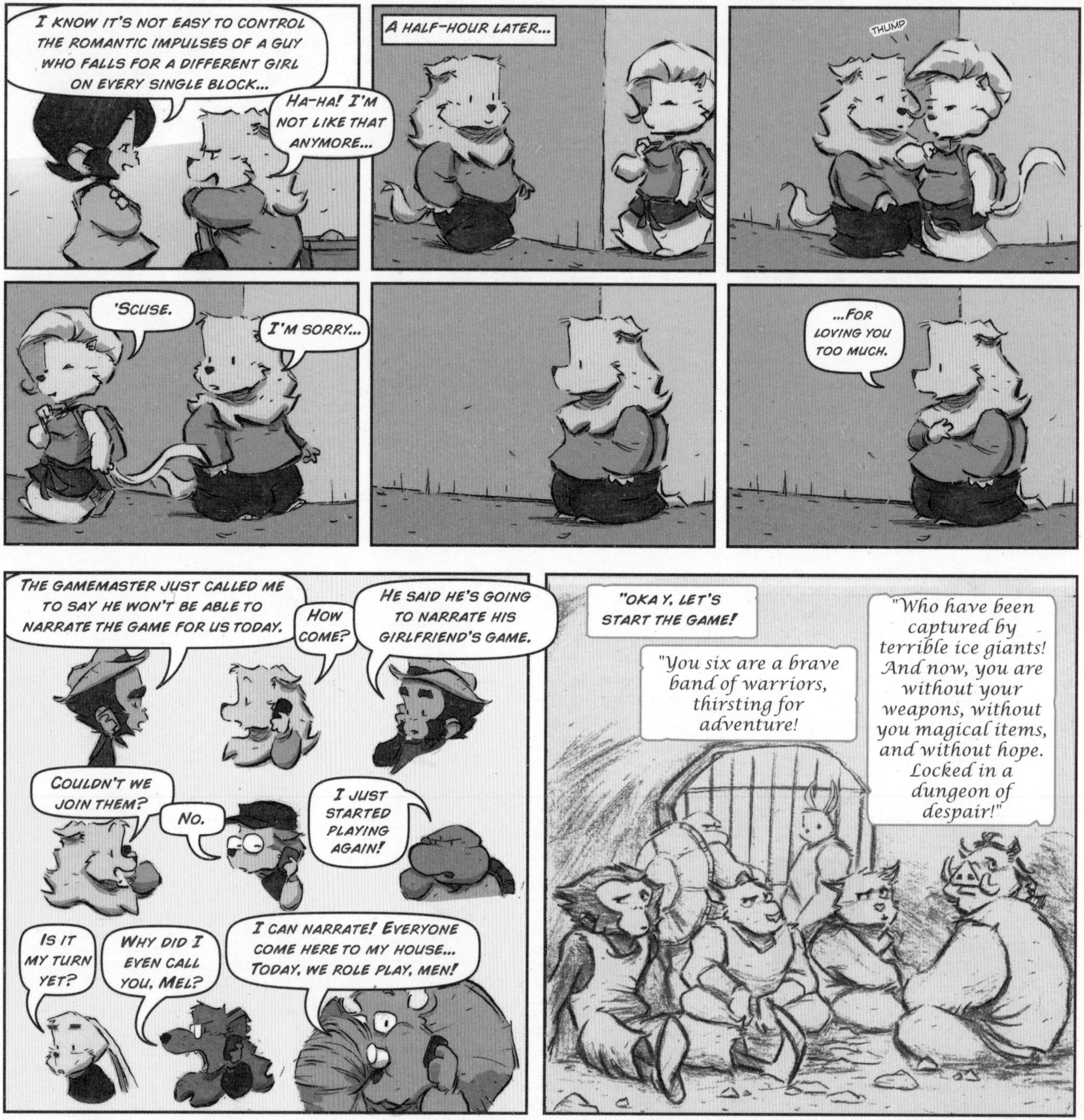
I KNOW IT'S NOT EASY TO CONTROL THE ROMANTIC IMPULSES OF A GUY WHO FALLS FOR A DIFFERENT GIRL ON EVERY SINGLE BLOCK...
HA-HA! I'M NOT LIKE THAT ANYMORE...
A HALF-HOUR LATER...
THUMP
'SCUSE.
I'M SORRY...
...FOR LOVING YOU TOO MUCH.
THE GAMEMASTER JUST CALLED ME TO SAY HE WON'T BE ABLE TO NARRATE THE GAME FOR US TODAY.
HOW COME?
HE SAID HE'S GOING TO NARRATE HIS GIRLFRIEND'S GAME.
COULDN'T WE JOIN THEM?
NO.
I JUST STARTED PLAYING AGAIN!
IS IT MY TURN YET?
WHY DID I EVEN CALL YOU, MEL?
I CAN NARRATE! EVERYONE COME HERE TO MY HOUSE... TODAY, WE ROLE PLAY, MEN!
"OKAY, LET'S START THE GAME!
"You six are a brave band of warriors, thirsting for adventure!
"Who have been captured by terrible ice giants! And now, you are without your weapons, without you magical items, and without hope. Locked in a dungeon of despair!"

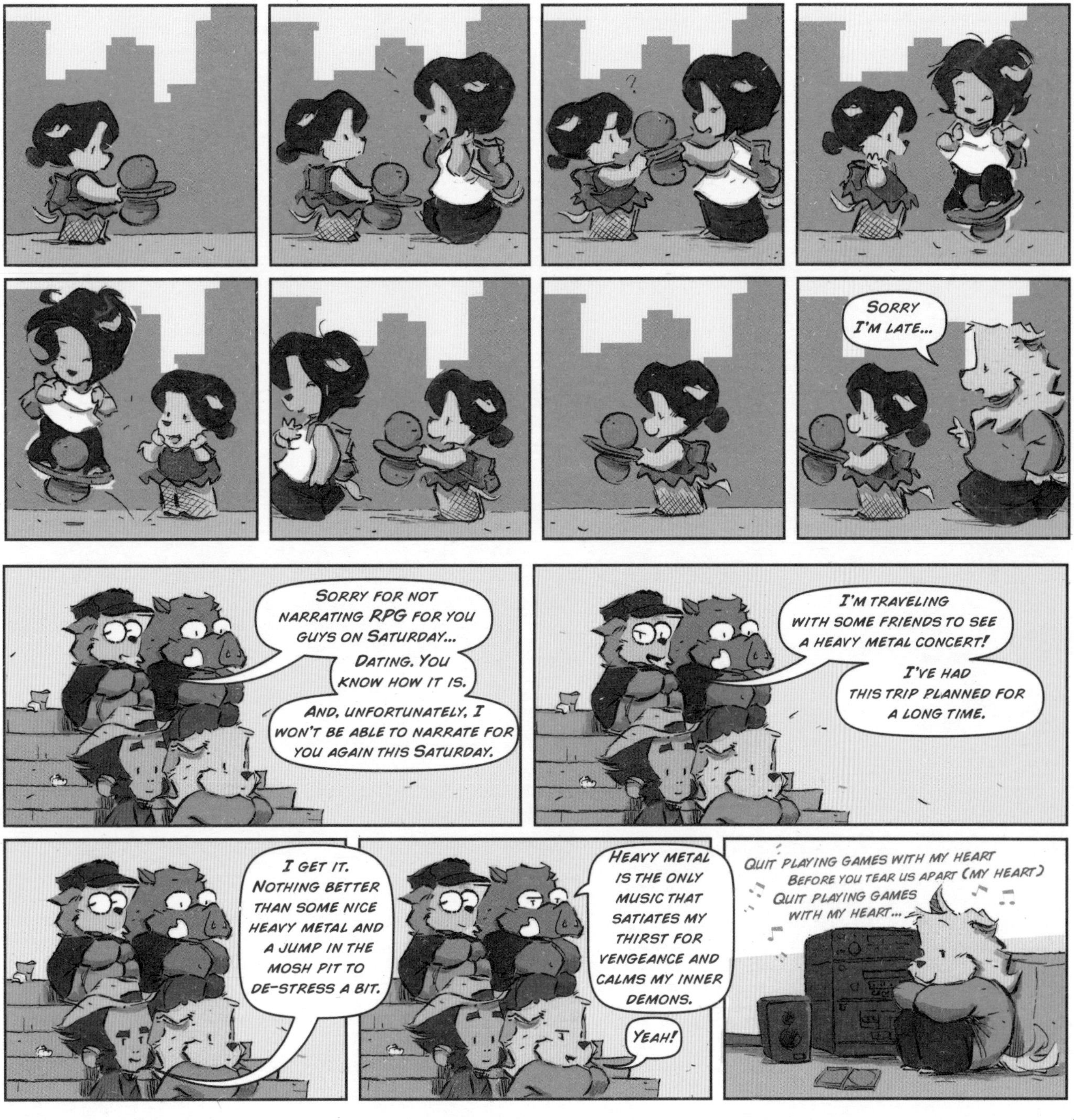
SORRY I'M LATE...
SORRY FOR NOT NARRATING RPG FOR YOU GUYS ON SATURDAY...
DATING. YOU KNOW HOW IT IS.
AND, UNFORTUNATELY, I WON'T BE ABLE TO NARRATE FOR YOU AGAIN THIS SATURDAY.
I'M TRAVELING WITH SOME FRIENDS TO SEE A HEAVY METAL CONCERT!
I'VE HAD THIS TRIP PLANNED FOR A LONG TIME.
I GET IT. NOTHING BETTER THAN SOME NICE HEAVY METAL AND A JUMP IN THE MOSH PIT TO DE-STRESS A BIT.
HEAVY METAL IS THE ONLY MUSIC THAT SATIATES MY THIRST FOR VENGEANCE AND CALMS MY INNER DEMONS.
YEAH!
QUIT PLAYING GAMES WITH MY HEART
BEFORE YOU TEAR US APART (MY HEART)
QUIT PLAYING GAMES WITH MY HEART...

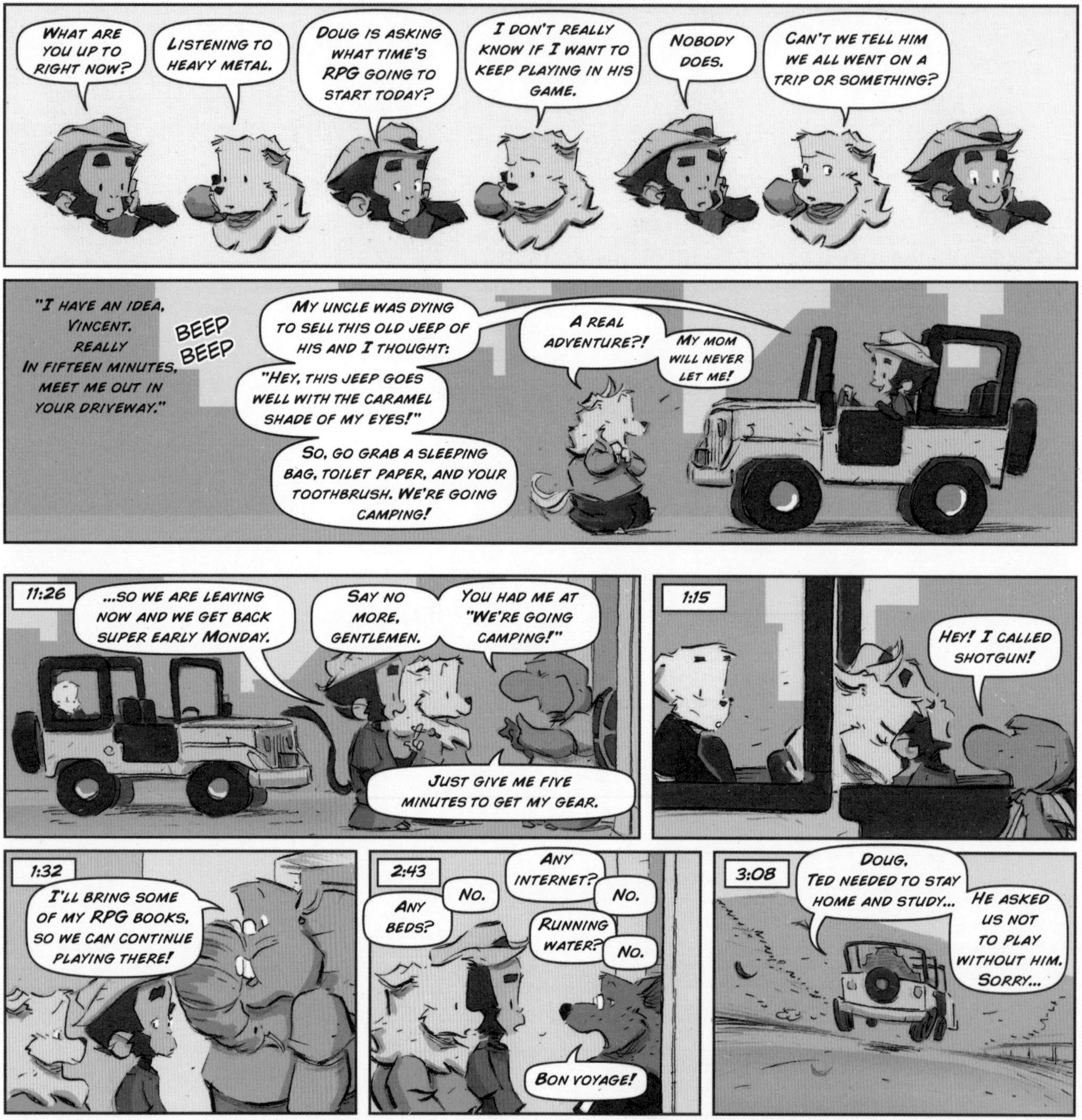
WHAT ARE YOU UP TO RIGHT NOW?
LISTENING TO HEAVY METAL.
DOUG IS ASKING WHAT TIME'S RPG GOING TO START TODAY?
I DON'T REALLY KNOW IF I WANT TO KEEP PLAYING IN HIS GAME.
NOBODY DOES.
CAN'T WE TELL HIM WE ALL WENT ON A TRIP OR SOMETHING?
"I HAVE AN IDEA, VINCENT. REALLY IN FIFTEEN MINUTES, MEET ME OUT IN YOUR DRIVEWAY."
BEEP BEEP
MY UNCLE WAS DYING TO SELL THIS OLD JEEP OF HIS AND I THOUGHT:
"HEY, THIS JEEP GOES WELL WITH THE CARAMEL SHADE OF MY EYES!"
SO, GO GRAB A SLEEPING BAG, TOILET PAPER, AND YOUR TOOTHBRUSH. WE'RE GOING CAMPING!
A REAL ADVENTURE?!
MY MOM WILL NEVER LET ME!
11:26
...SO WE ARE LEAVING NOW AND WE GET BACK SUPER EARLY MONDAY.
SAY NO MORE, GENTLEMEN.
YOU HAD ME AT "WE'RE GOING CAMPING!"
JUST GIVE ME FIVE MINUTES TO GET MY GEAR.
1:15
HEY! I CALLED SHOTGUN!
1:32
I'LL BRING SOME OF MY RPG BOOKS, SO WE CAN CONTINUE PLAYING THERE!
2:43
ANY BEDS?
NO.
ANY INTERNET?
NO.
RUNNING WATER?
NO.
BON VOYAGE!
3:08
DOUG, TED NEEDED TO STAY HOME AND STUDY...
HE ASKED US NOT TO PLAY WITHOUT HIM. SORRY...

Panel 1: I LOVE CAMPING!

Panel 2: I LOVE FEELING THE WIND IN MY FUR AND SLEEPING UNDER THE STARS, THE SMELL OF DEW ON THE GRASS.

Panel 3: I LOVE NATURE, THE FLORA, THE FAUNA, THE FEELING OF FREEDOM.

Panel 4: I ALSO LOVE DOING STRIPTEASE SHOWS FOR MY LITTLE SISTER'S STUFFED ANIMALS.

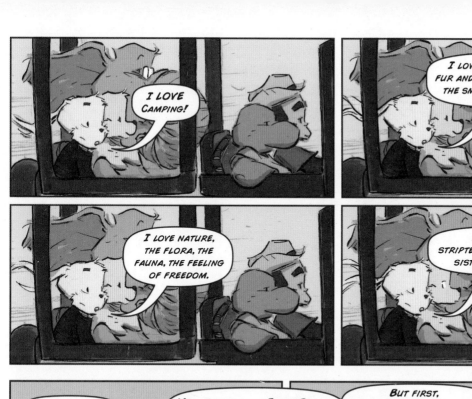

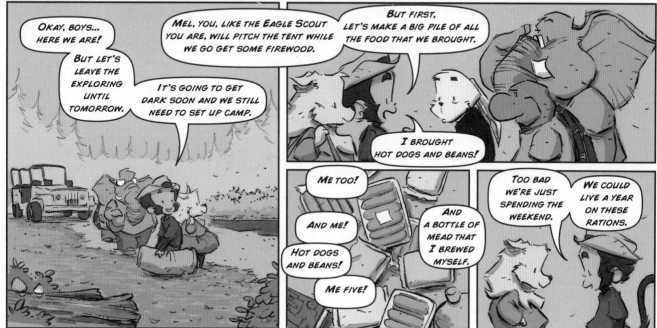

OKAY, BOYS... HERE WE ARE!

BUT LET'S LEAVE THE EXPLORING UNTIL TOMORROW.

MEL, YOU, LIKE THE EAGLE SCOUT YOU ARE, WILL PITCH THE TENT WHILE WE GO GET SOME FIREWOOD.

IT'S GOING TO GET DARK SOON AND WE STILL NEED TO SET UP CAMP.

BUT FIRST, LET'S MAKE A BIG PILE OF ALL THE FOOD THAT WE BROUGHT.

I BROUGHT HOT DOGS AND BEANS!

ME TOO!

AND ME!

HOT DOGS AND BEANS!

ME FIVE!

AND A BOTTLE OF MEAD THAT I BREWED MYSELF.

TOO BAD WE'RE JUST SPENDING THE WEEKEND.

WE COULD LIVE A YEAR ON THESE RATIONS.

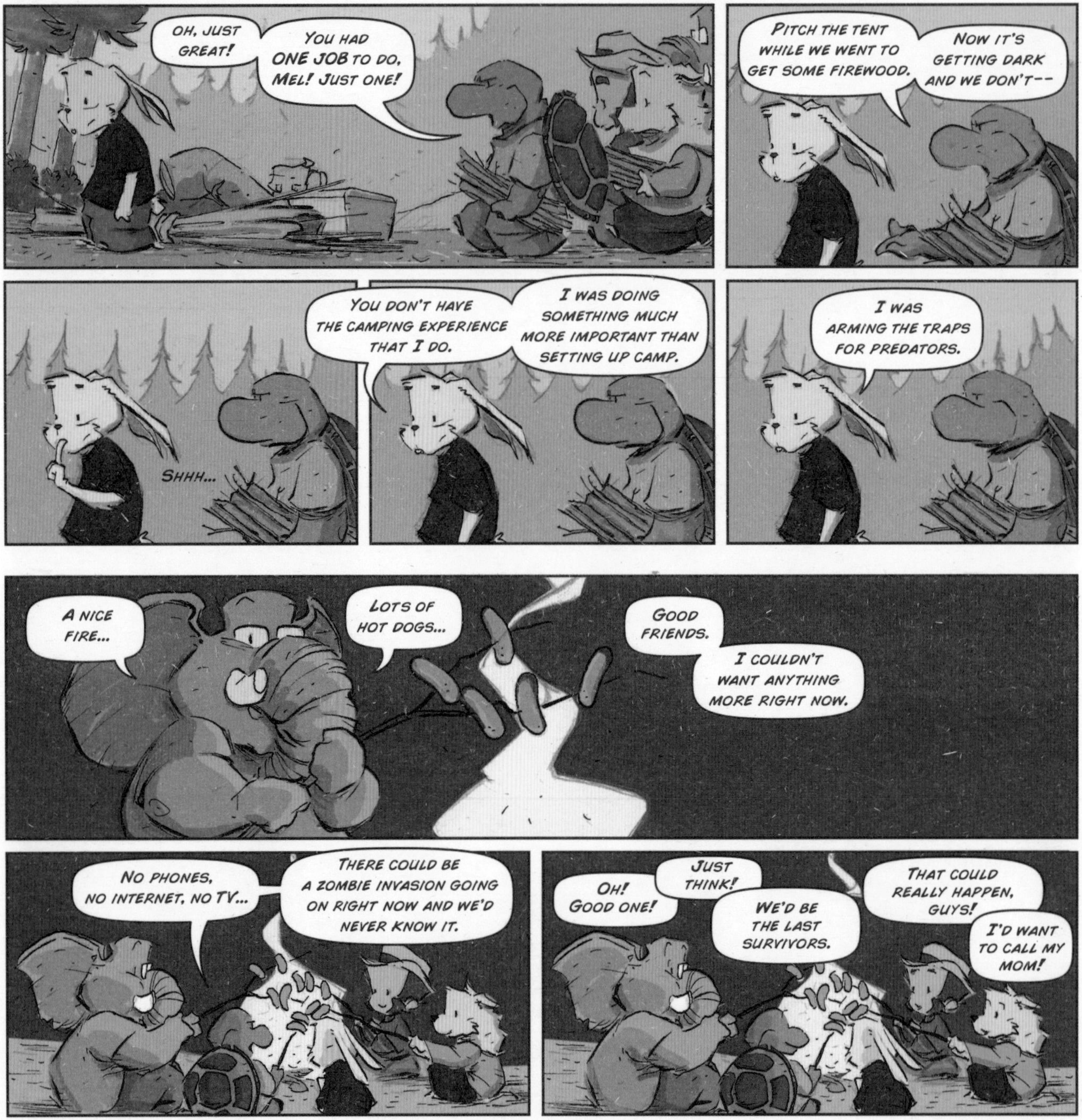
OH, JUST GREAT!
YOU HAD ONE JOB TO DO, MEL! JUST ONE!
PITCH THE TENT WHILE WE WENT TO GET SOME FIREWOOD.
NOW IT'S GETTING DARK AND WE DON'T--
SHHH...
YOU DON'T HAVE THE CAMPING EXPERIENCE THAT I DO.
I WAS DOING SOMETHING MUCH MORE IMPORTANT THAN SETTING UP CAMP.
I WAS ARMING THE TRAPS FOR PREDATORS.
A NICE FIRE...
LOTS OF HOT DOGS...
GOOD FRIENDS.
I COULDN'T WANT ANYTHING MORE RIGHT NOW.
NO PHONES, NO INTERNET, NO TV...
THERE COULD BE A ZOMBIE INVASION GOING ON RIGHT NOW AND WE'D NEVER KNOW IT.
OH! GOOD ONE!
JUST THINK!
WE'D BE THE LAST SURVIVORS.
THAT COULD REALLY HAPPEN, GUYS!
I'D WANT TO CALL MY MOM!

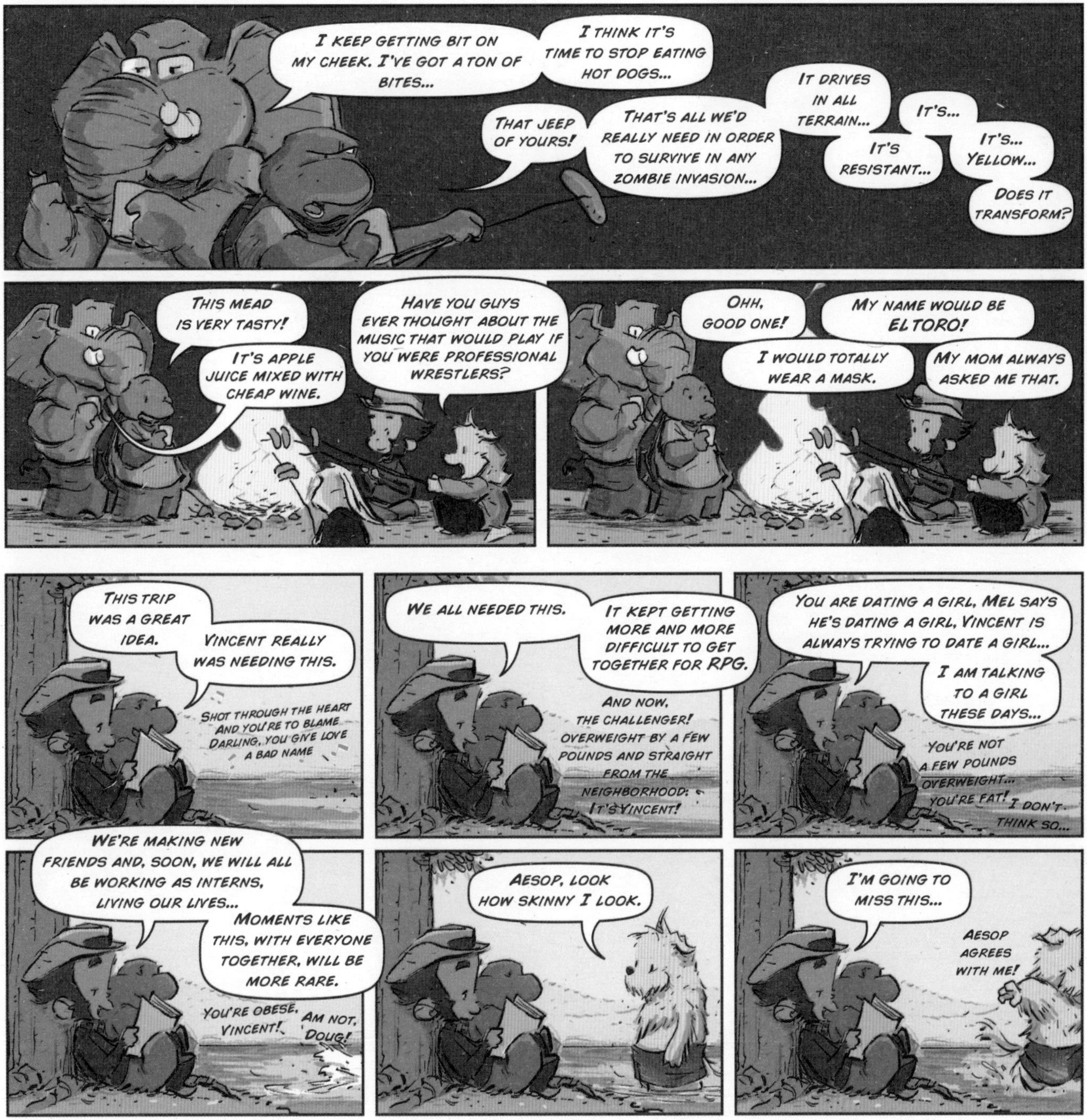
I KEEP GETTING BIT ON MY CHEEK. I'VE GOT A TON OF BITES...
I THINK IT'S TIME TO STOP EATING HOT DOGS...
THAT JEEP OF YOURS!
THAT'S ALL WE'D REALLY NEED IN ORDER TO SURVIVE IN ANY ZOMBIE INVASION...
IT DRIVES IN ALL TERRAIN...
IT'S RESISTANT...
IT'S...
IT'S... YELLOW...
DOES IT TRANSFORM?
THIS MEAD IS VERY TASTY!
IT'S APPLE JUICE MIXED WITH CHEAP WINE.
HAVE YOU GUYS EVER THOUGHT ABOUT THE MUSIC THAT WOULD PLAY IF YOU WERE PROFESSIONAL WRESTLERS?
OHH, GOOD ONE!
MY NAME WOULD BE EL TORO!
I WOULD TOTALLY WEAR A MASK.
MY MOM ALWAYS ASKED ME THAT.
THIS TRIP WAS A GREAT IDEA.
VINCENT REALLY WAS NEEDING THIS.
SHOT THROUGH THE HEART AND YOU'RE TO BLAME DARLING, YOU GIVE LOVE A BAD NAME
WE ALL NEEDED THIS.
IT KEPT GETTING MORE AND MORE DIFFICULT TO GET TOGETHER FOR RPG.
AND NOW, THE CHALLENGER! OVERWEIGHT BY A FEW POUNDS AND STRAIGHT FROM THE NEIGHBORHOOD: IT'S VINCENT!
YOU ARE DATING A GIRL, MEL SAYS HE'S DATING A GIRL, VINCENT IS ALWAYS TRYING TO DATE A GIRL...
I AM TALKING TO A GIRL THESE DAYS...
YOU'RE NOT A FEW POUNDS OVERWEIGHT... YOU'RE FAT!
I DON'T THINK SO...
WE'RE MAKING NEW FRIENDS AND, SOON, WE WILL ALL BE WORKING AS INTERNS, LIVING OUR LIVES...
MOMENTS LIKE THIS, WITH EVERYONE TOGETHER, WILL BE MORE RARE.
YOU'RE OBESE, VINCENT!
AM NOT, DOUG!
AESOP, LOOK HOW SKINNY I LOOK.
I'M GOING TO MISS THIS...
AESOP AGREES WITH ME!

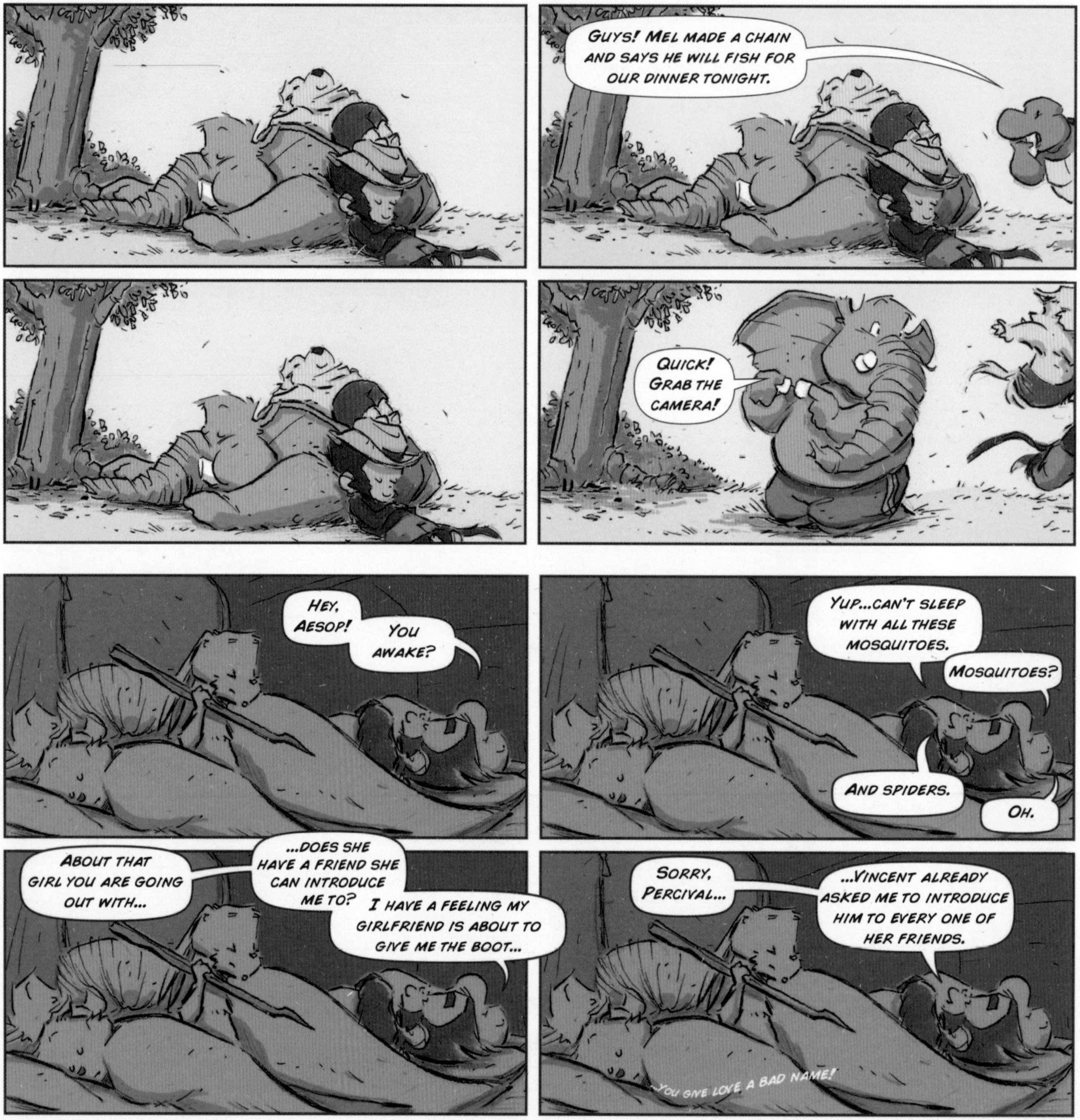
GUYS! MEL MADE A CHAIN AND SAYS HE WILL FISH FOR OUR DINNER TONIGHT.
QUICK! GRAB THE CAMERA!
HEY, AESOP!
YOU AWAKE?
YUP...CAN'T SLEEP WITH ALL THESE MOSQUITOES.
MOSQUITOES?
AND SPIDERS.
OH.
ABOUT THAT GIRL YOU ARE GOING OUT WITH...
...DOES SHE HAVE A FRIEND SHE CAN INTRODUCE ME TO?
I HAVE A FEELING MY GIRLFRIEND IS ABOUT TO GIVE ME THE BOOT...
SORRY, PERCIVAL...
...VINCENT ALREADY ASKED ME TO INTRODUCE HIM TO EVERY ONE OF HER FRIENDS.
...YOU GIVE LOVE A BAD NAME!

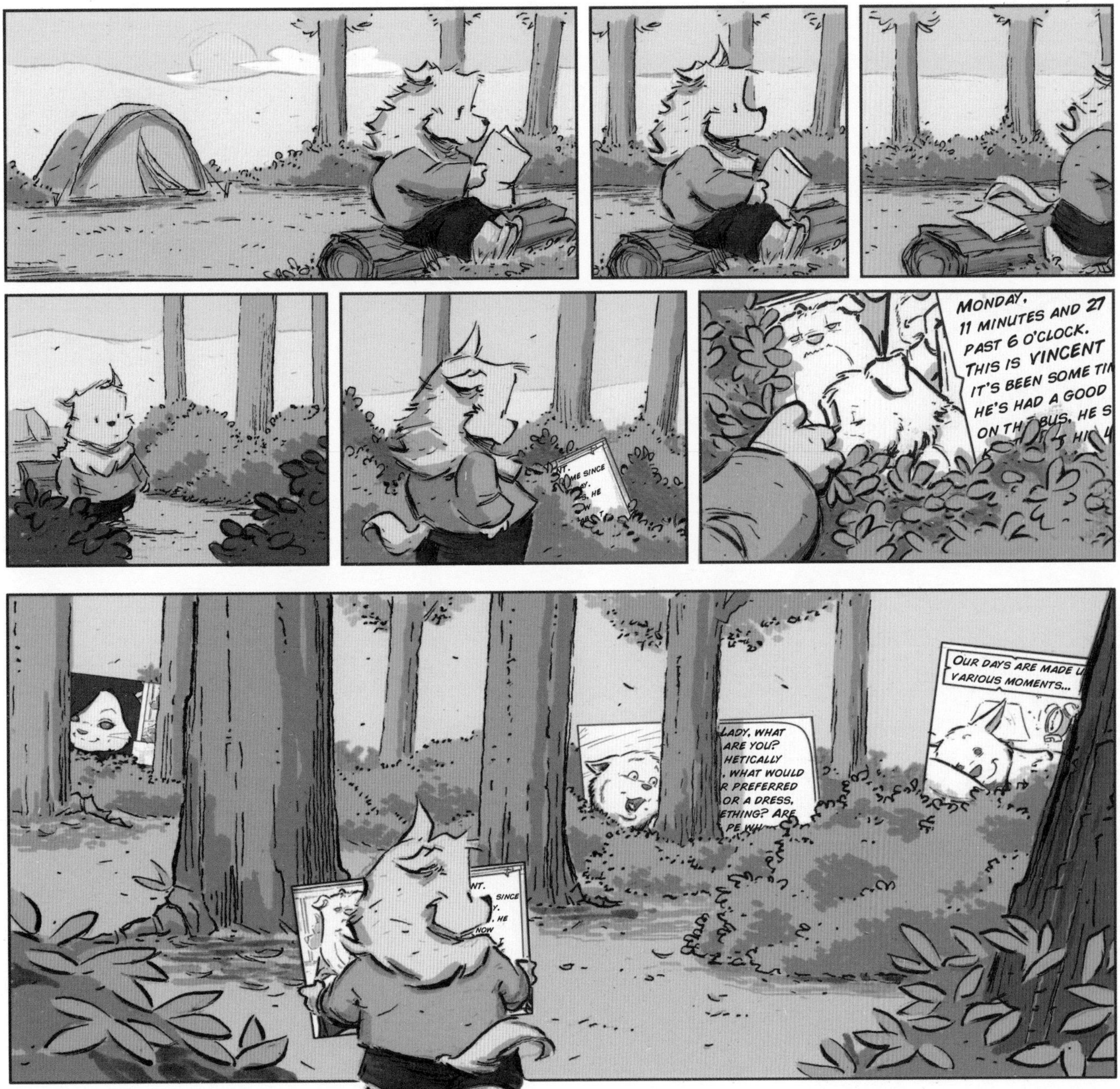
MONDAY,
11 MINUTES AND 27
PAST 6 O'CLOCK.
THIS IS VINCENT
IT'S BEEN SOME TI
HE'S HAD A GOOD
LADY, WHAT
ARE YOU?
HETICALLY
, WHAT WOULD
R PREFERRED
OR A DRESS,
ETHING? ARE
OUR DAYS ARE MADE U
VARIOUS MOMENTS...

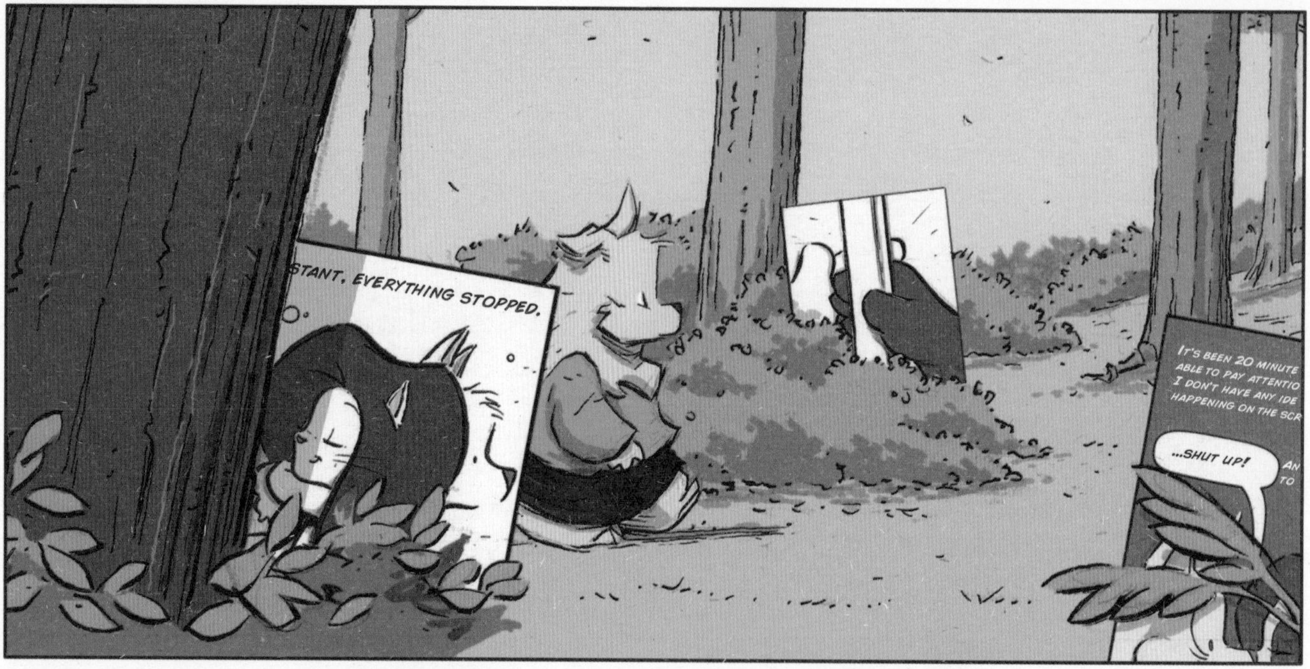
STANT, EVERYTHING STOPPED.
IT'S BEEN 20 MINUTE
ABLE TO PAY ATTENTIO
I DON'T HAVE ANY IDE
HAPPENING ON THE SCR
...SHUT UP!
AN
TO

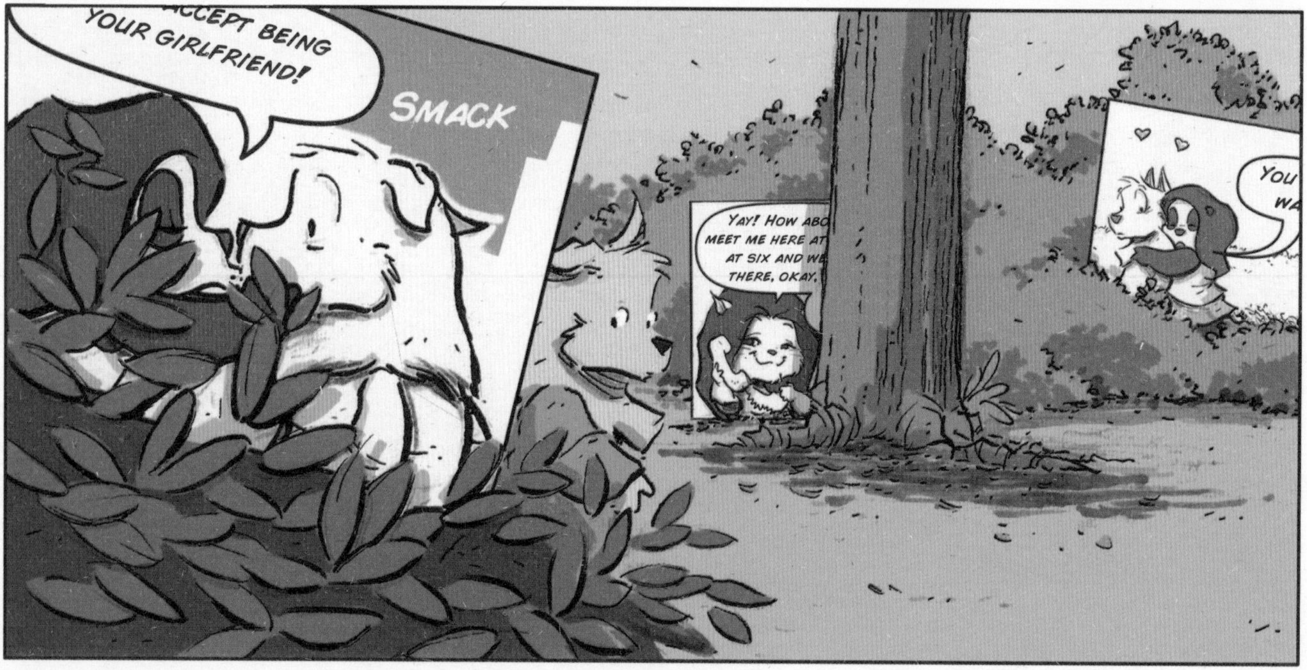
ACCEPT BEING YOUR GIRLFRIEND!
SMACK
YAY! HOW ABO
MEET ME HERE AT
AT SIX AND WE
THERE, OKAY.
YOU
WA

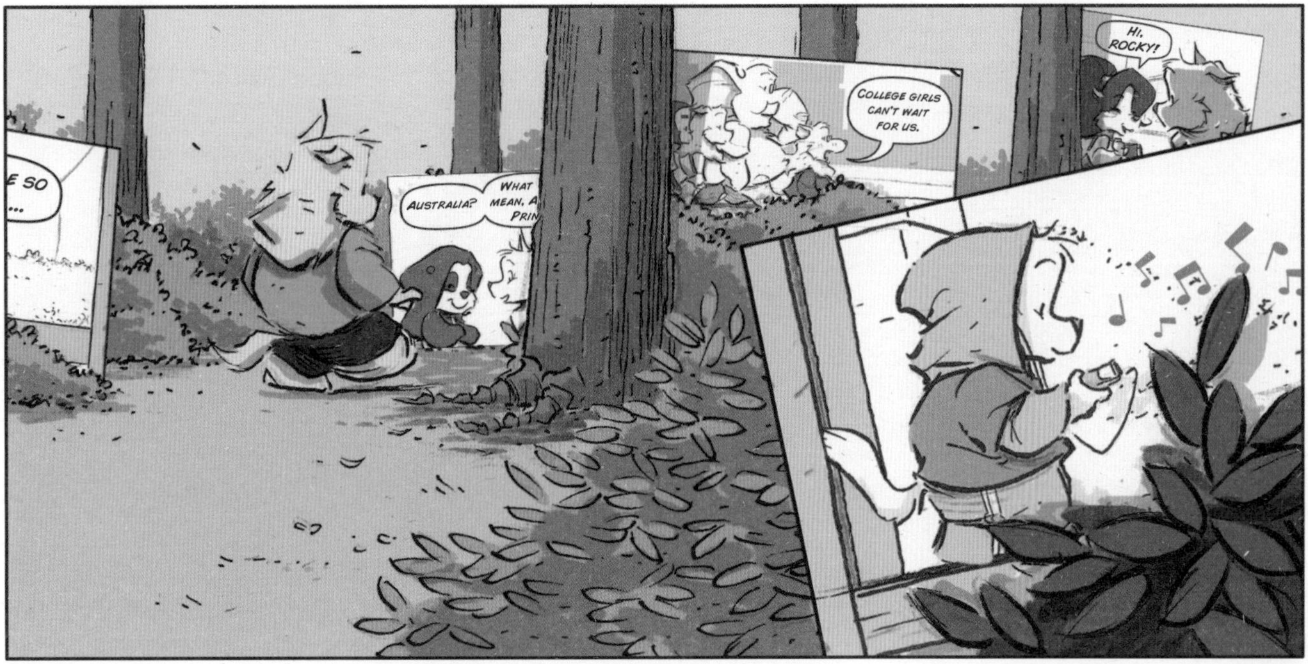
E SO
...
AUSTRALIA?
WHAT
MEAN, A
PRIN
COLLEGE GIRLS CAN'T WAIT FOR US.
HI, ROCKY!

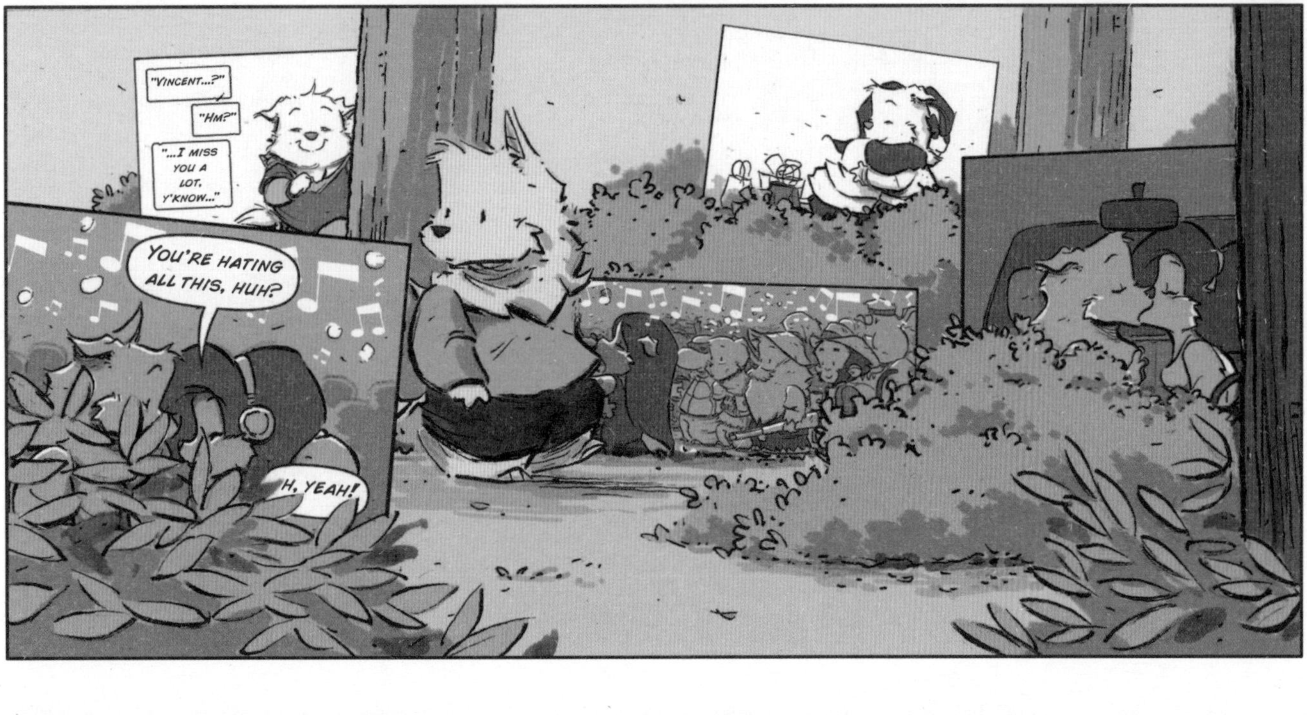
"VINCENT...?"
"HM?"
"...I MISS YOU A LOT, Y'KNOW..."
YOU'RE HATING ALL THIS, HUH?
H, YEAH!

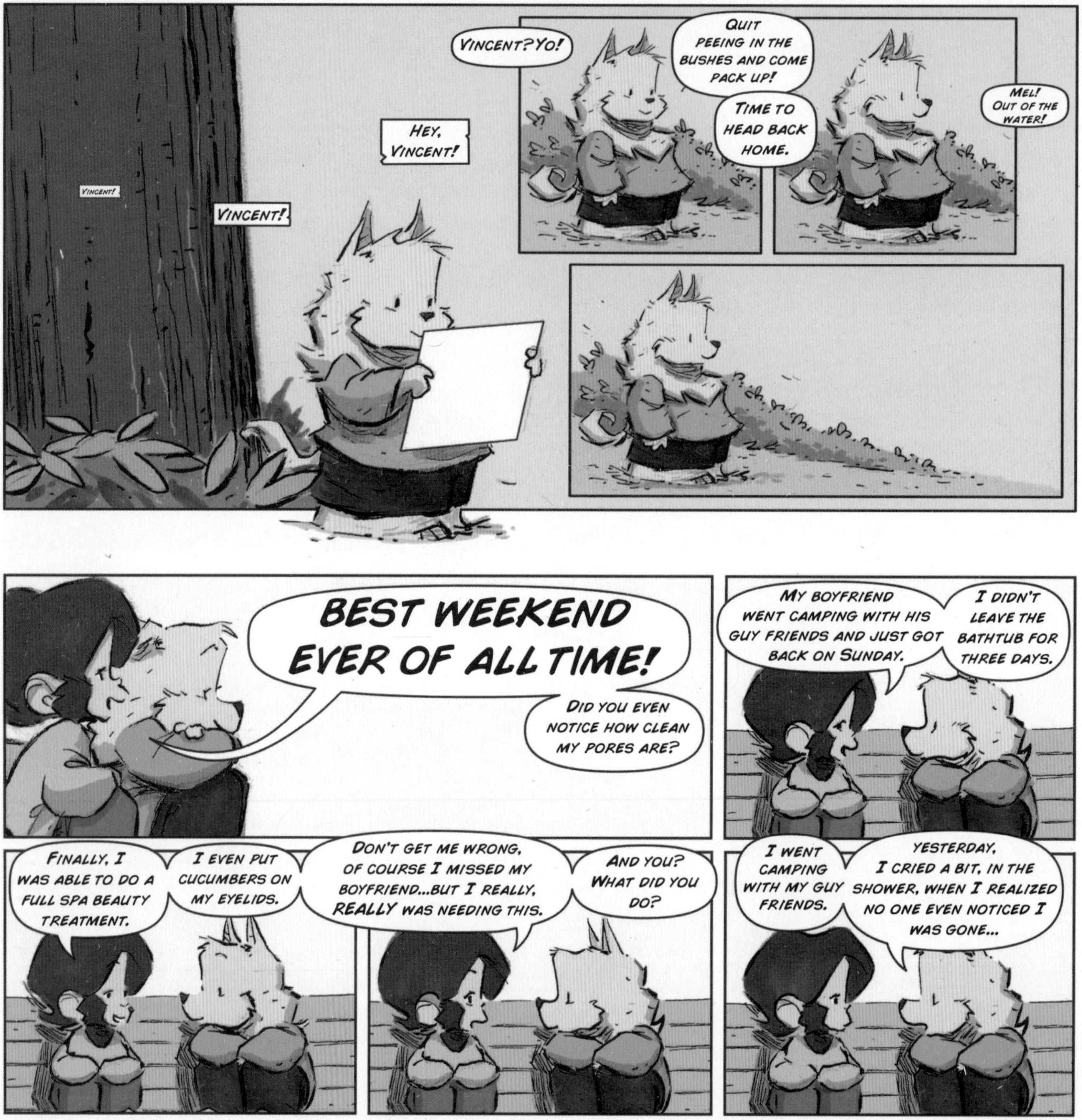
VINCENT!
VINCENT!
HEY, VINCENT!
VINCENT? YO!
QUIT PEEING IN THE BUSHES AND COME PACK UP!
TIME TO HEAD BACK HOME.
MEL! OUT OF THE WATER!
BEST WEEKEND EVER OF ALL TIME!
DID YOU EVEN NOTICE HOW CLEAN MY PORES ARE?
MY BOYFRIEND WENT CAMPING WITH HIS GUY FRIENDS AND JUST GOT BACK ON SUNDAY.
I DIDN'T LEAVE THE BATHTUB FOR THREE DAYS.
FINALLY, I WAS ABLE TO DO A FULL SPA BEAUTY TREATMENT.
I EVEN PUT CUCUMBERS ON MY EYELIDS.
DON'T GET ME WRONG, OF COURSE I MISSED MY BOYFRIEND...BUT I REALLY, REALLY WAS NEEDING THIS.
AND YOU? WHAT DID YOU DO?
I WENT CAMPING WITH MY GUY FRIENDS.
YESTERDAY, I CRIED A BIT, IN THE SHOWER, WHEN I REALIZED NO ONE EVEN NOTICED I WAS GONE...

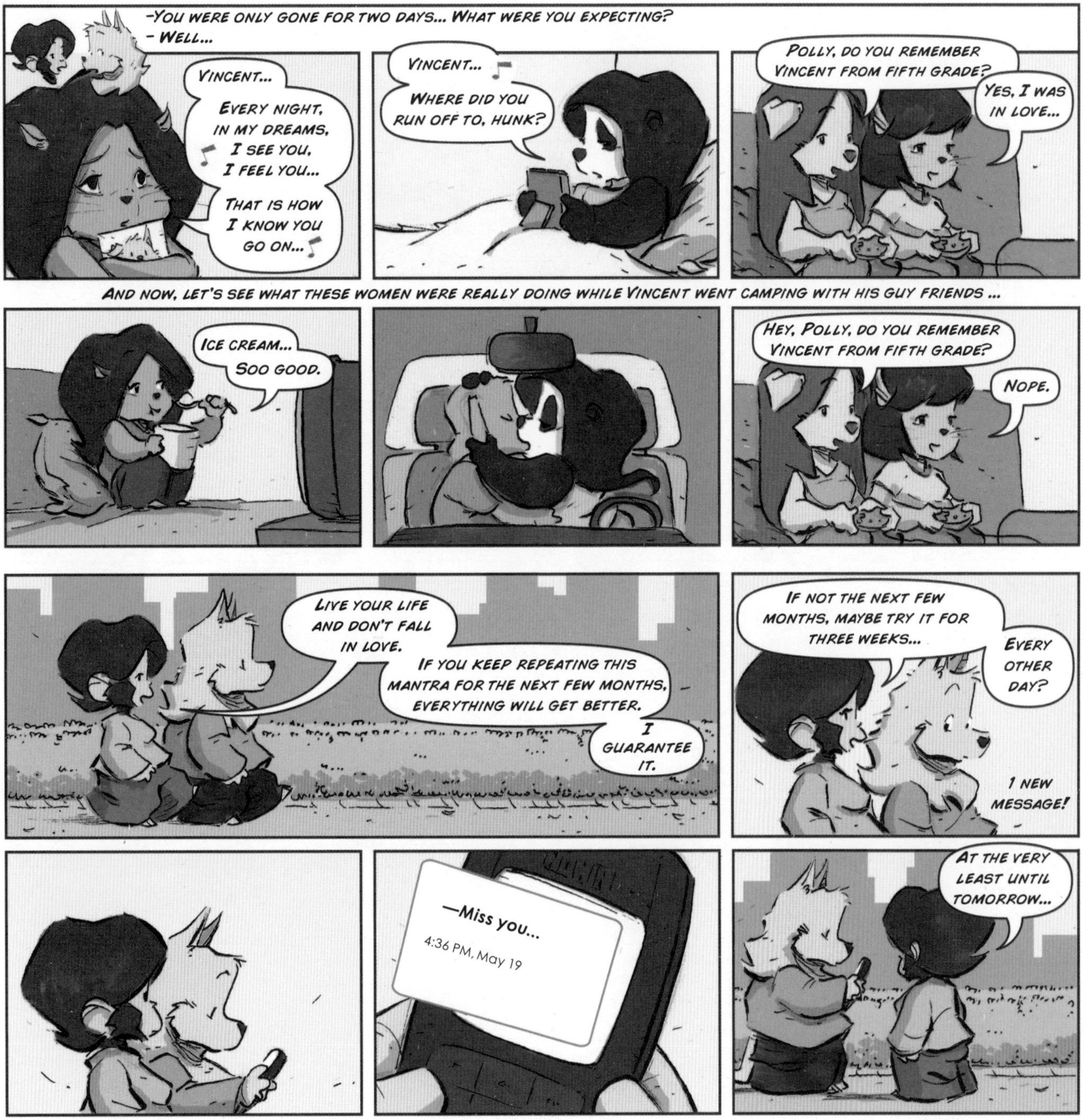
-YOU WERE ONLY GONE FOR TWO DAYS... WHAT WERE YOU EXPECTING?
- WELL...
VINCENT...
EVERY NIGHT, IN MY DREAMS, I SEE YOU, I FEEL YOU...
THAT IS HOW I KNOW YOU GO ON...
VINCENT...
WHERE DID YOU RUN OFF TO, HUNK?
POLLY, DO YOU REMEMBER VINCENT FROM FIFTH GRADE?
YES, I WAS IN LOVE...
AND NOW, LET'S SEE WHAT THESE WOMEN WERE REALLY DOING WHILE VINCENT WENT CAMPING WITH HIS GUY FRIENDS ...
ICE CREAM...
SOO GOOD.
HEY, POLLY, DO YOU REMEMBER VINCENT FROM FIFTH GRADE?
NOPE.
LIVE YOUR LIFE AND DON'T FALL IN LOVE.
IF YOU KEEP REPEATING THIS MANTRA FOR THE NEXT FEW MONTHS, EVERYTHING WILL GET BETTER.
I GUARANTEE IT.
IF NOT THE NEXT FEW MONTHS, MAYBE TRY IT FOR THREE WEEKS...
EVERY OTHER DAY?
1 NEW MESSAGE!
—Miss you...
4:36 PM, May 19
AT THE VERY LEAST UNTIL TOMORROW...

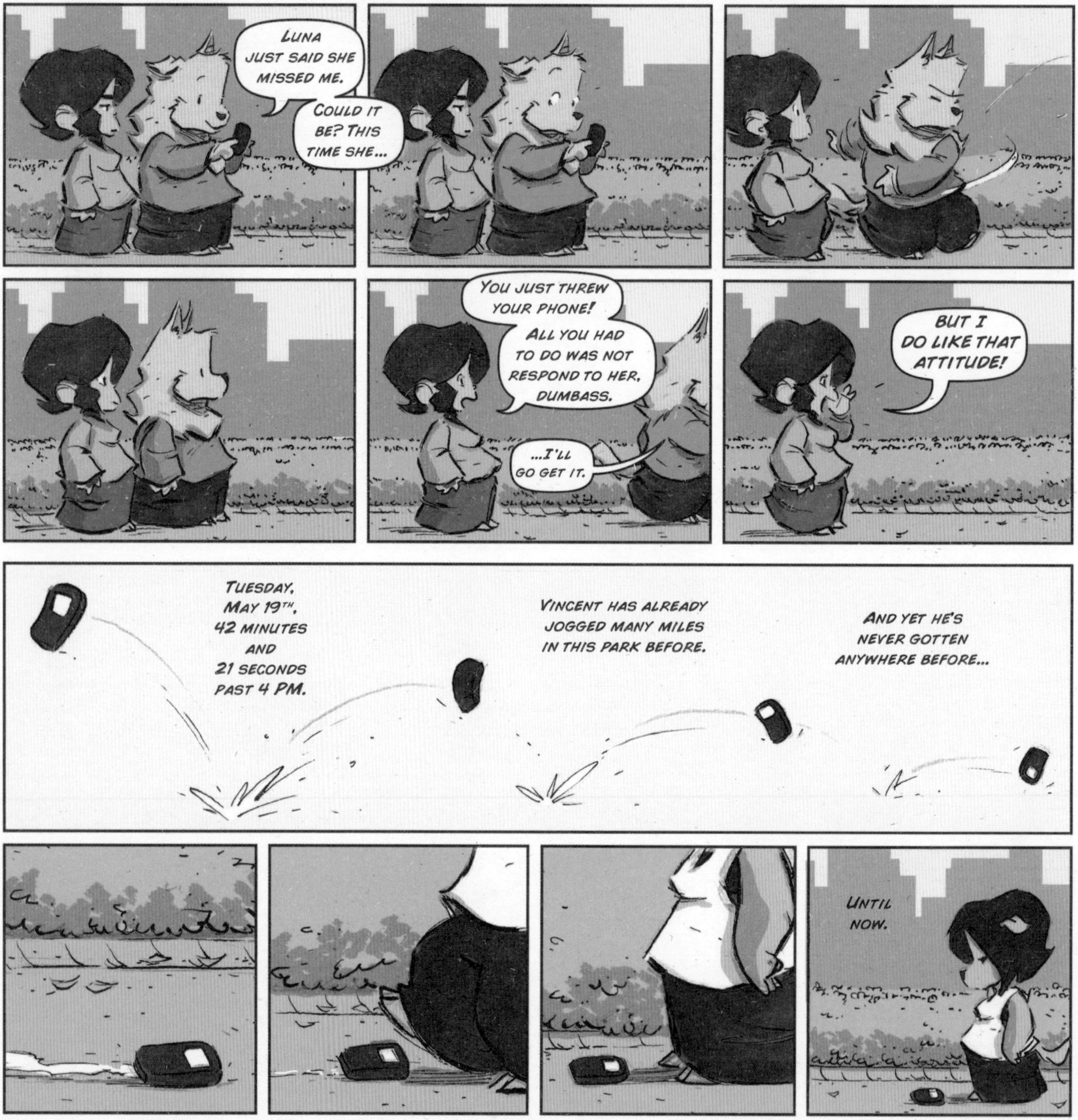
Luna just said she missed me.
Could it be? This time she...
You just threw your phone!
All you had to do was not respond to her, dumbass.
...I'll go get it.
But I do like that attitude!
Tuesday, May 19th, 42 minutes and 21 seconds past 4 PM.
Vincent has already jogged many miles in this park before.
And yet he's never gotten anywhere before...
Until now.

MARRIAGE CRAZY TALK

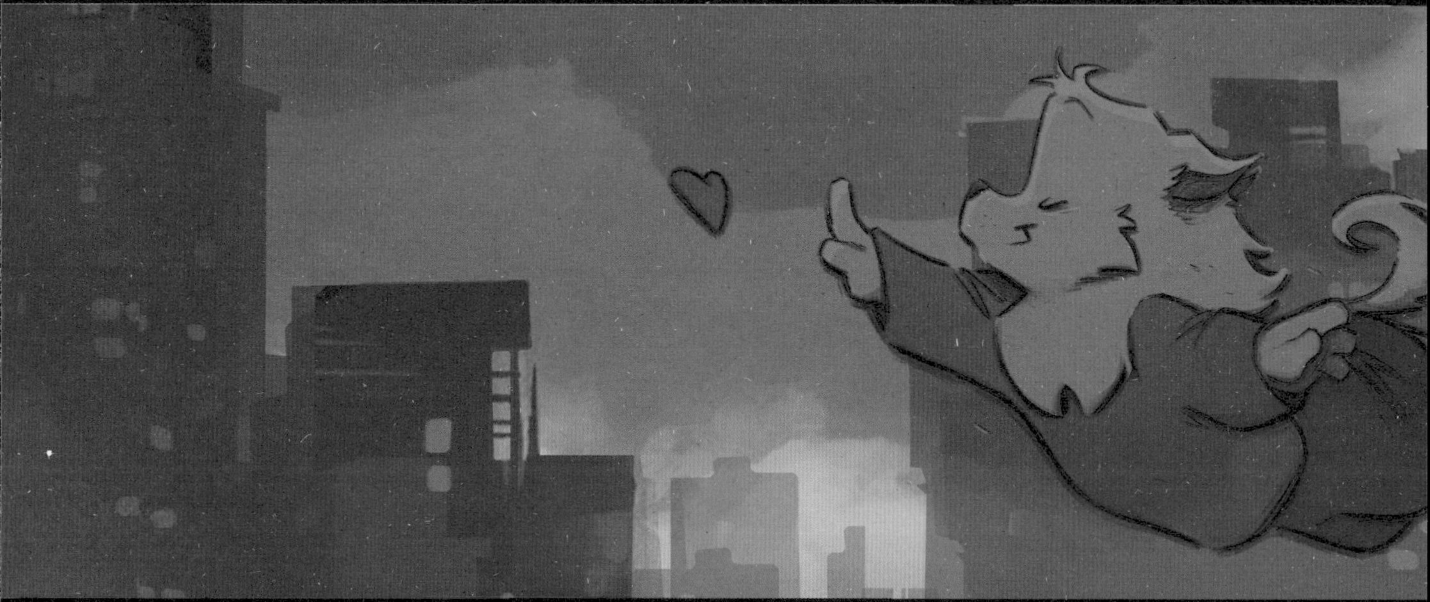

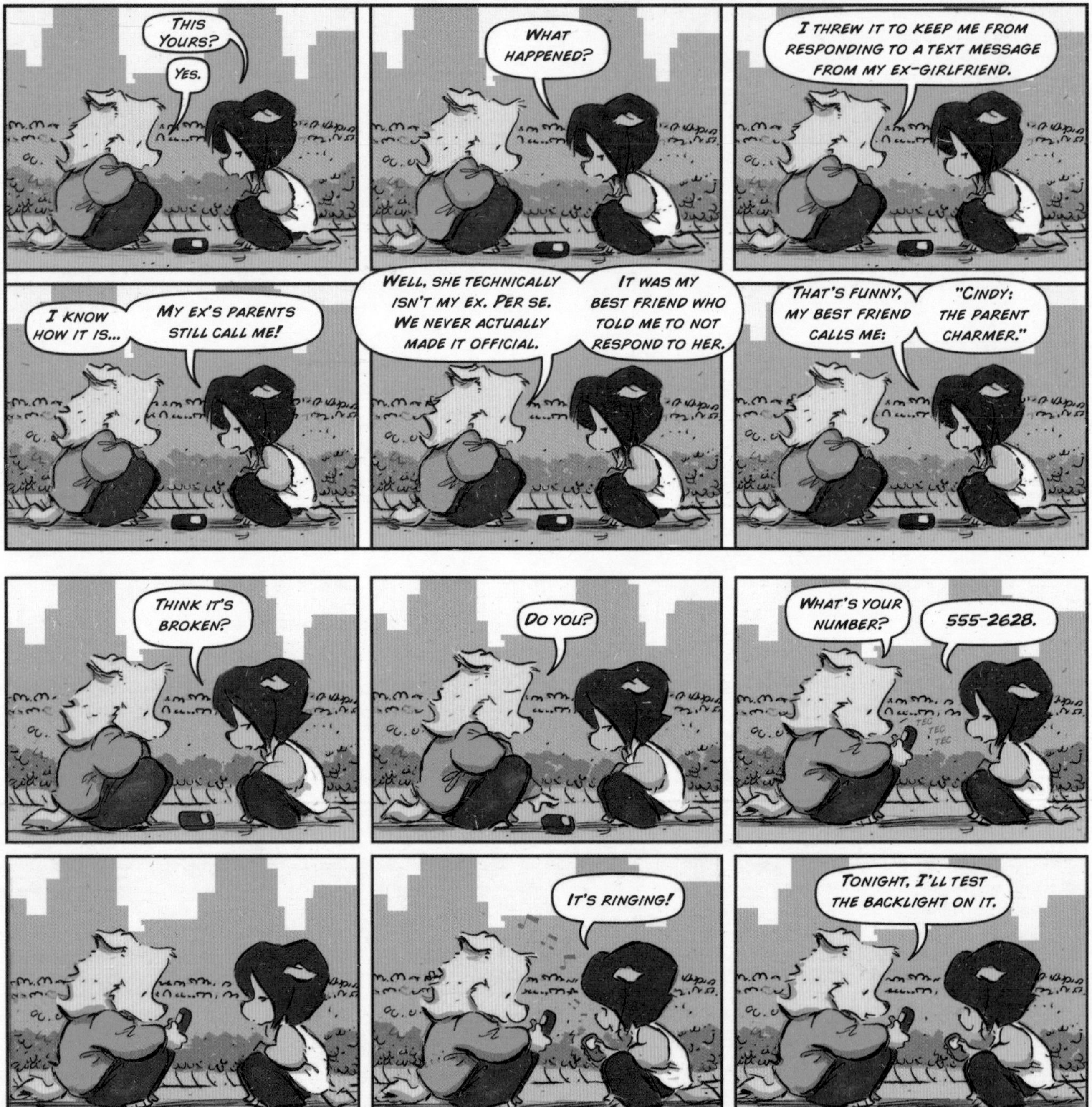
THIS YOURS?
YES.
WHAT HAPPENED?
I THREW IT TO KEEP ME FROM RESPONDING TO A TEXT MESSAGE FROM MY EX-GIRLFRIEND.
I KNOW HOW IT IS...
MY EX'S PARENTS STILL CALL ME!
WELL, SHE TECHNICALLY ISN'T MY EX. PER SE. WE NEVER ACTUALLY MADE IT OFFICIAL.
IT WAS MY BEST FRIEND WHO TOLD ME TO NOT RESPOND TO HER.
THAT'S FUNNY, MY BEST FRIEND CALLS ME:
"CINDY: THE PARENT CHARMER."
THINK IT'S BROKEN?
DO YOU?
WHAT'S YOUR NUMBER?
555-2628.
TEC TEC TEC
IT'S RINGING!
TONIGHT, I'LL TEST THE BACKLIGHT ON IT.

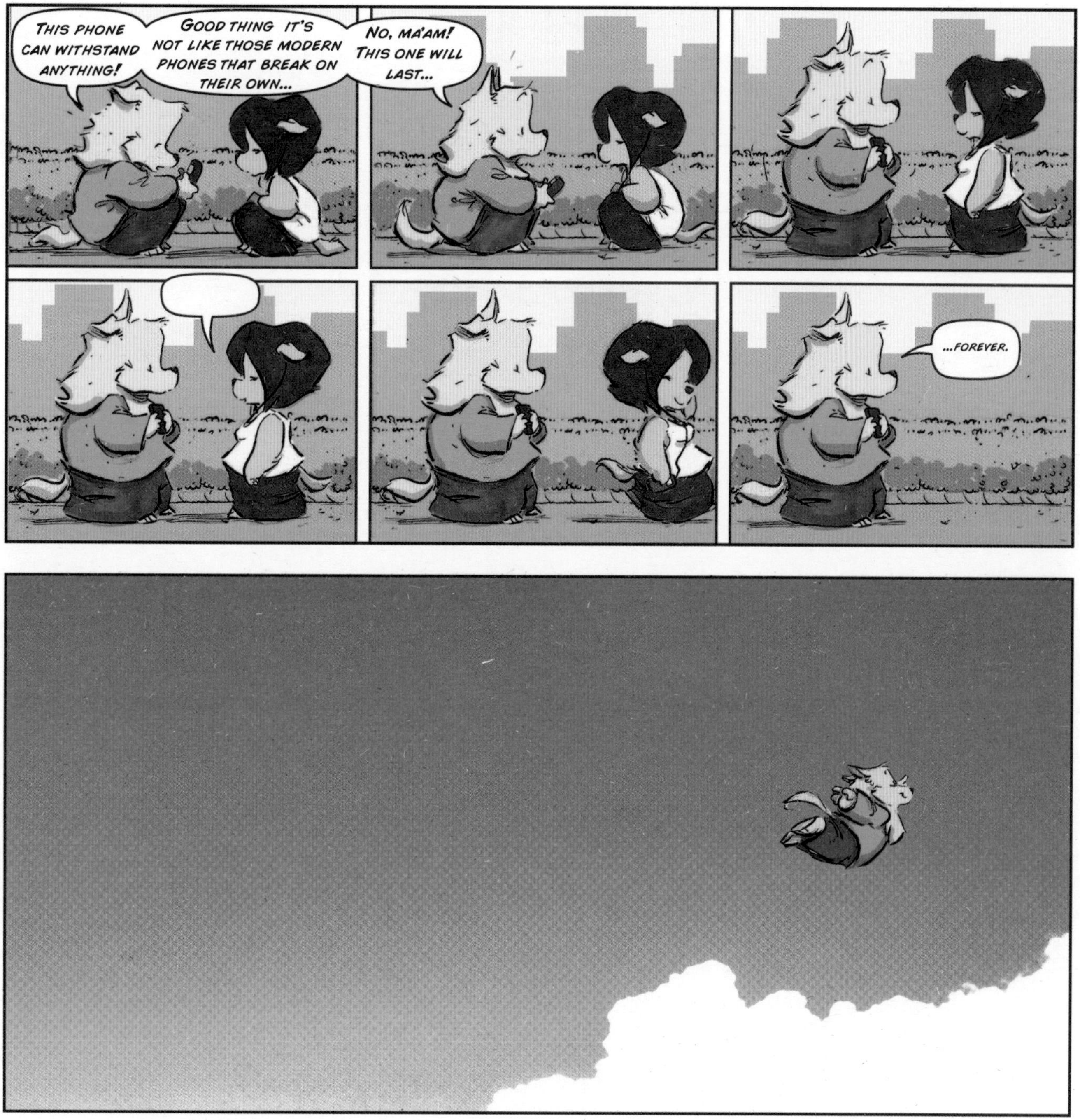
THIS PHONE CAN WITHSTAND ANYTHING!
GOOD THING IT'S NOT LIKE THOSE MODERN PHONES THAT BREAK ON THEIR OWN...
NO, MA'AM! THIS ONE WILL LAST...
...FOREVER.

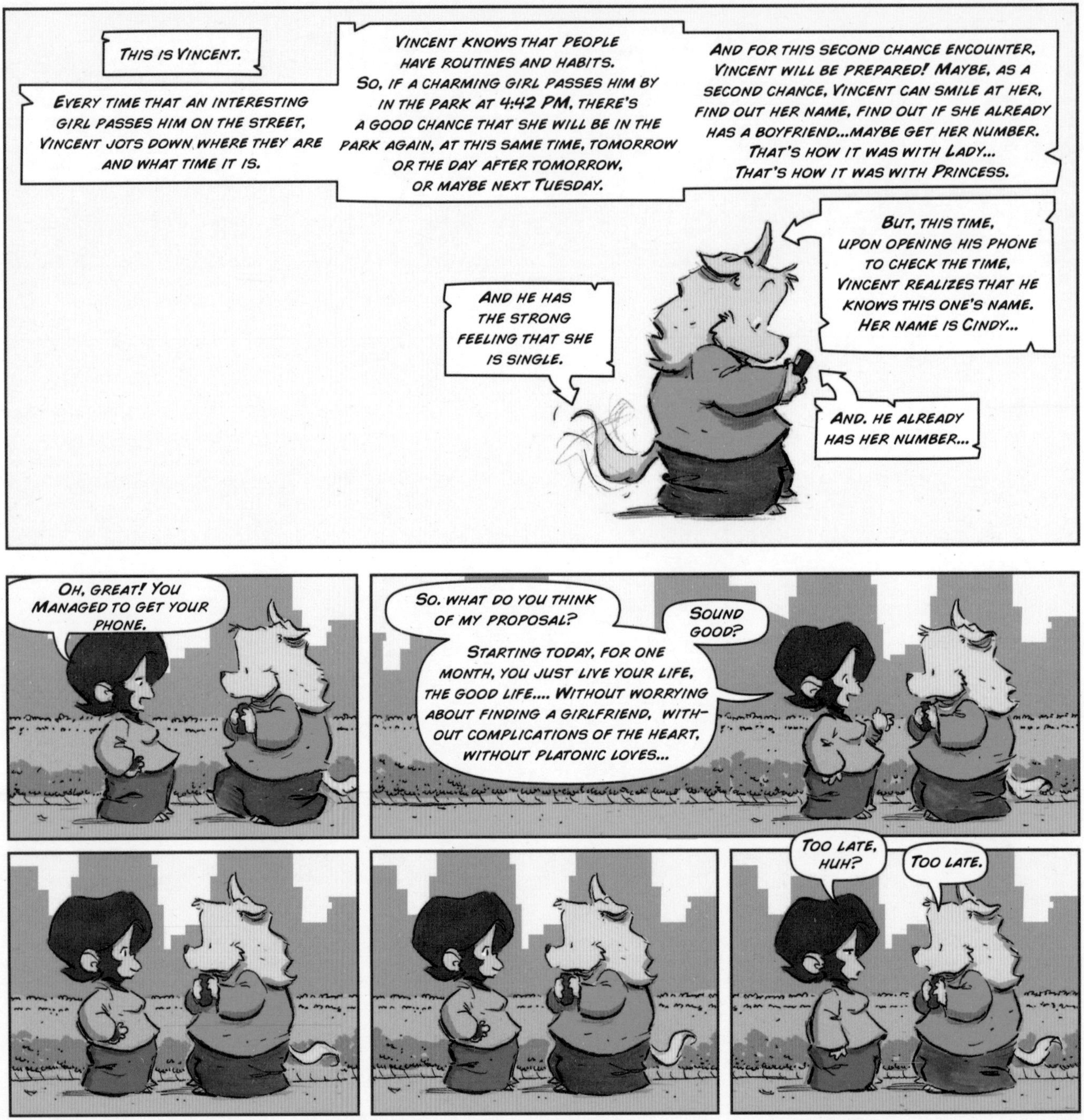

THIS IS VINCENT.
EVERY TIME THAT AN INTERESTING GIRL PASSES HIM ON THE STREET, VINCENT JOTS DOWN WHERE THEY ARE AND WHAT TIME IT IS.
VINCENT KNOWS THAT PEOPLE HAVE ROUTINES AND HABITS. SO, IF A CHARMING GIRL PASSES HIM BY IN THE PARK AT 4:42 PM, THERE'S A GOOD CHANCE THAT SHE WILL BE IN THE PARK AGAIN, AT THIS SAME TIME, TOMORROW OR THE DAY AFTER TOMORROW, OR MAYBE NEXT TUESDAY.
AND FOR THIS SECOND CHANCE ENCOUNTER, VINCENT WILL BE PREPARED! MAYBE, AS A SECOND CHANCE, VINCENT CAN SMILE AT HER, FIND OUT HER NAME, FIND OUT IF SHE ALREADY HAS A BOYFRIEND...MAYBE GET HER NUMBER. THAT'S HOW IT WAS WITH LADY... THAT'S HOW IT WAS WITH PRINCESS.
BUT, THIS TIME, UPON OPENING HIS PHONE TO CHECK THE TIME, VINCENT REALIZES THAT HE KNOWS THIS ONE'S NAME. HER NAME IS CINDY...
AND HE HAS THE STRONG FEELING THAT SHE IS SINGLE.
AND, HE ALREADY HAS HER NUMBER...
OH, GREAT! YOU MANAGED TO GET YOUR PHONE.
SO, WHAT DO YOU THINK OF MY PROPOSAL?
STARTING TODAY, FOR ONE MONTH, YOU JUST LIVE YOUR LIFE, THE GOOD LIFE.... WITHOUT WORRYING ABOUT FINDING A GIRLFRIEND, WITH-OUT COMPLICATIONS OF THE HEART, WITHOUT PLATONIC LOVES...
SOUND GOOD?
TOO LATE, HUH?
TOO LATE.

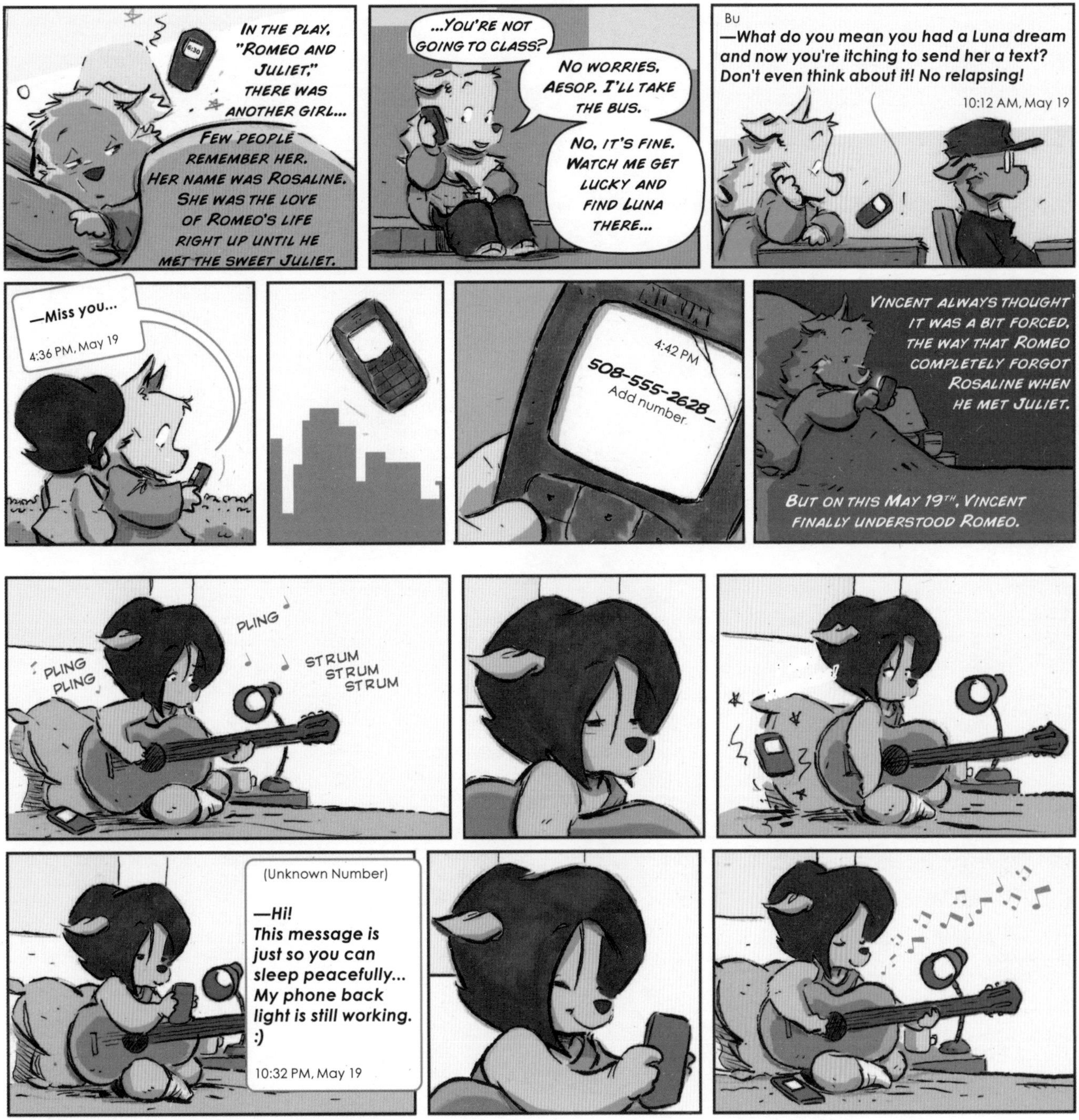
In the play, "Romeo and Juliet," there was another girl...
Few people remember her. Her name was Rosaline. She was the love of Romeo's life right up until he met the sweet Juliet.
...You're not going to class?
No worries, Aesop. I'll take the bus.
No, it's fine. Watch me get lucky and find Luna there...
Bu
—What do you mean you had a Luna dream and now you're itching to send her a text? Don't even think about it! No relapsing!
10:12 AM, May 19
—Miss you...
4:36 PM, May 19
4:42 PM
508-555-2628
Add number.
Vincent always thought it was a bit forced, the way that Romeo completely forgot Rosaline when he met Juliet.
But on this May 19th, Vincent finally understood Romeo.
Pling
Pling pling
Strum strum strum
(Unknown Number)
—Hi!
This message is just so you can sleep peacefully... My phone back light is still working. :)
10:32 PM, May 19

YOU LOOK REALLY TIRED TODAY, VINCENT...

I WAS UP UNTIL THREE IN THE MORNING TEXTING BACK AND FORTH WITH A GIRL...

LUNA?

NO, NO... A GIRL THAT I MET YESTERDAY.

YOU'RE GETTING GOOD AT THAT, HUH?

TEXT MESSAGING HAS CHANGED MY WHOLE LOVE LIFE, AESOP!

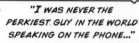

"I WAS NEVER THE PERKIEST GUY IN THE WORLD SPEAKING ON THE PHONE..."

...SO.... UMM... WHAT ARE YOU DOING... THIS WEEKEND?

LIST OF TOPICS

I DUNNO, YOU COULD COME HERE AND PLAY VIDEO GAMES?

"I REMEMBER VINCENT... YOU FLOUNDERED EVEN TALKING TO ME!"

IMAGINE IF YOU HAD A GIRL'S PHONE NUMBER IN THOSE DAYS?

I FROZE UP EVEN WHEN YOUR MOM ANSWERED...

TIME PASSES SO FAST THE OLDER AND OLDER WE GET...

BACK IN ELEMENTARY SCHOOL, THE YEAR CRAWLED... NOW, WE JUST BLINK AND BAM, IT'S ALREADY MAY!

SEEMS LIKE JUST YESTERDAY OUR SOCIOLOGY PROFESSOR ASSIGNED THAT GROUP PROJECT ON THE PROLETARIATS DURING THE INDUSTRIAL REVOLUTION.

BUT THAT WAS AT THE START OF APRIL...THE PROJECT IS DUE TOMORROW.

THE NOVICE TOLD US TO GO TO HIS HOUSE TO WORK ON THE PROJECT AT 7:30.

THAT'S WHEN HE GETS OFF HIS INTERNSHIP.

SPEAKING OF, WHERE IS HE?

HE'S ASLEEP IN THE CLASSROOM.

POOR THING LOOKED REALLY SLEEPY...

TRULY, ANOTHER VICTIM EXPLOITED BY THE BOURGEOIS CAPITALISTS.

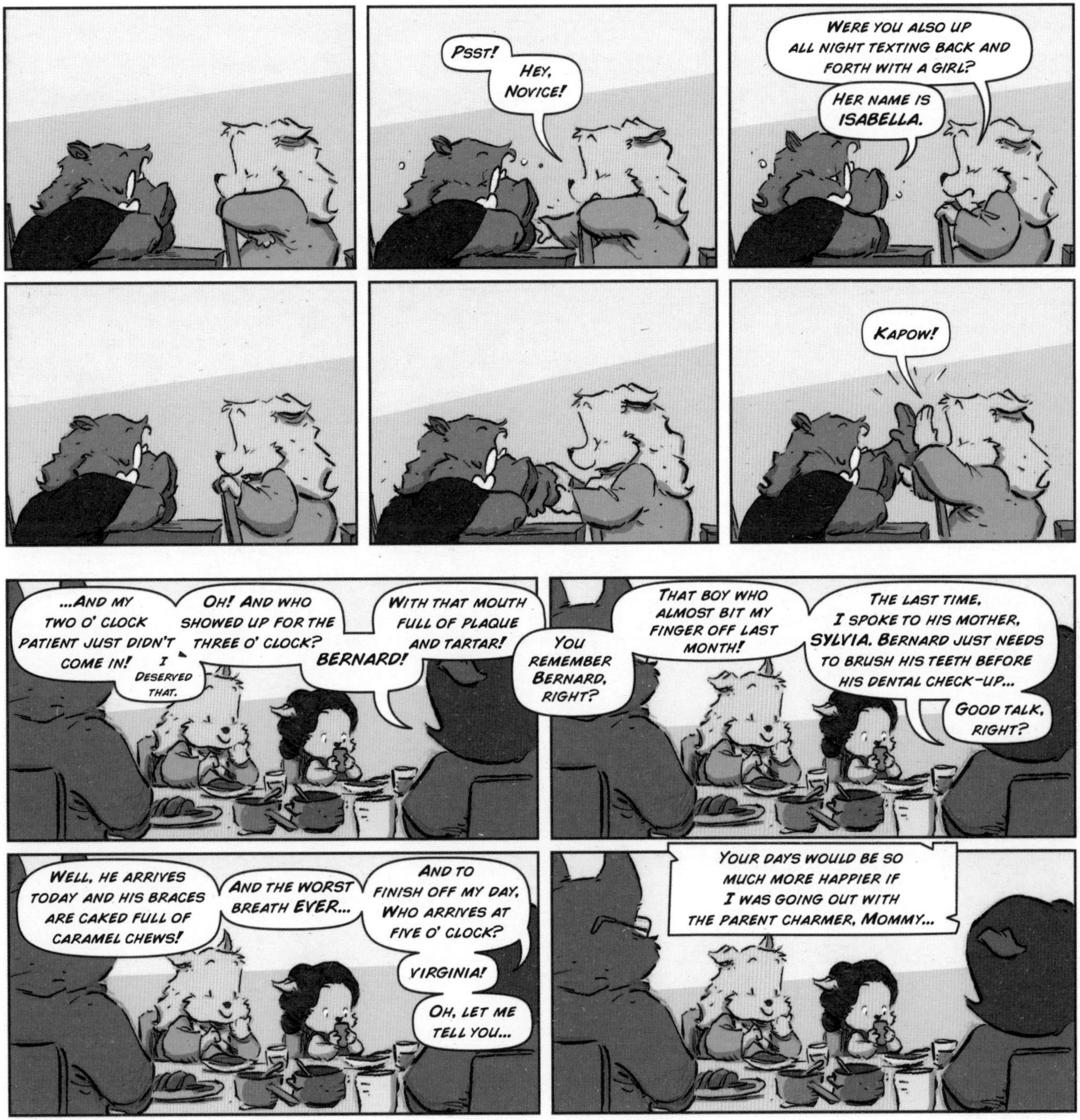
PSST!
HEY, NOVICE!
WERE YOU ALSO UP ALL NIGHT TEXTING BACK AND FORTH WITH A GIRL?
HER NAME IS ISABELLA.
KAPOW!
...AND MY TWO O' CLOCK PATIENT JUST DIDN'T COME IN!
OH! AND WHO SHOWED UP FOR THE THREE O' CLOCK?
I DESERVED THAT.
WITH THAT MOUTH FULL OF PLAQUE AND TARTAR!
BERNARD!
YOU REMEMBER BERNARD, RIGHT?
THAT BOY WHO ALMOST BIT MY FINGER OFF LAST MONTH!
THE LAST TIME, I SPOKE TO HIS MOTHER, SYLVIA. BERNARD JUST NEEDS TO BRUSH HIS TEETH BEFORE HIS DENTAL CHECK-UP...
GOOD TALK, RIGHT?
WELL, HE ARRIVES TODAY AND HIS BRACES ARE CAKED FULL OF CARAMEL CHEWS!
AND THE WORST BREATH EVER...
AND TO FINISH OFF MY DAY, WHO ARRIVES AT FIVE O' CLOCK?
VIRGINIA!
OH, LET ME TELL YOU...
YOUR DAYS WOULD BE SO MUCH MORE HAPPIER IF I WAS GOING OUT WITH THE PARENT CHARMER, MOMMY...

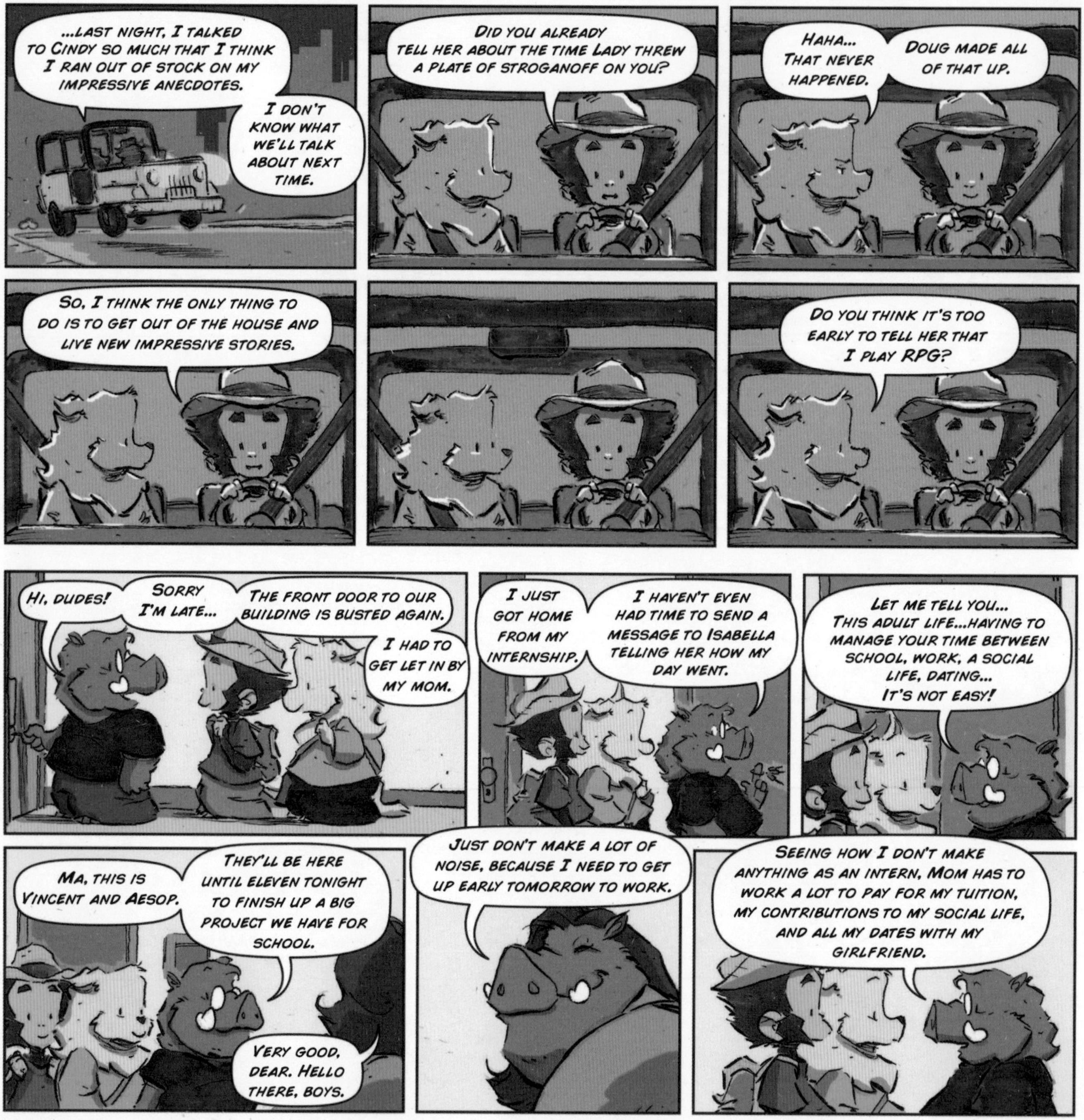
...LAST NIGHT, I TALKED TO CINDY SO MUCH THAT I THINK I RAN OUT OF STOCK ON MY IMPRESSIVE ANECDOTES.
I DON'T KNOW WHAT WE'LL TALK ABOUT NEXT TIME.
DID YOU ALREADY TELL HER ABOUT THE TIME LADY THREW A PLATE OF STROGANOFF ON YOU?
HAHA... THAT NEVER HAPPENED.
DOUG MADE ALL OF THAT UP.
SO, I THINK THE ONLY THING TO DO IS TO GET OUT OF THE HOUSE AND LIVE NEW IMPRESSIVE STORIES.
DO YOU THINK IT'S TOO EARLY TO TELL HER THAT I PLAY RPG?
HI, DUDES!
SORRY I'M LATE...
THE FRONT DOOR TO OUR BUILDING IS BUSTED AGAIN.
I HAD TO GET LET IN BY MY MOM.
I JUST GOT HOME FROM MY INTERNSHIP.
I HAVEN'T EVEN HAD TIME TO SEND A MESSAGE TO ISABELLA TELLING HER HOW MY DAY WENT.
LET ME TELL YOU... THIS ADULT LIFE...HAVING TO MANAGE YOUR TIME BETWEEN SCHOOL, WORK, A SOCIAL LIFE, DATING... IT'S NOT EASY!
MA, THIS IS VINCENT AND AESOP.
THEY'LL BE HERE UNTIL ELEVEN TONIGHT TO FINISH UP A BIG PROJECT WE HAVE FOR SCHOOL.
VERY GOOD, DEAR. HELLO THERE, BOYS.
JUST DON'T MAKE A LOT OF NOISE, BECAUSE I NEED TO GET UP EARLY TOMORROW TO WORK.
SEEING HOW I DON'T MAKE ANYTHING AS AN INTERN, MOM HAS TO WORK A LOT TO PAY FOR MY TUITION, MY CONTRIBUTIONS TO MY SOCIAL LIFE, AND ALL MY DATES WITH MY GIRLFRIEND.

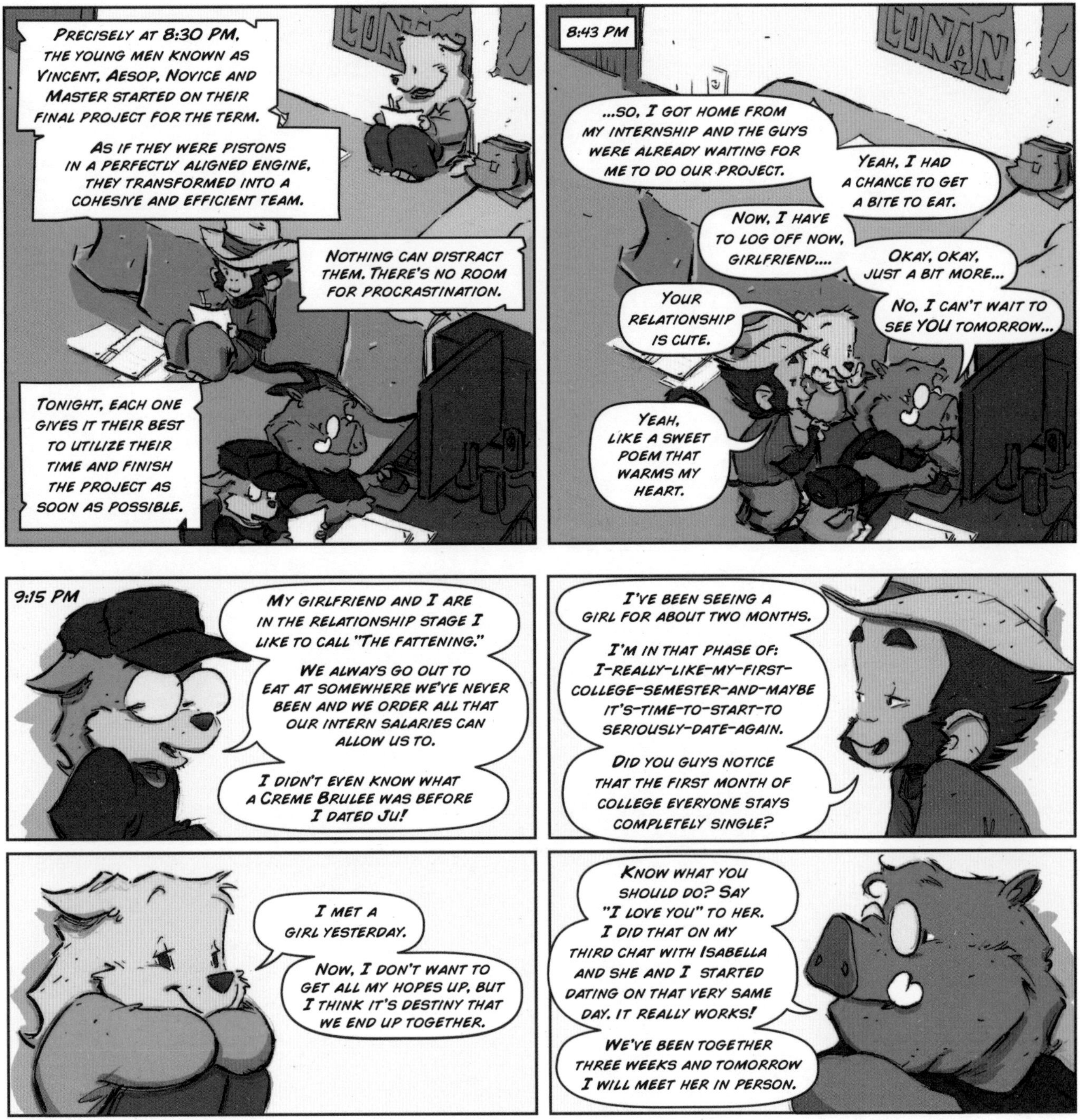
PRECISELY AT 8:30 PM, THE YOUNG MEN KNOWN AS VINCENT, AESOP, NOVICE AND MASTER STARTED ON THEIR FINAL PROJECT FOR THE TERM.
AS IF THEY WERE PISTONS IN A PERFECTLY ALIGNED ENGINE, THEY TRANSFORMED INTO A COHESIVE AND EFFICIENT TEAM.
NOTHING CAN DISTRACT THEM. THERE'S NO ROOM FOR PROCRASTINATION.
TONIGHT, EACH ONE GIVES IT THEIR BEST TO UTILIZE THEIR TIME AND FINISH THE PROJECT AS SOON AS POSSIBLE.
CONAN
8:43 PM
CONAN
...SO, I GOT HOME FROM MY INTERNSHIP AND THE GUYS WERE ALREADY WAITING FOR ME TO DO OUR PROJECT.
YEAH, I HAD A CHANCE TO GET A BITE TO EAT.
NOW, I HAVE TO LOG OFF NOW, GIRLFRIEND....
OKAY, OKAY, JUST A BIT MORE...
YOUR RELATIONSHIP IS CUTE.
NO, I CAN'T WAIT TO SEE YOU TOMORROW...
YEAH, LIKE A SWEET POEM THAT WARMS MY HEART.
9:15 PM
MY GIRLFRIEND AND I ARE IN THE RELATIONSHIP STAGE I LIKE TO CALL "THE FATTENING."
WE ALWAYS GO OUT TO EAT AT SOMEWHERE WE'VE NEVER BEEN AND WE ORDER ALL THAT OUR INTERN SALARIES CAN ALLOW US TO.
I DIDN'T EVEN KNOW WHAT A CREME BRULEE WAS BEFORE I DATED JU!
I'VE BEEN SEEING A GIRL FOR ABOUT TWO MONTHS.
I'M IN THAT PHASE OF: I-REALLY-LIKE-MY-FIRST-COLLEGE-SEMESTER-AND-MAYBE IT'S-TIME-TO-START-TO SERIOUSLY-DATE-AGAIN.
DID YOU GUYS NOTICE THAT THE FIRST MONTH OF COLLEGE EVERYONE STAYS COMPLETELY SINGLE?
I MET A GIRL YESTERDAY.
NOW, I DON'T WANT TO GET ALL MY HOPES UP, BUT I THINK IT'S DESTINY THAT WE END UP TOGETHER.
KNOW WHAT YOU SHOULD DO? SAY "I LOVE YOU" TO HER. I DID THAT ON MY THIRD CHAT WITH ISABELLA AND SHE AND I STARTED DATING ON THAT VERY SAME DAY. IT REALLY WORKS!
WE'VE BEEN TOGETHER THREE WEEKS AND TOMORROW I WILL MEET HER IN PERSON.

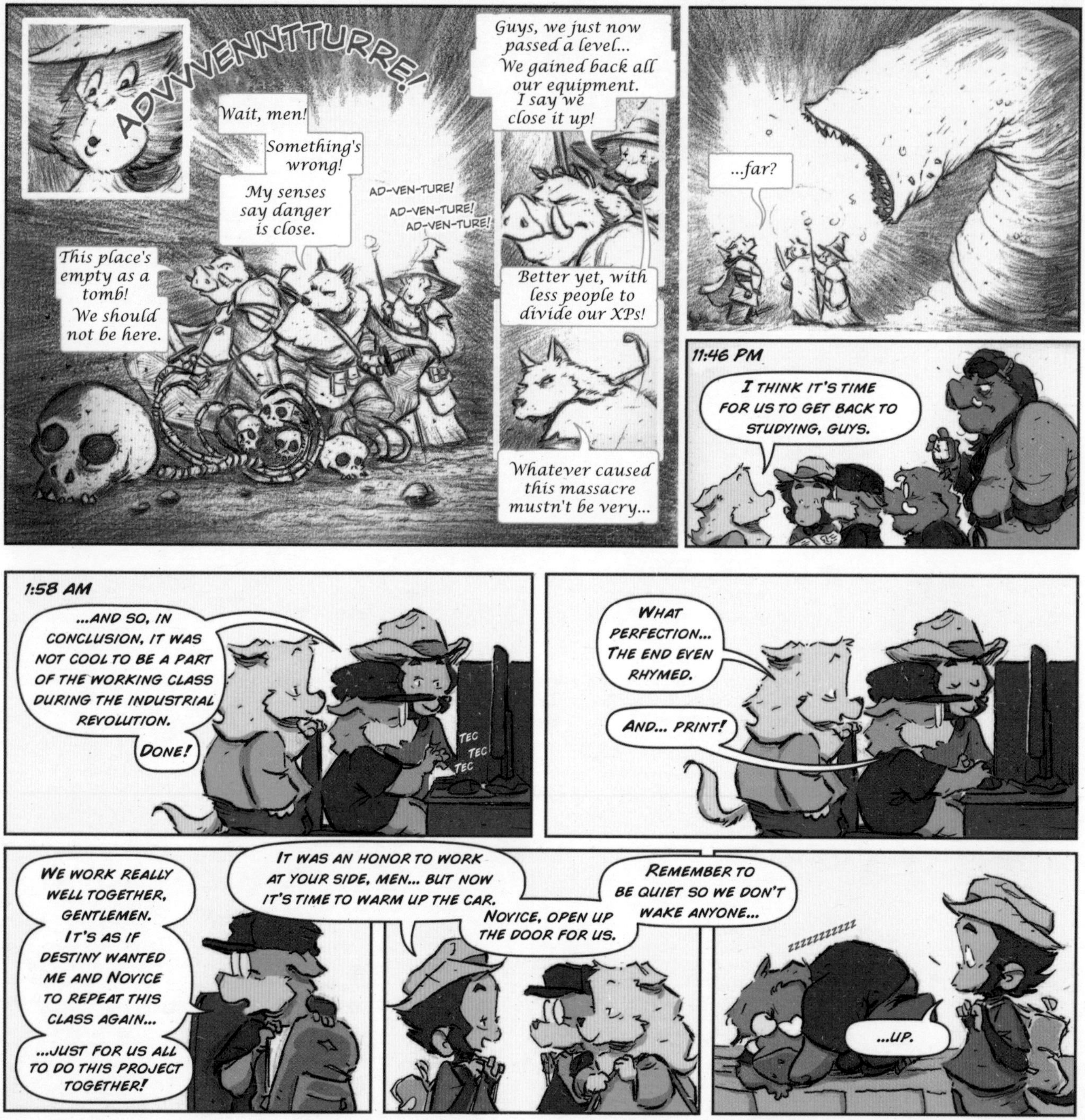
ADVVVENNTTURRE!
Wait, men!
Something's wrong!
My senses say danger is close.
AD-VEN-TURE!
AD-VEN-TURE!
AD-VEN-TURE!
This place's empty as a tomb!
We should not be here.
Guys, we just now passed a level... We gained back all our equipment.
I say we close it up!
Better yet, with less people to divide our XPs!
Whatever caused this massacre mustn't be very...
...far?
11:46 PM
I THINK IT'S TIME FOR US TO GET BACK TO STUDYING, GUYS.
1:58 AM
...AND SO, IN CONCLUSION, IT WAS NOT COOL TO BE A PART OF THE WORKING CLASS DURING THE INDUSTRIAL REVOLUTION.
DONE!
TEC TEC TEC
WHAT PERFECTION... THE END EVEN RHYMED.
AND... PRINT!
WE WORK REALLY WELL TOGETHER, GENTLEMEN.
IT'S AS IF DESTINY WANTED ME AND NOVICE TO REPEAT THIS CLASS AGAIN...
...JUST FOR US ALL TO DO THIS PROJECT TOGETHER!
IT WAS AN HONOR TO WORK AT YOUR SIDE, MEN... BUT NOW IT'S TIME TO WARM UP THE CAR.
NOVICE, OPEN UP THE DOOR FOR US.
REMEMBER TO BE QUIET SO WE DON'T WAKE ANYONE...
ZZZZZZZZZZ
...UP.

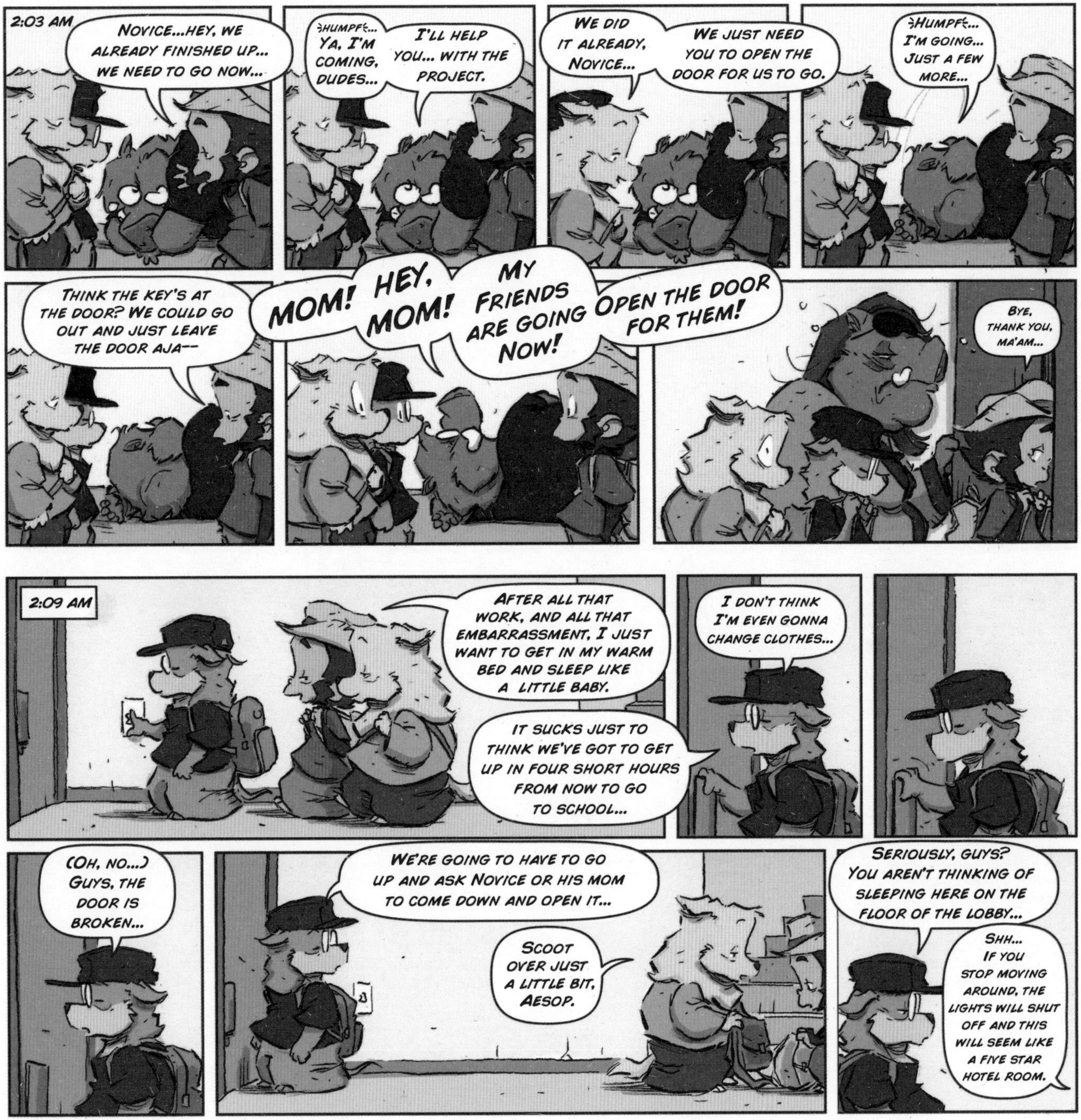
2:03 AM
NOVICE...HEY, WE ALREADY FINISHED UP... WE NEED TO GO NOW...
HUMPF... YA, I'M COMING, DUDES...
I'LL HELP YOU... WITH THE PROJECT.
WE DID IT ALREADY, NOVICE...
WE JUST NEED YOU TO OPEN THE DOOR FOR US TO GO.
HUMPF... I'M GOING... JUST A FEW MORE...
THINK THE KEY'S AT THE DOOR? WE COULD GO OUT AND JUST LEAVE THE DOOR AJA--
MOM! HEY, MOM!
MY FRIENDS ARE GOING NOW!
OPEN THE DOOR FOR THEM!
BYE, THANK YOU, MA'AM...
2:09 AM
AFTER ALL THAT WORK, AND ALL THAT EMBARRASSMENT, I JUST WANT TO GET IN MY WARM BED AND SLEEP LIKE A LITTLE BABY.
IT SUCKS JUST TO THINK WE'VE GOT TO GET UP IN FOUR SHORT HOURS FROM NOW TO GO TO SCHOOL...
I DON'T THINK I'M EVEN GONNA CHANGE CLOTHES...
(OH, NO...) GUYS, THE DOOR IS BROKEN...
WE'RE GOING TO HAVE TO GO UP AND ASK NOVICE OR HIS MOM TO COME DOWN AND OPEN IT...
SCOOT OVER JUST A LITTLE BIT, AESOP.
SERIOUSLY, GUYS? YOU AREN'T THINKING OF SLEEPING HERE ON THE FLOOR OF THE LOBBY...
SHH... IF YOU STOP MOVING AROUND, THE LIGHTS WILL SHUT OFF AND THIS WILL SEEM LIKE A FIVE STAR HOTEL ROOM.

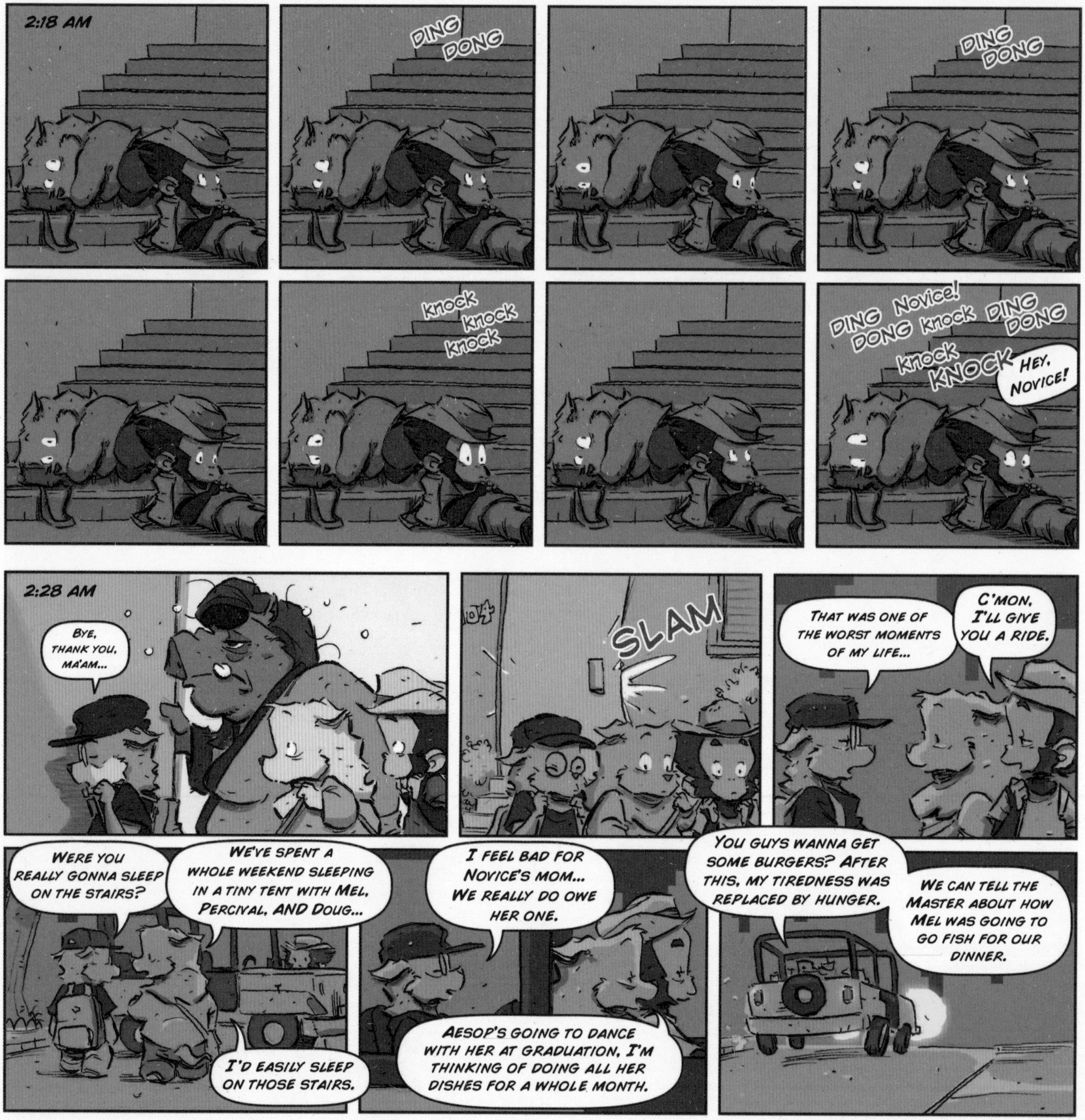

2:18 AM
DING DONG
DING DONG
knock knock knock
DING Novice! DONG knock DING DONG
knock KNOCK
HEY, NOVICE!
2:28 AM
BYE, THANK YOU, MA'AM...
SLAM
THAT WAS ONE OF THE WORST MOMENTS OF MY LIFE...
C'MON, I'LL GIVE YOU A RIDE.
WERE YOU REALLY GONNA SLEEP ON THE STAIRS?
WE'VE SPENT A WHOLE WEEKEND SLEEPING IN A TINY TENT WITH MEL, PERCIVAL, AND DOUG...
I'D EASILY SLEEP ON THOSE STAIRS.
I FEEL BAD FOR NOVICE'S MOM... WE REALLY DO OWE HER ONE.
AESOP'S GOING TO DANCE WITH HER AT GRADUATION. I'M THINKING OF DOING ALL HER DISHES FOR A WHOLE MONTH.
YOU GUYS WANNA GET SOME BURGERS? AFTER THIS, MY TIREDNESS WAS REPLACED BY HUNGER.
WE CAN TELL THE MASTER ABOUT HOW MEL WAS GOING TO GO FISH FOR OUR DINNER.

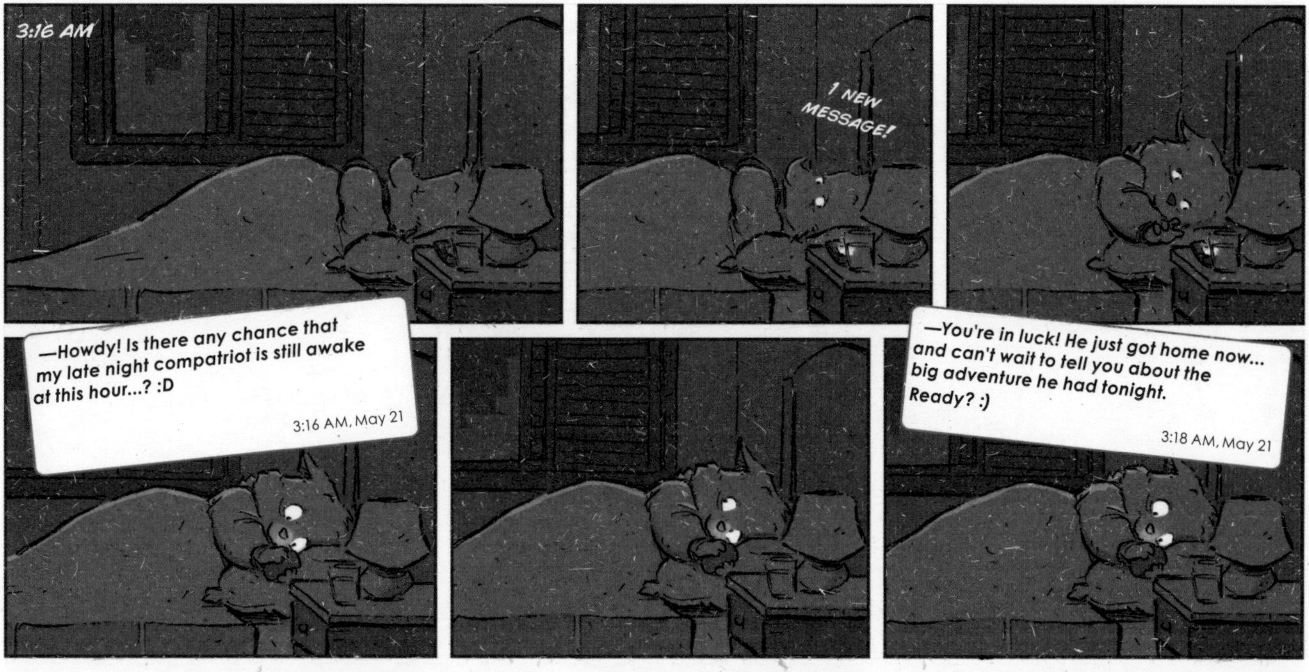
3:16 AM
1 NEW MESSAGE!
—Howdy! Is there any chance that my late night compatriot is still awake at this hour...? :D
3:16 AM, May 21
—You're in luck! He just got home now... and can't wait to tell you about the big adventure he had tonight. Ready? :)
3:18 AM, May 21

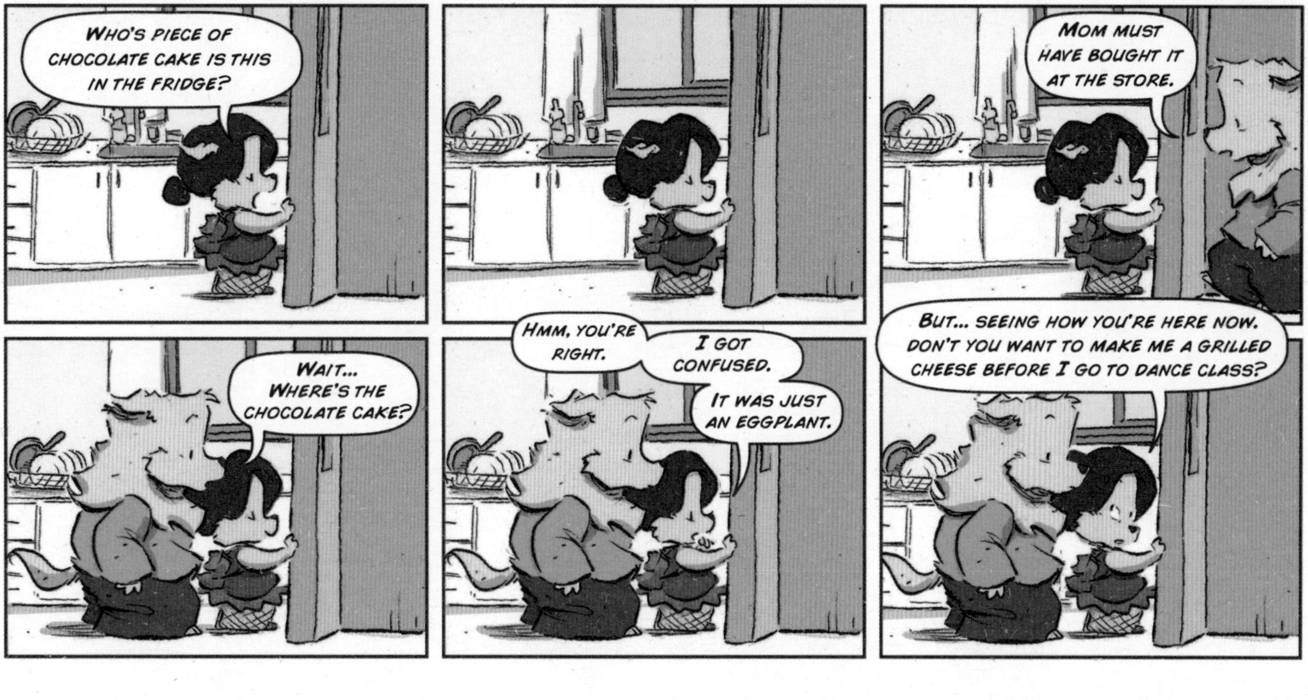
WHO'S PIECE OF CHOCOLATE CAKE IS THIS IN THE FRIDGE?
MOM MUST HAVE BOUGHT IT AT THE STORE.
WAIT... WHERE'S THE CHOCOLATE CAKE?
HMM, YOU'RE RIGHT.
I GOT CONFUSED.
IT WAS JUST AN EGGPLANT.
BUT... SEEING HOW YOU'RE HERE NOW. DON'T YOU WANT TO MAKE ME A GRILLED CHEESE BEFORE I GO TO DANCE CLASS?

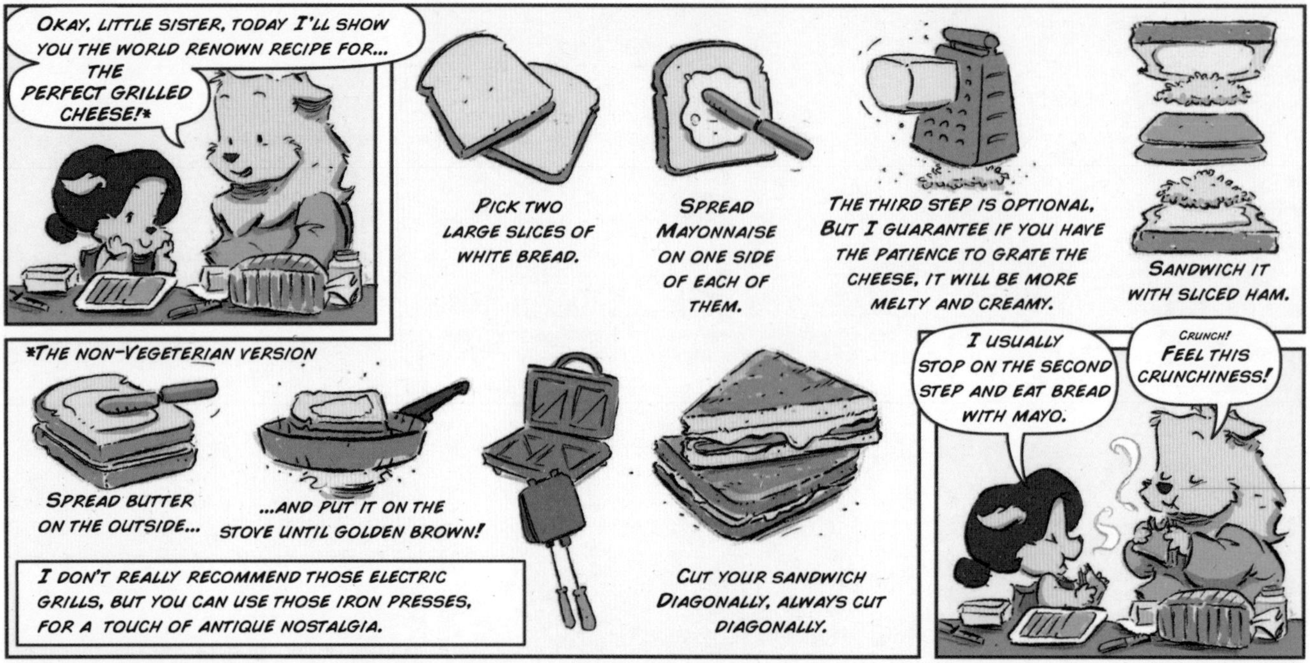
OKAY, LITTLE SISTER, TODAY I'LL SHOW YOU THE WORLD RENOWN RECIPE FOR... THE PERFECT GRILLED CHEESE!*
PICK TWO LARGE SLICES OF WHITE BREAD.
SPREAD MAYONNAISE ON ONE SIDE OF EACH OF THEM.
THE THIRD STEP IS OPTIONAL, BUT I GUARANTEE IF YOU HAVE THE PATIENCE TO GRATE THE CHEESE, IT WILL BE MORE MELTY AND CREAMY.
SANDWICH IT WITH SLICED HAM.
*THE NON-VEGETERIAN VERSION
SPREAD BUTTER ON THE OUTSIDE...
...AND PUT IT ON THE STOVE UNTIL GOLDEN BROWN!
I DON'T REALLY RECOMMEND THOSE ELECTRIC GRILLS, BUT YOU CAN USE THOSE IRON PRESSES, FOR A TOUCH OF ANTIQUE NOSTALGIA.
CUT YOUR SANDWICH DIAGONALLY, ALWAYS CUT DIAGONALLY.
I USUALLY STOP ON THE SECOND STEP AND EAT BREAD WITH MAYO.
CRUNCH!
FEEL THIS CRUNCHINESS!

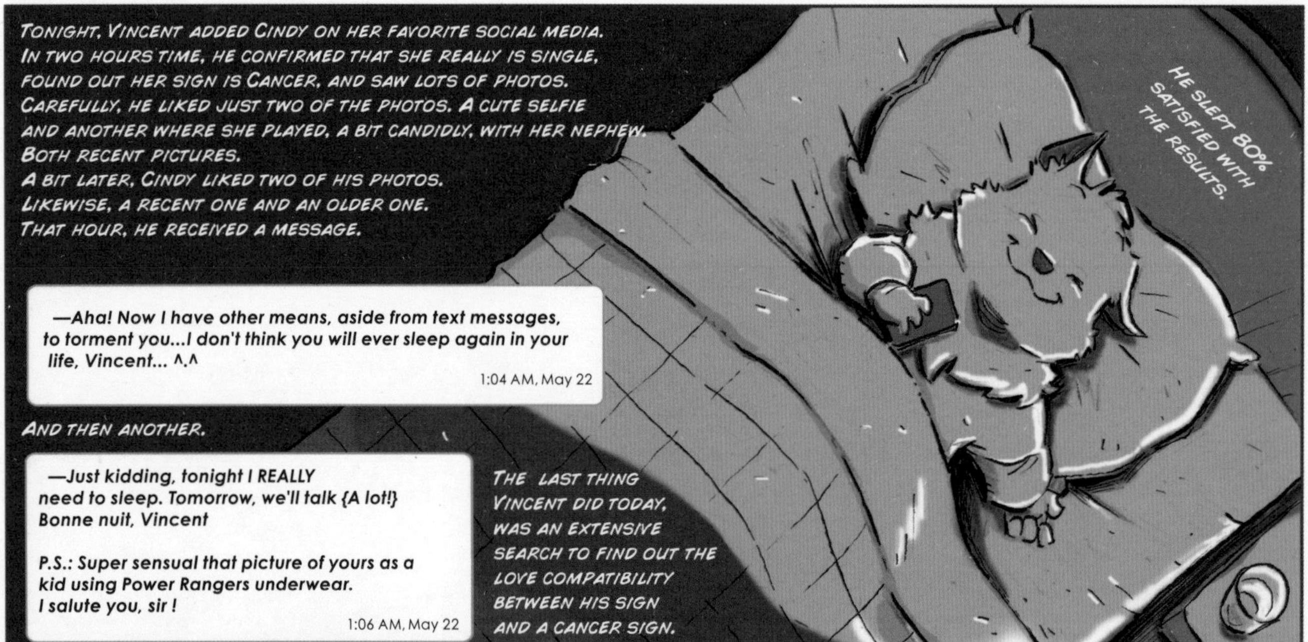
TONIGHT, VINCENT ADDED CINDY ON HER FAVORITE SOCIAL MEDIA. IN TWO HOURS TIME, HE CONFIRMED THAT SHE REALLY IS SINGLE, FOUND OUT HER SIGN IS CANCER, AND SAW LOTS OF PHOTOS. CAREFULLY, HE LIKED JUST TWO OF THE PHOTOS. A CUTE SELFIE AND ANOTHER WHERE SHE PLAYED, A BIT CANDIDLY, WITH HER NEPHEW. BOTH RECENT PICTURES. A BIT LATER, CINDY LIKED TWO OF HIS PHOTOS. LIKEWISE, A RECENT ONE AND AN OLDER ONE. THAT HOUR, HE RECEIVED A MESSAGE.
—Aha! Now I have other means, aside from text messages, to torment you...I don't think you will ever sleep again in your life, Vincent... ^.^
1:04 AM, May 22
AND THEN ANOTHER.
—Just kidding, tonight I REALLY need to sleep. Tomorrow, we'll talk {A lot!} Bonne nuit, Vincent
P.S.: Super sensual that picture of yours as a kid using Power Rangers underwear. I salute you, sir !
1:06 AM, May 22
THE LAST THING VINCENT DID TODAY, WAS AN EXTENSIVE SEARCH TO FIND OUT THE LOVE COMPATIBILITY BETWEEN HIS SIGN AND A CANCER SIGN.
HE SLEPT 80% SATISFIED WITH THE RESULTS.

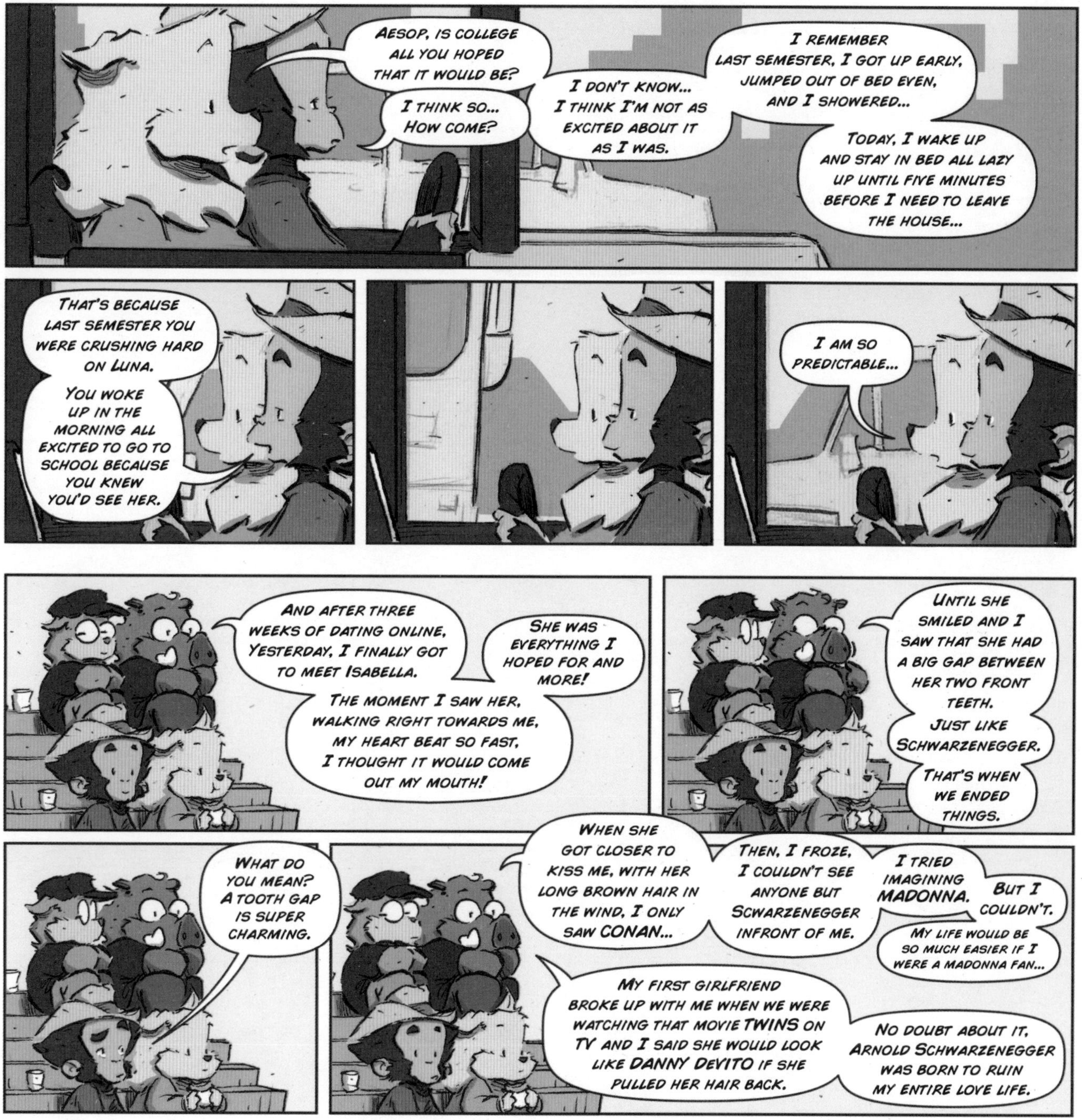
AESOP, IS COLLEGE ALL YOU HOPED THAT IT WOULD BE?
I THINK SO... HOW COME?
I DON'T KNOW... I THINK I'M NOT AS EXCITED ABOUT IT AS I WAS.
I REMEMBER LAST SEMESTER, I GOT UP EARLY, JUMPED OUT OF BED EVEN, AND I SHOWERED...
TODAY, I WAKE UP AND STAY IN BED ALL LAZY UP UNTIL FIVE MINUTES BEFORE I NEED TO LEAVE THE HOUSE...
THAT'S BECAUSE LAST SEMESTER YOU WERE CRUSHING HARD ON LUNA.
YOU WOKE UP IN THE MORNING ALL EXCITED TO GO TO SCHOOL BECAUSE YOU KNEW YOU'D SEE HER.
I AM SO PREDICTABLE...
AND AFTER THREE WEEKS OF DATING ONLINE, YESTERDAY, I FINALLY GOT TO MEET ISABELLA.
SHE WAS EVERYTHING I HOPED FOR AND MORE!
THE MOMENT I SAW HER, WALKING RIGHT TOWARDS ME, MY HEART BEAT SO FAST, I THOUGHT IT WOULD COME OUT MY MOUTH!
UNTIL SHE SMILED AND I SAW THAT SHE HAD A BIG GAP BETWEEN HER TWO FRONT TEETH.
JUST LIKE SCHWARZENEGGER.
THAT'S WHEN WE ENDED THINGS.
WHAT DO YOU MEAN? A TOOTH GAP IS SUPER CHARMING.
WHEN SHE GOT CLOSER TO KISS ME, WITH HER LONG BROWN HAIR IN THE WIND, I ONLY SAW CONAN...
THEN, I FROZE, I COULDN'T SEE ANYONE BUT SCHWARZENEGGER INFRONT OF ME.
I TRIED IMAGINING MADONNA.
BUT I COULDN'T.
MY LIFE WOULD BE SO MUCH EASIER IF I WERE A MADONNA FAN...
MY FIRST GIRLFRIEND BROKE UP WITH ME WHEN WE WERE WATCHING THAT MOVIE TWINS ON TV AND I SAID SHE WOULD LOOK LIKE DANNY DEVITO IF SHE PULLED HER HAIR BACK.
NO DOUBT ABOUT IT, ARNOLD SCHWARZENEGGER WAS BORN TO RUIN MY ENTIRE LOVE LIFE.

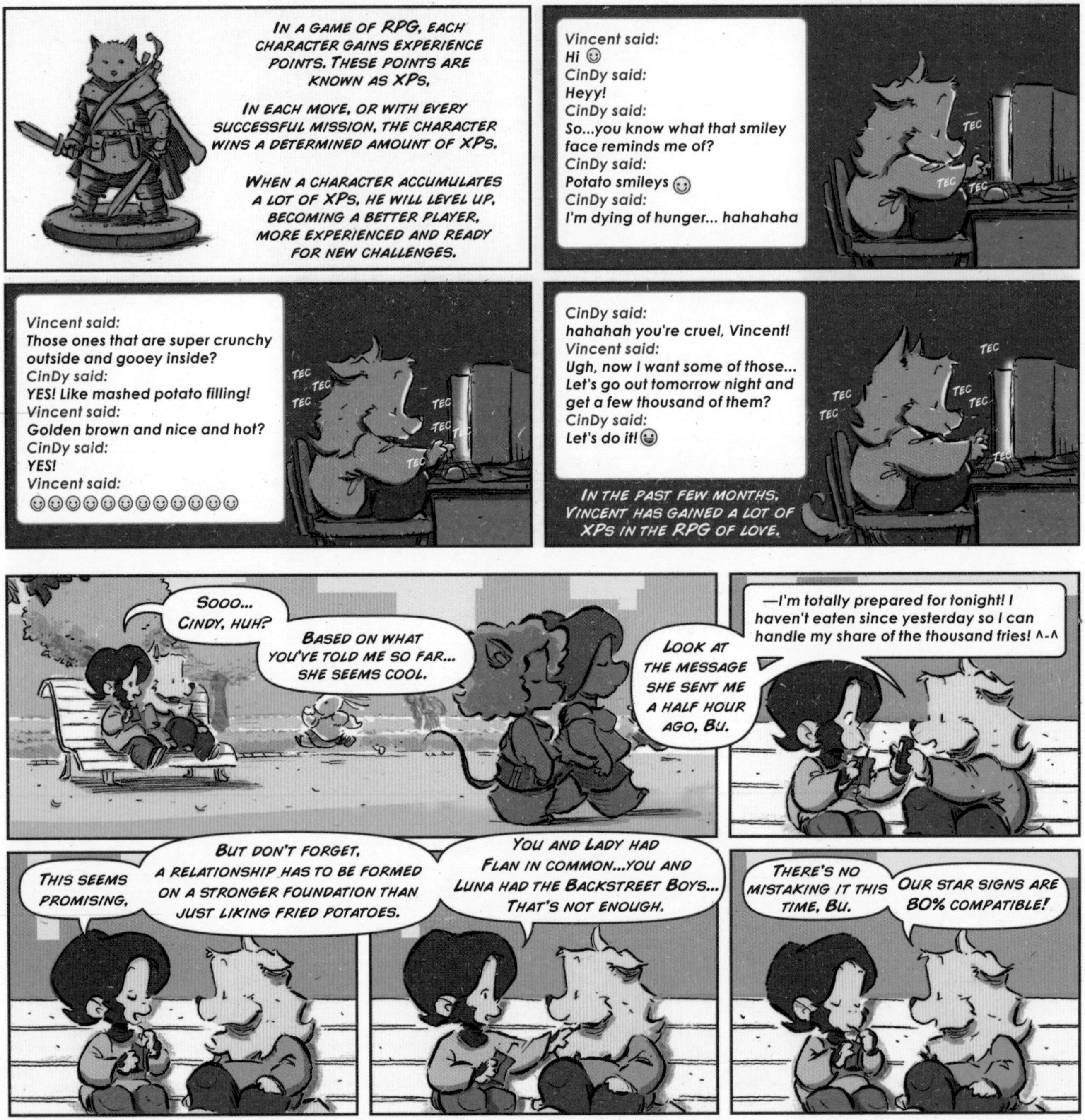

IN A GAME OF RPG, EACH CHARACTER GAINS EXPERIENCE POINTS. THESE POINTS ARE KNOWN AS XPS.
IN EACH MOVE, OR WITH EVERY SUCCESSFUL MISSION, THE CHARACTER WINS A DETERMINED AMOUNT OF XPS.
WHEN A CHARACTER ACCUMULATES A LOT OF XPS, HE WILL LEVEL UP, BECOMING A BETTER PLAYER, MORE EXPERIENCED AND READY FOR NEW CHALLENGES.
Vincent said:
Hi ☺
CinDy said:
Heyy!
CinDy said:
So...you know what that smiley face reminds me of?
CinDy said:
Potato smileys ☺
CinDy said:
I'm dying of hunger... hahahaha
TEC
TEC
TEC
Vincent said:
Those ones that are super crunchy outside and gooey inside?
CinDy said:
YES! Like mashed potato filling!
Vincent said:
Golden brown and nice and hot?
CinDy said:
YES!
Vincent said:
☺☺☺☺☺☺☺☺☺☺☺☺
TEC
TEC
TEC
TEC
TEC
TEC
TEC
CinDy said:
hahahah you're cruel, Vincent!
Vincent said:
Ugh, now I want some of those... Let's go out tomorrow night and get a few thousand of them?
CinDy said:
Let's do it!
TEC
TEC
TEC
TEC
TEC
TEC
IN THE PAST FEW MONTHS, VINCENT HAS GAINED A LOT OF XPS IN THE RPG OF LOVE.
SOOO... CINDY, HUH?
BASED ON WHAT YOU'VE TOLD ME SO FAR... SHE SEEMS COOL.
LOOK AT THE MESSAGE SHE SENT ME A HALF HOUR AGO, BU.
—I'm totally prepared for tonight! I haven't eaten since yesterday so I can handle my share of the thousand fries! ^-^
THIS SEEMS PROMISING.
BUT DON'T FORGET, A RELATIONSHIP HAS TO BE FORMED ON A STRONGER FOUNDATION THAN JUST LIKING FRIED POTATOES.
YOU AND LADY HAD FLAN IN COMMON...YOU AND LUNA HAD THE BACKSTREET BOYS... THAT'S NOT ENOUGH.
THERE'S NO MISTAKING IT THIS TIME, BU.
OUR STAR SIGNS ARE 80% COMPATIBLE!

So then, Bu... Do you have any wise advice that I could use on my date that's in a few hours?

This time, just be yourself... No lists, no little games, no over-rationalizing everything, got it?

You're ready for this, Vincent.

Just listen to your heart...like the song says.

That's exactly what Lady told me!

Lady? Lady-Loco? And when did she tell you this?

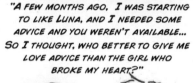

"A few months ago, I was starting to like Luna, and I needed some advice and you weren't available... So I thought, who better to give me love advice than the girl who broke my heart?"

You're not ready for this, at all.

About those three love tips, there's one that says...

3. DON'T FALL IN LOVE

(BEFORE IT'S TIME)

So...the right time, is that all measured in days, or in how many messages you send to that person...?

Why, Vincent?

Oh, nothing.

Do you have something to say?

Is someone falling for a girl when he hasn't even had a date yet...hm?

Look at me.

Who hasn't been a good boy, huh?

65

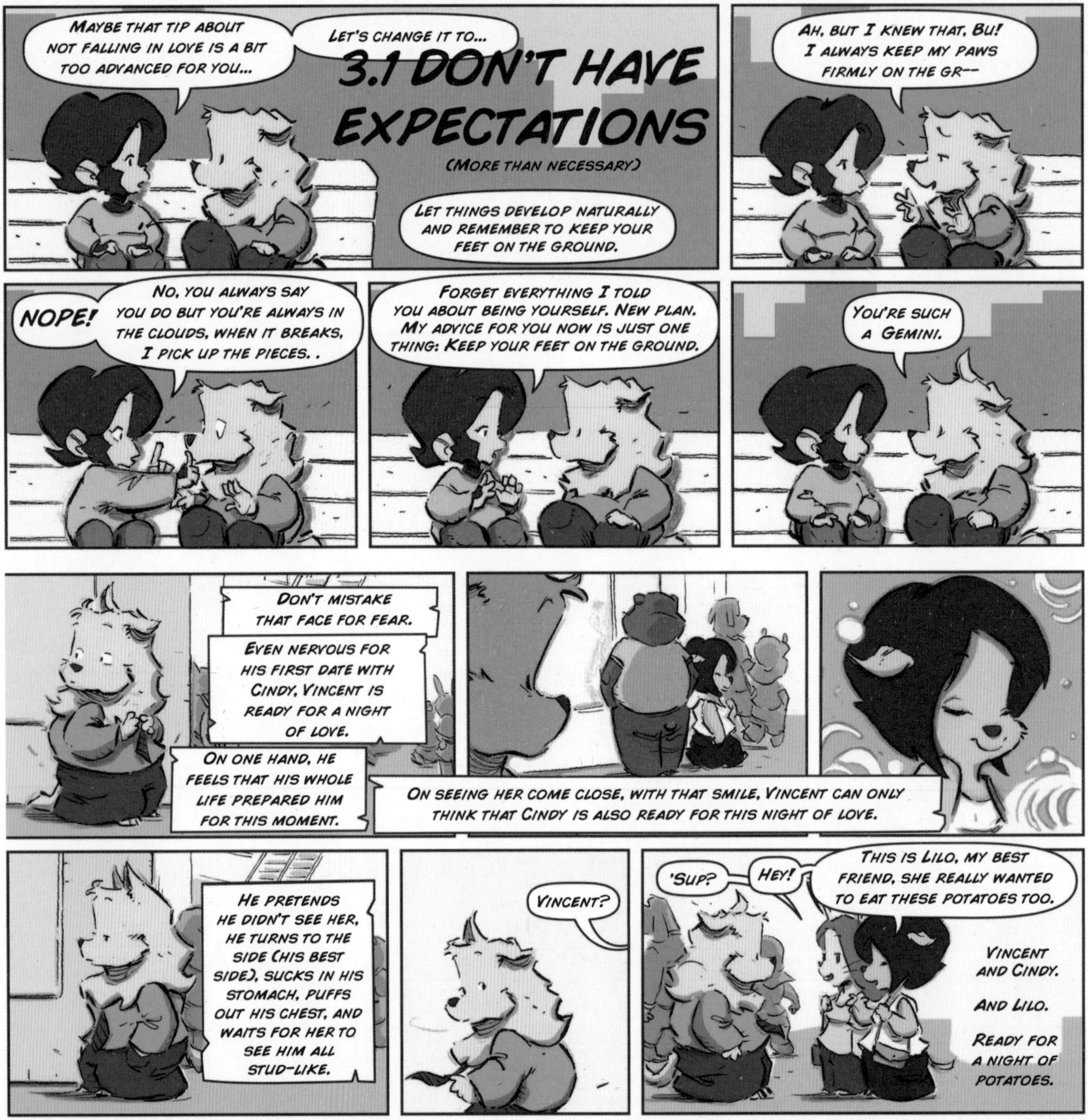
MAYBE THAT TIP ABOUT NOT FALLING IN LOVE IS A BIT TOO ADVANCED FOR YOU...
LET'S CHANGE IT TO...
3.1 DON'T HAVE EXPECTATIONS
(MORE THAN NECESSARY)
LET THINGS DEVELOP NATURALLY AND REMEMBER TO KEEP YOUR FEET ON THE GROUND.
AH, BUT I KNEW THAT, BU! I ALWAYS KEEP MY PAWS FIRMLY ON THE GR--
NOPE!
NO, YOU ALWAYS SAY YOU DO BUT YOU'RE ALWAYS IN THE CLOUDS. WHEN IT BREAKS, I PICK UP THE PIECES. .
FORGET EVERYTHING I TOLD YOU ABOUT BEING YOURSELF. NEW PLAN. MY ADVICE FOR YOU NOW IS JUST ONE THING: KEEP YOUR FEET ON THE GROUND.
YOU'RE SUCH A GEMINI.
DON'T MISTAKE THAT FACE FOR FEAR.
EVEN NERVOUS FOR HIS FIRST DATE WITH CINDY, VINCENT IS READY FOR A NIGHT OF LOVE.
ON ONE HAND, HE FEELS THAT HIS WHOLE LIFE PREPARED HIM FOR THIS MOMENT.
ON SEEING HER COME CLOSE, WITH THAT SMILE, VINCENT CAN ONLY THINK THAT CINDY IS ALSO READY FOR THIS NIGHT OF LOVE.
HE PRETENDS HE DIDN'T SEE HER, HE TURNS TO THE SIDE (HIS BEST SIDE), SUCKS IN HIS STOMACH, PUFFS OUT HIS CHEST, AND WAITS FOR HER TO SEE HIM ALL STUD-LIKE.
VINCENT?
'SUP?
HEY!
THIS IS LILO, MY BEST FRIEND. SHE REALLY WANTED TO EAT THESE POTATOES TOO.
VINCENT AND CINDY.
AND LILO.
READY FOR A NIGHT OF POTATOES.

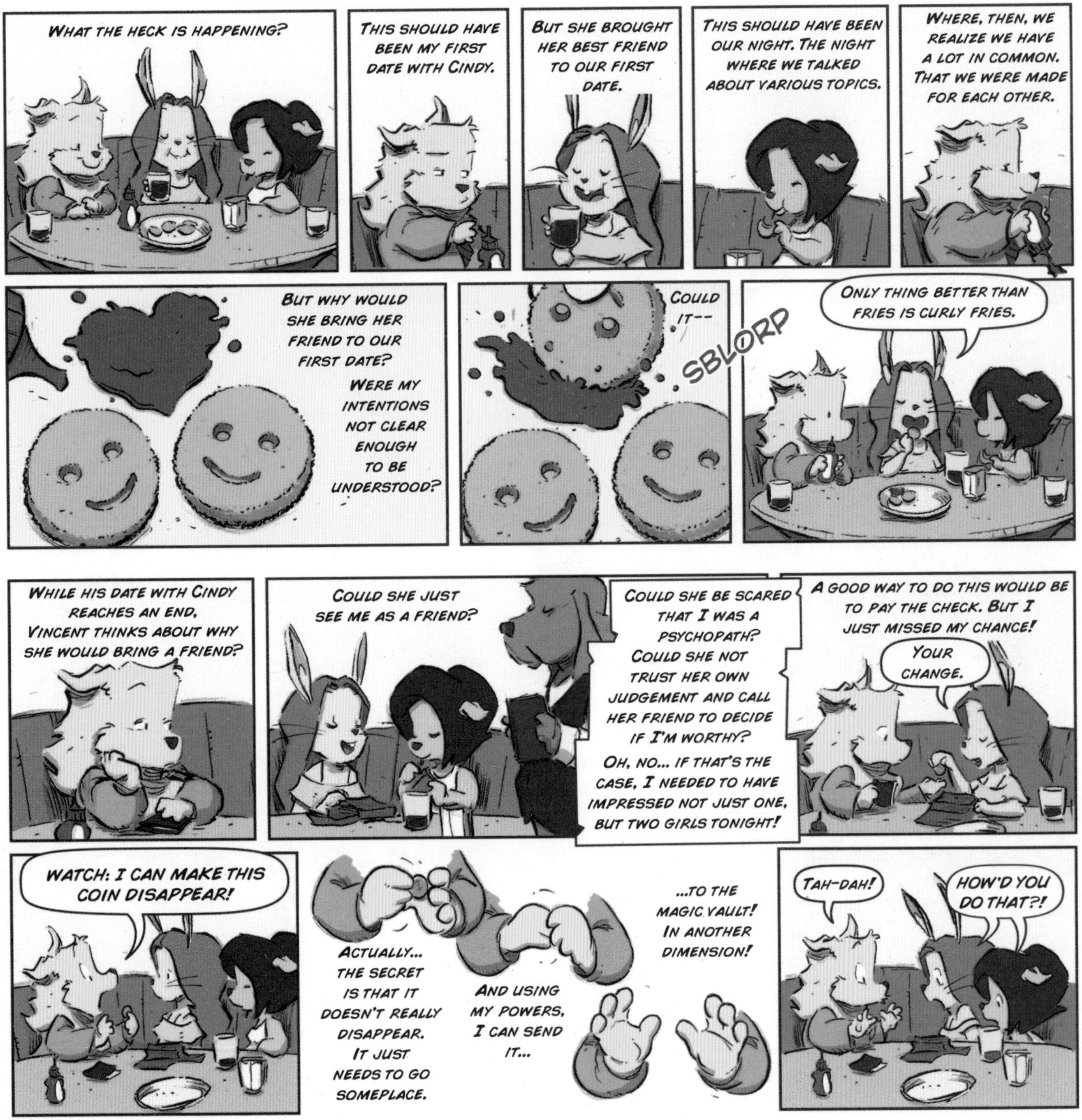

WHAT THE HECK IS HAPPENING?
THIS SHOULD HAVE BEEN MY FIRST DATE WITH CINDY.
BUT SHE BROUGHT HER BEST FRIEND TO OUR FIRST DATE.
THIS SHOULD HAVE BEEN OUR NIGHT. THE NIGHT WHERE WE TALKED ABOUT VARIOUS TOPICS.
WHERE, THEN, WE REALIZE WE HAVE A LOT IN COMMON. THAT WE WERE MADE FOR EACH OTHER.
BUT WHY WOULD SHE BRING HER FRIEND TO OUR FIRST DATE?
WERE MY INTENTIONS NOT CLEAR ENOUGH TO BE UNDERSTOOD?
COULD IT--
SBLORP
ONLY THING BETTER THAN FRIES IS CURLY FRIES.
WHILE HIS DATE WITH CINDY REACHES AN END, VINCENT THINKS ABOUT WHY SHE WOULD BRING A FRIEND?
COULD SHE JUST SEE ME AS A FRIEND?
COULD SHE BE SCARED THAT I WAS A PSYCHOPATH? COULD SHE NOT TRUST HER OWN JUDGEMENT AND CALL HER FRIEND TO DECIDE IF I'M WORTHY?
OH, NO... IF THAT'S THE CASE, I NEEDED TO HAVE IMPRESSED NOT JUST ONE, BUT TWO GIRLS TONIGHT!
A GOOD WAY TO DO THIS WOULD BE TO PAY THE CHECK. BUT I JUST MISSED MY CHANCE!
YOUR CHANGE.
WATCH: I CAN MAKE THIS COIN DISAPPEAR!
ACTUALLY... THE SECRET IS THAT IT DOESN'T REALLY DISAPPEAR. IT JUST NEEDS TO GO SOMEPLACE.
AND USING MY POWERS, I CAN SEND IT...
...TO THE MAGIC VAULT! IN ANOTHER DIMENSION!
TAH-DAH!
HOW'D YOU DO THAT?!

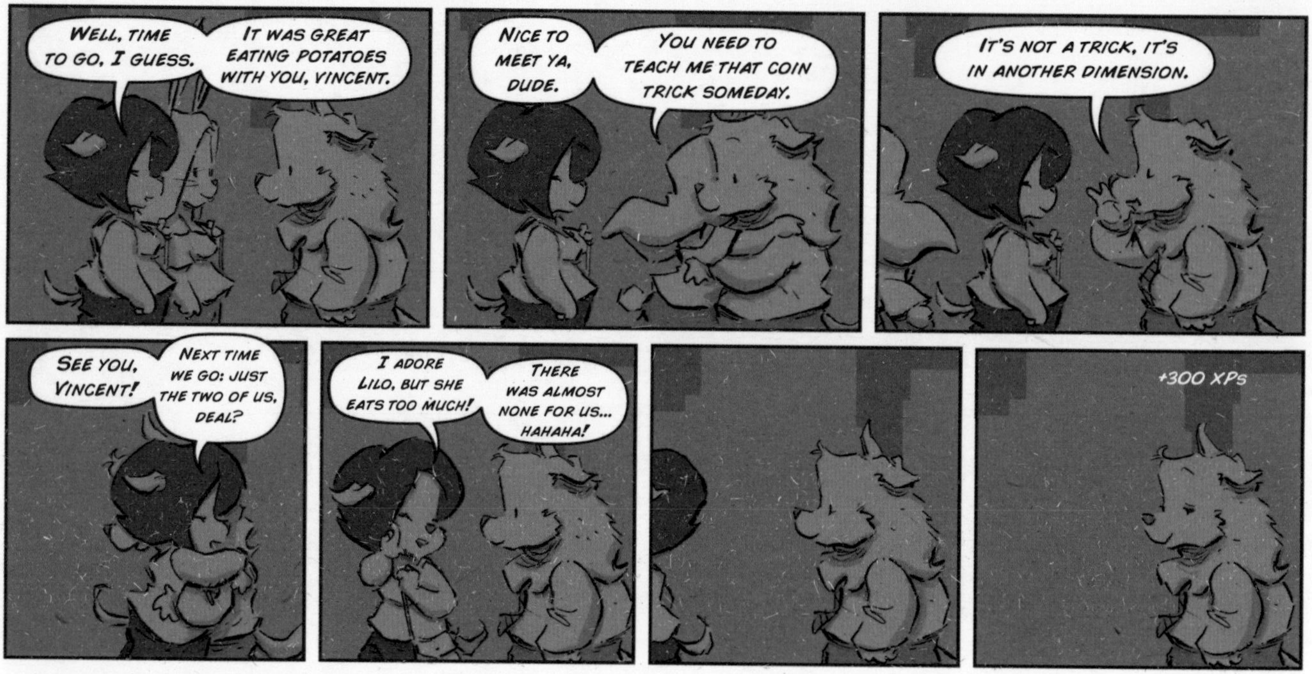
WELL, TIME TO GO, I GUESS.
IT WAS GREAT EATING POTATOES WITH YOU, VINCENT.
NICE TO MEET YA, DUDE.
YOU NEED TO TEACH ME THAT COIN TRICK SOMEDAY.
IT'S NOT A TRICK, IT'S IN ANOTHER DIMENSION.
SEE YOU, VINCENT!
NEXT TIME WE GO: JUST THE TWO OF US, DEAL?
I ADORE LILO, BUT SHE EATS TOO MUCH!
THERE WAS ALMOST NONE FOR US... HAHAHA!
+300 XPs

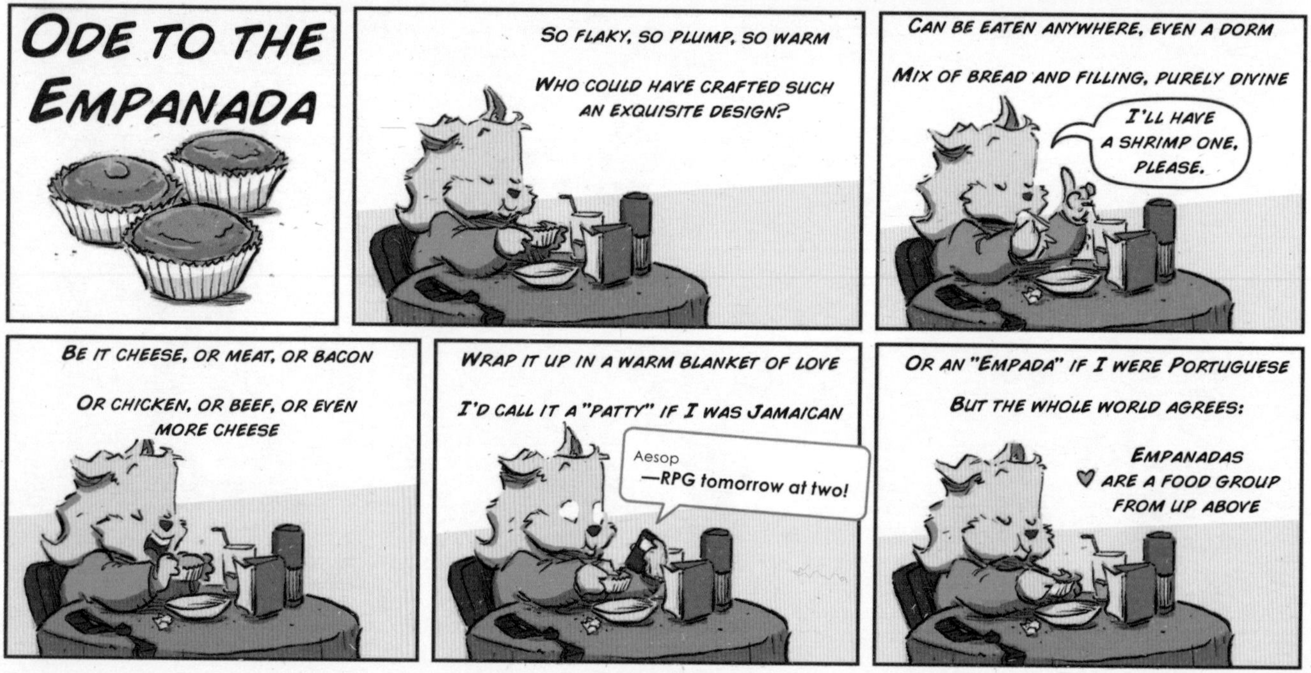
ODE TO THE EMPANADA
SO FLAKY, SO PLUMP, SO WARM
WHO COULD HAVE CRAFTED SUCH AN EXQUISITE DESIGN?
CAN BE EATEN ANYWHERE, EVEN A DORM
MIX OF BREAD AND FILLING, PURELY DIVINE
I'LL HAVE A SHRIMP ONE, PLEASE.
BE IT CHEESE, OR MEAT, OR BACON
OR CHICKEN, OR BEEF, OR EVEN MORE CHEESE
WRAP IT UP IN A WARM BLANKET OF LOVE
I'D CALL IT A "PATTY" IF I WAS JAMAICAN
Aesop
—RPG tomorrow at two!
OR AN "EMPADA" IF I WERE PORTUGUESE
BUT THE WHOLE WORLD AGREES:
EMPANADAS ♥ ARE A FOOD GROUP FROM UP ABOVE

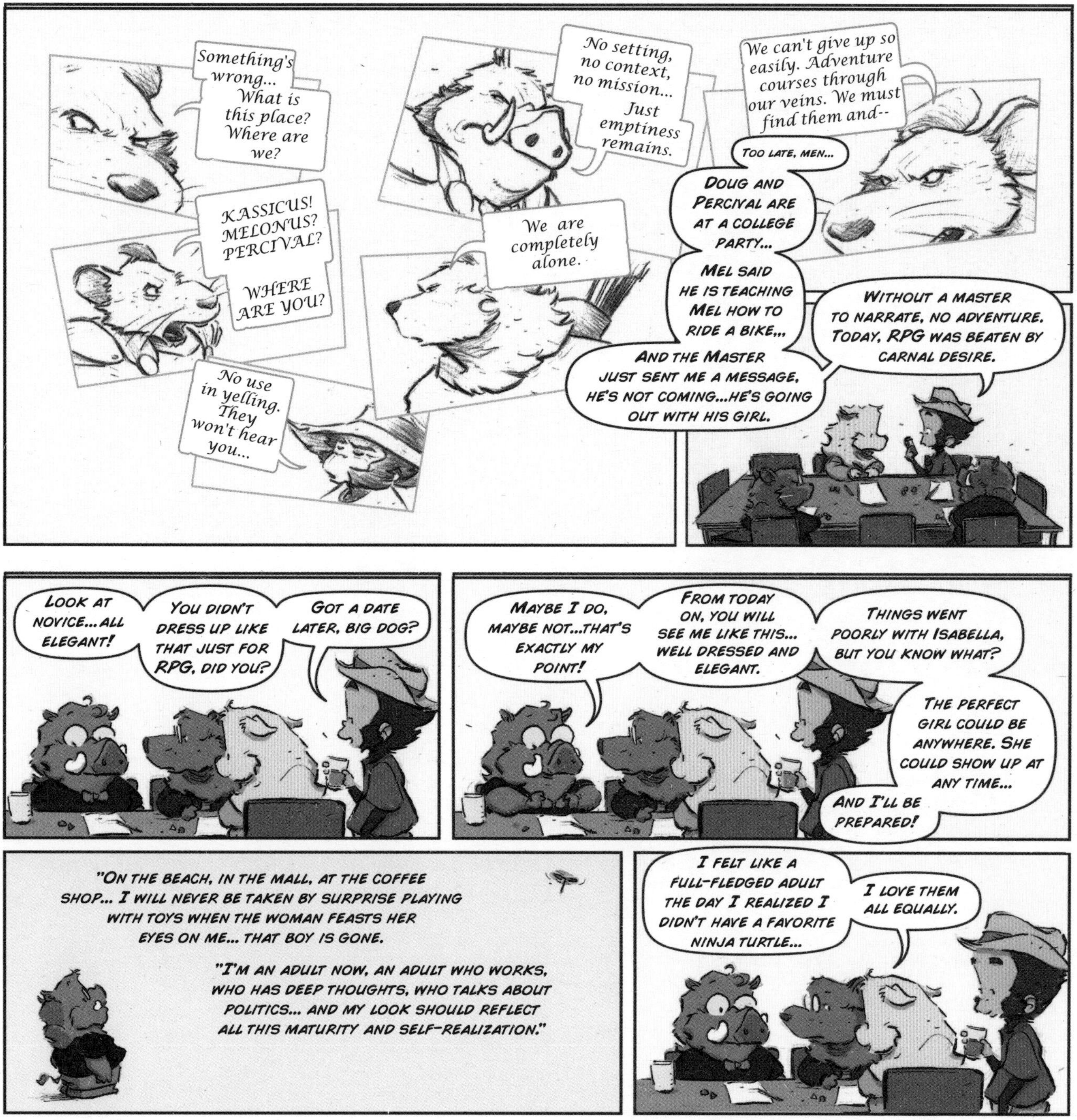
Something's wrong... What is this place? Where are we?
KASSICUS! MELONUS? PERCIVAL? WHERE ARE YOU?
No use in yelling. They won't hear you...
No setting, no context, no mission... Just emptiness remains.
We are completely alone.
We can't give up so easily. Adventure courses through our veins. We must find them and--
TOO LATE, MEN...
DOUG AND PERCIVAL ARE AT A COLLEGE PARTY...
MEL SAID HE IS TEACHING MEL HOW TO RIDE A BIKE...
AND THE MASTER JUST SENT ME A MESSAGE, HE'S NOT COMING...HE'S GOING OUT WITH HIS GIRL.
WITHOUT A MASTER TO NARRATE, NO ADVENTURE. TODAY, RPG WAS BEATEN BY CARNAL DESIRE.
LOOK AT NOVICE...ALL ELEGANT!
YOU DIDN'T DRESS UP LIKE THAT JUST FOR RPG, DID YOU?
GOT A DATE LATER, BIG DOG?
MAYBE I DO, MAYBE NOT...THAT'S EXACTLY MY POINT!
FROM TODAY ON, YOU WILL SEE ME LIKE THIS... WELL DRESSED AND ELEGANT.
THINGS WENT POORLY WITH ISABELLA, BUT YOU KNOW WHAT?
THE PERFECT GIRL COULD BE ANYWHERE. SHE COULD SHOW UP AT ANY TIME...
AND I'LL BE PREPARED!
"ON THE BEACH, IN THE MALL, AT THE COFFEE SHOP... I WILL NEVER BE TAKEN BY SURPRISE PLAYING WITH TOYS WHEN THE WOMAN FEASTS HER EYES ON ME... THAT BOY IS GONE.
"I'M AN ADULT NOW, AN ADULT WHO WORKS, WHO HAS DEEP THOUGHTS, WHO TALKS ABOUT POLITICS... AND MY LOOK SHOULD REFLECT ALL THIS MATURITY AND SELF-REALIZATION."
I FELT LIKE A FULL-FLEDGED ADULT THE DAY I REALIZED I DIDN'T HAVE A FAVORITE NINJA TURTLE...
I LOVE THEM ALL EQUALLY.

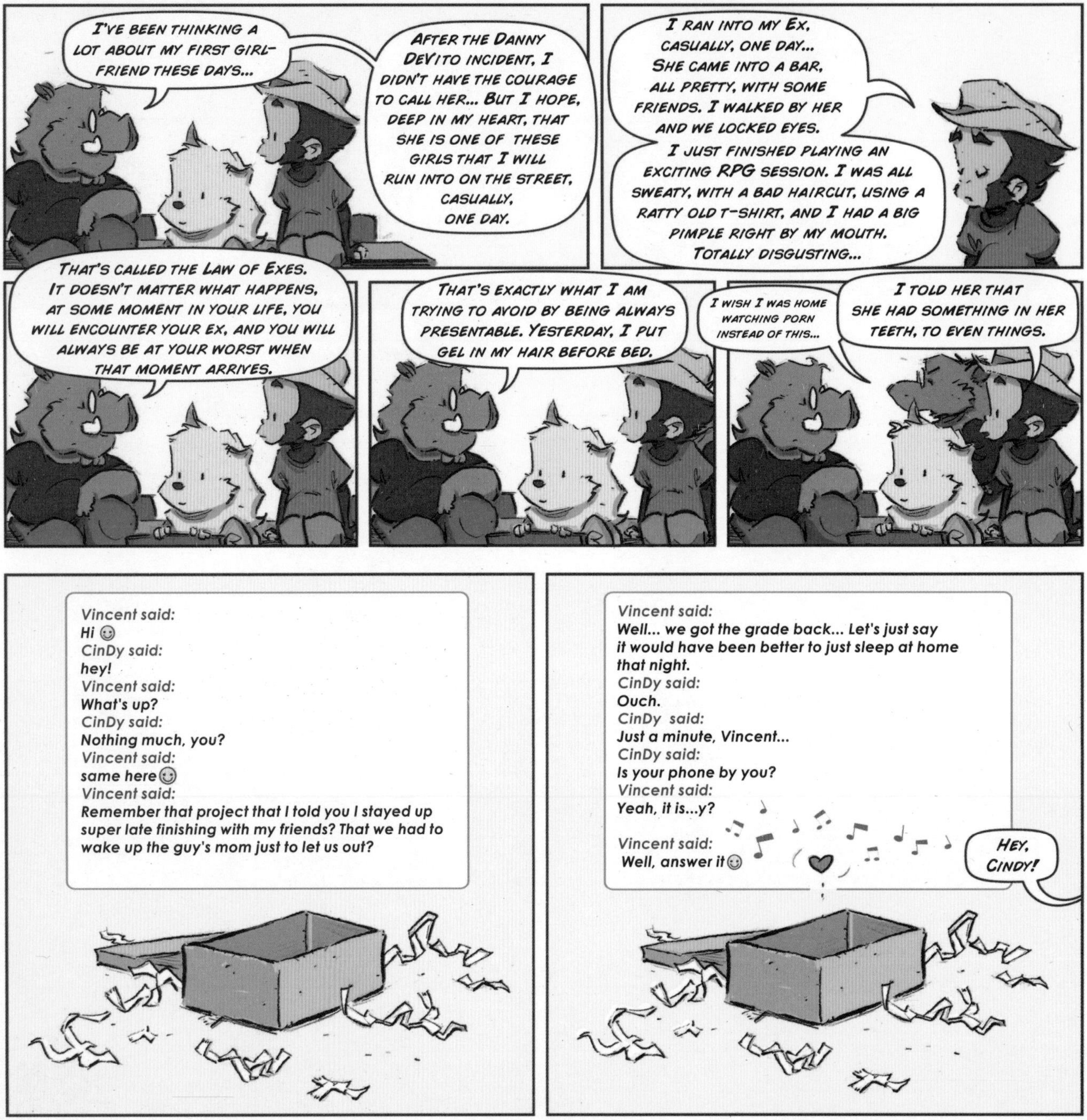
I'VE BEEN THINKING A LOT ABOUT MY FIRST GIRL-FRIEND THESE DAYS...
AFTER THE DANNY DEVITO INCIDENT, I DIDN'T HAVE THE COURAGE TO CALL HER... BUT I HOPE, DEEP IN MY HEART, THAT SHE IS ONE OF THESE GIRLS THAT I WILL RUN INTO ON THE STREET, CASUALLY, ONE DAY.
I RAN INTO MY EX, CASUALLY, ONE DAY... SHE CAME INTO A BAR, ALL PRETTY, WITH SOME FRIENDS. I WALKED BY HER AND WE LOCKED EYES.
I JUST FINISHED PLAYING AN EXCITING RPG SESSION. I WAS ALL SWEATY, WITH A BAD HAIRCUT, USING A RATTY OLD T-SHIRT, AND I HAD A BIG PIMPLE RIGHT BY MY MOUTH. TOTALLY DISGUSTING...
THAT'S CALLED THE LAW OF EXES. IT DOESN'T MATTER WHAT HAPPENS, AT SOME MOMENT IN YOUR LIFE, YOU WILL ENCOUNTER YOUR EX, AND YOU WILL ALWAYS BE AT YOUR WORST WHEN THAT MOMENT ARRIVES.
THAT'S EXACTLY WHAT I AM TRYING TO AVOID BY BEING ALWAYS PRESENTABLE. YESTERDAY, I PUT GEL IN MY HAIR BEFORE BED.
I WISH I WAS HOME WATCHING PORN INSTEAD OF THIS...
I TOLD HER THAT SHE HAD SOMETHING IN HER TEETH, TO EVEN THINGS.
Vincent said:
Hi ☺
CinDy said:
hey!
Vincent said:
What's up?
CinDy said:
Nothing much, you?
Vincent said:
same here ☺
Vincent said:
Remember that project that I told you I stayed up super late finishing with my friends? That we had to wake up the guy's mom just to let us out?
Vincent said:
Well... we got the grade back... Let's just say it would have been better to just sleep at home that night.
CinDy said:
Ouch.
CinDy said:
Just a minute, Vincent...
CinDy said:
Is your phone by you?
Vincent said:
Yeah, it is...y?
Vincent said:
Well, answer it ☺
HEY, CINDY!

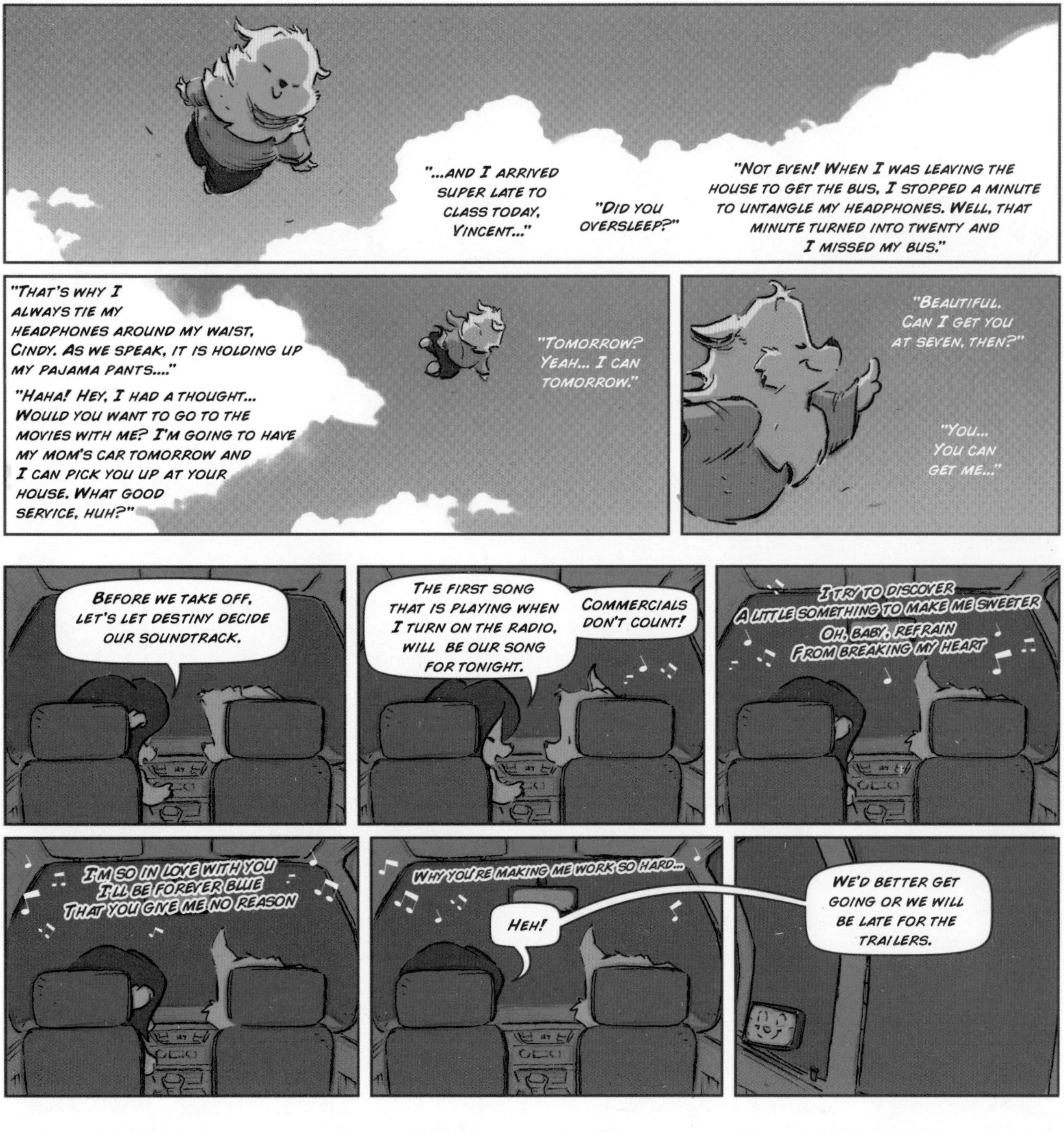
"...AND I ARRIVED SUPER LATE TO CLASS TODAY, VINCENT..."
"DID YOU OVERSLEEP?"
"NOT EVEN! WHEN I WAS LEAVING THE HOUSE TO GET THE BUS, I STOPPED A MINUTE TO UNTANGLE MY HEADPHONES. WELL, THAT MINUTE TURNED INTO TWENTY AND I MISSED MY BUS."
"THAT'S WHY I ALWAYS TIE MY HEADPHONES AROUND MY WAIST, CINDY. AS WE SPEAK, IT IS HOLDING UP MY PAJAMA PANTS...."
"HAHA! HEY, I HAD A THOUGHT... WOULD YOU WANT TO GO TO THE MOVIES WITH ME? I'M GOING TO HAVE MY MOM'S CAR TOMORROW AND I CAN PICK YOU UP AT YOUR HOUSE. WHAT GOOD SERVICE, HUH?"
"TOMORROW? YEAH... I CAN TOMORROW."
"BEAUTIFUL. CAN I GET YOU AT SEVEN, THEN?"
"YOU... YOU CAN GET ME..."
BEFORE WE TAKE OFF, LET'S LET DESTINY DECIDE OUR SOUNDTRACK.
THE FIRST SONG THAT IS PLAYING WHEN I TURN ON THE RADIO, WILL BE OUR SONG FOR TONIGHT.
COMMERCIALS DON'T COUNT!
I TRY TO DISCOVER
A LITTLE SOMETHING TO MAKE ME SWEETER
OH, BABY, REFRAIN
FROM BREAKING MY HEART
I'M SO IN LOVE WITH YOU
I'LL BE FOREVER BLUE
THAT YOU GIVE ME NO REASON
WHY YOU'RE MAKING ME WORK SO HARD...
HEH!
WE'D BETTER GET GOING OR WE WILL BE LATE FOR THE TRAILERS.

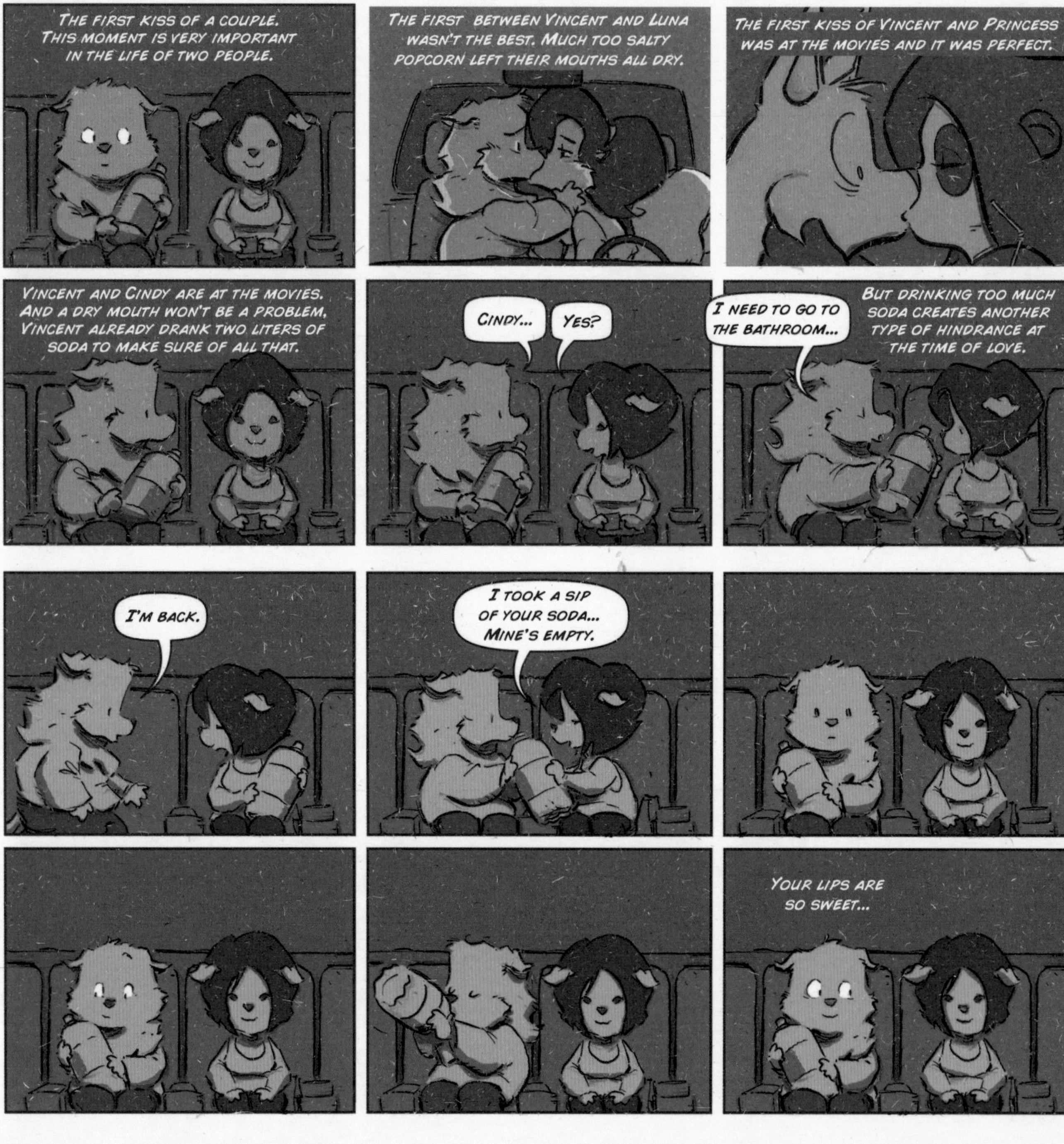
THE FIRST KISS OF A COUPLE. THIS MOMENT IS VERY IMPORTANT IN THE LIFE OF TWO PEOPLE.
THE FIRST BETWEEN VINCENT AND LUNA WASN'T THE BEST. MUCH TOO SALTY POPCORN LEFT THEIR MOUTHS ALL DRY.
THE FIRST KISS OF VINCENT AND PRINCESS WAS AT THE MOVIES AND IT WAS PERFECT.
VINCENT AND CINDY ARE AT THE MOVIES. AND A DRY MOUTH WON'T BE A PROBLEM, VINCENT ALREADY DRANK TWO LITERS OF SODA TO MAKE SURE OF ALL THAT.
CINDY...
YES?
I NEED TO GO TO THE BATHROOM...
BUT DRINKING TOO MUCH SODA CREATES ANOTHER TYPE OF HINDRANCE AT THE TIME OF LOVE.
I'M BACK.
I TOOK A SIP OF YOUR SODA... MINE'S EMPTY.
YOUR LIPS ARE SO SWEET...

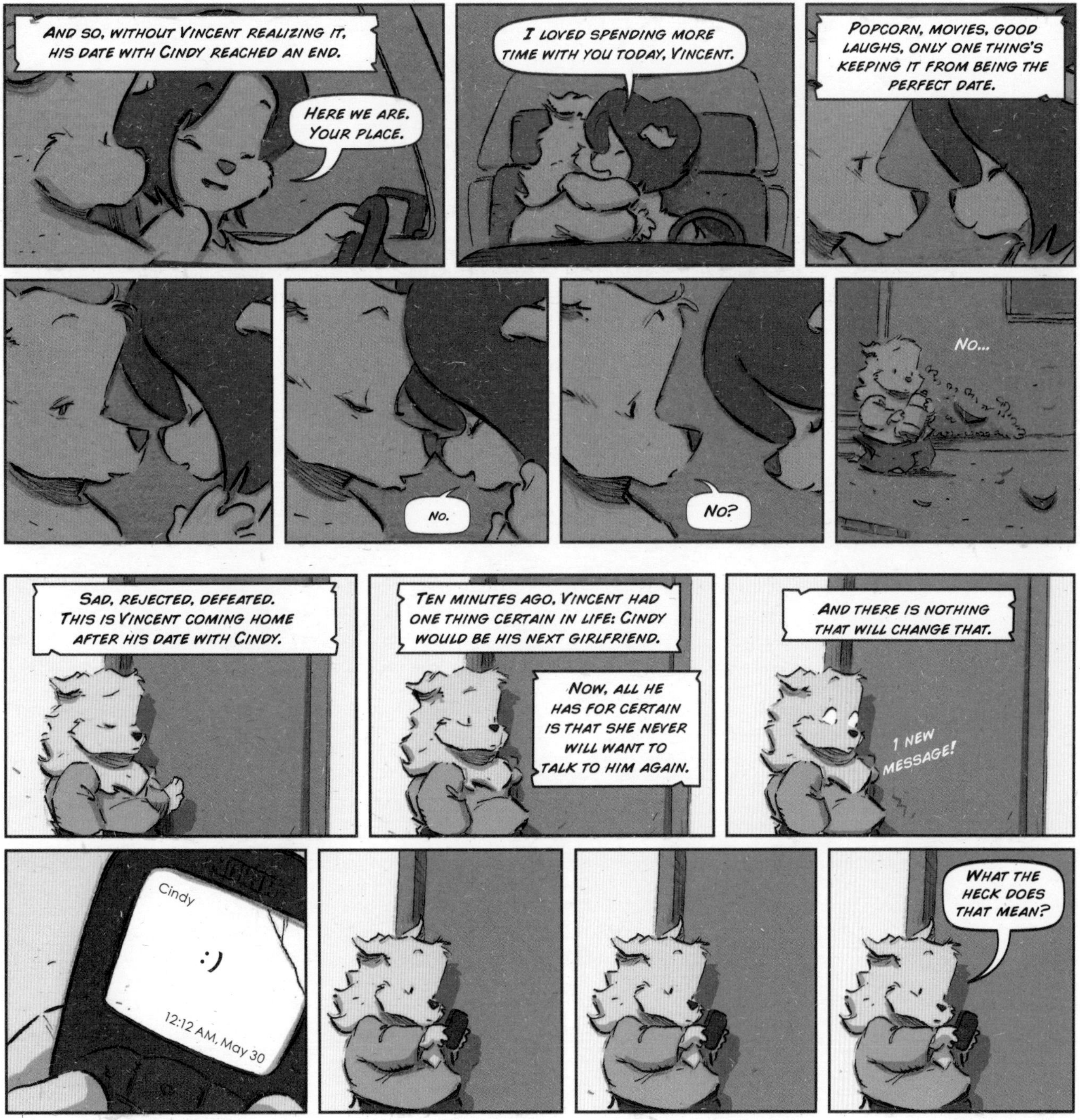

And so, without Vincent realizing it, his date with Cindy reached an end.
Here we are. Your place.
I loved spending more time with you today, Vincent.
Popcorn, movies, good laughs, only one thing's keeping it from being the perfect date.
No.
No?
No...
Sad, rejected, defeated. This is Vincent coming home after his date with Cindy.
Ten minutes ago, Vincent had one thing certain in life: Cindy would be his next girlfriend.
Now, all he has for certain is that she never will want to talk to him again.
And there is nothing that will change that.
1 new message!
Cindy
:)
12:12 AM, May 30
What the heck does that mean?

Cindy

:)

12:12 AM, May 30

WHAT THE HECK DOES THAT MEAN?

IS IT A SMILEY FACE LIKE:

"HI, IT'S OKAY YOU TRIED TO KISS ME. I'M NOT MAD AT YOU AND YOU AND I CAN STILL CONTINUE TO BE GOOD FRIENDS?"

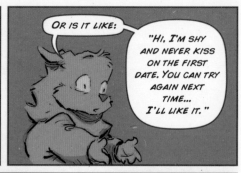

OR IS IT LIKE:

"HI, I'M SHY AND NEVER KISS ON THE FIRST DATE. YOU CAN TRY AGAIN NEXT TIME... I'LL LIKE IT."

IT WAS ALL SO RIGHT... THE DARKNESS, THE SILENCE, THE EXCHANGE OF GLANCES, HER IN MY ARMS...

HOW COULD IT'VE GONE WRONG?

HOW DID YOU GET IN HERE?

I DON'T GET IT, BU... WHY DID CINDY REJECT ME?

SINCE I'VE MET YOU, YOU'VE BEEN OBSESSED WITH FINDING A GIRLFRIEND.

REMEMBER OLIVIA FROM FIFTH GRADE?

I THOUGHT, THIS TIME, I FINALLY FOUND MYSELF THE PERFECT GIRLFRIEND...

"ONE DAY, SHE SAID THAT YOUR EYES LOOKED PRETTY AND WHAT DID YOU DO?"

AND THAT IS YOUR FIRST MISTAKE. YOU DIDN'T EVEN KISS AND SHE IS STILL "THE PERFECT GIRLFRIEND."

SHE'D SAID "GOOD MORNING" TO ME THAT WEEK TOO.

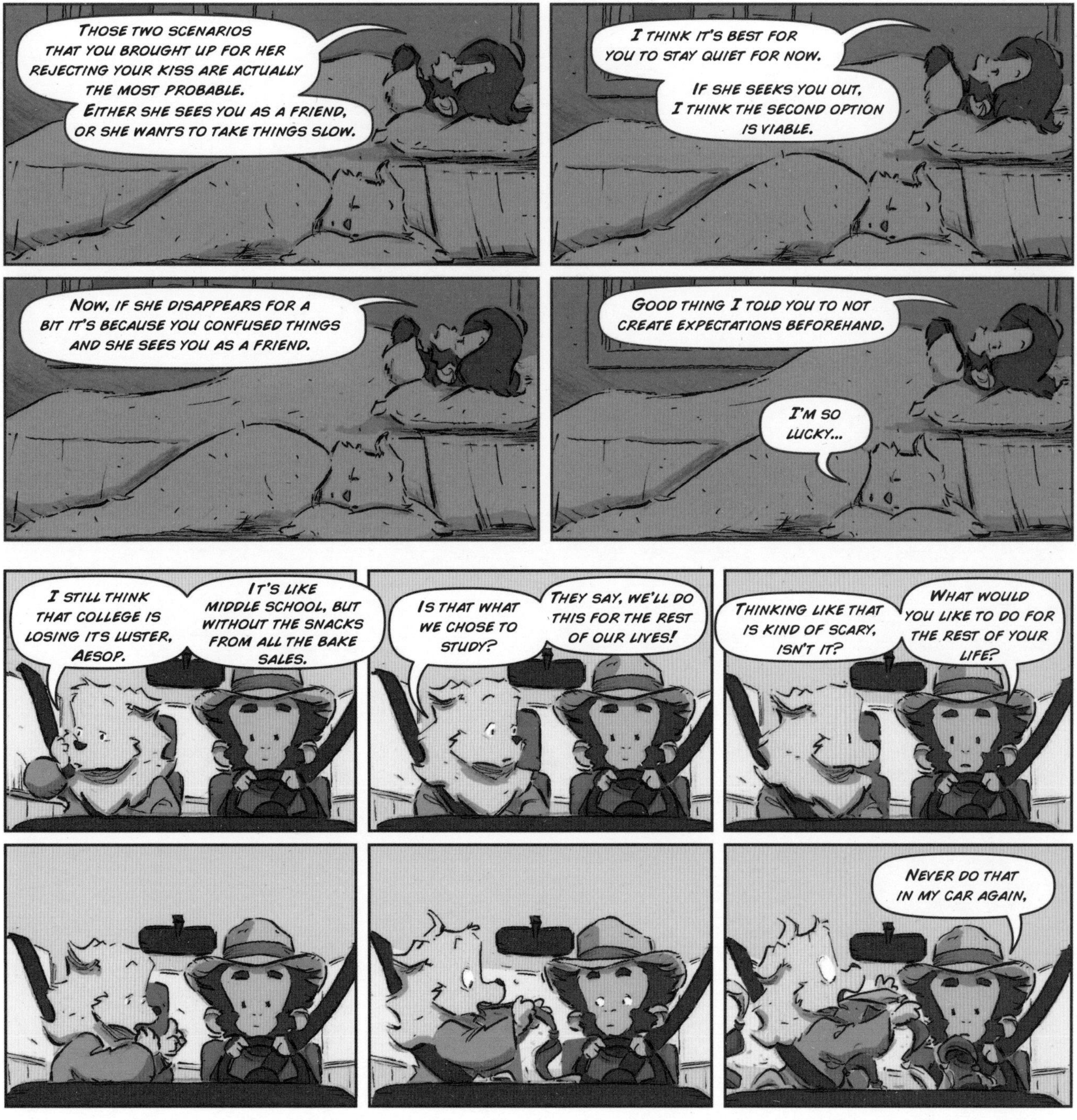
THOSE TWO SCENARIOS THAT YOU BROUGHT UP FOR HER REJECTING YOUR KISS ARE ACTUALLY THE MOST PROBABLE.
EITHER SHE SEES YOU AS A FRIEND, OR SHE WANTS TO TAKE THINGS SLOW.
I THINK IT'S BEST FOR YOU TO STAY QUIET FOR NOW.
IF SHE SEEKS YOU OUT, I THINK THE SECOND OPTION IS VIABLE.
NOW, IF SHE DISAPPEARS FOR A BIT IT'S BECAUSE YOU CONFUSED THINGS AND SHE SEES YOU AS A FRIEND.
GOOD THING I TOLD YOU TO NOT CREATE EXPECTATIONS BEFOREHAND.
I'M SO LUCKY...
I STILL THINK THAT COLLEGE IS LOSING ITS LUSTER, AESOP.
IT'S LIKE MIDDLE SCHOOL, BUT WITHOUT THE SNACKS FROM ALL THE BAKE SALES.
IS THAT WHAT WE CHOSE TO STUDY?
THEY SAY, WE'LL DO THIS FOR THE REST OF OUR LIVES!
THINKING LIKE THAT IS KIND OF SCARY, ISN'T IT?
WHAT WOULD YOU LIKE TO DO FOR THE REST OF YOUR LIFE?
NEVER DO THAT IN MY CAR AGAIN.

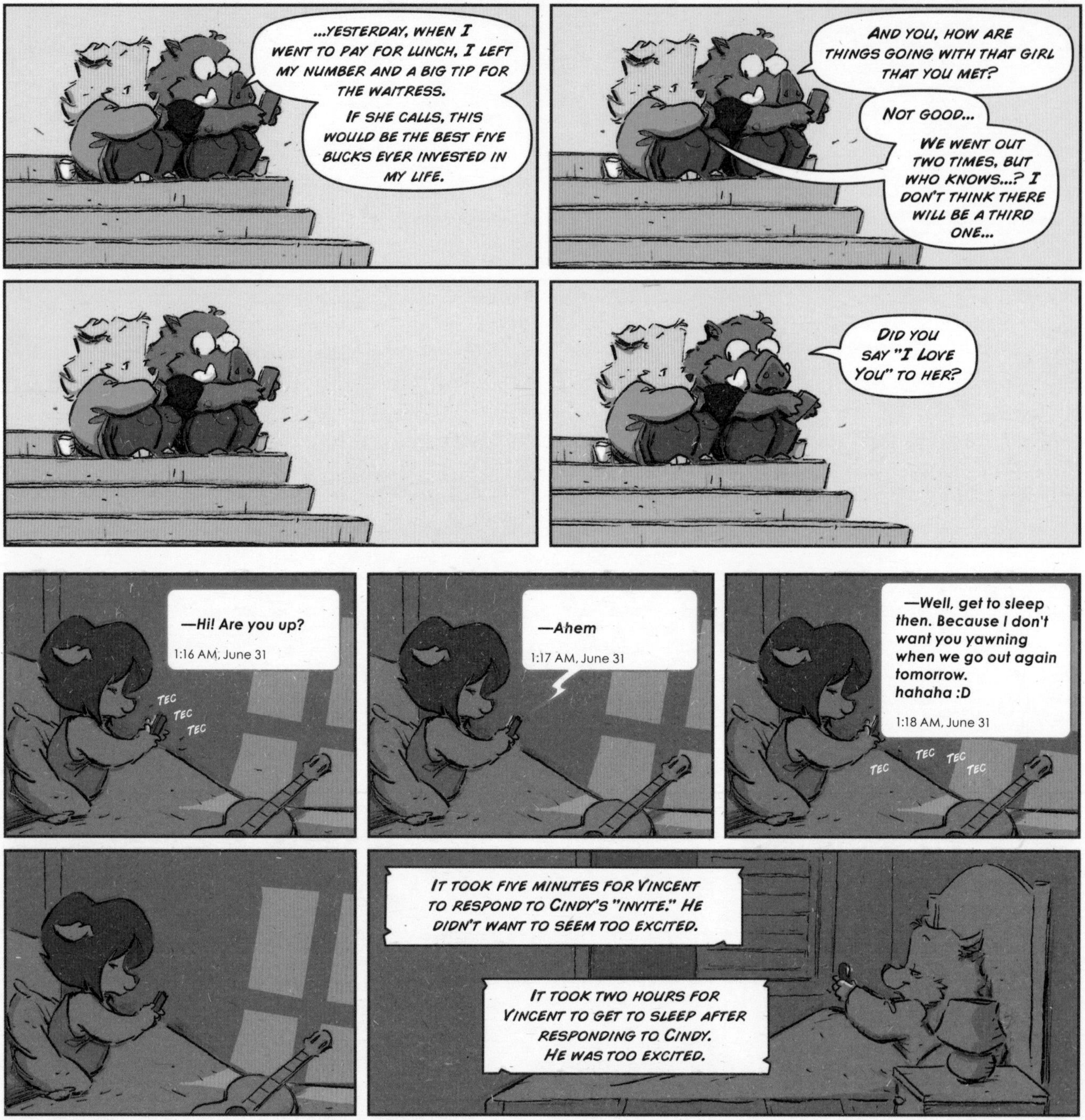
...YESTERDAY, WHEN I WENT TO PAY FOR LUNCH, I LEFT MY NUMBER AND A BIG TIP FOR THE WAITRESS.
IF SHE CALLS, THIS WOULD BE THE BEST FIVE BUCKS EVER INVESTED IN MY LIFE.
AND YOU, HOW ARE THINGS GOING WITH THAT GIRL THAT YOU MET?
NOT GOOD...
WE WENT OUT TWO TIMES, BUT WHO KNOWS...? I DON'T THINK THERE WILL BE A THIRD ONE...
DID YOU SAY "I LOVE YOU" TO HER?
—Hi! Are you up?
1:16 AM, June 31
TEC TEC TEC
—Ahem
1:17 AM, June 31
—Well, get to sleep then. Because I don't want you yawning when we go out again tomorrow.
hahaha :D
1:18 AM, June 31
TEC TEC TEC TEC
IT TOOK FIVE MINUTES FOR VINCENT TO RESPOND TO CINDY'S "INVITE." HE DIDN'T WANT TO SEEM TOO EXCITED.
IT TOOK TWO HOURS FOR VINCENT TO GET TO SLEEP AFTER RESPONDING TO CINDY. HE WAS TOO EXCITED.

SO, WHERE TO TODAY?

I DON'T KNOW... YOU CAN PICK.

ALRIGHT... IF I'M PICKING, I MIGHT AS WELL ENJOY IT.

IT'S A BIT OUT THERE, BUT SOMETIMES I REALLY, REALLY FEEL LIKE GETTING...

... EMPANADAS.

YOU IN?

I'M SO IN LOVE WITH YOU.... I'LL BE FOREVER BLUE...

COULD BE.

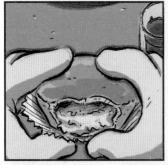

WHAT ARE YOU LOOKING AT?

OH, NOTHING.

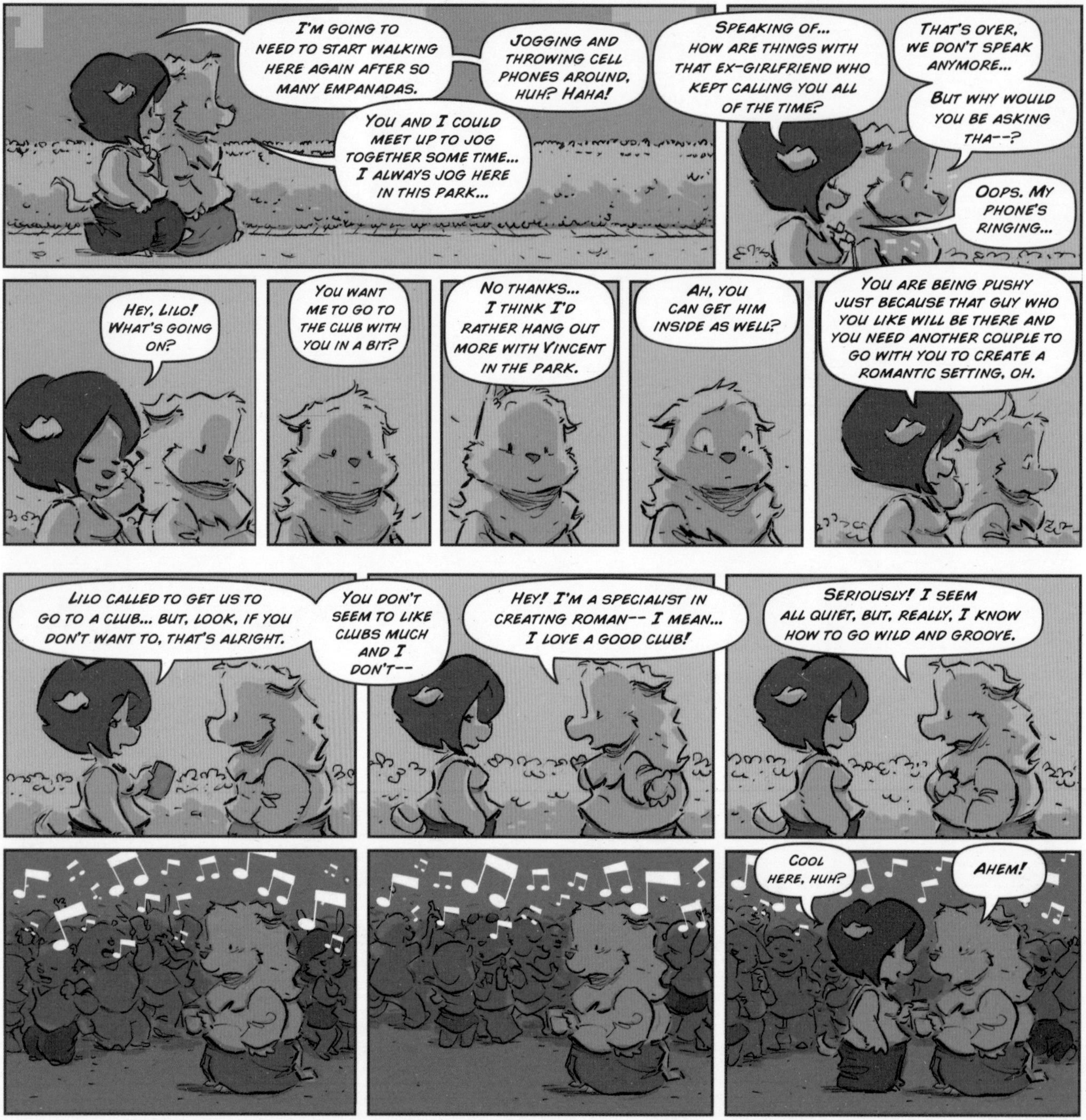
I'M GOING TO NEED TO START WALKING HERE AGAIN AFTER SO MANY EMPANADAS.
JOGGING AND THROWING CELL PHONES AROUND, HUH? HAHA!
YOU AND I COULD MEET UP TO JOG TOGETHER SOME TIME... I ALWAYS JOG HERE IN THIS PARK...
SPEAKING OF... HOW ARE THINGS WITH THAT EX-GIRLFRIEND WHO KEPT CALLING YOU ALL OF THE TIME?
THAT'S OVER, WE DON'T SPEAK ANYMORE...
BUT WHY WOULD YOU BE ASKING THA--?
OOPS. MY PHONE'S RINGING...
HEY, LILO! WHAT'S GOING ON?
YOU WANT ME TO GO TO THE CLUB WITH YOU IN A BIT?
NO THANKS... I THINK I'D RATHER HANG OUT MORE WITH VINCENT IN THE PARK.
AH, YOU CAN GET HIM INSIDE AS WELL?
YOU ARE BEING PUSHY JUST BECAUSE THAT GUY WHO YOU LIKE WILL BE THERE AND YOU NEED ANOTHER COUPLE TO GO WITH YOU TO CREATE A ROMANTIC SETTING, OH.
LILO CALLED TO GET US TO GO TO A CLUB... BUT, LOOK, IF YOU DON'T WANT TO, THAT'S ALRIGHT.
YOU DON'T SEEM TO LIKE CLUBS MUCH AND I DON'T--
HEY! I'M A SPECIALIST IN CREATING ROMAN-- I MEAN... I LOVE A GOOD CLUB!
SERIOUSLY! I SEEM ALL QUIET, BUT, REALLY, I KNOW HOW TO GO WILD AND GROOVE.
COOL HERE, HUH?
AHEM!

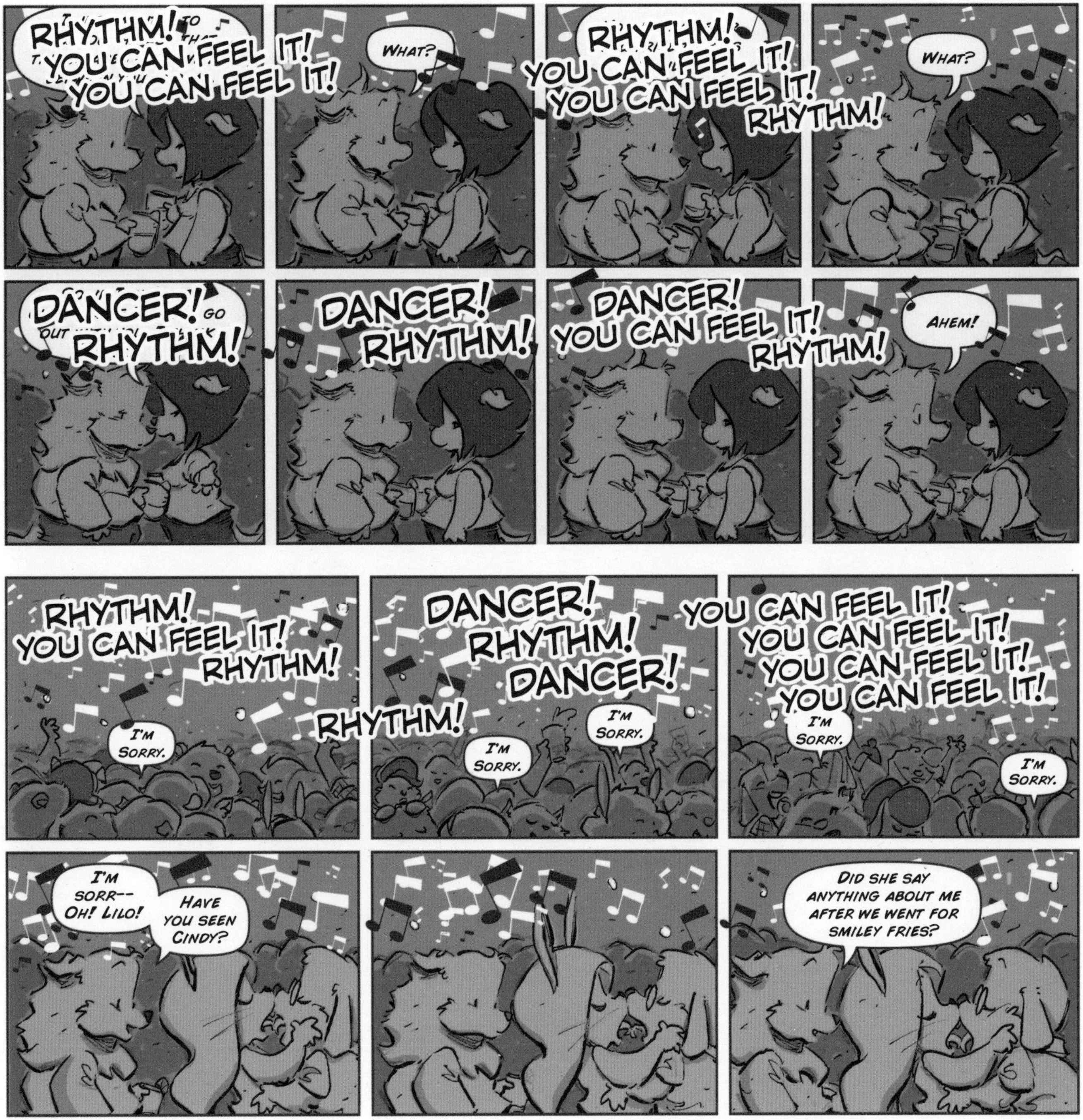
RHYTHM! YOU CAN FEEL IT! YOU CAN FEEL IT!
WHAT?
RHYTHM! YOU CAN FEEL IT! YOU CAN FEEL IT! RHYTHM!
WHAT?
DANCER! RHYTHM!
DANCER! RHYTHM!
DANCER! YOU CAN FEEL IT! RHYTHM!
AHEM!
RHYTHM! YOU CAN FEEL IT! RHYTHM!
I'M SORRY.
DANCER! RHYTHM! DANCER!
RHYTHM!
I'M SORRY.
I'M SORRY.
YOU CAN FEEL IT! YOU CAN FEEL IT! YOU CAN FEEL IT! YOU CAN FEEL IT!
I'M SORRY.
I'M SORRY.
I'M SORR-- OH! LILO!
HAVE YOU SEEN CINDY?
DID SHE SAY ANYTHING ABOUT ME AFTER WE WENT FOR SMILEY FRIES?

VINCENT AND CINDY ARRIVED TO THE CLUB AT 56 MINUTES AND 12 SECONDS PAST 11 O' CLOCK.

FIFTEEN MINUTES LATER, CINDY LEFT HIM TO GO HELP HER FRIEND LILO LAND HER SUITOR.

VINCENT SPENT THE NEXT HALF HOUR LOOKING FOR CINDY ON THE DANCE FLOOR. FINALLY, EXHAUSTED, HE SAT DOWN ON THE SOFA, AND TWENTY MINUTES LATER, HE SLEPT.

VINCENT PREFERRED TO NOT WASTE MORE TIME LOOKING FOR CINDY AROUND THE CLUB. WITH ALL HIS EXPERIENCE, HE KNOWS WHEN A RELATIONSHIP IS DESTINED TO FIZZLE.

AT THIS TIME, SHE SHOULD BE HANGING OUT WITH SOME LUCKY GUY THERE.

SORRY I'M LATE, GANG!

MY FINGERS ARE BURNING TODAY! I'M READY TO PLAY, I'M READY TO NARRATE... I'M READY FOR ANY--

...THING?

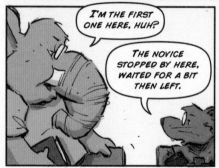

I'M THE FIRST ONE HERE, HUH?

THE NOVICE STOPPED BY HERE, WAITED FOR A BIT THEN LEFT.

WHERE'S EVERYONE ELSE?

EVERYONE CANCELLED AT THE LAST MINUTE. EACH ONE WITH A DIFFERENT SCAPEGOAT.

ONLY VINCENT DIDN'T SEND WORD.

"HE SHOULD BE HERE ANY MINUTE NOW, THEN."

...SO THEN, I WAS WOKEN UP BY A COUPLE GOING AT IT LIKE CRAZY RIGHT NEXT TO ME ON THE COUCH.

I LOOKED FOR CINDY AGAIN, DIDN'T FIND HER, AND WENT ON HOME.

HAVE YOU TALKED TO HER AFTER THIS?

LATER I'M GOING TO SEND HER A MESSAGE, BUT I HAVEN'T FELT UP TO IT YET.

LAST NIGHT LEFT IT VERY CLEAR TO ME THAT WE DON'T HAVE ANYTHING TOGETHER...

I'VE ALREADY GONE THROUGH THAT. DECEIVING MYSELF WHEN ALL SIGNS POINT TOWARDS THE TRUTH.

I WENT TO A PARTY YESTERDAY.

THE BOY I LIKE WAS THERE. I SAW HIM EATING A HOT DOG WITH HIS MOUTH WIDE OPEN.

I DON'T LIKE HIM ANYMORE.

IT'S NOT EASY THIS WAY... YOU CAN'T STAND CLUBS AND YOU ARE ALWAYS FALLING FOR THE BIGGEST CLUBBERS...

AFTER LAST NIGHT, I CAN SAY THAT I HATE CLUBS NOW MORE THAN EVER.

I SPENT WAY TOO MUCH AT THAT PLACE, JUST TO ENTER, DRINK SOME BITTER GINGER CONCOTION, AND TO WATCH GUYS WEARING TUCKED-IN POLOS MAKE OUT WITH ALL THE GIRLS.

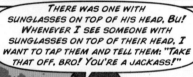

THERE WAS ONE WITH SUNGLASSES ON TOP OF HIS HEAD, BU! WHENEVER I SEE SOMEONE WITH SUNGLASSES ON TOP OF THEIR HEAD, I WANT TO TAP THEM AND TELL THEM: "TAKE THAT OFF, BRO! YOU'RE A JACKASS!"

WOW! IS THAT JUST WITH GUYS, OR DO YOU FEEL THE SAME WHEN YOU SEE GIRLS WITH GLASSES ON THEIR HEADS?

HEY, I'M A GUY. WHO AM I TO SAY WHAT A GIRL CAN OR CAN'T DO, Y'KNOW?

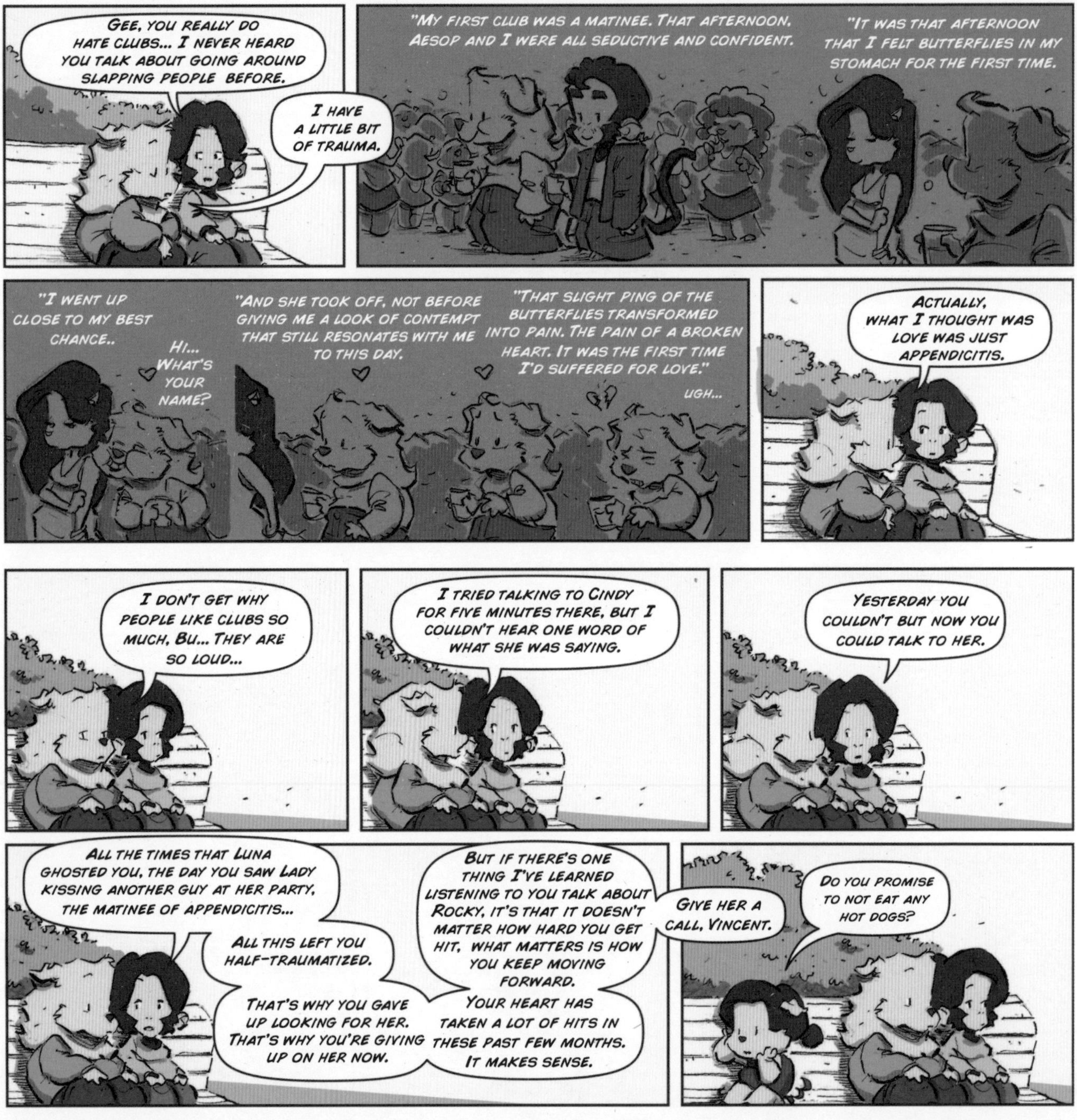

GEE, YOU REALLY DO HATE CLUBS... I NEVER HEARD YOU TALK ABOUT GOING AROUND SLAPPING PEOPLE BEFORE.
I HAVE A LITTLE BIT OF TRAUMA.
"MY FIRST CLUB WAS A MATINEE. THAT AFTERNOON, AESOP AND I WERE ALL SEDUCTIVE AND CONFIDENT.
"IT WAS THAT AFTERNOON THAT I FELT BUTTERFLIES IN MY STOMACH FOR THE FIRST TIME.
"I WENT UP CLOSE TO MY BEST CHANCE..
HI... WHAT'S YOUR NAME?
"AND SHE TOOK OFF, NOT BEFORE GIVING ME A LOOK OF CONTEMPT THAT STILL RESONATES WITH ME TO THIS DAY.
"THAT SLIGHT PING OF THE BUTTERFLIES TRANSFORMED INTO PAIN. THE PAIN OF A BROKEN HEART. IT WAS THE FIRST TIME I'D SUFFERED FOR LOVE."
UGH...
ACTUALLY, WHAT I THOUGHT WAS LOVE WAS JUST APPENDICITIS.
I DON'T GET WHY PEOPLE LIKE CLUBS SO MUCH, BU... THEY ARE SO LOUD...
I TRIED TALKING TO CINDY FOR FIVE MINUTES THERE, BUT I COULDN'T HEAR ONE WORD OF WHAT SHE WAS SAYING.
YESTERDAY YOU COULDN'T BUT NOW YOU COULD TALK TO HER.
ALL THE TIMES THAT LUNA GHOSTED YOU, THE DAY YOU SAW LADY KISSING ANOTHER GUY AT HER PARTY, THE MATINEE OF APPENDICITIS...
ALL THIS LEFT YOU HALF-TRAUMATIZED.
THAT'S WHY YOU GAVE UP LOOKING FOR HER. THAT'S WHY YOU'RE GIVING UP ON HER NOW.
BUT IF THERE'S ONE THING I'VE LEARNED LISTENING TO YOU TALK ABOUT ROCKY, IT'S THAT IT DOESN'T MATTER HOW HARD YOU GET HIT, WHAT MATTERS IS HOW YOU KEEP MOVING FORWARD.
YOUR HEART HAS TAKEN A LOT OF HITS IN THESE PAST FEW MONTHS. IT MAKES SENSE.
GIVE HER A CALL, VINCENT.
DO YOU PROMISE TO NOT EAT ANY HOT DOGS?

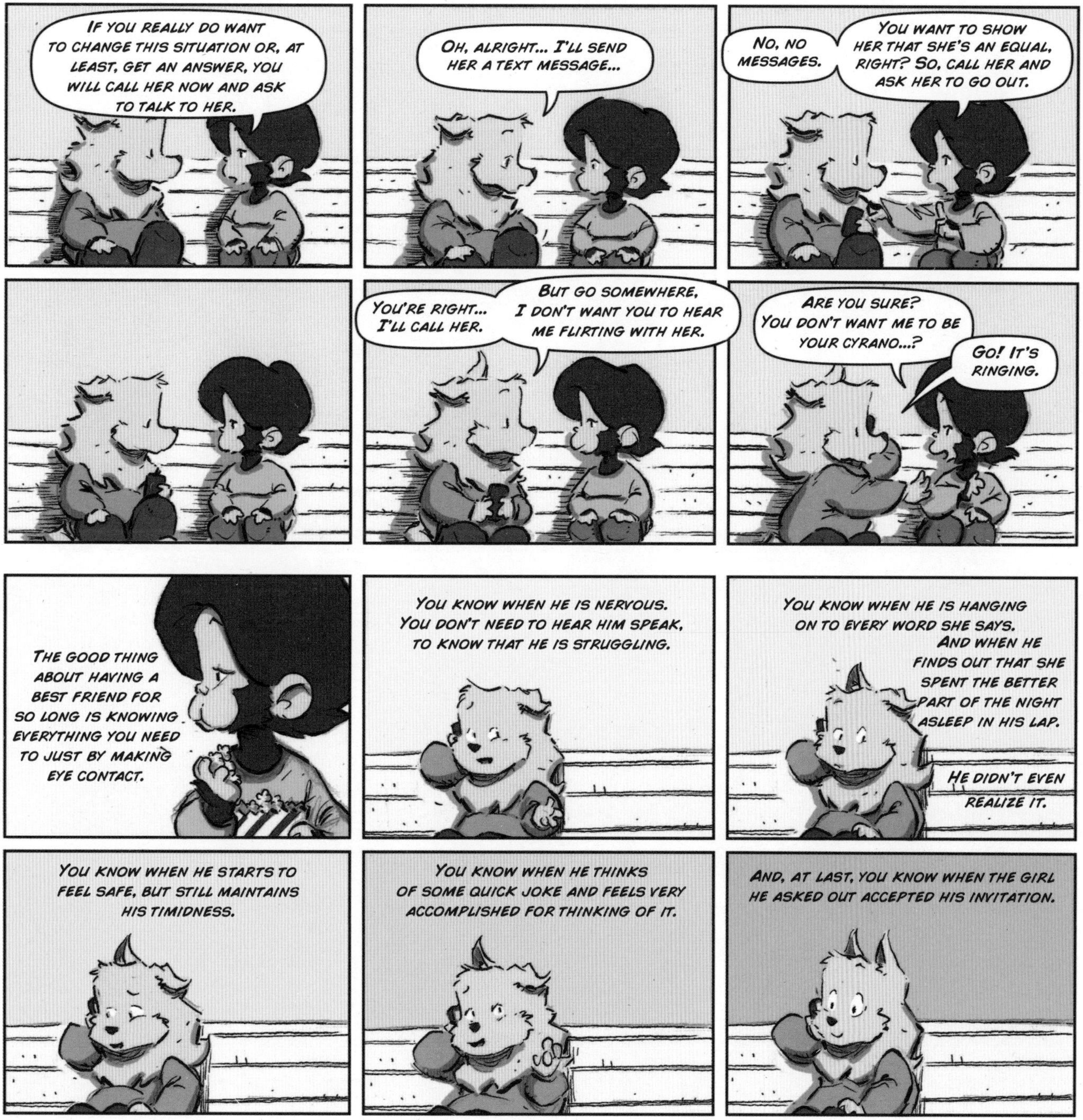
IF YOU REALLY DO WANT TO CHANGE THIS SITUATION OR, AT LEAST, GET AN ANSWER, YOU WILL CALL HER NOW AND ASK TO TALK TO HER.
OH, ALRIGHT... I'LL SEND HER A TEXT MESSAGE...
NO, NO MESSAGES.
YOU WANT TO SHOW HER THAT SHE'S AN EQUAL, RIGHT? SO, CALL HER AND ASK HER TO GO OUT.
YOU'RE RIGHT... I'LL CALL HER.
BUT GO SOMEWHERE, I DON'T WANT YOU TO HEAR ME FLIRTING WITH HER.
ARE YOU SURE? YOU DON'T WANT ME TO BE YOUR CYRANO...?
GO! IT'S RINGING.
THE GOOD THING ABOUT HAVING A BEST FRIEND FOR SO LONG IS KNOWING EVERYTHING YOU NEED TO JUST BY MAKING EYE CONTACT.
YOU KNOW WHEN HE IS NERVOUS. YOU DON'T NEED TO HEAR HIM SPEAK, TO KNOW THAT HE IS STRUGGLING.
YOU KNOW WHEN HE IS HANGING ON TO EVERY WORD SHE SAYS.
AND WHEN HE FINDS OUT THAT SHE SPENT THE BETTER PART OF THE NIGHT ASLEEP IN HIS LAP.
HE DIDN'T EVEN REALIZE IT.
YOU KNOW WHEN HE STARTS TO FEEL SAFE, BUT STILL MAINTAINS HIS TIMIDNESS.
YOU KNOW WHEN HE THINKS OF SOME QUICK JOKE AND FEELS VERY ACCOMPLISHED FOR THINKING OF IT.
AND, AT LAST, YOU KNOW WHEN THE GIRL HE ASKED OUT ACCEPTED HIS INVITATION.

OKAY, YOU'VE BEEN THROUGH THIS BEFORE, AT THIS STAGE OF LIFE, YOU KNOW WELL WHAT TO DO BEFORE A DATE.

BEFORE ANYTHING ELSE, YOU HIDE AWAY THOSE FEELINGS WELL.

THEN, YOU RESERVE A TABLE AT A FANCY RESTAURANT.

WOULD IT BE ALRIGHT IF I PAID WITH MY MOM'S CREDIT CARD?

YOU SEARCH WHAT WINE GOES WELL WITH SPAGHETTI AND MEAT BALLS.

AND THEN, TAKE A NICE SHOWER WITH THAT SOAP THAT YOUR AUNT GAVE YOU.

YOU DO SOME EXERCISE TO GET ALL HUNKY FOR THE DATE.

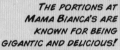

(WHICH MEANS A SECOND SHOWER)

YOU SAID WE WERE GOING TO A FANCY RESTAURANT... SO, I WANTED TO DRESS UP... IS THIS OKAY?

YEAH.

BUT THE MOMENT YOU SEE HER, YOU REALIZE HOW DIFFICULT IT WILL BE TO HIDE AWAY YOUR FEELINGS.

NOW'S THE TIME FOR VINCENT TO PUT INTO PRACTICE HIS PLAN TO KISS CINDY!

THE PORTIONS AT MAMA BIANCA'S ARE KNOWN FOR BEING GIGANTIC AND DELICIOUS!

AND THAT'S WHY SINCE YESTERDAY, VINCENT ALREADY DECIDED WHAT HE'D ORDER TONIGHT.

...AND THE HOUSE SPECIAL, VEAL LASAGNA IN A WINE SAUCE.

I'LL HAVE ONE OF THOSE, PLEASE.

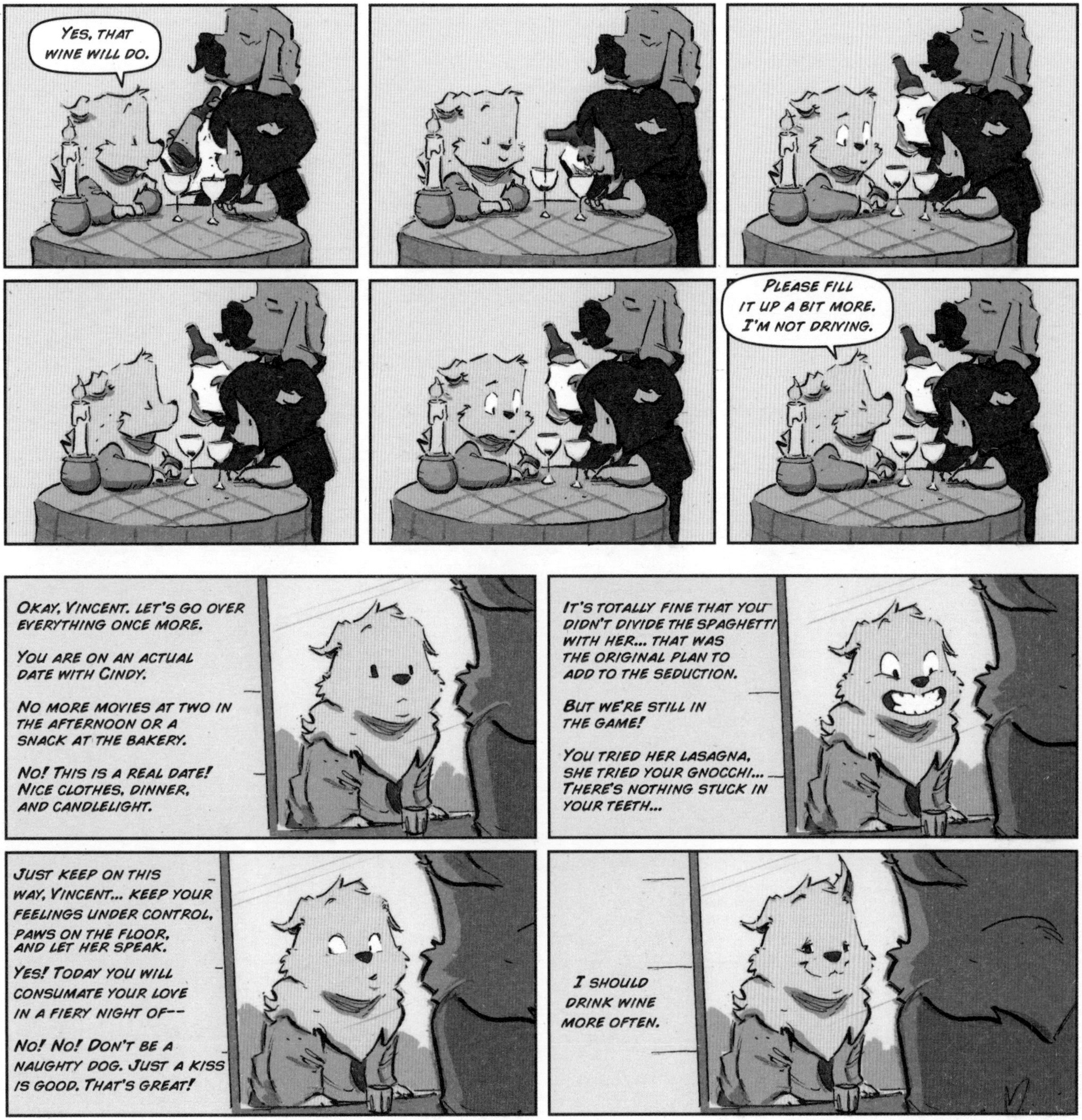
YES, THAT WINE WILL DO.
PLEASE FILL IT UP A BIT MORE. I'M NOT DRIVING.
OKAY, VINCENT. LET'S GO OVER EVERYTHING ONCE MORE.
YOU ARE ON AN ACTUAL DATE WITH CINDY.
NO MORE MOVIES AT TWO IN THE AFTERNOON OR A SNACK AT THE BAKERY.
NO! THIS IS A REAL DATE! NICE CLOTHES, DINNER, AND CANDLELIGHT.
IT'S TOTALLY FINE THAT YOU DIDN'T DIVIDE THE SPAGHETTI WITH HER... THAT WAS THE ORIGINAL PLAN TO ADD TO THE SEDUCTION.
BUT WE'RE STILL IN THE GAME!
YOU TRIED HER LASAGNA, SHE TRIED YOUR GNOCCHI... THERE'S NOTHING STUCK IN YOUR TEETH...
JUST KEEP ON THIS WAY, VINCENT... KEEP YOUR FEELINGS UNDER CONTROL, PAWS ON THE FLOOR, AND LET HER SPEAK.
YES! TODAY YOU WILL CONSUMATE YOUR LOVE IN A FIERY NIGHT OF--
NO! NO! DON'T BE A NAUGHTY DOG. JUST A KISS IS GOOD. THAT'S GREAT!
I SHOULD DRINK WINE MORE OFTEN.

LIKE ANY GOOD ITALIAN RESTAURANT, MAMA BIANCA'S MUSICAL AMBIENCE IS FILLED WITH THE GREAT CLASSICS OF ITALIAN MUSICIANS..

WHEN THE WILD GUITAR SOLO OF EROS RAMAZZOTTI ANNOUNCES THE ARRIVAL OF THE COSE DELLA VITA, VINCENT BEGAN TO FEEL A WARMTH IN HIS CHEST.

RAMAZZOTTI IS LIKE AN ITALIAN MAROON 5. PAIR HIM WITH A CANDLELIT DINNER, TOP IT OFF WITH A GOOD WINE, AND WE HAVE A TRUE ART OF SEDUCTION.

BUT OF COURSE THIS ALL COMES AT A PRICE.

WE COULD HAVE SPLIT THE BILL, VINCENT. BUT THANK YOU ANYWAYS, THAT DINNER WAS AMAZING.

HERE, CLOSE YOUR EYES. LET ME PAY YOU BACK FOR MY PART.

TRUST ME.

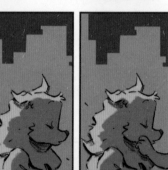

READY.

I TOOK IT FROM YOUR EAR. BUT LET'S SAY IT WAS IN A MAGIC SAFE IN ANOTHER DIMENSION, OKAY?

HAHAH. GOOD NIGHT, VINCENT.

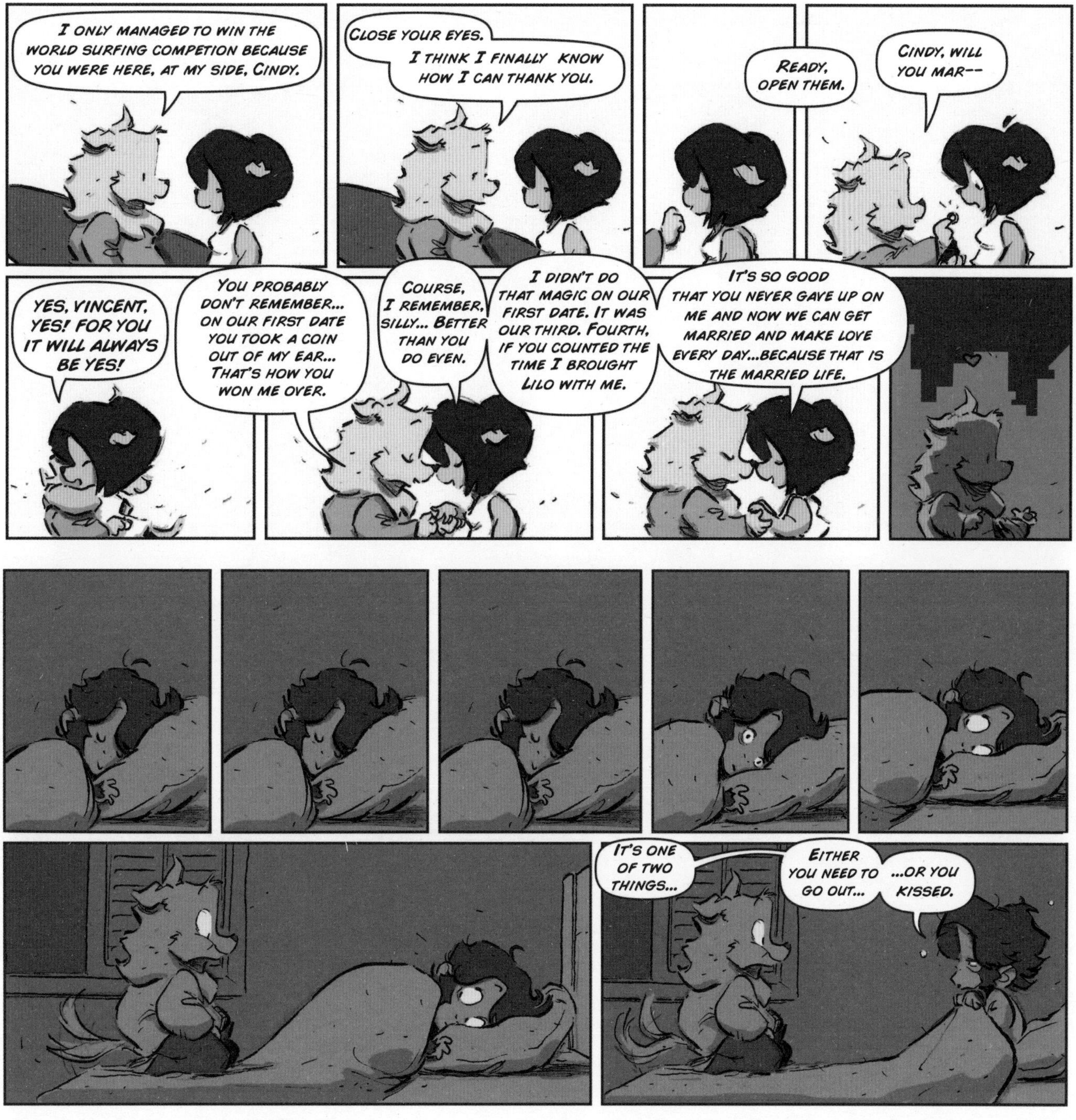
I ONLY MANAGED TO WIN THE WORLD SURFING COMPETION BECAUSE YOU WERE HERE, AT MY SIDE, CINDY.
CLOSE YOUR EYES.
I THINK I FINALLY KNOW HOW I CAN THANK YOU.
READY, OPEN THEM.
CINDY, WILL YOU MAR--
YES, VINCENT, YES! FOR YOU IT WILL ALWAYS BE YES!
YOU PROBABLY DON'T REMEMBER... ON OUR FIRST DATE YOU TOOK A COIN OUT OF MY EAR... THAT'S HOW YOU WON ME OVER.
COURSE, I REMEMBER, SILLY... BETTER THAN YOU DO EVEN.
I DIDN'T DO THAT MAGIC ON OUR FIRST DATE. IT WAS OUR THIRD. FOURTH, IF YOU COUNTED THE TIME I BROUGHT LILO WITH ME.
IT'S SO GOOD THAT YOU NEVER GAVE UP ON ME AND NOW WE CAN GET MARRIED AND MAKE LOVE EVERY DAY...BECAUSE THAT IS THE MARRIED LIFE.
IT'S ONE OF TWO THINGS...
EITHER YOU NEED TO GO OUT...
...OR YOU KISSED.

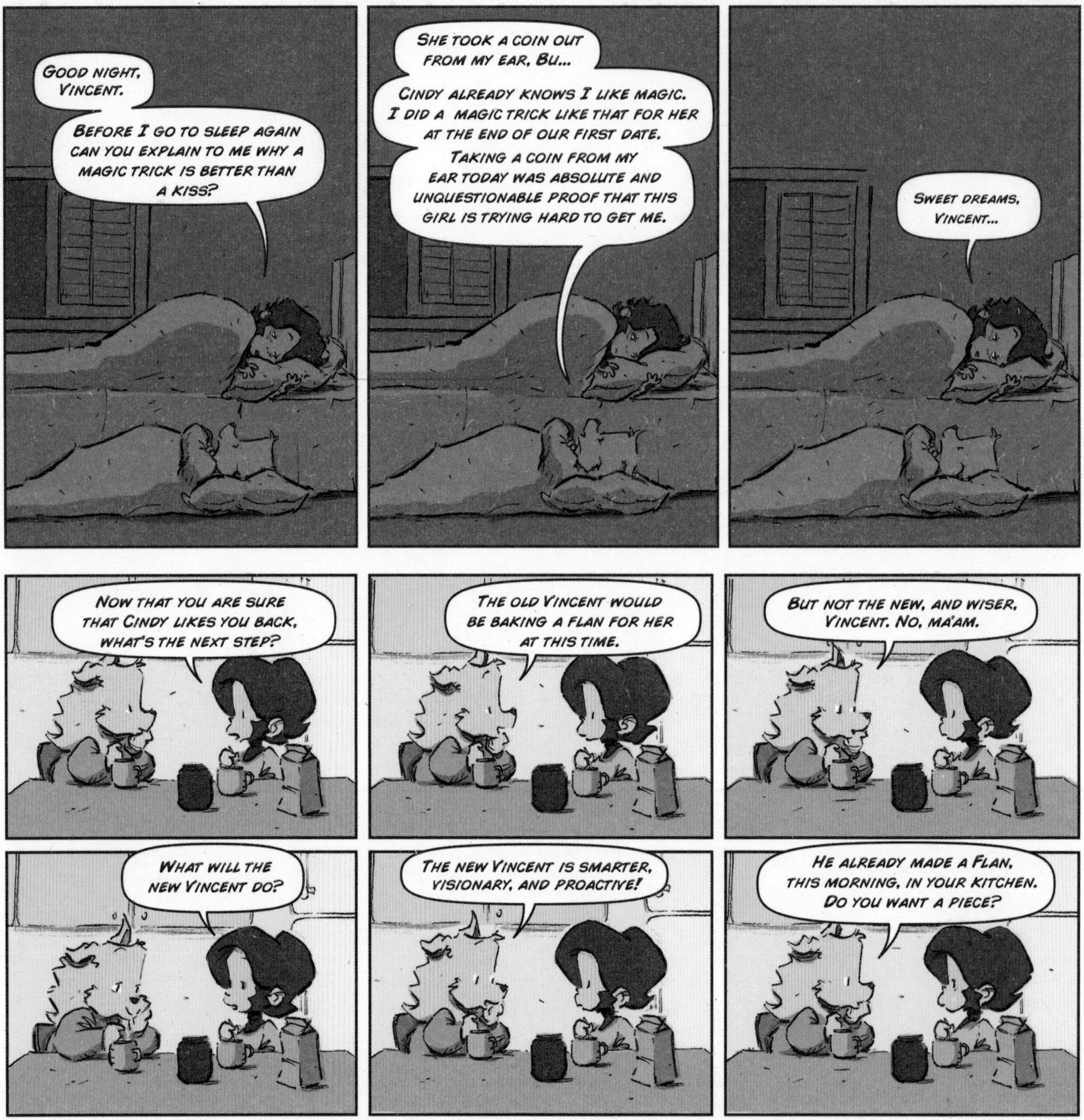

GOOD NIGHT, VINCENT.
BEFORE I GO TO SLEEP AGAIN CAN YOU EXPLAIN TO ME WHY A MAGIC TRICK IS BETTER THAN A KISS?
SHE TOOK A COIN OUT FROM MY EAR, BU...
CINDY ALREADY KNOWS I LIKE MAGIC. I DID A MAGIC TRICK LIKE THAT FOR HER AT THE END OF OUR FIRST DATE.
TAKING A COIN FROM MY EAR TODAY WAS ABSOLUTE AND UNQUESTIONABLE PROOF THAT THIS GIRL IS TRYING HARD TO GET ME.
SWEET DREAMS, VINCENT...
NOW THAT YOU ARE SURE THAT CINDY LIKES YOU BACK, WHAT'S THE NEXT STEP?
THE OLD VINCENT WOULD BE BAKING A FLAN FOR HER AT THIS TIME.
BUT NOT THE NEW, AND WISER, VINCENT. NO, MA'AM.
WHAT WILL THE NEW VINCENT DO?
THE NEW VINCENT IS SMARTER, VISIONARY, AND PROACTIVE!
HE ALREADY MADE A FLAN, THIS MORNING, IN YOUR KITCHEN. DO YOU WANT A PIECE?

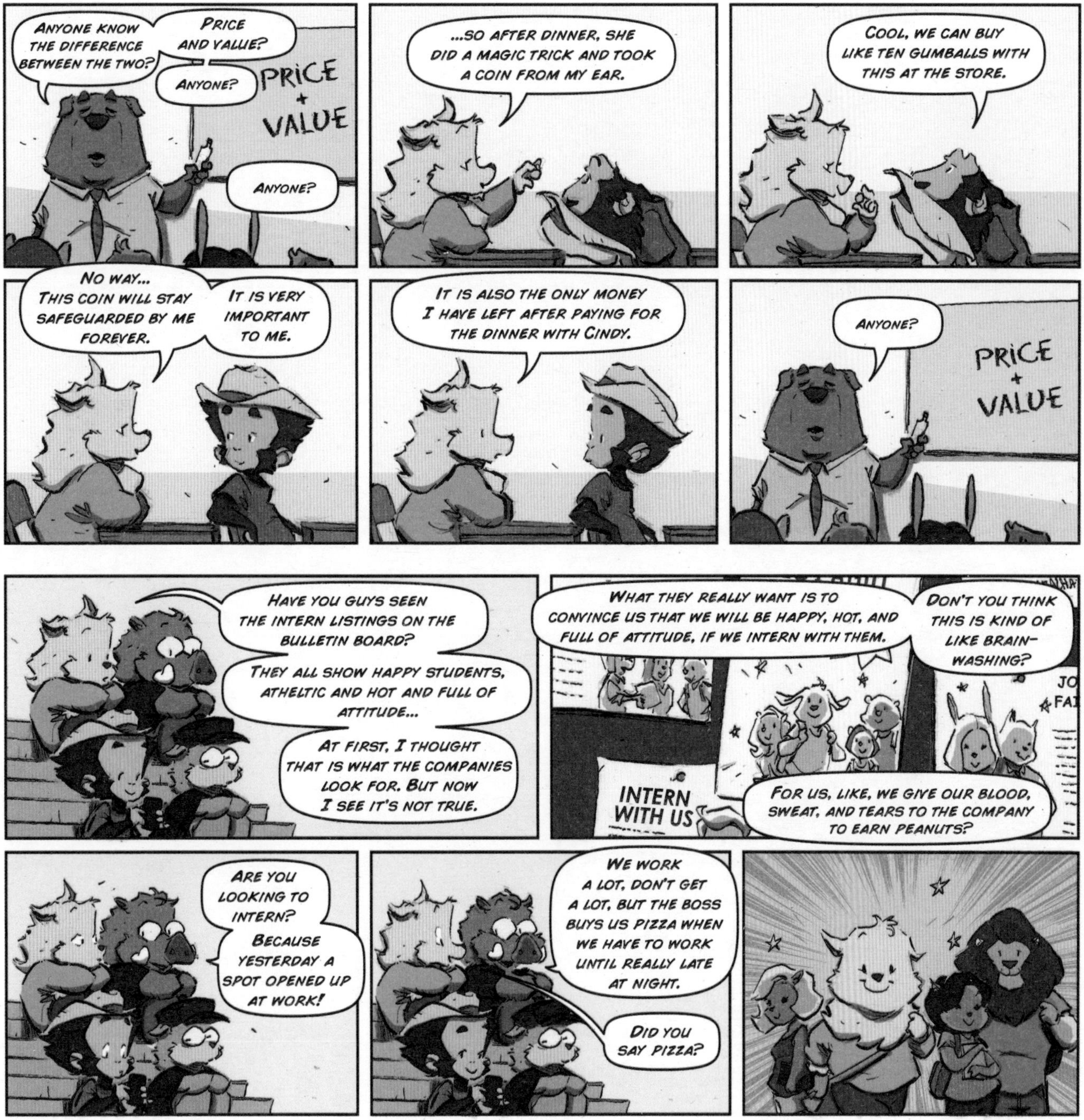
ANYONE KNOW THE DIFFERENCE BETWEEN THE TWO?
PRICE AND VALUE?
ANYONE?
PRICE + VALUE
ANYONE?
...SO AFTER DINNER, SHE DID A MAGIC TRICK AND TOOK A COIN FROM MY EAR.
COOL, WE CAN BUY LIKE TEN GUMBALLS WITH THIS AT THE STORE.
NO WAY... THIS COIN WILL STAY SAFEGUARDED BY ME FOREVER.
IT IS VERY IMPORTANT TO ME.
IT IS ALSO THE ONLY MONEY I HAVE LEFT AFTER PAYING FOR THE DINNER WITH CINDY.
ANYONE?
PRICE + VALUE
HAVE YOU GUYS SEEN THE INTERN LISTINGS ON THE BULLETIN BOARD?
THEY ALL SHOW HAPPY STUDENTS, ATHELTIC AND HOT AND FULL OF ATTITUDE...
AT FIRST, I THOUGHT THAT IS WHAT THE COMPANIES LOOK FOR. BUT NOW I SEE IT'S NOT TRUE.
WHAT THEY REALLY WANT IS TO CONVINCE US THAT WE WILL BE HAPPY, HOT, AND FULL OF ATTITUDE, IF WE INTERN WITH THEM.
DON'T YOU THINK THIS IS KIND OF LIKE BRAIN-WASHING?
INTERN WITH US
FOR US, LIKE, WE GIVE OUR BLOOD, SWEAT, AND TEARS TO THE COMPANY TO EARN PEANUTS?
ARE YOU LOOKING TO INTERN?
BECAUSE YESTERDAY A SPOT OPENED UP AT WORK!
WE WORK A LOT, DON'T GET A LOT, BUT THE BOSS BUYS US PIZZA WHEN WE HAVE TO WORK UNTIL REALLY LATE AT NIGHT.
DID YOU SAY PIZZA?

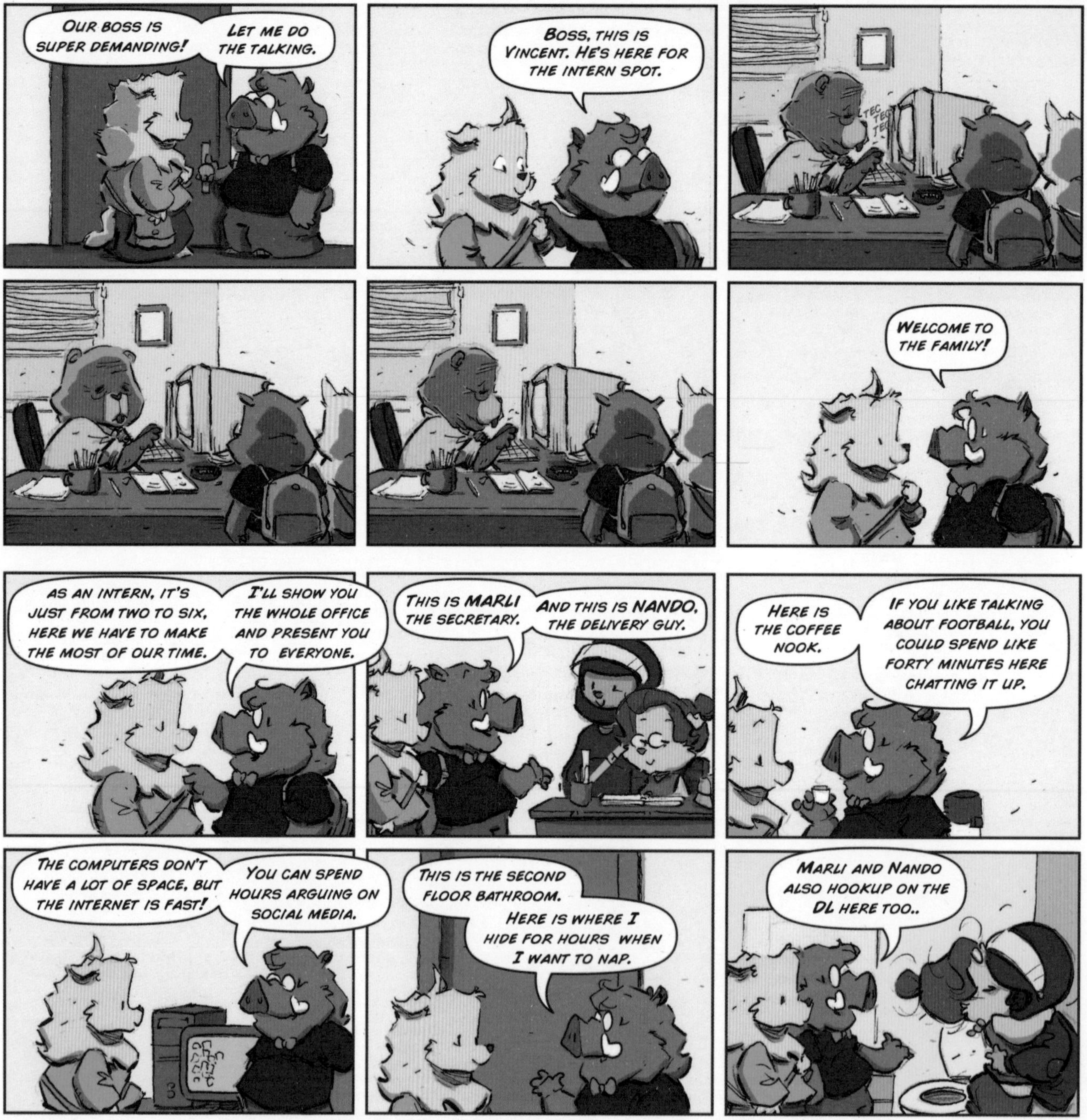

OUR BOSS IS SUPER DEMANDING!
LET ME DO THE TALKING.
BOSS, THIS IS VINCENT. HE'S HERE FOR THE INTERN SPOT.
TEC TEC TEC
WELCOME TO THE FAMILY!
AS AN INTERN, IT'S JUST FROM TWO TO SIX, HERE WE HAVE TO MAKE THE MOST OF OUR TIME.
I'LL SHOW YOU THE WHOLE OFFICE AND PRESENT YOU TO EVERYONE.
THIS IS MARLI THE SECRETARY.
AND THIS IS NANDO, THE DELIVERY GUY.
HERE IS THE COFFEE NOOK.
IF YOU LIKE TALKING ABOUT FOOTBALL, YOU COULD SPEND LIKE FORTY MINUTES HERE CHATTING IT UP.
THE COMPUTERS DON'T HAVE A LOT OF SPACE, BUT THE INTERNET IS FAST!
YOU CAN SPEND HOURS ARGUING ON SOCIAL MEDIA.
THIS IS THE SECOND FLOOR BATHROOM.
HERE IS WHERE I HIDE FOR HOURS WHEN I WANT TO NAP.
MARLI AND NANDO ALSO HOOKUP ON THE DL HERE TOO..

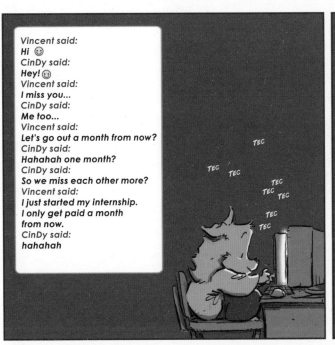

Vincent said:
Hi 😊
CinDy said:
Hey! 😊
Vincent said:
I miss you...
CinDy said:
Me too...
Vincent said:
Let's go out a month from now?
CinDy said:
Hahahah one month?
CinDy said:
So we miss each other more?
Vincent said:
I just started my internship. I only get paid a month from now.
CinDy said:
hahahah

TEC TEC TEC TEC TEC TEC TEC TEC

CinDy said:
We could do something that doesn't cost money... Like a picnic in the park! Bring whatever's in your fridge and I will bring what's in mine
Vincent said:
All we have in the fridge is eggplant.
CinDy said:
That's specific hahahaha
CinDy said:
No problem. I will bring anything in my fridge that goes with eggplant.
Vincent said:
So Saturday ? 😊
CinDy said:
It's a date, Mr. Intern.

GET A JOB +250 XPs

TEC TEC TEC TEC TEC

DAYS LATER, CINDY AND VINCENT MEET UP TO HAVE A PICNIC IN THE PARK.

LIKE ANY GOOD COLLEGE STUDENT, THE TWO OF THEM COULD NOT AFFORD TO BUY FOOD. SO, THEY PLANNED TO EACH BRING WHATEVER THEY COULD FIND FROM RAIDING THEIR PARENT'S FRIDGES.

VINCENT BROUGHT A WEDGE OF CHEESE, A HALF PACK OF SANDWICH COOKIES, AND THE HOPE THAT DESTINY WILL UNITE HIM AND CINDY.

I SURE HOPE YOU'RE NOT SUPER HUNGRY...

WE ONLY HAD SOME MANGO AND MILK IN THE FRIDGE!

MILK

NOTHING THAT GOES GOOD WITH EGGPLANT, SADLY...

THIS IS VINCENT.

THIS IS CINDY.

   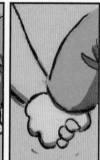

HE LOVES A GOOD STEAK.

SO DOES SHE.

LISTEN TO THIS SONG I CAME UP WITH...

DON'T LAUGH, 'KAY?

VALIANT VINCENT, VINCENT...

WHY ARE YOU SO, SO, SO...

VALIANT, VALIANT VINCENT...?

I JUST HAVE THE CHORUS FOR NOW...

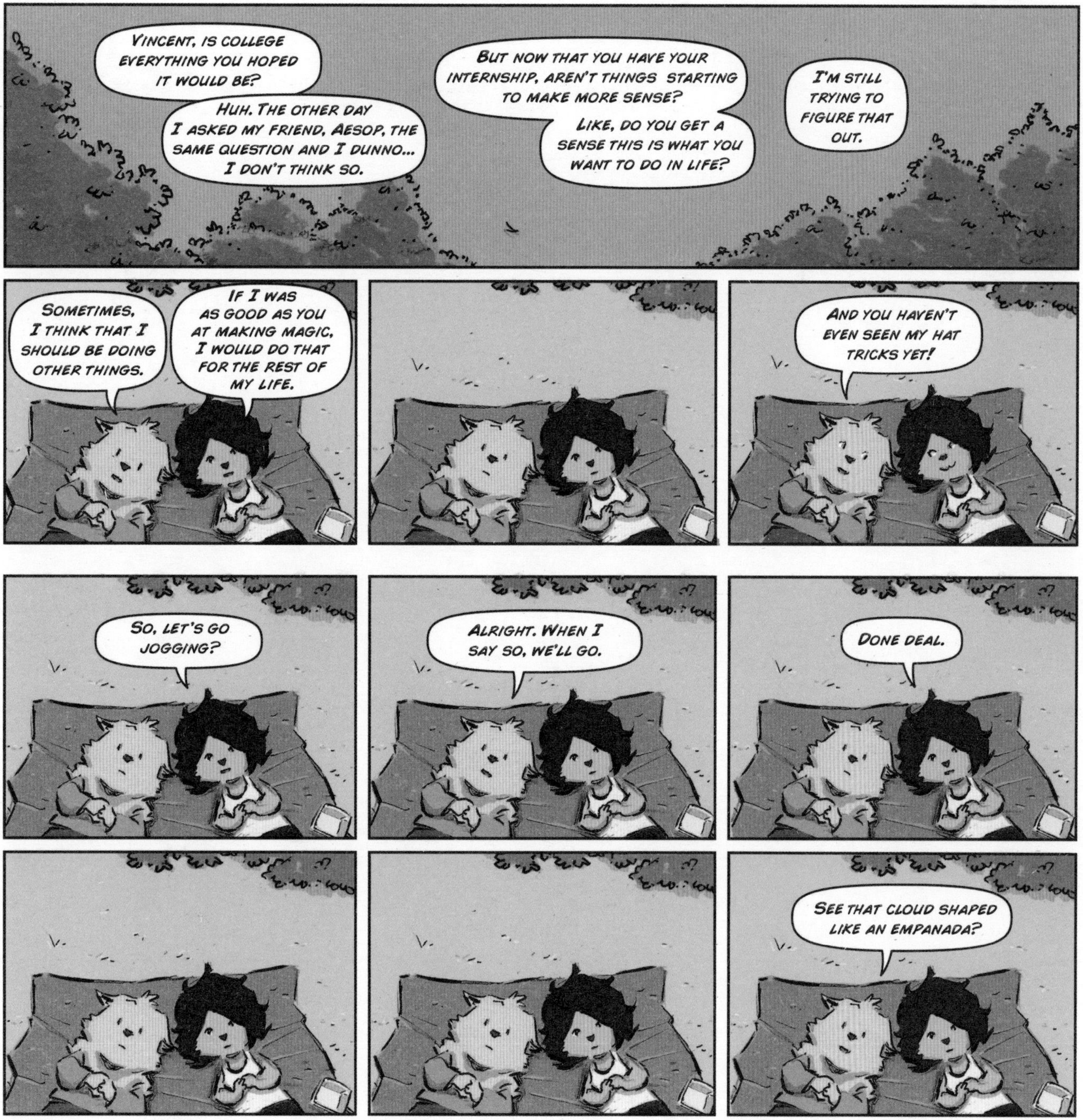
VINCENT, IS COLLEGE EVERYTHING YOU HOPED IT WOULD BE?
HUH. THE OTHER DAY I ASKED MY FRIEND, AESOP, THE SAME QUESTION AND I DUNNO... I DON'T THINK SO.
BUT NOW THAT YOU HAVE YOUR INTERNSHIP, AREN'T THINGS STARTING TO MAKE MORE SENSE?
LIKE, DO YOU GET A SENSE THIS IS WHAT YOU WANT TO DO IN LIFE?
I'M STILL TRYING TO FIGURE THAT OUT.
SOMETIMES, I THINK THAT I SHOULD BE DOING OTHER THINGS.
IF I WAS AS GOOD AS YOU AT MAKING MAGIC, I WOULD DO THAT FOR THE REST OF MY LIFE.
AND YOU HAVEN'T EVEN SEEN MY HAT TRICKS YET!
SO, LET'S GO JOGGING?
ALRIGHT. WHEN I SAY SO, WE'LL GO.
DONE DEAL.
SEE THAT CLOUD SHAPED LIKE AN EMPANADA?

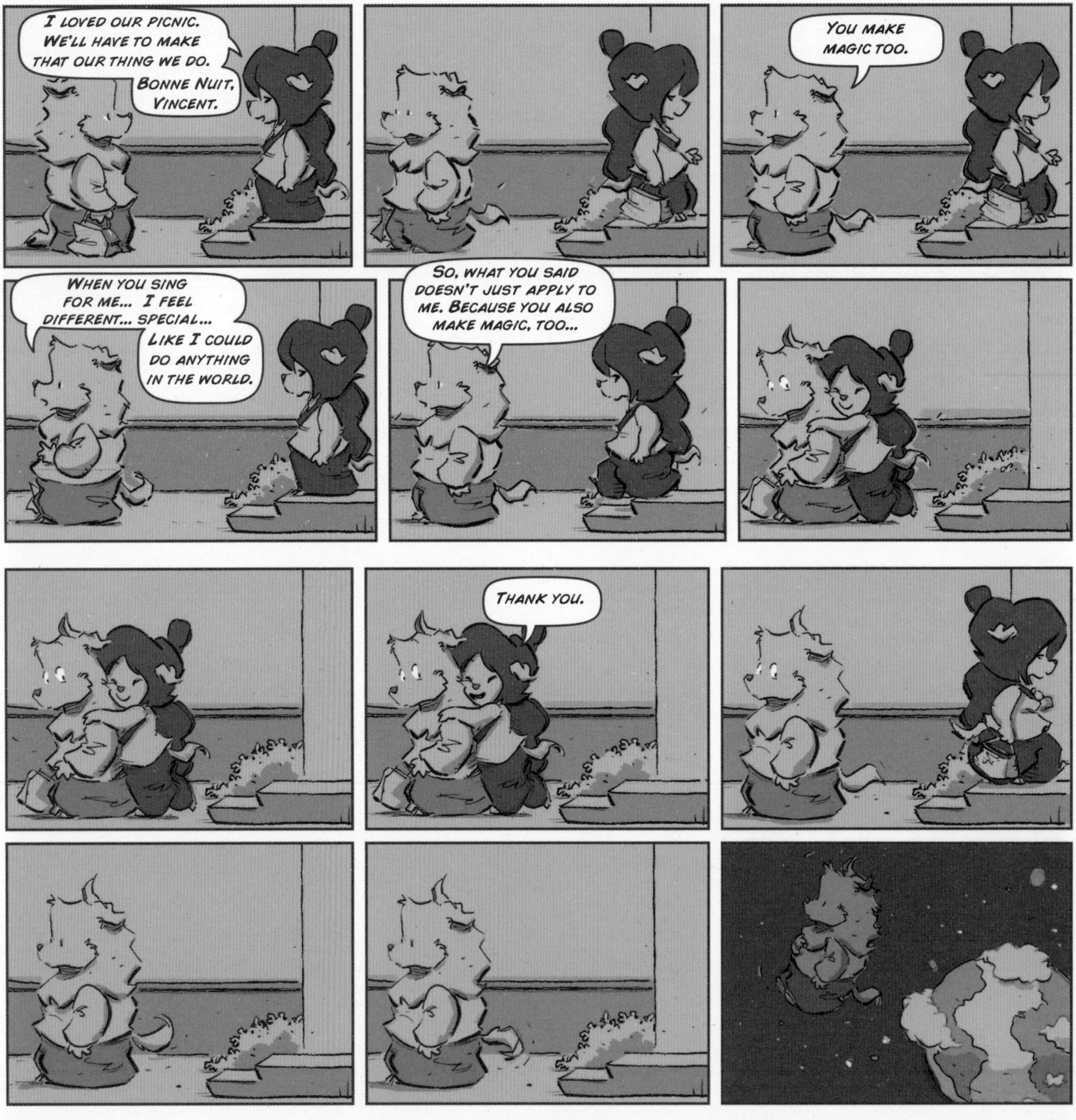
I LOVED OUR PICNIC. WE'LL HAVE TO MAKE THAT OUR THING WE DO.
BONNE NUIT, VINCENT.
YOU MAKE MAGIC TOO.
WHEN YOU SING FOR ME... I FEEL DIFFERENT... SPECIAL...
LIKE I COULD DO ANYTHING IN THE WORLD.
SO, WHAT YOU SAID DOESN'T JUST APPLY TO ME. BECAUSE YOU ALSO MAKE MAGIC, TOO...
THANK YOU.

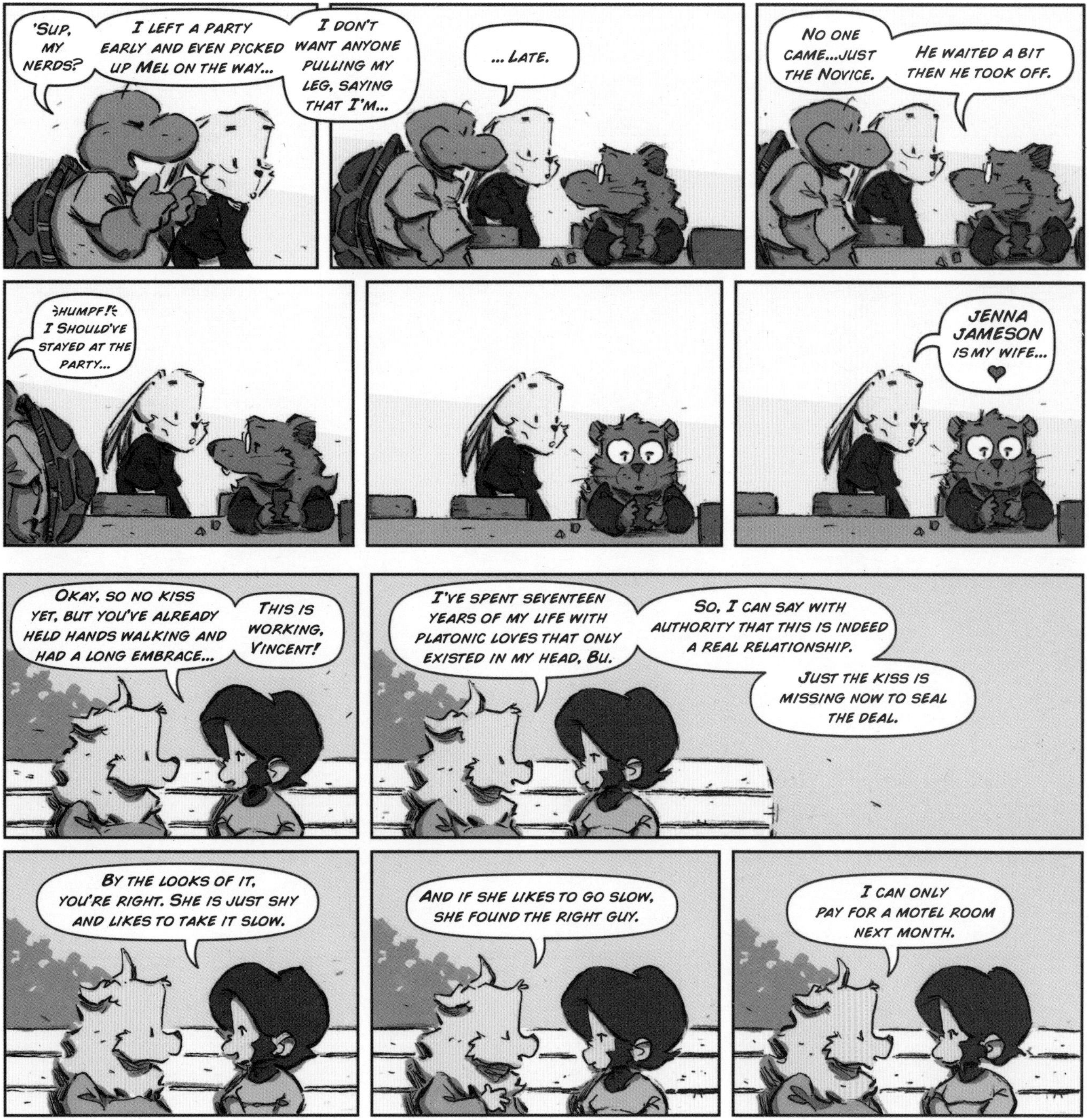
'SUP, MY NERDS?
I LEFT A PARTY EARLY AND EVEN PICKED UP MEL ON THE WAY...
I DON'T WANT ANYONE PULLING MY LEG, SAYING THAT I'M...
... LATE.
NO ONE CAME...JUST THE NOVICE.
HE WAITED A BIT THEN HE TOOK OFF.
HUMPF! I SHOULD'VE STAYED AT THE PARTY...
JENNA JAMESON IS MY WIFE...
OKAY, SO NO KISS YET, BUT YOU'VE ALREADY HELD HANDS WALKING AND HAD A LONG EMBRACE...
THIS IS WORKING, VINCENT!
I'VE SPENT SEVENTEEN YEARS OF MY LIFE WITH PLATONIC LOVES THAT ONLY EXISTED IN MY HEAD, BU.
SO, I CAN SAY WITH AUTHORITY THAT THIS IS INDEED A REAL RELATIONSHIP.
JUST THE KISS IS MISSING NOW TO SEAL THE DEAL.
BY THE LOOKS OF IT, YOU'RE RIGHT. SHE IS JUST SHY AND LIKES TO TAKE IT SLOW.
AND IF SHE LIKES TO GO SLOW, SHE FOUND THE RIGHT GUY.
I CAN ONLY PAY FOR A MOTEL ROOM NEXT MONTH.

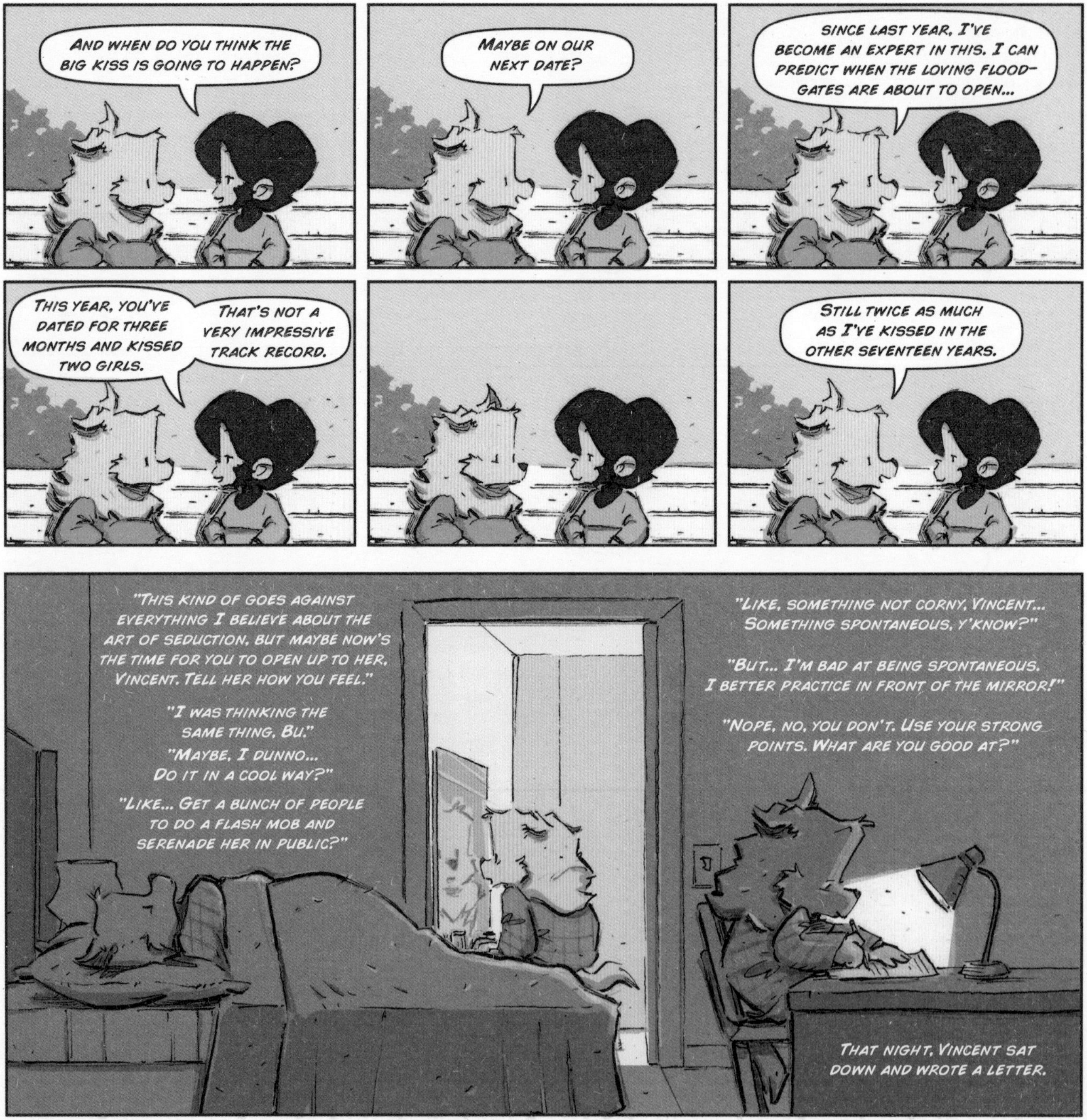
AND WHEN DO YOU THINK THE BIG KISS IS GOING TO HAPPEN?
MAYBE ON OUR NEXT DATE?
SINCE LAST YEAR, I'VE BECOME AN EXPERT IN THIS. I CAN PREDICT WHEN THE LOVING FLOOD-GATES ARE ABOUT TO OPEN...
THIS YEAR, YOU'VE DATED FOR THREE MONTHS AND KISSED TWO GIRLS.
THAT'S NOT A VERY IMPRESSIVE TRACK RECORD.
STILL TWICE AS MUCH AS I'VE KISSED IN THE OTHER SEVENTEEN YEARS.
"THIS KIND OF GOES AGAINST EVERYTHING I BELIEVE ABOUT THE ART OF SEDUCTION, BUT MAYBE NOW'S THE TIME FOR YOU TO OPEN UP TO HER, VINCENT. TELL HER HOW YOU FEEL."
"I WAS THINKING THE SAME THING, BU."
"MAYBE, I DUNNO... DO IT IN A COOL WAY?"
"LIKE... GET A BUNCH OF PEOPLE TO DO A FLASH MOB AND SERENADE HER IN PUBLIC?"
"LIKE, SOMETHING NOT CORNY, VINCENT... SOMETHING SPONTANEOUS, Y'KNOW?"
"BUT... I'M BAD AT BEING SPONTANEOUS. I BETTER PRACTICE IN FRONT OF THE MIRROR!"
"NOPE, NO, YOU DON'T. USE YOUR STRONG POINTS. WHAT ARE YOU GOOD AT?"
THAT NIGHT, VINCENT SAT DOWN AND WROTE A LETTER.

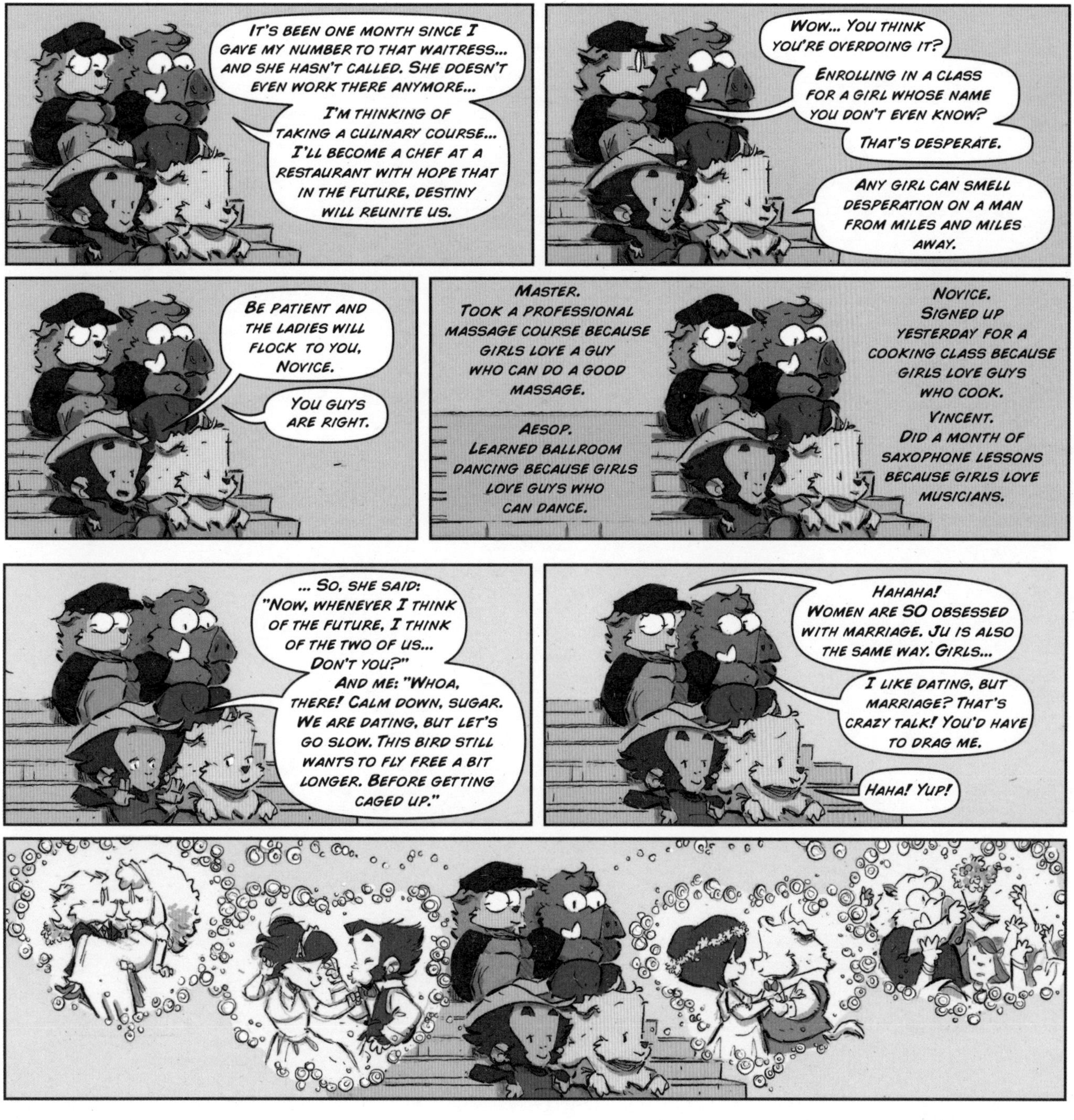
IT'S BEEN ONE MONTH SINCE I GAVE MY NUMBER TO THAT WAITRESS... AND SHE HASN'T CALLED. SHE DOESN'T EVEN WORK THERE ANYMORE...
I'M THINKING OF TAKING A CULINARY COURSE... I'LL BECOME A CHEF AT A RESTAURANT WITH HOPE THAT IN THE FUTURE, DESTINY WILL REUNITE US.
WOW... YOU THINK YOU'RE OVERDOING IT?
ENROLLING IN A CLASS FOR A GIRL WHOSE NAME YOU DON'T EVEN KNOW?
THAT'S DESPERATE.
ANY GIRL CAN SMELL DESPERATION ON A MAN FROM MILES AND MILES AWAY.
BE PATIENT AND THE LADIES WILL FLOCK TO YOU, NOVICE.
YOU GUYS ARE RIGHT.
MASTER. TOOK A PROFESSIONAL MASSAGE COURSE BECAUSE GIRLS LOVE A GUY WHO CAN DO A GOOD MASSAGE.
AESOP. LEARNED BALLROOM DANCING BECAUSE GIRLS LOVE GUYS WHO CAN DANCE.
NOVICE. SIGNED UP YESTERDAY FOR A COOKING CLASS BECAUSE GIRLS LOVE GUYS WHO COOK.
VINCENT. DID A MONTH OF SAXOPHONE LESSONS BECAUSE GIRLS LOVE MUSICIANS.
... SO, SHE SAID: "NOW, WHENEVER I THINK OF THE FUTURE, I THINK OF THE TWO OF US... DON'T YOU?" AND ME: "WHOA, THERE! CALM DOWN, SUGAR. WE ARE DATING, BUT LET'S GO SLOW. THIS BIRD STILL WANTS TO FLY FREE A BIT LONGER. BEFORE GETTING CAGED UP."
HAHAHA! WOMEN ARE SO OBSESSED WITH MARRIAGE. JU IS ALSO THE SAME WAY. GIRLS...
I LIKE DATING, BUT MARRIAGE? THAT'S CRAZY TALK! YOU'D HAVE TO DRAG ME.
HAHA! YUP!

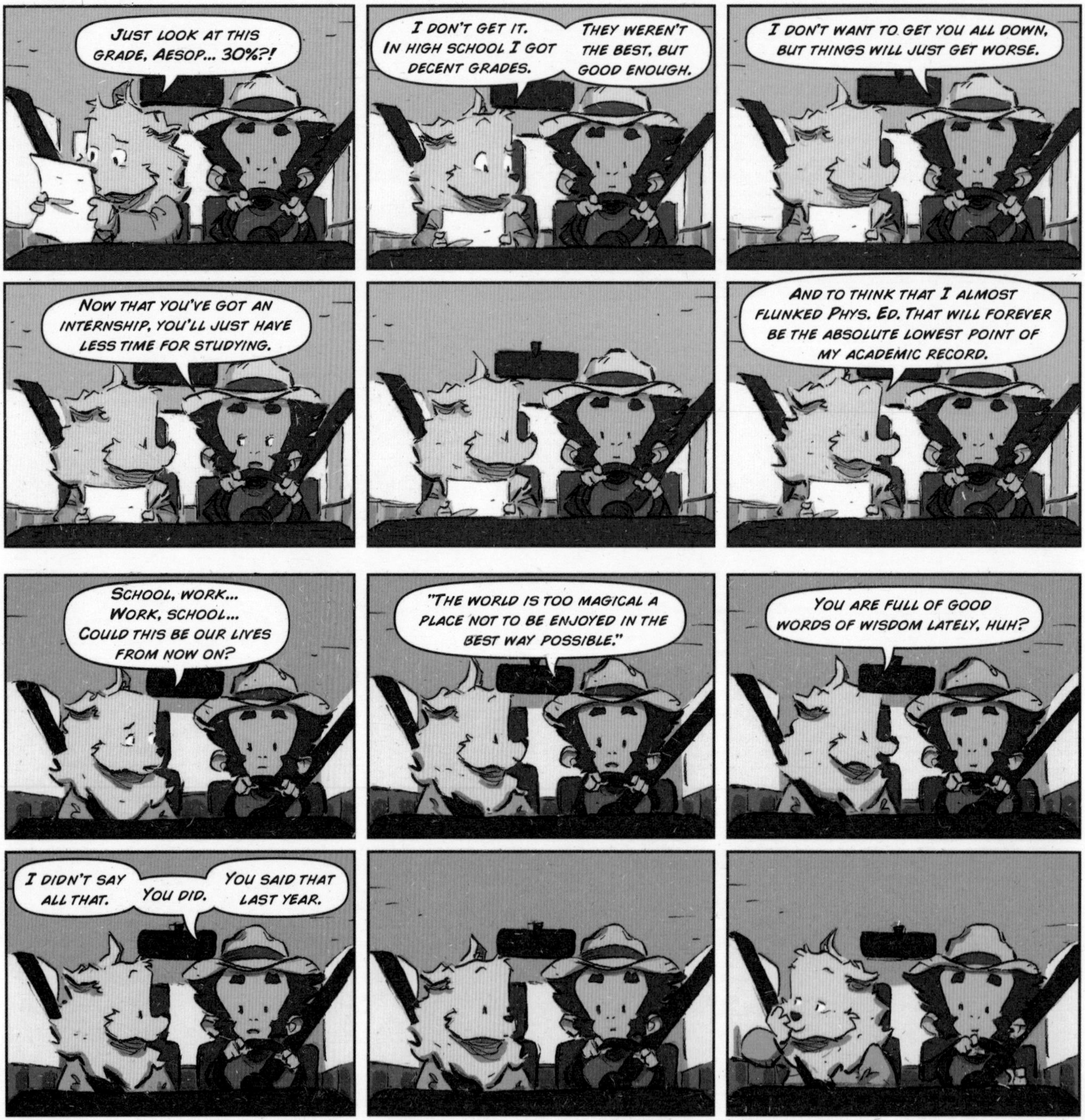
JUST LOOK AT THIS GRADE, AESOP... 30%?!
I DON'T GET IT. IN HIGH SCHOOL I GOT DECENT GRADES.
THEY WEREN'T THE BEST, BUT GOOD ENOUGH.
I DON'T WANT TO GET YOU ALL DOWN, BUT THINGS WILL JUST GET WORSE.
NOW THAT YOU'VE GOT AN INTERNSHIP, YOU'LL JUST HAVE LESS TIME FOR STUDYING.
AND TO THINK THAT I ALMOST FLUNKED PHYS. ED. THAT WILL FOREVER BE THE ABSOLUTE LOWEST POINT OF MY ACADEMIC RECORD.
SCHOOL, WORK... WORK, SCHOOL... COULD THIS BE OUR LIVES FROM NOW ON?
"THE WORLD IS TOO MAGICAL A PLACE NOT TO BE ENJOYED IN THE BEST WAY POSSIBLE."
YOU ARE FULL OF GOOD WORDS OF WISDOM LATELY, HUH?
I DIDN'T SAY ALL THAT.
YOU DID.
YOU SAID THAT LAST YEAR.

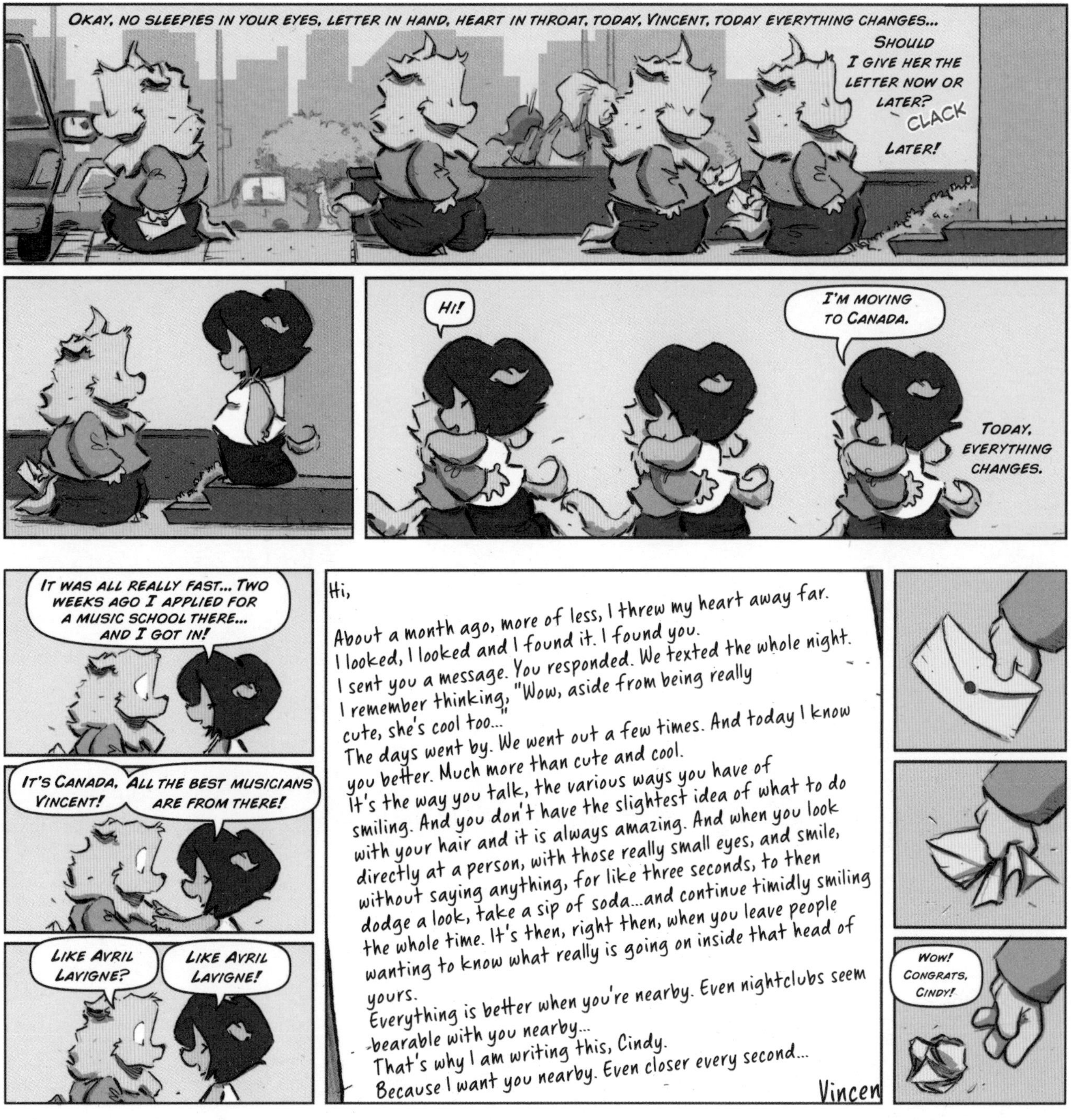
OKAY, NO SLEEPIES IN YOUR EYES, LETTER IN HAND, HEART IN THROAT, TODAY, VINCENT, TODAY EVERYTHING CHANGES...
SHOULD I GIVE HER THE LETTER NOW OR LATER?
CLACK
LATER!
HI!
I'M MOVING TO CANADA.
TODAY, EVERYTHING CHANGES.
IT WAS ALL REALLY FAST... TWO WEEKS AGO I APPLIED FOR A MUSIC SCHOOL THERE... AND I GOT IN!
IT'S CANADA, VINCENT!
ALL THE BEST MUSICIANS ARE FROM THERE!
LIKE AVRIL LAVIGNE?
LIKE AVRIL LAVIGNE!
Hi,
About a month ago, more of less, I threw my heart away far.
I looked, I looked and I found it. I found you.
I sent you a message. You responded. We texted the whole night.
I remember thinking, "Wow, aside from being really
cute, she's cool too..."
The days went by. We went out a few times. And today I know
you better. Much more than cute and cool.
It's the way you talk, the various ways you have of
smiling. And you don't have the slightest idea of what to do
with your hair and it is always amazing. And when you look
directly at a person, with those really small eyes, and smile,
without saying anything, for like three seconds, to then
dodge a look, take a sip of soda...and continue timidly smiling
the whole time. It's then, right then, when you leave people
wanting to know what really is going on inside that head of
yours.
Everything is better when you're nearby. Even nightclubs seem
bearable with you nearby...
That's why I am writing this, Cindy.
Because I want you nearby. Even closer every second...
Vincen
WOW! CONGRATS, CINDY!

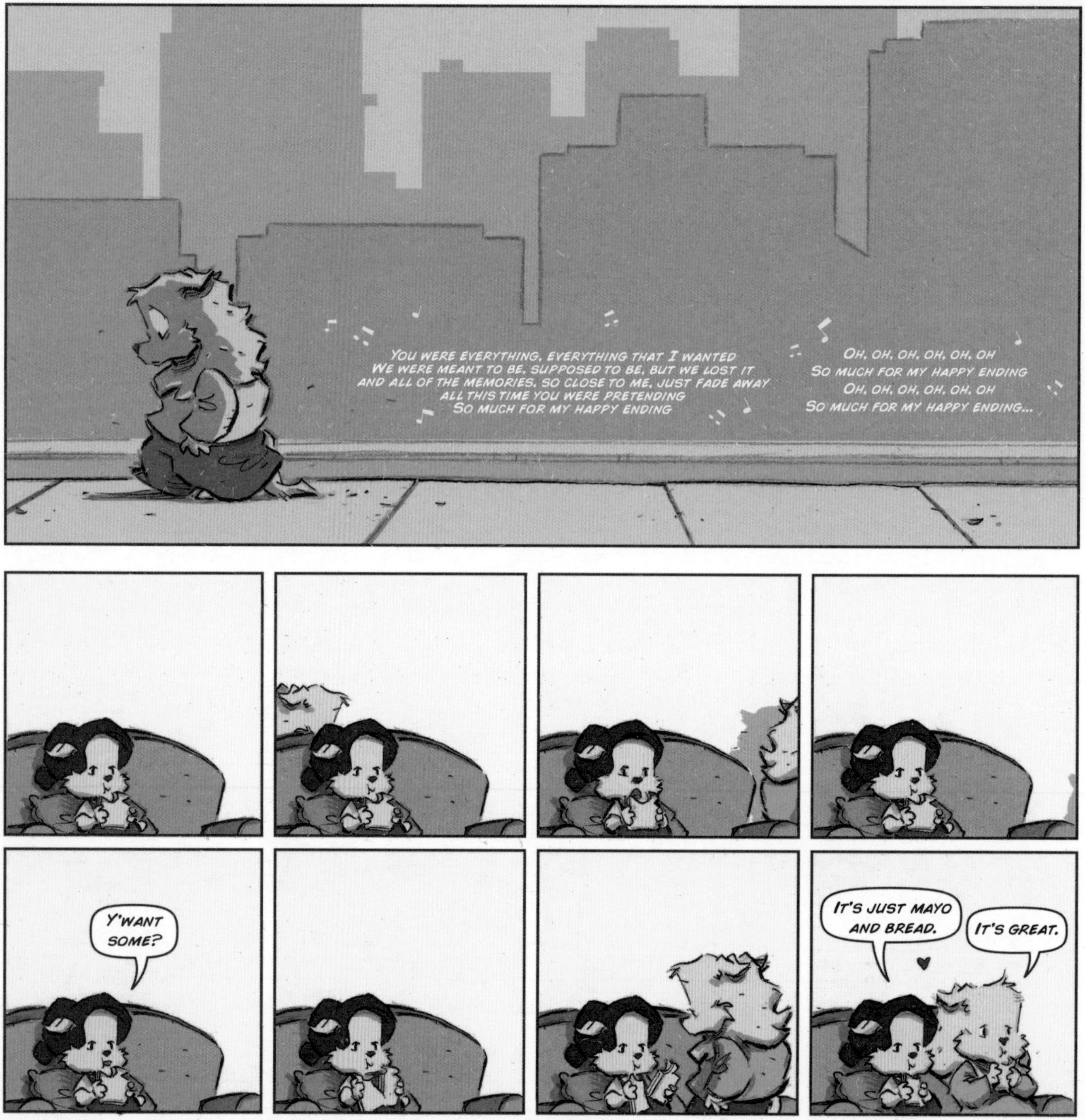
YOU WERE EVERYTHING, EVERYTHING THAT I WANTED
WE WERE MEANT TO BE, SUPPOSED TO BE, BUT WE LOST IT
AND ALL OF THE MEMORIES, SO CLOSE TO ME, JUST FADE AWAY
ALL THIS TIME YOU WERE PRETENDING
SO MUCH FOR MY HAPPY ENDING
OH, OH, OH, OH, OH, OH
SO MUCH FOR MY HAPPY ENDING
OH, OH, OH, OH, OH, OH
SO MUCH FOR MY HAPPY ENDING...
Y'WANT SOME?
IT'S JUST MAYO AND BREAD.
IT'S GREAT.

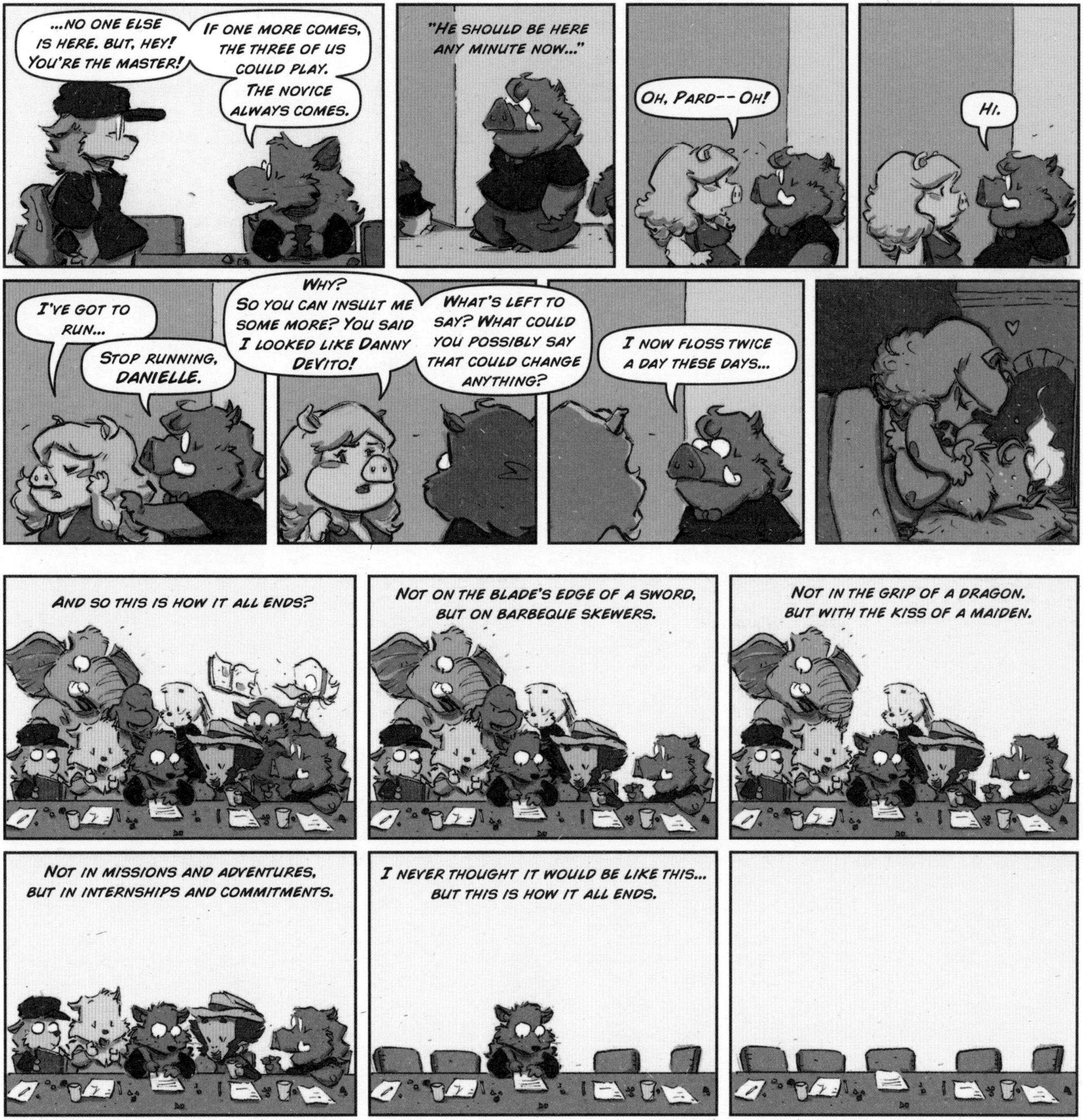

...NO ONE ELSE IS HERE. BUT, HEY! YOU'RE THE MASTER!
IF ONE MORE COMES, THE THREE OF US COULD PLAY. THE NOVICE ALWAYS COMES.
"HE SHOULD BE HERE ANY MINUTE NOW..."
OH, PARD-- OH!
HI.
I'VE GOT TO RUN...
STOP RUNNING, DANIELLE.
WHY? SO YOU CAN INSULT ME SOME MORE? YOU SAID I LOOKED LIKE DANNY DEVITO!
WHAT'S LEFT TO SAY? WHAT COULD YOU POSSIBLY SAY THAT COULD CHANGE ANYTHING?
I NOW FLOSS TWICE A DAY THESE DAYS...
AND SO THIS IS HOW IT ALL ENDS?
NOT ON THE BLADE'S EDGE OF A SWORD, BUT ON BARBEQUE SKEWERS.
NOT IN THE GRIP OF A DRAGON, BUT WITH THE KISS OF A MAIDEN.
NOT IN MISSIONS AND ADVENTURES, BUT IN INTERNSHIPS AND COMMITMENTS.
I NEVER THOUGHT IT WOULD BE LIKE THIS... BUT THIS IS HOW IT ALL ENDS.

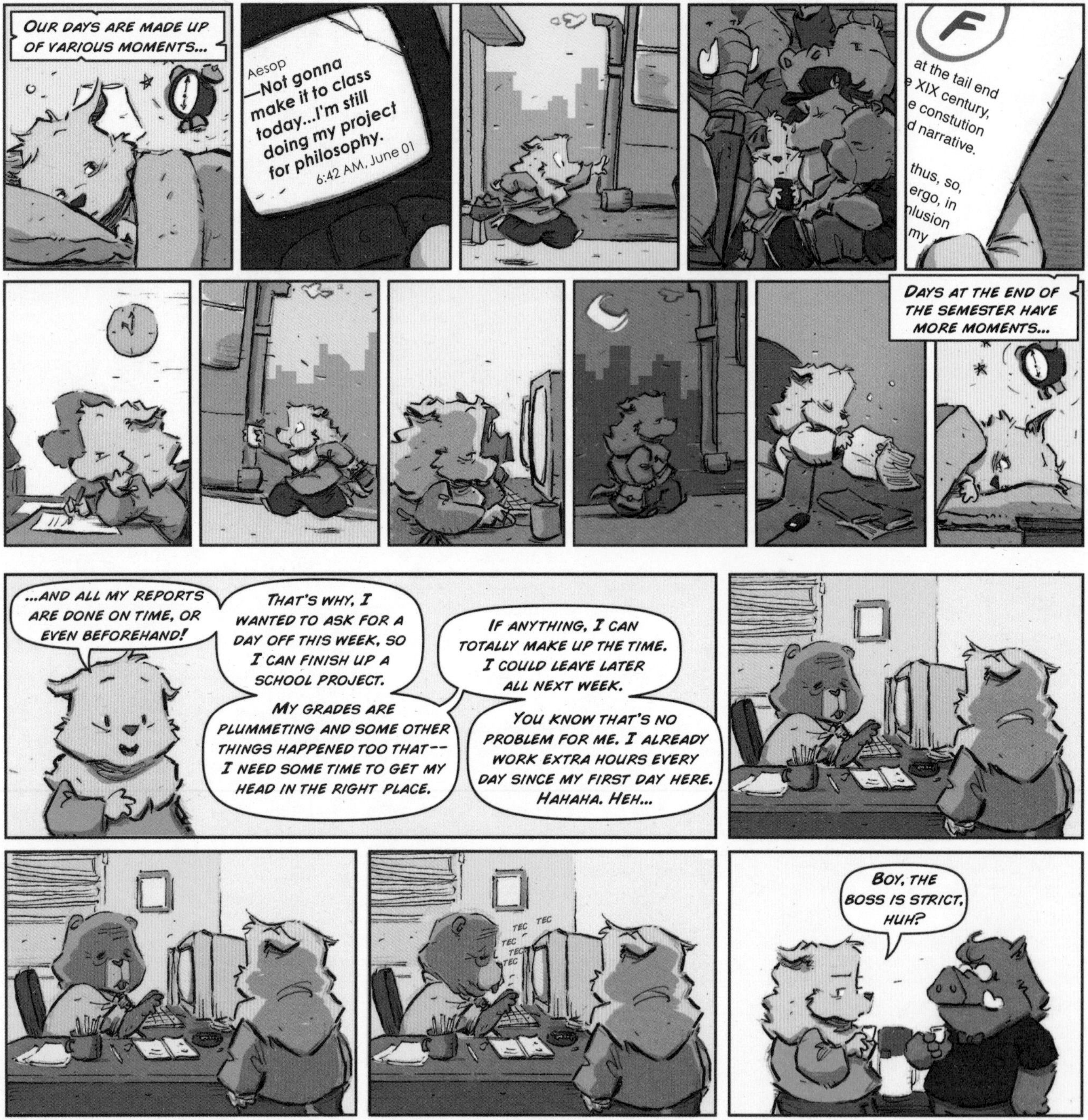
OUR DAYS ARE MADE UP OF VARIOUS MOMENTS...
Aesop
—Not gonna make it to class today...I'm still doing my project for philosophy.
6:42 AM, June 01
F
at the tail end
e XIX century,
e constution
d narrative.
thus, so,
ergo, in
nlusion
my
DAYS AT THE END OF THE SEMESTER HAVE MORE MOMENTS...
...AND ALL MY REPORTS ARE DONE ON TIME, OR EVEN BEFOREHAND!
THAT'S WHY, I WANTED TO ASK FOR A DAY OFF THIS WEEK, SO I CAN FINISH UP A SCHOOL PROJECT.
MY GRADES ARE PLUMMETING AND SOME OTHER THINGS HAPPENED TOO THAT-- I NEED SOME TIME TO GET MY HEAD IN THE RIGHT PLACE.
IF ANYTHING, I CAN TOTALLY MAKE UP THE TIME. I COULD LEAVE LATER ALL NEXT WEEK.
YOU KNOW THAT'S NO PROBLEM FOR ME. I ALREADY WORK EXTRA HOURS EVERY DAY SINCE MY FIRST DAY HERE. HAHAHA. HEH...
TEC TEC TEC TEC TEC
BOY, THE BOSS IS STRICT, HUH?

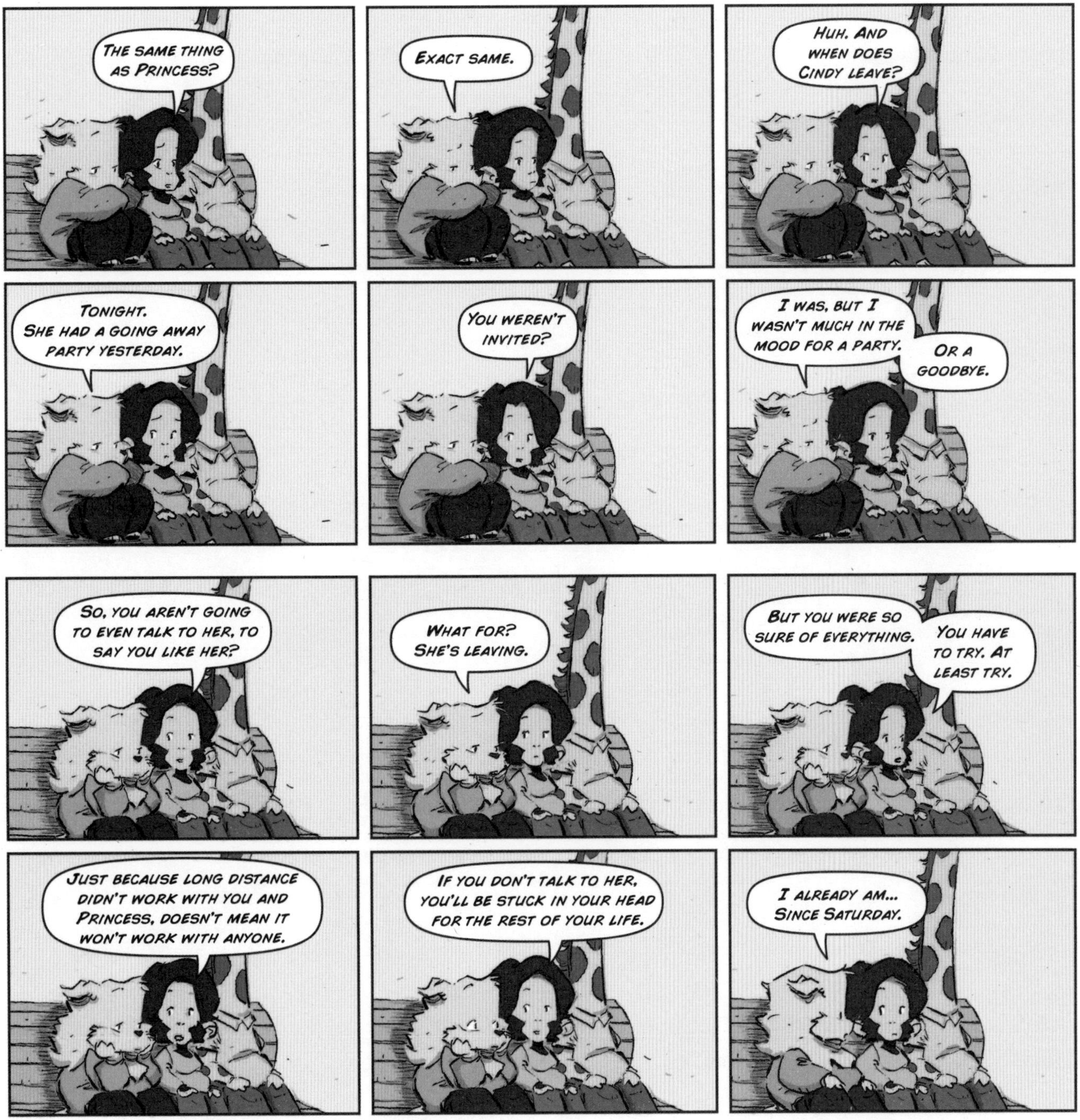

THE SAME THING AS PRINCESS?
EXACT SAME.
HUH. AND WHEN DOES CINDY LEAVE?
TONIGHT. SHE HAD A GOING AWAY PARTY YESTERDAY.
YOU WEREN'T INVITED?
I WAS, BUT I WASN'T MUCH IN THE MOOD FOR A PARTY.
OR A GOODBYE.
SO, YOU AREN'T GOING TO EVEN TALK TO HER, TO SAY YOU LIKE HER?
WHAT FOR? SHE'S LEAVING.
BUT YOU WERE SO SURE OF EVERYTHING.
YOU HAVE TO TRY. AT LEAST TRY.
JUST BECAUSE LONG DISTANCE DIDN'T WORK WITH YOU AND PRINCESS, DOESN'T MEAN IT WON'T WORK WITH ANYONE.
IF YOU DON'T TALK TO HER, YOU'LL BE STUCK IN YOUR HEAD FOR THE REST OF YOUR LIFE.
I ALREADY AM... SINCE SATURDAY.

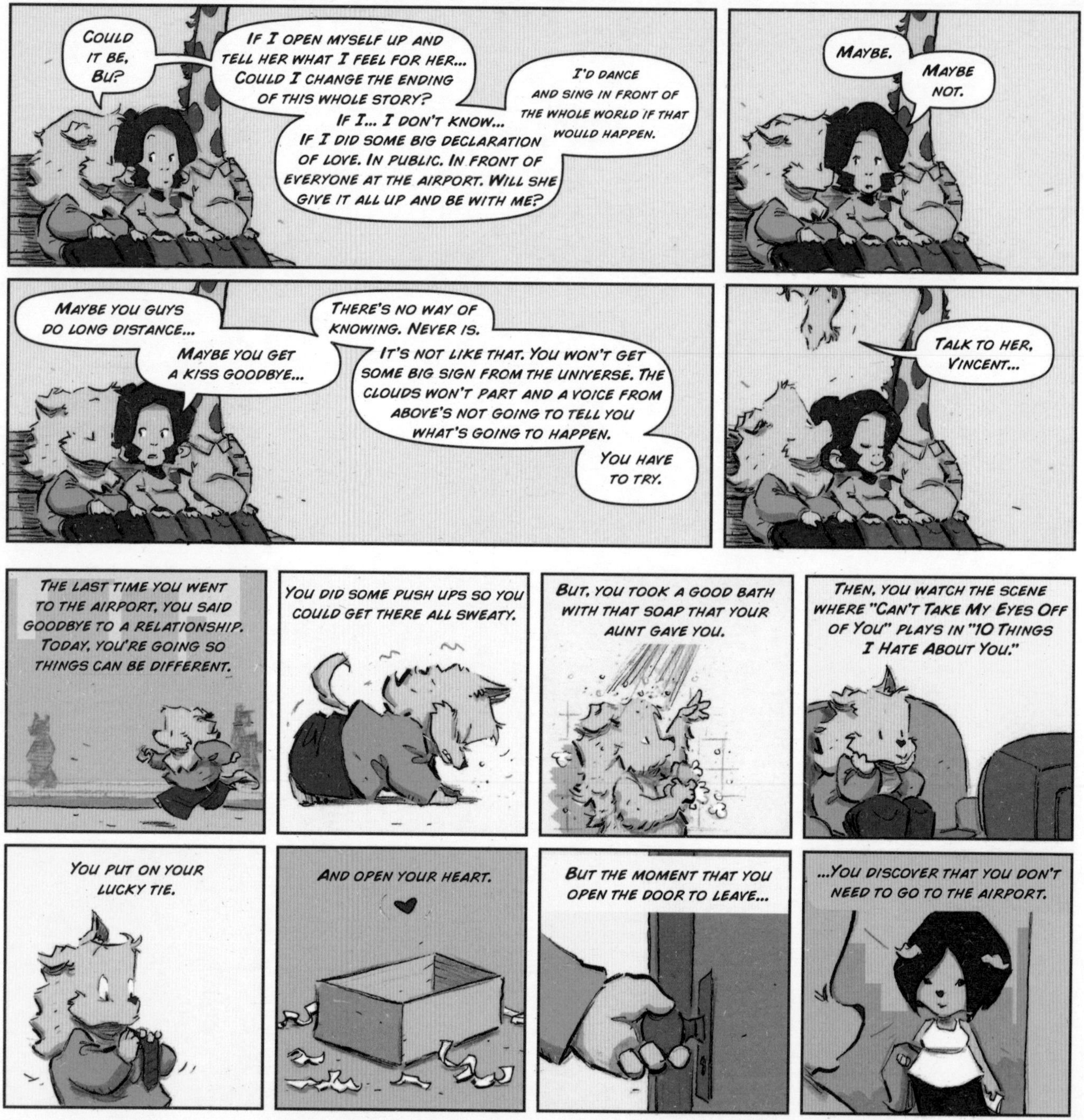
COULD IT BE, BU?
IF I OPEN MYSELF UP AND TELL HER WHAT I FEEL FOR HER... COULD I CHANGE THE ENDING OF THIS WHOLE STORY?
IF I... I DON'T KNOW... IF I DID SOME BIG DECLARATION OF LOVE. IN PUBLIC. IN FRONT OF EVERYONE AT THE AIRPORT. WILL SHE GIVE IT ALL UP AND BE WITH ME?
I'D DANCE AND SING IN FRONT OF THE WHOLE WORLD IF THAT WOULD HAPPEN.
MAYBE.
MAYBE NOT.
MAYBE YOU GUYS DO LONG DISTANCE...
MAYBE YOU GET A KISS GOODBYE...
THERE'S NO WAY OF KNOWING. NEVER IS.
IT'S NOT LIKE THAT. YOU WON'T GET SOME BIG SIGN FROM THE UNIVERSE. THE CLOUDS WON'T PART AND A VOICE FROM ABOVE'S NOT GOING TO TELL YOU WHAT'S GOING TO HAPPEN.
YOU HAVE TO TRY.
TALK TO HER, VINCENT...
THE LAST TIME YOU WENT TO THE AIRPORT, YOU SAID GOODBYE TO A RELATIONSHIP. TODAY, YOU'RE GOING SO THINGS CAN BE DIFFERENT.
YOU DID SOME PUSH UPS SO YOU COULD GET THERE ALL SWEATY.
BUT, YOU TOOK A GOOD BATH WITH THAT SOAP THAT YOUR AUNT GAVE YOU.
THEN, YOU WATCH THE SCENE WHERE "CAN'T TAKE MY EYES OFF OF YOU" PLAYS IN "10 THINGS I HATE ABOUT YOU."
YOU PUT ON YOUR LUCKY TIE.
AND OPEN YOUR HEART.
BUT THE MOMENT THAT YOU OPEN THE DOOR TO LEAVE...
...YOU DISCOVER THAT YOU DON'T NEED TO GO TO THE AIRPORT.

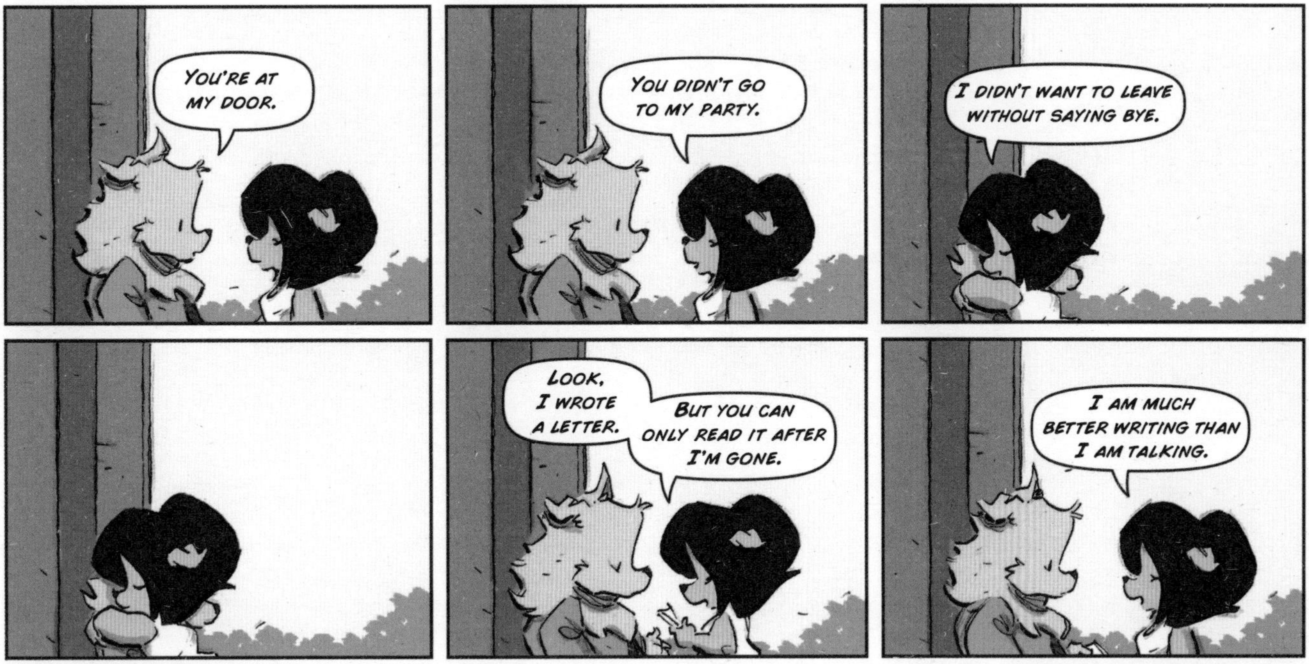
YOU'RE AT MY DOOR.
YOU DIDN'T GO TO MY PARTY.
I DIDN'T WANT TO LEAVE WITHOUT SAYING BYE.
LOOK, I WROTE A LETTER.
BUT YOU CAN ONLY READ IT AFTER I'M GONE.
I AM MUCH BETTER WRITING THAN I AM TALKING.

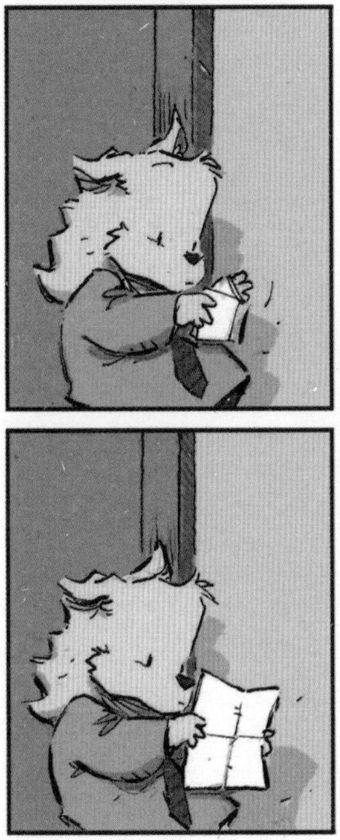

Hi Vincent,

I am writing this letter because tomorrow I leave and I still have something I want to say to you. Actually, to say to you again:
Thank you :)

Thank you for being the best friend I could ask for in these almost two months.
Thank you for giving me courage. It was when you told me I make magic with my music, that's when I had the courage to apply for this scholarship in Canada. That was when everything changed for me.

Thank you for accepting me as I am, when not even I knew who I was. That night at the nightclub, when I told you I liked girls, that was the first time I told anyone that.

Not even Lilo knows yet. And the way you handled it, you treated me exactly the same as you treated me before, made me feel really good.

I am even speaking to a girl in Canada lately. Her name is Amanda.
She seems pretty cool ;)

I am still a bit nervous for all these changes in my life, but I think it will all be okay. I think I need this. Root for me, okay? I think I need that courage one more time that you gave me. Even long distance.

Love, Cindy

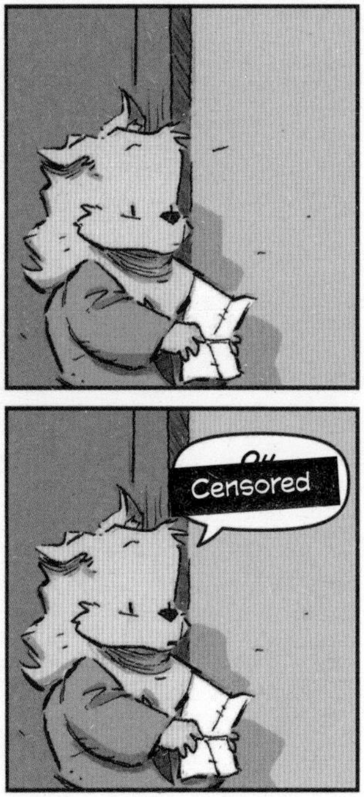
Censored

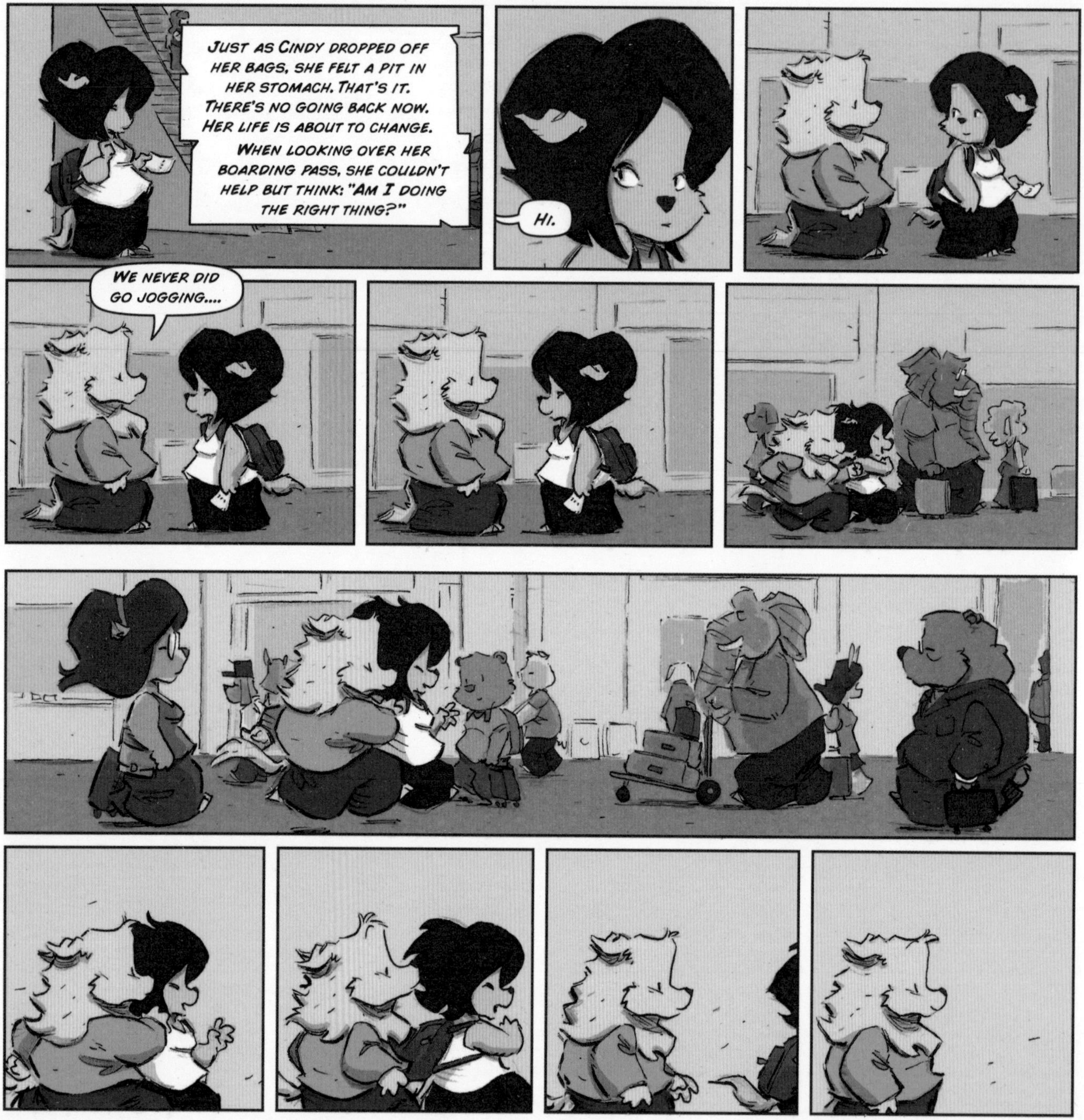
JUST AS CINDY DROPPED OFF HER BAGS, SHE FELT A PIT IN HER STOMACH. THAT'S IT. THERE'S NO GOING BACK NOW. HER LIFE IS ABOUT TO CHANGE.
WHEN LOOKING OVER HER BOARDING PASS, SHE COULDN'T HELP BUT THINK: "AM I DOING THE RIGHT THING?"
HI.
WE NEVER DID GO JOGGING....

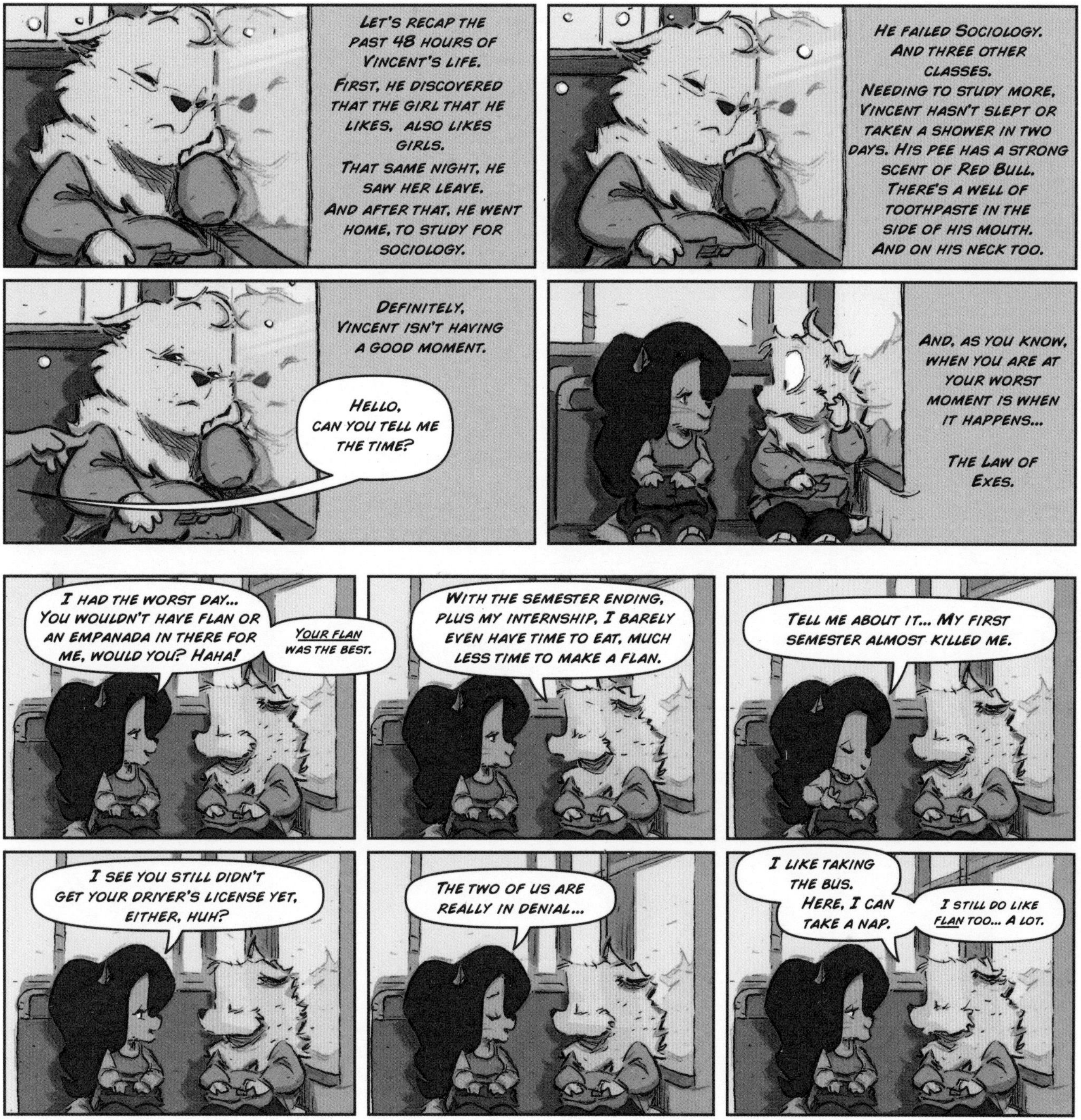

Let's recap the past 48 hours of Vincent's life.
First, he discovered that the girl that he likes, also likes girls.
That same night, he saw her leave.
And after that, he went home, to study for sociology.
He failed Sociology. And three other classes.
Needing to study more, Vincent hasn't slept or taken a shower in two days. His pee has a strong scent of Red Bull.
There's a well of toothpaste in the side of his mouth.
And on his neck too.
Definitely, Vincent isn't having a good moment.
Hello, can you tell me the time?
And, as you know, when you are at your worst moment is when it happens...
The Law of Exes.
I had the worst day... You wouldn't have flan or an empanada in there for me, would you? Haha!
Your flan was the best.
With the semester ending, plus my internship, I barely even have time to eat, much less time to make a flan.
Tell me about it... My first semester almost killed me.
I see you still didn't get your driver's license yet, either, huh?
The two of us are really in denial...
I like taking the bus. Here, I can take a nap.
I still do like flan too... a lot.

You

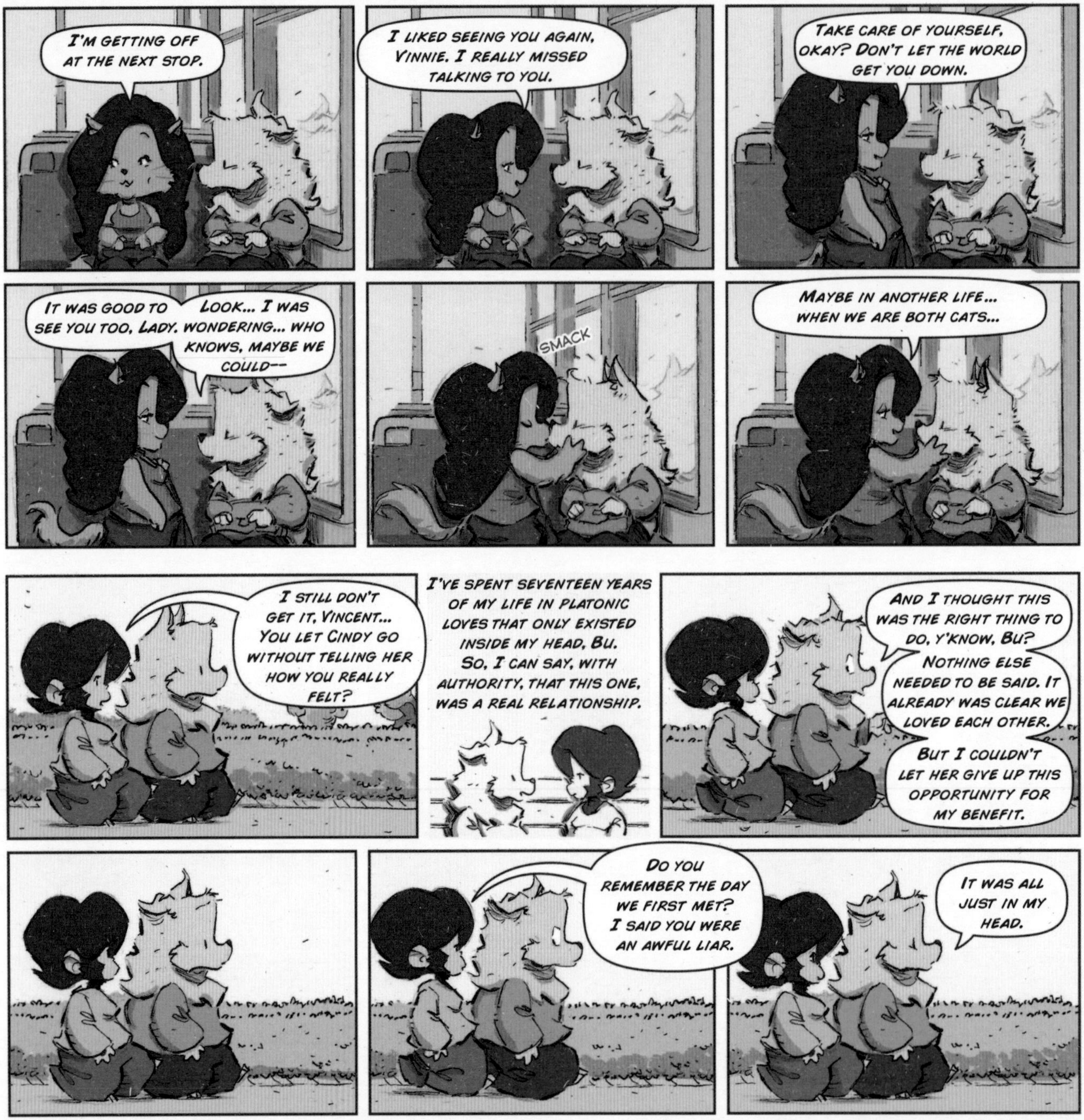
I'M GETTING OFF AT THE NEXT STOP.
I LIKED SEEING YOU AGAIN, VINNIE. I REALLY MISSED TALKING TO YOU.
TAKE CARE OF YOURSELF, OKAY? DON'T LET THE WORLD GET YOU DOWN.
IT WAS GOOD TO SEE YOU TOO, LADY.
LOOK... I WAS WONDERING... WHO KNOWS, MAYBE WE COULD--
SMACK
MAYBE IN ANOTHER LIFE... WHEN WE ARE BOTH CATS...
I STILL DON'T GET IT, VINCENT... YOU LET CINDY GO WITHOUT TELLING HER HOW YOU REALLY FELT?
I'VE SPENT SEVENTEEN YEARS OF MY LIFE IN PLATONIC LOVES THAT ONLY EXISTED INSIDE MY HEAD, BU. SO, I CAN SAY, WITH AUTHORITY, THAT THIS ONE, WAS A REAL RELATIONSHIP.
AND I THOUGHT THIS WAS THE RIGHT THING TO DO, Y'KNOW, BU?
NOTHING ELSE NEEDED TO BE SAID. IT ALREADY WAS CLEAR WE LOVED EACH OTHER.
BUT I COULDN'T LET HER GIVE UP THIS OPPORTUNITY FOR MY BENEFIT.
DO YOU REMEMBER THE DAY WE FIRST MET? I SAID YOU WERE AN AWFUL LIAR.
IT WAS ALL JUST IN MY HEAD.

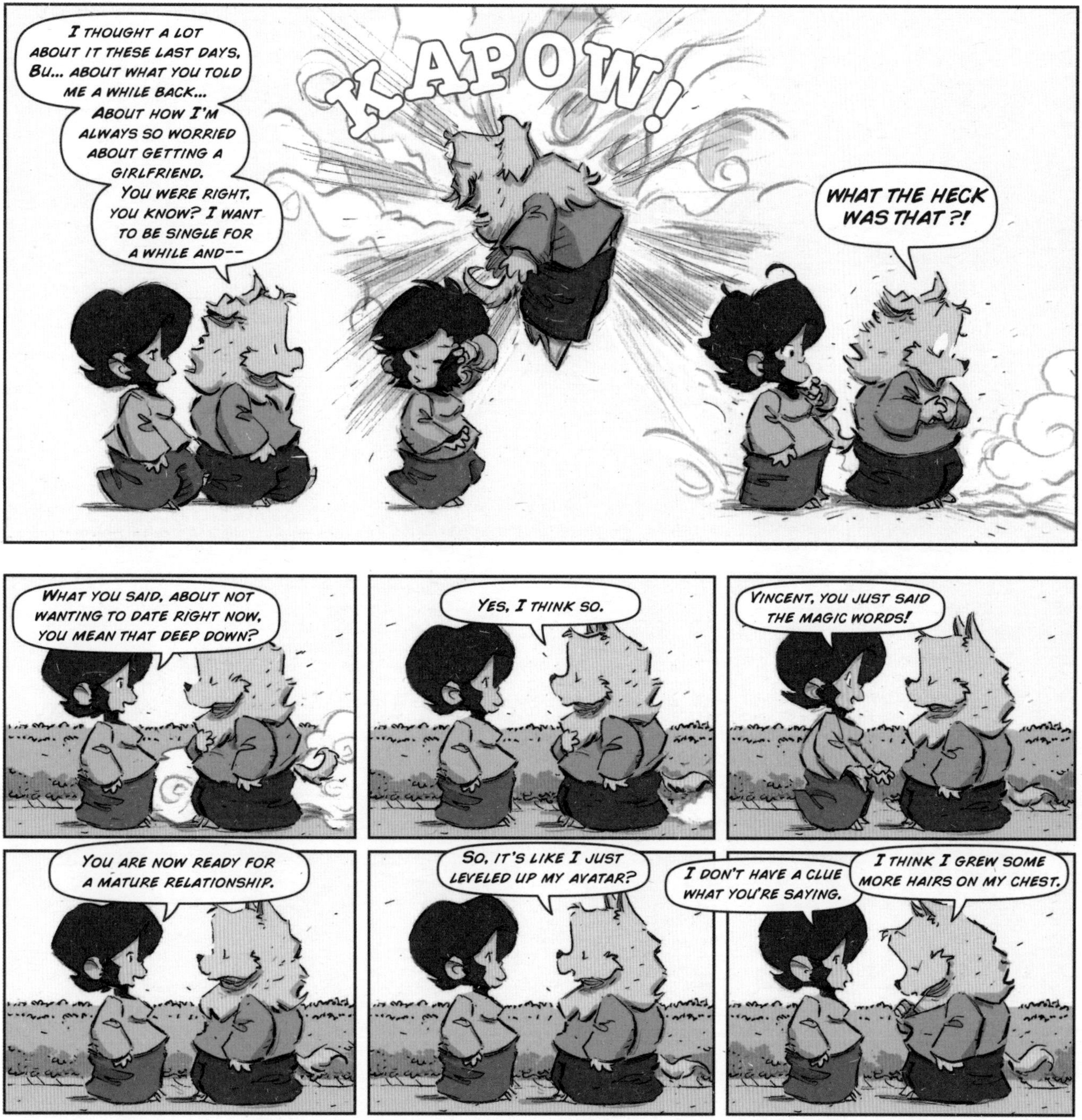
I THOUGHT A LOT ABOUT IT THESE LAST DAYS, BU... ABOUT WHAT YOU TOLD ME A WHILE BACK... ABOUT HOW I'M ALWAYS SO WORRIED ABOUT GETTING A GIRLFRIEND. YOU WERE RIGHT, YOU KNOW? I WANT TO BE SINGLE FOR A WHILE AND--
KAPOW!
WHAT THE HECK WAS THAT ?!
WHAT YOU SAID, ABOUT NOT WANTING TO DATE RIGHT NOW, YOU MEAN THAT DEEP DOWN?
YES, I THINK SO.
VINCENT, YOU JUST SAID THE MAGIC WORDS!
YOU ARE NOW READY FOR A MATURE RELATIONSHIP.
SO, IT'S LIKE I JUST LEVELED UP MY AVATAR?
I DON'T HAVE A CLUE WHAT YOU'RE SAYING.
I THINK I GREW SOME MORE HAIRS ON MY CHEST.

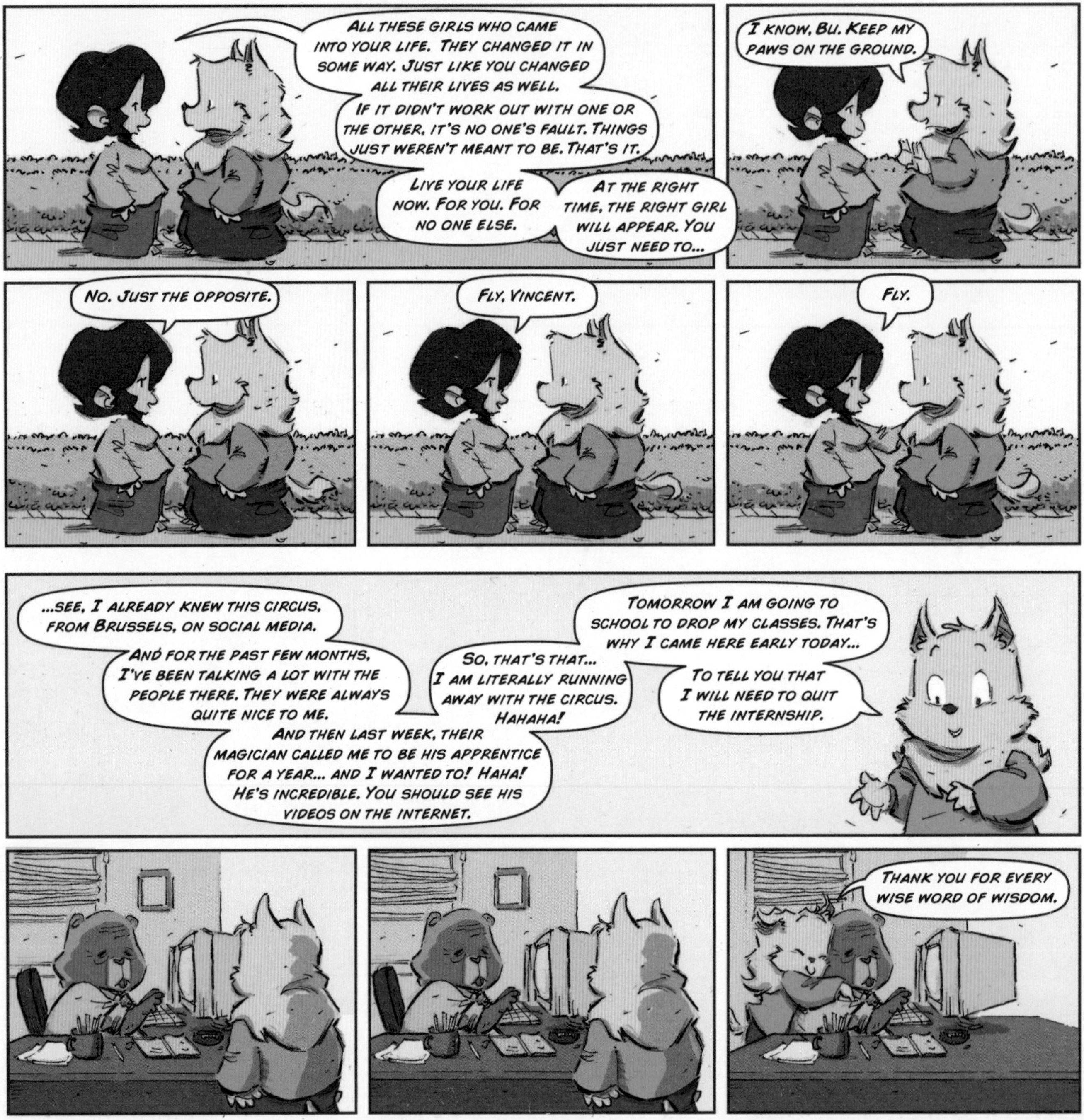
ALL THESE GIRLS WHO CAME INTO YOUR LIFE. THEY CHANGED IT IN SOME WAY. JUST LIKE YOU CHANGED ALL THEIR LIVES AS WELL.
IF IT DIDN'T WORK OUT WITH ONE OR THE OTHER, IT'S NO ONE'S FAULT. THINGS JUST WEREN'T MEANT TO BE. THAT'S IT.
LIVE YOUR LIFE NOW. FOR YOU. FOR NO ONE ELSE.
AT THE RIGHT TIME, THE RIGHT GIRL WILL APPEAR. YOU JUST NEED TO...
I KNOW, BU. KEEP MY PAWS ON THE GROUND.
NO. JUST THE OPPOSITE.
FLY, VINCENT.
FLY.
...SEE, I ALREADY KNEW THIS CIRCUS, FROM BRUSSELS, ON SOCIAL MEDIA.
AND FOR THE PAST FEW MONTHS, I'VE BEEN TALKING A LOT WITH THE PEOPLE THERE. THEY WERE ALWAYS QUITE NICE TO ME.
AND THEN LAST WEEK, THEIR MAGICIAN CALLED ME TO BE HIS APPRENTICE FOR A YEAR... AND I WANTED TO! HAHA! HE'S INCREDIBLE. YOU SHOULD SEE HIS VIDEOS ON THE INTERNET.
SO, THAT'S THAT... I AM LITERALLY RUNNING AWAY WITH THE CIRCUS. HAHAHA!
TOMORROW I AM GOING TO SCHOOL TO DROP MY CLASSES. THAT'S WHY I CAME HERE EARLY TODAY...
TO TELL YOU THAT I WILL NEED TO QUIT THE INTERNSHIP.
THANK YOU FOR EVERY WISE WORD OF WISDOM.

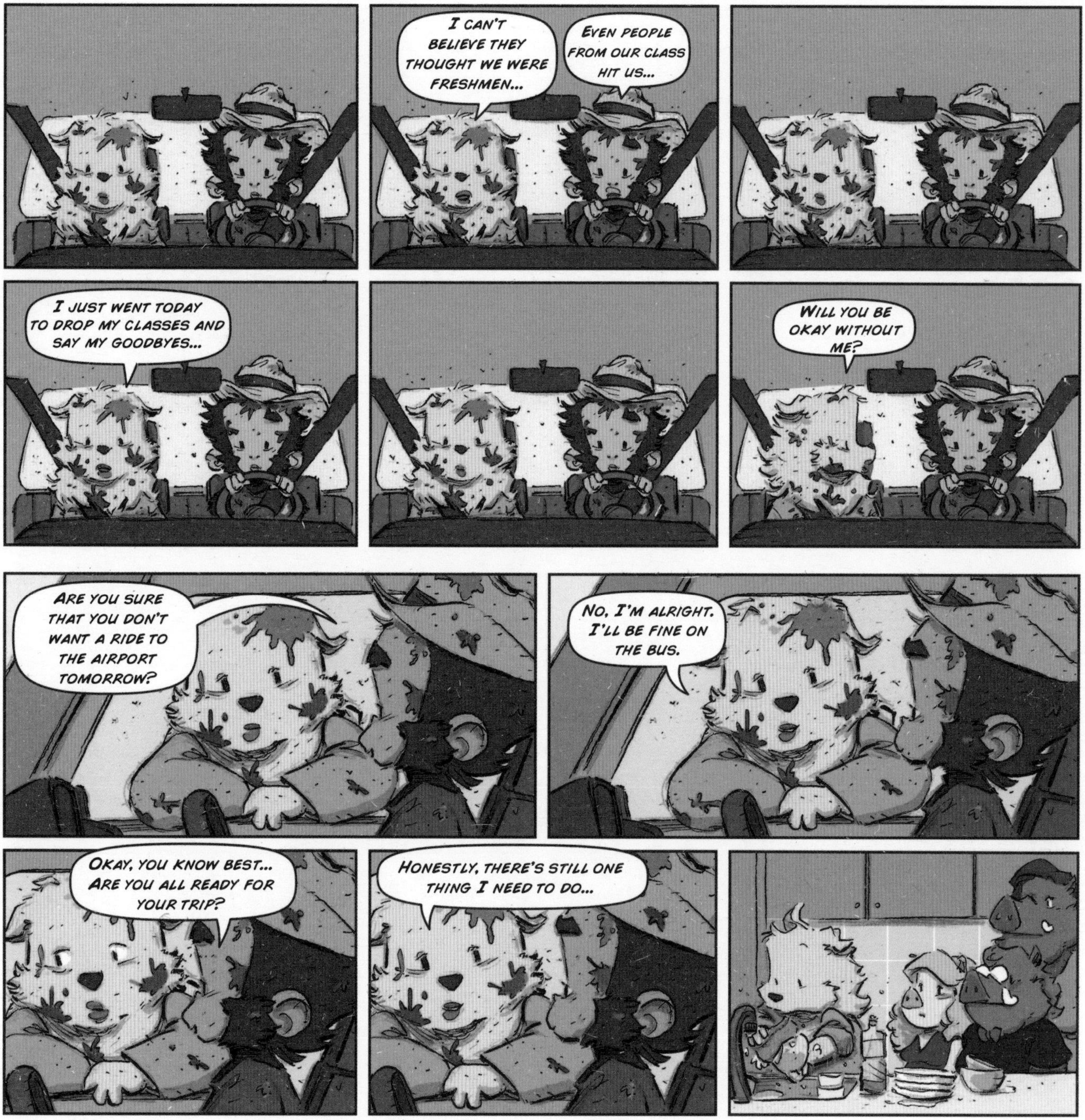
I CAN'T BELIEVE THEY THOUGHT WE WERE FRESHMEN...
EVEN PEOPLE FROM OUR CLASS HIT US...
I JUST WENT TODAY TO DROP MY CLASSES AND SAY MY GOODBYES...
WILL YOU BE OKAY WITHOUT ME?
ARE YOU SURE THAT YOU DON'T WANT A RIDE TO THE AIRPORT TOMORROW?
NO, I'M ALRIGHT. I'LL BE FINE ON THE BUS.
OKAY, YOU KNOW BEST... ARE YOU ALL READY FOR YOUR TRIP?
HONESTLY, THERE'S STILL ONE THING I NEED TO DO...

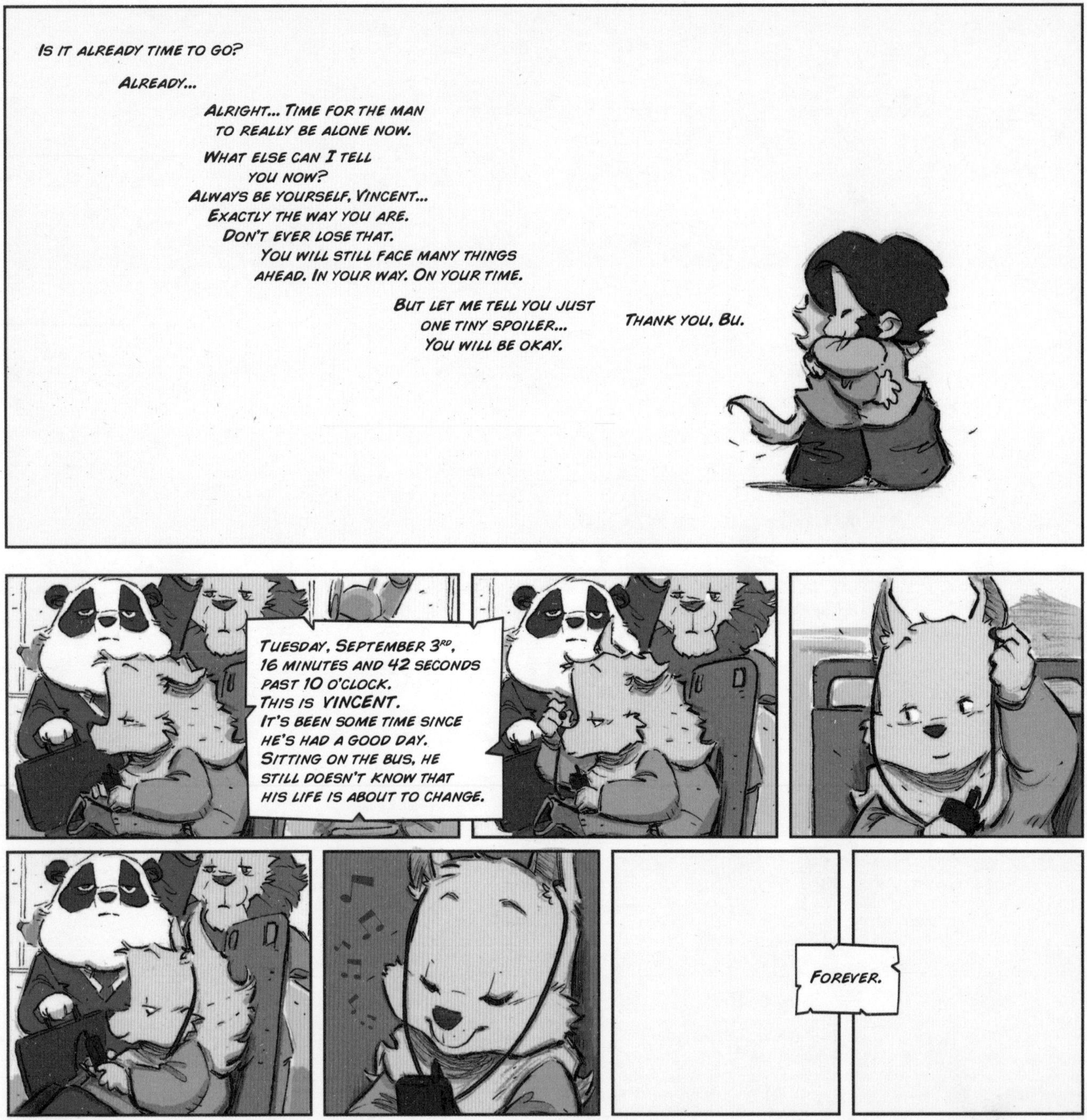

IS IT ALREADY TIME TO GO?

ALREADY...

ALRIGHT... TIME FOR THE MAN
TO REALLY BE ALONE NOW.

WHAT ELSE CAN I TELL
YOU NOW?
ALWAYS BE YOURSELF, VINCENT...
EXACTLY THE WAY YOU ARE.
DON'T EVER LOSE THAT.
YOU WILL STILL FACE MANY THINGS
AHEAD. IN YOUR WAY. ON YOUR TIME.

BUT LET ME TELL YOU JUST
ONE TINY SPOILER...
YOU WILL BE OKAY.

THANK YOU, BU.

TUESDAY, SEPTEMBER 3RD,
16 MINUTES AND 42 SECONDS
PAST 10 O'CLOCK.
THIS IS VINCENT.
IT'S BEEN SOME TIME SINCE
HE'S HAD A GOOD DAY.
SITTING ON THE BUS, HE
STILL DOESN'T KNOW THAT
HIS LIFE IS ABOUT TO CHANGE.

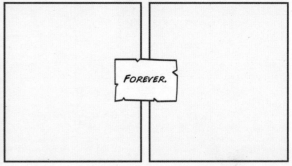

FOREVER.